The
Buffalo
Soldier

ALSO BY

Chris Bohjalian

Trans-Sister Radio
(2 0 0 0)

The Law of Similars
(1 9 9 9)

Midwives
(1 9 9 7)

Water Witches
(1 9 9 5)

Past the Bleachers
(1 9 9 2)

Hangman
(1 9 9 1)

A Killing in the Real World
(1 9 8 8)

THE
Buffalo
Soldier

A NOVEL

Chris Bohjalian

SHAYE AREHEART BOOKS

NEW YORK

―――――――

Published by Shaye Areheart Books, New York, New York.
Member of the Crown Publishing Group, a division of Random House, Inc.

www.randomhouse.com

SHAYE AREHEART BOOKS is a registered trademark and
the Shaye Areheart Books colophon is a trademark of Random House, Inc.

Printed in the United States of America

DESIGN BY LYNNE AMFT

Library of Congress Cataloging-in-Publication Data
Bohjalian, Christopher A.
The buffalo soldier: a novel / by Chris Bohjalian.
1. African-American boys—Fiction. 2. Children—Death—Fiction.
3. Married people—Fiction. 4. Foster parents—Fiction. 5. Adultery—Fiction.
6. Vermont—Fiction. I. Title.

PS3552.O495 B84 2002
813'.54—dc21   2001049042

ISBN 0-609-60833-9

10   9   8   7   6   5   4   3

For Grace

If you know your history
Then you would know where you coming from.

———

BOB MARLEY, "Buffalo Soldier"

The
Buffalo
Soldier

The
Flood

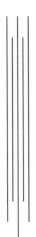

It rained throughout September and October, and people made jokes about Biblical floods before the Sheldon girls drowned. But their jokes weren't serious, because there were intermittent days when the clouds would continue on their way to the east and leave behind nothing but blue skies and crisp autumn air. If people worried about anything, they fretted over the numbers of leaf peepers and flatlanders who hadn't made their customary fall pilgrimages to Vermont that year—and what effect that lost revenue might have on their purses—or they complained about the mud.

After all, the fall rains had made the ground as boggy as March, and the earth showed no signs of freezing up soon. The dirt roads were so laden with runnels that drivers would wince as they lurched their cars forward, while the paved ones often were layered with diaphanous sheets of moisture that in the night reflected a vehicle's headlights like mirrors.

Certainly the water was high in the lakes: Bomoseen and Champlain to the west of the Green Mountains, that range of hills that rose like a great animal's spine across the vertical center of the state, and Willoughby and Memphremagog to the east. Likewise, the rivers of any size often had small crests of albescent foam. There must have been a half-dozen days when the counties north of Rutland had lived with flash-flood advisories and warnings, especially the two occasions when the remnants of late-season Caribbean hurricanes tracked deep into New England and dumped torrents of rain onto ground that was already soaked, and into lakes and rivers that already had about all the water they could handle. One Saturday in late October the Cornish Volunteer Fire Company went so far as to move its two attack pumpers and heavy rescue truck over the bridge that spanned the Gale River, so the vehicles would be on the more populated side of the water if the bridge was brought down by the rapids.

That had happened once before: The original bridge had washed away in the Great Flood of 1927, on the very day that S. Hollister Jackson, the state's lieutenant governor, had drowned in another part of the state when his car stalled in a rivulet on the road near his house and he tried to walk home through the waters. Instead he had been swept away in the current, his body washing up a mile downriver in Potash Brook.

But the rivers never topped their banks the fall the Sheldon girls died, at least not while the phantasmagoric red and yellow leaves remained on the trees, and lake water only oozed into the basements of the people who lived on the shore. For most of northern Vermont the rains were a mere inconvenience.

THE HUNTERS TRAIPSED into the woods that November despite the storms and the showers. They trudged along paths in which they sunk ankle-deep in wet leaves, their boots sometimes swallowed in turbid mountain runoff, and even the thinner tree branches would whip water in their faces when they gently pushed them aside as they walked.

On the second day of deer season, a Sunday, the Sheldon girls were playing with their friend Alicia Montgomery. It had rained heavily all Friday night, Saturday, and much of Sunday morning—dropping close to eight inches in the thirty-six-hour period.

A little past two the rain stopped, and the three girls donned their raincoats and mud boots and wandered outside. They, like so many children that autumn, had been cooped up indoors for whole weekends at a time, and any opportunity to run outside to jump and shriek was taken. Alicia's mother, a woman in her late forties who had three sons older than Alicia, assumed they were going to slosh in the mud around the family's swing set in the backyard, or see how much water had trickled into the wooden clubhouse Alicia's older brothers had built on the property some years before. She thought she might have told them to stay away from the river, but she admitted she honestly wasn't sure. Certainly her daughter didn't recall any such warning.

The Sheldon girls were nine, and they were twins—though not identical twins. They were small-boned, but not at all frail-looking. Rather, with their long legs and arms, they reminded some people of baby colts: They were known for running everywhere, though Megan had never shown any interest in organized sports. Hillary had, but not Megan. Their hair was just a shade closer to blond than brown, and very, very fine. It fell to their shoulders. Hillary was likely to wear her hair down, except on those days when she was playing youth soccer—then she would allow her mother to put it back in a ponytail. Megan usually had her mother braid her hair in the morning, or try one of the bolder statements—a poodle pony or a French twist—that she found described in a hairstylist's handbook she had bought at a yard sale for a dime.

Alicia had been more Hillary's friend than Megan's, because she, too, loved sports. Some days it was just easier for everyone, however, if the twins played together. The two were in the same Girl Scout troop and the same classroom at school, and it couldn't have been otherwise. The small town only had one Girl Scout troop and one classroom filled with fourth-graders. There were only so many eight-, nine-, and ten-year-old girls in the whole village, and so the pair tended to be together more often than they were apart.

Most years, the Gale River meandered lazily through the canyon it had carved over centuries through Cornish and Durham. The water ran down from the mountains, working its way west through rocks and boulders into the Otter Creek, and then, eventually, into Lake Champlain. In summer, the water fell to barely a foot or two in some sections, though there were always areas where it was considerably deeper and people would congregate in large groups to swim or in small groups to fish. The river had stretches that were rich with rainbow and brown trout.

At its thinnest point, the Gale narrowed to fifteen feet; at its widest, it swelled to fifty.

The water paralleled the road that linked Cornish with the more substantial village of Durham, the asphalt and aqua almost perfectly aligned for close to six miles. The riverbanks were steeply pitched, and thick with moss and oak and maple saplings. There were clusters of raspberry bushes that were resplendent with claret-red fruit in July. The side of the river opposite the road was forest until you reached the small collection of houses and public buildings that most people considered the Cornish village center: the elementary school, a church, and a general store on one side of the water, a fire department and Little League baseball field on the other. Depending upon the angle of the road, the river could be either obvious or completely invisible.

Occasionally people swam naked in those sections where the river could not be seen from the street.

THE MONTGOMERY FAMILY lived no more than a hundred yards from the section of the Gale River that was traversed by the bridge—the very bridge over which the fire company had moved its trucks a few weeks earlier. On summer nights when their windows were open, the family could hear the water as it burbled through the thin clove next to the road.

The Sheldons lived outside of the tiny village, on the street that led past the Cousinos' dairy farm and on to the cemetery. That meant Hillary and Megan usually only visited the river in the summer, when they might venture to the swimming hole most frequented by the families with younger children—a section of the river that formed a cozy lagoon near a waterfall, and the depth rose to five or six feet. You could feel a slight current in the spot, but it wasn't enough to pull one from the pool.

To get there, either one of their parents or the parents of one of their friends would have to drive them. You couldn't walk to that swimming hole—not from the town or from their house—and on the hottest summer days there would be a conga line of cars and trucks parked as far to the side of the winding road as possible. Often an automobile would pull in so close to the brush that everyone would have to exit the vehicle on the driver's side.

The waters were high the day the Sheldon girls drowned—according to Alicia, this alone had drawn the three of them to the Gale—and there was in fact a flood warning. But there had been flood warnings on any given day throughout the fall, and no one was unduly alarmed.

While tromping aimlessly through the mud in the Montgomery family's yard, the three girls heard the low roar of the high water in the distance, and—despite the fact that the rain had resumed in earnest—went to see just how close to the bank the river really was. The general store was open until three on Sunday afternoons, and periodically that day people had ventured to either the bridge or the bank itself after getting their newspaper, cigarettes, or milk, and watched the water as it tumbled by. The waves weren't yet lapping at the very tops of the riverbank, but they were close. Alicia recalled that almost all of the adults who wandered by had remarked in some way on the whitewater, raising their voices so they could be heard over the sound of the rapids.

Just before two-thirty, Jeremy Stern left the general store with a six-pack of beer and a frozen pizza, and glanced at the bridge where the three nine-year-old girls were standing. Far down the street that led from the village up into the mountains he heard someone honking madly on a car horn. The toots were distant, but there was a frenzied quality to them. He returned to his own pickup to drive toward them, wondering what the fuss was all about and whether there was anything he could do to help. He backed into the street, not realizing that the person who was pounding furiously on his car horn was actually driving into the village as fast as he could, hoping to warn people that the Gale was already over its banks up on the mountain, and a wall of water was sure to hit the town any minute.

Other than Alicia Montgomery, Jeremy was the last person to see the Sheldon girls when they were alive.

THE WATER WOULD carve chasms in the road that were forty feet deep and, in one case, forty-five feet wide. Wherever the road bent to the south, there was at the very least erosion of the dirt beneath the asphalt, and in four cases there was complete destruction of the pavement—massive holes hewed abruptly into the hillsides. It was a miracle that the half-dozen or so cars on the road that moment were in sections of pavement that survived the flash flood, and so none of the motorists were hurt. Granted, the Willards' car was trapped for a week and a half between two canyons, and the elderly couple had to traverse one of the deep holes in the ground by foot to get home that afternoon. But they made it. Other cars had to turn back, returning to either Cornish or Durham.

And the property damage was immense. The Federal Emergency Management Agency would spend a month in the county—a week in Cornish alone. People who lived along the river lost the washing machines, dryers, and furnaces they kept in their basements. Small structures were upended and swept downriver, where they were smashed against the remains of a modest hydroelectric plant—largely boulders and cement pilings now—the power company had built along the river in 1922.

It had been the flood of 1927 that destroyed the generating station, so that the only traces left were a part of the foundation below the waterline and the concrete buttresses above it.

Once the wall of water had passed, there was an enormous heap of scrap wood at the site of the old plant, a mound easily as large as the woodpiles at the state's landfills and dumps. There were parts of two small barns there, including the Nuners' elegant carriage barn, and a gazebo. There were at least a half-dozen of the small outbuildings and lean-tos people used to store their sap buckets and plastic sugaring tubes, any tools they were likely to use outdoors, and their snowmobiles or their boats.

These items crashed into the power station stanchions as well, and usually broke apart.

The Murrays lost both of their horses, and the Dillons lost all three of their sheep. The animal carcasses somehow wound their way through the dam of debris by the old generator site, and washed ashore six miles away, where the river forked into a second branch that wound its way through the considerably larger towns of Durham, New Haven, and Middlebury.

The village Little League field was flooded, as was the library. The library sat in a room beside the town clerk's office, and it lost its entire collection of children's books—every book, that is, that wasn't checked out at that moment—because those books were kept on the lowest shelves and the water inside the building climbed to three feet before it started to recede.

The center of the town and a great many of the homes with basements that filled with water smelled liked river mud for days: earthy and musty and—because of the havoc that had been wrought—a little putrid.

The only fatalities, however, were Hillary and Megan Sheldon.

Along with Alicia Montgomery, they were still standing on the bridge in the shower when Jeremy Stern roared east to the sound of the honking. Alicia said they heard the wave before they saw it: It was a rumble that was not necessarily louder than the waters that had been rushing below them for minutes, but it was deeper and steadier, and they could hear it despite the thrumming of the rain. She had never been in an earthquake, but the nine-year-old had certainly learned about them in school and from movies, and she thought she was about to experience one.

She started to run from the bridge, and she presumed the Sheldon girls were right behind her. From the corner of her eye she saw the water sluicing through the riverbed, much more than the channel could handle, and it was obvious to her that the water was higher than the spot on the bridge where they'd been standing. It was clearly going to wash over the bridge, perhaps even take the bridge with it, and she was terrified. Scared to death. She didn't stop running until she was on the steps of the general store, where she saw grown-ups congregating: Even inside the store they had heard the sound of the wave and come outside.

When she finally turned around, she realized the water was indeed streaming over the bridge, and for a brief moment it reminded her of a fountain she knew of in Burlington: The fountain was a wide black wall, and water poured down it like a curtain. The bridge, of course, was perpendicular to the fountain, but she imagined the bridge at that moment would resemble the fountain if viewed from above.

For a short while her fear disappeared. She was with a small group of adults who were awed by what they were witnessing, but they clearly weren't viewing it as the end of the world. The water, as powerful as it was, was no more than a foot or a foot and a half above the asphalt on the bridge. Moreover, twenty or twenty-five seconds after the wave passed, the water fell once again beneath the bottom of the cement and steel span—not far below it, but below it nevertheless.

Across the bridge they could see that the Little League field was underwater, and the river was oozing toward the middle of the road on their side of the torrent, too—it looked to Alicia like a giant glass of cola had spilled and was spreading across the ground—but the grown-ups seemed more impressed than panicked. Then, almost at once, everyone turned toward the building that housed the town clerk's office and someone screamed, The library!

It was clear instantly that a great many books had been ruined. The papers in the town clerk's office were probably safe because the clerk and the selectmen used the front of the building—away from the wave. But the library was going to be a mess to clean up. All those books? Pulpy sponges, no doubt.

Alicia turned to share her fear for the books with Hillary and Megan. She had assumed all along that the girls were somewhere in the midst of the people around her. When she realized they weren't, she went into the store but found they weren't there, either. No one, of course, was inside the store—not when there was a wall of water to watch just outside the front door.

So she went back outside, hoping that the girls had run to her house. But she wasn't confident they had. Why would they? She looked in that direction anyway, but there was no sign of them.

She approached Alan Goodyear, one of the adults in the group who she knew, and asked him if he had seen Hillary or Megan Sheldon. Alan had children a few years behind her in the school. She had to ask him twice to be heard over the rain and the rumbling din of the water.

No, I haven't seen them, he said. You looking for them? He was cradling a bag of groceries in one arm.

They were with me on the bridge, she answered, and as the reality of what had happened began to grow concrete in her mind, she started to cry, swallowing the last word in her short sentence in her sobs, so once again she had to repeat herself for the adult. She went to wipe her eyes with her sleeve, but she was wearing a raincoat slick with spray, and she only made her face wetter. When she pulled her arm away, she realized that everyone was staring at her. Then, all at once, everyone started to move. Adrianna Palmore disappeared inside the store to call the rescue squad, and Alan Goodyear and Tad Russo began running toward the bridge. A man whose face she recognized but whose name she didn't know snuffed out his cigarette on the cement step and murmured something about going to find Terry and Laura—Hillary and Megan's parents. As he climbed into his SUV, he said to no one in particular that he thought Terry was at deer camp, but he wasn't positive, and then he shut the car door and backed out of the small parking lot.

For a moment she feared she'd been left alone, but that concern came and went fast: An older woman she knew named Sue Wallace was suddenly kneeling before her. Sue was wearing a heavy ski sweater, and when she wrapped her wet arms around her, Alicia could smell the damp wool as easily as she could feel it. But she didn't care, she didn't care at all, and she buried her face in the grown-up's wet sweater and continued to cry.

THE TWO BODIES hit a partial dam anchored by Will Richmond's fourteen-foot motorboat and the trailer on which he carted it to and from Lakes Dunmore and Champlain. The boat and the trailer had been under a tarp in the Richmonds' backyard.

The dam was a mile and a half west of the bridge, but well east of the even bigger pileup that would occur further downriver at the site of the old generator. It was between the village and the first of the great chasms in the asphalt road. The dam cut the width of the channel in half, but it didn't back up the water, and much—though far from all—of the debris either went up and over the boat and the bodies or around them.

When the river was back between its banks by three-thirty, the bodies were buried deep in a partly submerged wedge that in addition to the small boat and trailer included bicycles, garden carts, and the remains of an ice-fishing shanty. There was shredded metal roofing that looked like crumpled tinfoil, piles of wooden shutters in desperate need of scraping and painting, and a pair of antique carousel horses that belonged to a retired IBM engineer who was planning to restore them someday for his grandchildren. They'd been stabled since the summer in an outbuilding that had washed away.

For a time that afternoon there had been some hope that the girls would be found alive. Not much, but until the bodies were recovered, no one was going to tell Laura Sheldon that her girls must have died, and the mere act of verbalizing the notion that they might turn up at any moment kept the idea on a respirator.

Terry Sheldon, their father, was indeed away at deer camp that weekend. It would be evening before he would know what had occurred.

Laura, however, learned of the girls' fate around sunset—or what would have been sunset if the sky hadn't been an endless sheet of gunmetal gray. The bodies were not visible from the side of the river, but the rescue squad, the volunteer fire companies from both Durham and Cornish, and the state police moved methodically west from the bridge in their search, and started pulling apart the dam with the two carousel horses about a quarter past four.

They might have been found sooner if the people who did not live in Cornish had been able to get there more quickly. But with the main road destroyed, they'd had to approach the town from Middlebury and Ripton, an eighteen-mile detour as it was, made all the more time-consuming by the fact that the roads were dirt and had become severely rutted quagmires from the rain.

The bodies were first spotted by a volunteer firefighter from Durham who had never met the girls or their mother but knew Terry: Their paths had crossed at the scenes of numerous car accidents and fires, and even at a pair of hazardous-materials spills on Route 116.

It was clear instantly that the children were dead. One of the girls—no one could tell if it was Hillary or Megan—was completely naked: Every piece of clothing she'd worn had been ripped off by the litany of obstructions against which the body had banged as it cascaded downriver. The other child still had on her jeans and her sweater, but she was barefoot and her raincoat had disappeared.

Both girls were a mass of deep red scratches and cuts, and there were lengthy gashes along the legs of the twin who was nude. Her skin had a crimson cast to it, because of the way the cold water had caused the blood to settle near the surface after death.

Their eyes were closed, their hair was tangled with thin twigs and leaves, and there were great clods of mud in the small hollows cast by their joints. Their bodies were bent into shapes that no living person—even a contortionist—could bear.

Nevertheless, an EMS technician took the pulse of each girl just to be sure.

Then, much to the despair of their mother, the bodies were left where they were until someone could reach the state's attorney—and by the time someone was able to get to a telephone that worked (radios and cell phones were always useless in the spoonlike valley of the Gale), it was already five-thirty.

But the rescue squad and the volunteers and the state police hadn't a choice. It was against the law to remove the bodies without the state's attorney's explicit authorization.

As a courtesy to Laura, whose friends were keeping her home so she was far from the spot in the river where her children's damp bodies had grown cold, one rescue worker suggested they claim they had a pulse so they could cart the girls away in the ambulance. But there must have been twenty-five people at the scene by that point, and so no one took the idea seriously. Instead they gently covered each body with one of the blankets that were stored inside the rescue vehicle.

The person who told Laura that her children's bodies had been found worked for her husband—or, to be precise, reported to him. Terry was a sergeant with the state police, and it was one of his very own troopers, Henry Labarge, who stood in the kitchen in his boss's house with his winter campaign hat in his hands and told his boss's disconsolate wife that her children had drowned.

Later that evening he would also be the one to inform Terry. There was some talk that the station commander up in Derby would track Terry down and tell him, but Henry would have none of that idea. Though he was so fatigued his lids would loll shut and he would have to clutch the steering wheel to wake himself up, Henry drove all the way to the Sheldon family's deer camp in the northeast corner of the state to tell his sergeant in person, and then in that cruiser he drove him home.

PART ONE

Deer
Season

———

"I have no idea who my father is and I was very young when my mother was given or sold to Mr. Rowe's brother. Sixteen dollars a month may sound like a meager wage to you, but it's more, I believe, than your newspaper would pay me."

———

SERGEANT GEORGE ROWE,
TENTH REGIMENT, UNITED STATES CAVALRY,
QUOTED IN THE *ST. LOUIS POST-DISPATCH*,
AUGUST 11, 1869

———

Alfred

The boy sat on the wooden porch steps, his back flat against the peeling white column. He was oblivious to the paint flecks that surrounded his sneakers like gravel. In his hands was a black-and-yellow ball cap with the insignia for the Tenth Cavalry, a buffalo, stitched above the bill on the front. Along with a book about the buffalo soldiers, the old couple across the street had brought it back to him from Kansas, where they had recently been on a trip.

Behind him he heard the woman in the front hallway, just inside the glass storm door. For a long time she stood there, watching him, but he was resolved to neither look up nor turn around. She was being needy again. Needy, he knew, was a hard place to be and he had always avoided it at all costs. Instead of turning around, he focused on the embroidered animal on the cap, and the hump on its back that looked like a mountain. He knew he was making her uncomfortable.

Are you hungry? she asked after a moment, opening the door and leaning outside. I know it's early, but I can make us supper. Her voice was light—almost chipper—and a ripple of annoyance passed through him because it always seemed she was trying so hard.

Okay.

What would you like?

Whatever, he said. He told himself he was trying to be easy, but he knew after the word had escaped his lips that he'd sounded only difficult—which, on another level, had been his intention.

You like my macaroni and cheese, right?

Sure.

It's going to rain, the woman said, clicking her tongue in her mouth after she'd spoken. The boy could hear concern in her voice—needless, in his mind—but he'd heard enough in his ten weeks in Cornish to know why it was there: Two years earlier it had rained throughout the fall, and in some nearby pond or river her children had drowned. Two girls. He slept in the room that had belonged to one of them, probably in the very same bed.

Could it snow? the boy asked. It was cold, and in the distance they could both see the front coming in with the wind, and the rain—or, perhaps, the snow—falling like lead pencil shading to the west.

It's November, she answered, it always might snow. But I didn't hear anything on the radio about a storm. No one was talking like that.

You must get a lot of snow this high up.

I guess. Probably a little more than you're used to.

He heard the storm door glide shut. She hadn't left the doorway while they'd decided upon dinner and discussed the weather, and he hadn't looked up from the cap. He found himself wondering why they called them buffalo soldiers, and for a moment he worried that it might have had something to do with their hair.

DINNER WAS GOING to be an hour away since Laura had to boil the macaroni before baking it. And so he came inside and asked her if he could go to the cemetery up the hill.

Do you think you should? she asked. That sky looks awfully nasty.

I'll put on those mittens, he offered, referring to the hunting mittens he'd come across in the hall closet that he had commandeered as his own. Each had a single long slit midway up the inside of the wide pocket, parallel to the joints, that allowed a hunter to expose his fingers when he needed to point and shoot his gun.

I know you will. Still . . .

The kitchen cabinets were painted white, but they were built of metal instead of wood, and they made a tinny *ping* whenever the woman closed them. The handles were metal, too. Already there was a pot of water on the stove, with a flame below it gas blue.

And I'll wear a hat, he said.

She was standing on a ladder-back chair when he entered the kitchen, rummaging among the tins and cake mixes on the highest shelf for a can of Cheddar cheese soup, and he was embarrassed that he could see so much of the backs of her legs. She was wearing a corduroy dress that fell to just above her knees when she was standing but climbed higher now that she was stretching her arms high over head. Her cats—two girl cats she'd brought home from the shelter soon after she started working there, a pair of common-looking black-and-white kitties with markings that looked vaguely tuxedo-like—were watching her from the kitchen counter.

Okay, she said finally. Just come right back if it starts to drizzle—or snow! Don't wait. Okay?

He nodded and took the parka they'd bought for him off the cherry coat-rack across from the door, and replaced it with the blue-jeans jacket he'd been wearing. The coatrack had feet that looked like tree roots, and he knew it was one of Laura's favorite things in the house. Certainly it was one of the most elegant. He figured she would prefer that he wear a wool hat—that was actually what he'd had in mind when he offered—but at the last moment he decided to wear the souvenir ball cap with the buffalo on it instead. It wouldn't keep his ears as warm, but he liked the way it felt on his head. Then he reached into his school backpack for his portable CD player—it wasn't much bigger than a CD case and had a clip on the back for his belt—and left the woman alone in the kitchen.

IN THE CEMETERY he scuffed his way through the fallen leaves, kicking them before him as he walked. The wind was picking up, but it still hadn't started to rain.

When he reached a monument in the old section for some family named Granger, he pushed aside the tendrils and twigs from the massive hydrangea tree and crawled underneath. It was like being inside a cave, except that it was neither damp nor musty nor dark. At least not too dark. Though some of the conical flowers had turned brown and fallen off, many of the dead blossoms still clung to the talonlike branches of the tree. Enough foliage remained both to offer him the illusion that he was completely hidden and to keep him dry if the rain didn't become more pronounced than a shower.

He placed the headphones for the CD player over his ears as gently as he could, because his right lobe and the cartilage that ran like a seashell up the side had never healed properly, and would still smart if he failed to slip the headset on carefully. He didn't miss the studs he'd worn there that summer as much as he'd thought he would, but there had nevertheless been moments when he wished he still had them. They hadn't simply looked cool, they'd looked scary on a kid his size, and he knew that made him look tougher. Bigger.

When the earpieces were comfortably in place, he rested the cap loosely on his head.

He wished Terry or Laura smoked. If they did, he could have swiped a cigarette and had one right now. The Pattersons—the older couple he'd lived with in Burlington until they'd grown tired of chasing him down—had smoked, and he'd found that on any given day he could take a cigarette or two from the opened packs that littered the house and no one was ever the wiser.

A cigarette, the music cranked up loud on the CD player, a little peace. Not a bad moment to imagine. Still, he was vaguely content even without the cigarette.

He leaned against the boxy monument, wondering if other boys in the fifth grade knew of this spot. None of them ever talked about hanging out at the cemetery. The few afternoons he'd wandered aimlessly around the town with Tim Acker, another boy in the fifth grade, they'd never even considered heading up the hill to the graveyard. Maybe it was just too far, but maybe it was something more. For an instant he grew alarmed that his presence here was a sacrilege he didn't quite understand. After all, the other boys had family buried in this graveyard, grandmothers and grandfathers and great-aunts and -uncles. Schuyler Jackman's granddad was buried no more than forty or fifty feet from where he was sitting right now: Alfred had studied the headstone a half-dozen times, he'd even touched the cold marble. Tim Acker's cousin was here somewhere, too, a much older boy—a teenager—who'd died in a car accident further up the mountain near the gap. He figured that tombstone had to be in the new section, a part of the cemetery he rarely visited. It wasn't as interesting there. The tombstones were more recent, and there were no Civil War soldiers with their rusty G.A.R. stars.

Maybe, Alfred worried, it wasn't right for him to be here now. Or, perhaps, ever. He could be violating some country code or local tradition.

In Burlington no one would have cared if he and Tien—a Vietnamese girl who'd become his best friend in the year he was with the Pattersons—had felt like hanging out in the graveyard. It was a real city, and they went wherever they wanted. He figured the high-school kids there went to the cemetery all the time, especially when they needed a quiet place to get high. But never once had he met a soul in the cemetery in Cornish during the many times he'd roamed inside the wrought-iron fencing.

He decided he'd allow himself a few more minutes of solitude—that was something he had here that he'd never had anyplace else—and in one almost simultaneous motion he pulled his knees up to his chest and his cap down as far as his eyebrows. It was odd being the only kid in the house, and he wasn't sure what he thought about it. Often he felt lonely. It was, as far as he knew, a first for him since he'd been a baby with Renee. At the very least, it was the first time that he'd been alone in Vermont. Maybe when he was very young and they still lived in Philadelphia there'd been a time when he was the only kid around. But who knew? Maybe Renee did, but he had no expectations he'd ever see her again, and it probably wouldn't be the first thing he'd bother to ask her if he did.

One good thing about being the only child was that it meant he wasn't at the absolute bottom of the pecking order. In almost every other house where he'd lived, he had been. First there were the biologic children, and then there were the foster kids who'd gotten there before him. At one place—two houses ago—there had only been foster kids, but he was the last in and so he was still the low man on the totem pole. Not that it mattered. There they were all just a money-making scheme, anyway. They all knew they were just income so the woman could stay home, watch her soaps, and drink long-necks.

Yet even though he had more space now than he'd ever had in his life, he didn't feel as if he had much privacy. Here—at first he meant only the house, but as the word formed in his head, he realized he meant the town—he felt as if he was constantly being studied. Inside, outside. Everywhere, it seemed. It was the exact opposite of being ignored, which was something he was used to and understood. He knew how to get by on his own.

But between Terry and Laura and the neighbors and the teachers and the pastor and the kids at school, he felt like a zoo animal—and maybe not even a zoo animal you liked. More like a zoo animal you didn't quite trust. It was like they always thought he was up to something.

Maybe that was how come he felt lonely.

He was, as far as he could tell, the only black child for miles, and that didn't help, either. He wasn't just the new foster kid, he was the black foster kid. He couldn't begin to figure out what the deal was with that, or what the people who shuffled him around were trying to do now. At first he had figured this was just an emergency placement because he'd pissed off the Pattersons once and for all, but then he realized he was expected to stay here awhile.

He wasn't completely sure how he felt about that, even now after ten weeks.

Occasionally he wondered if he might have been adopted by someone if he'd been white, and that uncertainty crossed his mind now. He was five when it first dawned on him that skin color was an issue, and he'd been living with the Howards for close to three years. Suddenly Mr. Howard became ill, seriously ill, and within weeks he was living in a group home in Burlington. Alfred thought there may have been a place between the man getting sick and his spending time in a group home—an apartment, maybe, somewhere in the city's North End—but he couldn't quite remember. It was in that brief period when he'd stopped talking completely, and in hindsight he'd come to suspect that the grown-ups around him must have feared he was truly fucked up.

At some point since then he'd grown to believe—either because it was something someone had said to him or because it was something he simply had to assume was true to get on with his life—that the Howards would have adopted him if Mr. Howard hadn't gotten so sick. How much was real and how much he was making up was unclear to him. But he was quite sure that he had loved living with the Howards, and he had been happy.

He remembered the smell of the clean clothes that he wore, and the way Mrs. Howard always seemed to be dressing him straight from the dryer: The clothes were warm. He remembered a swing set made of wood, with a small fort beside the very top of a yellow slide. He remembered Mr. Howard driving him and a girl who was eight—a biologic child of theirs—to the elementary school in the morning on his way to an office nearby where he worked. He went to kindergarten in that school for a couple of months, leaving the class—and the Howards—either just before or just after Thanksgiving.

The Howards were white, and he was with them since he was a toddler. In those days, Renee still showed up once or twice a year. He remembered moments from those visits, too, but only because she always ended up shouting at the Howards.

Then she had another baby and moved to Jamaica, and gave up all her rights to him.

He only spent a couple of weeks in the group home, but it was there that he first began to fear—and fear, at least then, was indeed the right word—that he might never be adopted because he was black. Apparently that was one of the first things he had told a social worker when he started to speak again. After all, the kids in the home were all either Asian or black, while most of the people he saw on the streets were white. White grown-ups with white kids. That's what he saw out the window, at the playground, and in the kindergarten.

For a time he had expected the Howards to come back for him, but they never did. He thought Mr. Howard had died, but he wasn't completely sure. He knew he might have made that up to explain their disappearance from his life.

He squinted, and the tree branches looked like pencil lines against the gray sky. A spider's web, maybe.

He was afraid of spiders, and so he quickly opened his eyes all the way. He liked the cemetery, and he didn't want the place ruined for him. Here there was the undeniable relief that came with being completely invisible—of not being watched—and he wanted to retreat beneath the hydrangea until, at the very least, it was time to go back to the house for his supper.

"[Rowe] spoke very well for a colored, and rode much better than most. A superior horseman, I'd say. Of course, the settlers didn't much like him, but then he didn't like them a whole hell of a lot, either."

LIEUTENANT T. R. MCKEEVER,
TENTH REGIMENT, UNITED STATES CAVALRY,
WPA INTERVIEW,
AUGUST 1937

Laura

Laura crumbled the toast over the macaroni and cheese in the casserole dish and slipped their dinner into the oven. Then she sat down at the kitchen table, a slim woman with hair the color of sand when the surf has just receded and a complexion as pale as the skin on the inside of her palms. She was still in her mid-thirties, but her face and her eyes had been aged prematurely by grief, and she hadn't felt her age in two years. She'd felt, always, considerably older. She stopped in mid-turn and tried to remember what it was that she wanted to do next. Clear away the catalogs that had come with the mail? Set the table? Pour Alfred's milk?

No, the casserole needed forty minutes in the oven. If she poured his milk now, it would be warm when they sat down to eat. Maybe she should get the carrots up from the basement. They still had summer carrots left in the sand barrel.

She wished she had remembered to ask Alfred about his day at school. What he'd done, who he'd talked to. What they'd studied in social studies or history. Anything. Even whether he'd done his homework.

She wished, she decided simply, that she wasn't so out of practice at this, she wished there was some sort of muscle memory that went with parenting. She knew she hadn't wanted him to wander up to the cemetery right now—except for school, when he wasn't in her sight she grew worried and frightened—but she also wasn't sure she could have stopped him (or, for that matter, whether she should have). If she told him to stay around the house, she feared he would just ignore her and go anyway. He had done that a couple of times when Terry wasn't home. He'd treated

25

her like she was a giant paper doll and simply disregarded whatever she'd said.

The worst had been that Saturday morning in early October when he hitchhiked to Burlington. Just up and left, and thumbed rides the thirty-plus miles to the city to see that girl named Tien and—if he could—find some apparently loathsome teenager named Digger. When he got to the apartment where the girl lived, however, he discovered that she, too, had a new home, and her old foster father wouldn't say where. The man had called Social Services and the boy had been brought back to Cornish, and no one that day had looked very good. Certainly, Laura believed, she hadn't. And yet she had offered to set up a play date with the girl, hadn't she? And Alfred had declined. Afterward, he insisted he no longer had any interest in anyone he'd known in Burlington, and—she had to admit—from the little she knew of those friends, she was glad.

She wondered now if the real reason why she didn't want Alfred at the cemetery was her fear that he'd find the girls' graves. She wasn't sure why this idea disturbed her, but it did.

She would have called Terry at the shack his family used as a deer camp so she could hear his voice, but there wasn't a telephone. And, of course, there wasn't a tower nearby, so the cell phone wouldn't function.

She tried not to be angry with Terry for going hunting, but it was inescapable: She was mad. Alfred had only been with them a couple of months, and they were all still getting to know one another. Figure each other out. And Terry had gone off to deer camp Friday night, as if it were just any other November, and he wouldn't be back until tomorrow. Tuesday.

Reflexively, she looked up at the Humane Society calendar on the corkboard on the kitchen wall. Terry had been gone a weekend and a day. She'd spoken to him twice when he called from the pay phone at the general store near the neglected cabin they called their camp, but neither time had Alfred been home, and so neither time had he and the boy connected.

She and Terry hadn't discussed it, but she knew the only reason he was going to be back tomorrow was that Wednesday was the anniversary of the twins' deaths. Two years now. Far enough in the past that whole hours might pass without her thinking about them.

Had last year not been a leap year, the anniversary would have been Tuesday. Tomorrow.

She went to the den, a small room that faced north and so it was dark even at noon in the peak of the summer, and took a photo album out from a cabinet in the bookshelf a previous owner had built into the wall. Long ago she had taken down all the photos of the girls that once hung on the walls or sat on tables and bureaus in frames, because she couldn't bear to be reminded of them every moment. She would pause before the images as she'd pass by them in the hallway or the kitchen, and grow oblivious to the grilled cheese that was burning on the stove or the bath that she'd started to run for herself minutes before. She had never actually allowed the water to spill over the sides of the tub, but twice she'd stared for so long at a photograph of the girls in a tree in her mother-in-law's yard that the hot water had run out and her bath had been tepid.

Now, with the boy up the hill and her husband at deer camp, she sat on the couch beside the sleeping cats and flipped the heavy sheets that held the snapshots of the girls, occasionally dabbing at her nose with a Kleenex.

SHE UNDERSTOOD THAT everyone responded to personal tragedies in personal ways. She understood firsthand the one universal: Grief comes upon a person in increments. Reality becomes more painful as the magnitude of the loss sets in, and the body slowly emerges from the shock that only briefly envelopes it. Things have to get a lot worse before they get better.

But a loss this great? There were months when she didn't believe she'd ever get better—and, what was more important for everyone around her, it was clear that she didn't want to.

For a time, for her, there had been Prozac. And there had been the church, though she wasn't exactly sure there had been God. She was haunted by, among other Sunday-school memories, the Lord God's dictum to Ezekiel that though his wife was about to die, he might sigh, but not aloud, and he should make no mourning for the dead. Still, she had found it helpful to sit with the pastor on weekday mornings before she would go to the animal shelter where she worked. The two of them would find seats in the last pew in the sanctuary, completely alone in the big room, and she would cry and talk and he would listen.

One time she went to a bereavement group for parents in Burlington, but it had been a long drive for little comfort. She hadn't found it helpful to hear other women—and the group was entirely female—talk about the deaths of other children, and she hadn't returned for a second visit. Certainly some of her friends had tried to be there for her, but without children of her own anymore, her connections to them began to fray: She would never see these other women at the weekly Girl Scout meetings or T-ball practices or the annual "authors" tea at the elementary school. She would never run into them at the kids' swimming lessons or ballet, and there was no longer any need to speak with them to coordinate play dates and sleepovers.

Besides, she didn't want their sympathy. She wanted only one thing in the world and that was her children, and no one could give her that. And so she retreated completely into a space that consisted only of the animals at the shelter and the work they demanded, her talks with the minister, and her evenings and late afternoons with her husband. She saw nobody else, and for another period after the girls' deaths there had been the rediscovery—the reinvention, actually—of sex with Terry. About six months after the flood, when the days were long and the summer still stretched out before them, she decided to stop taking her antidepressants, and suddenly she and her husband entered a phase in which they were having sex all the time. She was behind it, and that made it even better. She had felt incredibly powerful, because the sex was not for one minute about trying to re-create a family or have another child. They both knew that wasn't going to happen. She'd had her tubes tied when the girls were three, after she and Terry concluded that their particular family unit worked well with four people. There were two grown-ups and there were two girls, and this meant that (as Terry put it, only half-kidding) you could play a man-to-man defense. If they had another child, however, the grown-ups would be outnumbered and reduced to a zone.

For a while, the sex alone had gotten her through it, and she was doing things she had never before imagined. She would surprise Terry in the shower and lather his penis with soap till he came, she would be waiting for him in only a slip or a G-string when he'd come home from work. She wouldn't care that he hadn't bathed since that morning, and he'd spent the day in his wool uniform. It didn't matter that he might smell like his cruiser. They'd make love on the couch, and sometimes when he would kneel on the floor and lick her, her orgasms would be so long and intense that she would cry out and fear that she had peed on the cushions.

She felt (had she heard the term on the radio?) deliciously slutty.

But then the days grew short once again, and the first anniversary of the girls' deaths began to draw near. And she could no longer sit in the den in only a slip or a chemise, because it was simply too cold. She tried waiting for him in the bedroom but it wasn't the same.

By Halloween, they were rarely having sex—two and three weeks would pass between couplings—and she considered calling in another prescription for the antidepressant. But she already felt dazed, and she hadn't liked the drug's side effects: She was sure it had been the pills that kept her awake at night, and given her an upset stomach almost daily.

She was aware that her mood swing had badly confused her poor husband. He'd gone from sleeping with a vital, sensuous woman to living with a zombie. Some nights that winter he tried to seduce her, and she did her best to respond. But it was clear that she was, literally, just going through the motions, and by the middle of January he, too, grew disinterested. He grew tired of trying.

Once, near Valentine's Day, they fought about her sterilization. She understood they were both being unreasonable, that this was a decision they'd made together, but it had seemed to her at that moment that she'd only done it to please him. Maybe this wasn't true, but she was also confident that she would never have minded a third child or being a family of five, and she told him so. And then after she added how she wished it wouldn't be so difficult—if not impossible—to reverse the procedure, he responded in a way that really set her off, because she realized on some level he was dead-on: He told her she couldn't handle a child right now, she wasn't ready. He added that he wasn't ready either, but that second part didn't matter. She'd barely been listening by then.

Nevertheless, as the second summer after the girls' deaths approached, her spirits once again lightened. She found herself planting a vegetable garden for the first time in two years, and she began to care for the flower gardens that had been left largely to their own devices the previous summer. She pulled up the grass that had migrated into the beds and ruthlessly yanked from the soil the Johnny-jump-ups that had overrun entire sections. She cut back the phlox that lined the walk from the end of the driveway to the front door, and added a pair by the steps that were a gray-blue that matched her little girls' eyes.

Then, when she found two ornamental clay tubs at a lawn sale, she brought them home and filled them with pink ageratum. They were, she decided, the rural Vermont equivalent of stone lions, and she placed them at the end of their driveway.

The house sat just beyond the village, midway up a small ridge that offered magnificent views of Mount Ellen and Abraham to the east, but was so sheltered by the bluff and the high trees behind it that evening always came early. Good sunrises, bad sunsets. They were separated from the rest of the town first by the Cousinos' dairy farm, and then by a wide finger of forest that snaked into the valley and hadn't yet been logged or cleared for another of the small clusters of houses that seemed to be springing up everywhere within thirty-five miles of Burlington. When the Cousinos would spread manure, she was grateful for those trees and the buffer they offered. There was a house across the street that belonged to a retired college professor and his wife, but otherwise there were no buildings in sight—really no structures even, except for the shed for the cemetery up the hill.

By the Fourth of July that year she was even seriously considering the possibility of bringing a child into the house via adoption or a foster care program. Maybe, she thought one day as she painted tiny flags on her fingernails, she and Terry might wind up with a little baby, and together they could rediscover the hard work that came with an infant. The girls had been nine when they died, and so their parents' memories of colic and sleep deprivation were sketchy at best.

Laura was so inspired by the prospect of another child that she agreed to teach Sunday school the following autumn, giving her at least an hour a week around kids. She couldn't have handled such a thing the previous year, but she could now. When the fall arrived, she would teach the first- and second-graders in a classroom in the wing off the sanctuary, using a standardized curriculum that seemed to stress word games and coloring and snacks. She wouldn't, as she had feared at first, need a degree in theology or the ability to make sense of the prophets. Mostly, she was told, she would just need patience, and she had plenty of that now.

It had actually been the pastor who suggested a foster child. He'd offered his idea toward the end of May, presenting the notion to her as if she were a wounded bird in his palm, but one he was sure he could heal: He spoke quietly, but with great concentration and will. He said the kids—some of them, anyway—were less troubled than one would imagine, and in many ways they were easier than a baby. After all, they were older. But, he had stressed, they were no less in need of love.

At first Terry had been tepid to the idea. He said he wasn't sure how emotionally invested he could become in a child who wasn't going to be his.

Sometimes foster children become yours, she explained.

Not the older ones, I expect.

Maybe sometimes.

So how should I view it, then? As a trial adoption?

I guess if you wanted to, you could.

He admitted that he could get used to the idea that there wouldn't be any diapers to deal with, and he said he certainly liked the notion that she'd be happy. Happier, anyway.

She wasn't sure if he understood that the state would help subsidize any child they agreed to take in, and she wasn't sure she should tell him. Terry had a lot of pride, and she didn't think he'd appreciate public assistance. Moreover, she wasn't completely sure what she thought of the money, either. She feared that it made them seem mercenary, and their intentions look suspect. She didn't like herself much when she took a calculator from the kitchen drawer by the refrigerator and multiplied out thirteen dollars and eighty cents, the per diem stipend they'd receive from the state, by the thirty days that fell in so many months. But she also couldn't stop herself. And while a little less than fourteen dollars a day didn't sound like a lot of money, it added up quickly—especially since it was all tax-free, and none of it would have to go toward health insurance. Apparently that would be covered by the state.

But when she broached the subject of a foster child again a few days later, she decided she should be honest with Terry about the money. Maybe if he didn't want it, they didn't have to take it.

But he'd been fine. She noticed that he didn't ask how much money was involved—his way, she decided, of making it clear that the money had nothing to do with either his interest or his consent.

And so she had filled out a surprisingly short application (why, she wondered, had she been so sure there would be essay questions?), and she and Terry had both taken a brief course on how being a foster parent differed from being a regular parent: What, in essence, would be expected of them, and what was involved. How these kids might differ from the children they had seen on the school bus that for years had arrived at the end of their driveway twice a day. She gave something called the Department of Social and Rehabilitation Services the permission to do criminal background checks on herself and her husband, and to make sure that neither was a known child abuser.

The irony was not lost on her: Her husband was a sergeant with the state police. In less than two years his lieutenant would retire, and in all likelihood he would be promoted and given command of the barracks—one of the reasons they'd decided to stay in Cornish after the flood.

She was the possible wild card in their minds. Not him.

Two weeks later, a woman from SRS came to their house at the end of the day, and she and Terry were interviewed together in the living room about child-rearing practices and discipline. About how their daughters had died. The woman tried to make sure they understood the program, and—depending upon the child—what they might be in for. She wanted to make sure they were ready. A few days after that another lady from the state came by for a visit, and this one wanted a tour of their home. It was clear to both Terry and Laura that she was impressed. She observed that the bedroom they would give to the child was airy and bright, and that one of the two windows was over the front porch and therefore could serve as an exit in the event of a fire.

She noted that Terry's guns were locked in a metal cabinet, and that the ammunition was kept in a separate sideboard—also locked—and she said that was proper. For a moment Laura feared that Terry was going to say something defensive, but he didn't. He simply nodded.

They both knew as soon as the woman left that they would get a child. It was, as Terry said, a slam dunk. A sure thing.

They even assumed their child would be a girl, though they decided she'd be younger than Hillary and Megan had been when they died. They envisioned her at six or seven, and they imagined almost daily how gentle they'd be with her. After all, who knew what scars the child would be carrying inside her?

They told themselves they were silly to anticipate with tangible certainty who their child would be, but it was hard not to hope for someone who might resemble the daughters they'd lost—especially after all they'd endured—and that this child would, as the SRS folks clearly hoped, be a youngster they would someday want to adopt. Still, when they discussed what sort of child would wind up under their roof, they were always careful to remind each other that this person might be nothing at all like their dreams.

Nevertheless, they were caught completely off guard when, barely two months after they had entered the system, they were offered what was described to them as a quiet, slightly troubled ten-year-old boy with skin, they would see, as dark as their mahogany headboard.

———

"Only a few braves went, but Lone Bear was among them. They took horses and mules from the ranchers, maybe some livestock. I don't remember. It's only the horses I can see now. The currents were always strong where the Pecos and the Canyon Creek met, but the men had been able to cross it before the thunderstorms. Then the rains came and the water rose. Two days it rained. Otherwise, the soldiers would never have been able to catch them. They were that close to the village."

———

VERONICA ROWE (FORMERLY POPPING TREES),
WPA INTERVIEW,
MARCH 1938

———

Terry

erry Sheldon—not tall in reality, but trim and athletic and with posture so impressive that he looked considerably taller than five-eight—watched the woman adjust the deer on the metal scale, pushing its haunches back onto the platform so she could get a more exact reading. The platform—a wire-mesh grill, actually, that dangled a good four feet off the ground—was hitched to a brace that extended out like a diving board from the red clapboard outbuilding just to the side of the general store.

Beside him, his younger brother was sipping a beer and grinning. Russell had popped the top of the can the moment they slid the dead buck onto the scale.

Hundred and eighty pounds, I say, his brother said. Maybe two hundred.

Oh, please, Terry said, and he resisted the urge to roll his eyes. He's healthy, all right, but you're acting like you just brought down Big Foot. He wondered if that was a muffler clamp the store was using to link the scale to the brace above it. It was the only new metal anywhere on the device, the only alloy that still had a trace of sparkle.

His brother shook his head and snickered. I should have entered the buck pool, he said. Just so I could take my loving older brother out to dinner and watch him squirm.

You can take me out to dinner anytime, Terry said.

But it would be so much better if it was with money I'd won in a buck pool.

Cast out those little demons you got with being young and green?

Squash 'em like grapes.

The deer had ten points, and a hole right behind the shoulder where the bullet had penetrated the animal's body. Near them two local dogs watched, hoping there would be some blood on the ground or on the scale when the two men put the buck back in Terry's red pickup.

Hundred and fifty pounds, the woman said finally, and she wrote down the number on a piece of paper on a brown clipboard.

Terry couldn't help himself, and he started to laugh.

That scale can't be right, Russell said, and then he turned to Terry. 'Cause if it is, we have gotten very lame in our old age. Hundred and fifty? Really?

The woman—thirty, maybe, with creosote-colored hair that fell to her shoulders, and a moist cherry lipstick that Terry thought was more than a little provocative—shrugged. It's still big, she said, her voice cheerful and light. Biggest I've seen today.

Well, thank you, Terry told her. That's the first time a woman's ever said anything like that to my kid brother. Do you have any idea how happy you just made him?

The woman stood up a little straighter and smiled. You want me to take a picture for the wall? she asked. Beginning along the trim beside the inside of the front door and continuing into the store were columns of Polaroids of hunters and their kills, with the name of each hunter written in black Magic Marker on the white strip below the image. By the time hunting season was over, the pictures would have taken over a good stretch of that wall.

You bet, Russell said.

By the scale, or the truck?

If you do the scale, Terry said, be sure to focus in on the weight.

His brother glared at him. The truck will be just fine, thank you very much, he said.

Terry helped his brother pull the buck from the rear of the scale, and they dropped it with a small thud into the back of the truck. The head bounced just a bit on the metal. The younger man then sat beside the animal, shifting the carcass slightly so that none of it would be hidden behind his orange vest, and held up the deer's head for the camera. The woman reached for the boxy Polaroid on a rock by the outbuilding, took the picture, and then started back toward the store. She was waving the print in her hands, drying it despite the chill in the air. Both men followed her.

Inside, Russell watched her tack the image to the wall and mumbled, Hundred and fifty. Yeah, right. Terry saw that his brother had left his beer in the back of the truck, and he was relieved. He certainly didn't want him walking around the shop with an open beer in his hands.

Maybe there is something wrong with my scale, the woman said. Maybe a hundred and ninety will win this year.

His brother studied each picture on the wall, and Terry figured he was trying to guess the weight of each animal. He came up here a lot more often than Terry did, and so he probably knew more of the faces in the Polaroids.

The woman strolled back behind the counter and helped a friend of hers, another woman somewhere in her late twenties or early thirties but nowhere near as attractive, bag a small collection of groceries. A box of sugar dough-nuts, some bread. Deli meat. Beer. A newspaper. Two packs of cigarettes. The customer was a man with hair the gray and black of the ash in a wood-stove, and it was piled thick on his head. He was still in his camouflage jacket and pants, and, as the man was leaving the store, Terry wondered if he'd gotten his buck for the year.

Unsure what he was going to say or why he was doing it, Terry asked the woman who'd weighed his brother's deer what her name was. He'd noticed there weren't any rings on her finger.

Phoebe, she said.

I'm Terry.

She raised one eyebrow, a small movement that always impressed him because he couldn't do it. Only Terrys I've ever known have been girls, she said.

It's short for Terrance.

I see.

You live around here? he asked.

No, I live an hour and a half away, but I commute here for the benefits. Of course I live around here! She shook her head and grinned, and folded her arms across her chest. Briefly he imagined her breasts under her turtle-neck shirt and denim jacket, and then he thought of Laura.

It's a beautiful part of the state, he said. My family has a camp just off the Lunenburg road.

I saw you and your friend—

Brother.

I saw you and your brother over the weekend. As a matter of fact, there were four of you, right?

Still are. Two of my cousins are in the woods right now.

You got your deer yet?

Nope. He didn't tell her that he hadn't even fired his rifle, despite ample opportunities. He understood that once he'd brought down his animal, he'd have to go home and face the anniversary of his little girls' deaths.

It is beautiful here, she said. I lived in Montpelier for seven years, and I was surprised by how much I missed it.

What brought you back?

She looked to Terry's right, and he saw that two teenage boys wanted to buy a six-pack of Pepsi and a handful of Slim Jims. He took a step back so she could ring them up. The other woman, he noticed, was slicing sandwich meats in the back of the store.

When the boys had moved on, Phoebe answered, My mom got sick.

I'm sorry. I presume you mean seriously sick.

Lung cancer.

My father died of lung cancer, he said. How is she doing now?

She died.

He nodded. Recently?

August.

You've had a tough fall. Is your father alive?

Yup. Healthy as a bear.

How's he doing otherwise?

He's okay. He doesn't talk about it much.

Are you going to go back to Montpelier?

Probably after the holidays. I had a good job in Waterbury with the state. I can get it back whenever I want it.

What part?

Developmental and Mental Health Services.

He thought instantly of Alfred because Mental Health Services and SRS were both part of the same massive state agency, and how quickly the foster family program had found him and Laura a child. He couldn't believe that Phoebe could possibly have crossed paths with any of the caseworkers they'd met in Social Services: It was a small world, all right, but it wasn't that small. Still, he figured he'd better find out.

What did you do there?

My business card said financial specialist. Translation? I'm a bean counter.

I'm sure counting beans can be very satisfying work, he said, surprised by how much her short, crisp answer had relieved him. The woman spent her time with numbers, not people.

She leaned against the shelves behind the cash register and then rested her hands on the wood. You do ask a lot of questions, Terry . . .

Sheldon. Terry Sheldon.

Any special reason you're so inquisitive?

He shrugged. I'm a state trooper. I guess I'm just likely to ask questions. Force of habit.

She glanced at his hand, and reflexively he followed her eyes. He realized he was still wearing his gloves. You married, Terry Sheldon? she asked.

I am.

Then I'm just going to assume you're inquisitive by nature, and there's nothing more to it. Okay?

There probably isn't more to it than that.

Uh-huh, she said.

Then she did something, and he realized that she was doing it to punish him for flirting with her despite the fact that he was married. She took a small matchbook-sized packet with a wet wipe inside it, tore it open, and reached toward him across the counter. So close to him that he could smell the floral odor of the powder or antiperspirant that she had used under her arms, she unfolded the wipe and ran it along his cheek at the edge of his immaculately trimmed mustache. She concentrated on his face, and her lips were within inches of his.

Then she pulled away. I thought I saw a smudge there, she said, or just maybe something of interest. But I guess I was mistaken.

His brother came up beside them and clapped him on the shoulder. I got nothing to be ashamed of, he said to Terry. That buck is just fine.

Terry turned to him and nodded. He realized his legs were a little bit shaky.

HIS COUSINS AND his brother were listening to the Celtics on the portable radio and playing cards, but Terry was annoyed by the static and had decided to leave the game. The cabin still smelled of fried meat, and

Terry was grateful because the earthy smell of the venison was considerably better in his opinion than the earthy smell of the three other men.

A part of him was relieved that Laura hadn't let him bring Alfred along. She said it was because the boy would have had to miss two days of school, and that was, probably, a factor. But he knew there was more to it than that. She lived in fear that something awful would happen to the child when he was out of her sight, and she wanted him nowhere near four men with a small arsenal in the woods. Still, he, too, was glad that the child wasn't with him: Deer camp was always a gamier place than he remembered, and though he always tried to recapture the joy he'd felt here as a boy, it just hadn't been the same since his father had passed away.

There was little light in the corner of the room he had staked out with the newspaper, but he wasn't doing much more than scanning the headlines and daydreaming. He'd spread the paper out on the massive picnic table that for two generations had been the table on which they'd butchered the animals and eaten their dinners. They usually ate by a kerosene lamp someone would place in the middle, or by candles in the two glass-enclosed hurricane lamps. They'd always played hearts or pinochle on the folding card table they set up near the woodstove, some years squeezing seven or eight men and boys around it.

He'd thought of Phoebe off and on since he and Russell had left the store, and the smell—was it roses?—that he'd taken in when she leaned toward him. He didn't feel guilty, reminding himself that thoughts weren't actions. Isn't that what the radio shrinks he sometimes listened to always said? Nope, thoughts were definitely not actions, and he knew as well as anyone that you certainly didn't arrest anyone for a thought.

Still, a part of him wasn't proud of himself. He loved Laura, they'd been married for almost fifteen years.

Yet he also felt that once again there was a distance between them, once more she was shutting him out. As soon as the boy had come into their lives, she'd fallen back inside herself—or, to be precise, away from him. It was not unlike the way she had been right after the girls died. But then at least he had understood what she was experiencing. He had known as well as she had the way the frustration and the anger could cause the adrenaline to rush through you in waves, make you frantic for a time, and then leave you only exhausted, despairing, and sad. He knew firsthand what it was like to sit in a cruiser on the side of Route 7 with your radar shut off, and wail so loudly that you half-expected some entitled son of a bitch in a sleek SUV to hear you and stop.

But this was different. Now that they had Alfred, Terry felt completely irrelevant. He'd never been able to help her before, that was clear, but at least he hadn't felt irrelevant.

He wished he understood the boy better, he wished the boy enjoyed the same kinds of things he did. But it just wasn't happening. The kid had absolutely no interest in Scouting, wouldn't even talk to the local troop leader. Didn't want to play soccer after school, even though there was a pretty good program, or go to the gym to shoot baskets. *Disassociative* was the word Louise, the caseworker, had used. Mostly he just groused that there was no cable in Cornish, and so he couldn't watch music videos and trash TV. Big loss, that, it seemed.

Sometimes Terry wasn't even sure that he liked the child, and that thought always made him feel guilty. He didn't believe it had a damn thing to do with the fact that the boy was black. Still, he'd probably said about a thousand words to black people in his whole life. When his lieutenant— a guy pushing forty-nine who'd be gone in fifteen months—had called him a multicultural wanna-be one afternoon in the barracks, he'd taken great comfort in the remark. It suggested that he was well-meaning and big-hearted.

His boss, of course, hadn't meant it quite like that. When he heard about Alfred, he'd nodded thoughtfully, his massive boots resting on the wastebasket beside his desk, and said to Terry, Noble notion, taking in a black boy. But what do you and Laura really know about a kid like that—or, for that matter, raising a kid like that? You ever done anything more with a black person than bust one?

And he was right. He told himself that he was no more likely to pull over an African-American for speeding or for driving a rust bucket without blinkers than he was anyone else. But how could he be certain? He saw so few, so very few. How could he really know? Moreover, he had to admit that, pure and simple, he didn't have a whole lot in common with a black boy who'd been born in Philadelphia and then lived most of his life in Burlington. Burlington may not have been a major metropolis, but it was considerably more urban than any place he'd ever lived. When the kid had arrived at their house, he had a line of metal studs in his ear that some sociopathic teen had placed there in a shopping mall men's room. Terry didn't even want to know what kind of needle the older boy had used to pierce the lobe and tough cartilage.

Sometimes he wondered what the hell those SRS people were thinking when they sent a black child to live in rural Vermont. He'd look at the boy over dinner as he and Laura talked about what they had done with their days at their jobs, and he'd realize he didn't have the slightest idea what he should be telling this kid about the black experience.

That was his lieutenant's expression, not his. But he understood what the lieutenant had been driving at. Laura had bought some books on black history, and they'd both read articles on interracial parenting. One afternoon he spent forty-five minutes on the phone trying to find a barber closer than Burlington who would have the slightest idea how to cut the boy's hair. It was proving to be a real stretch for them both, and most of the time they just tried to be decent parents and hoped the rest would work itself out.

Unfortunately, it was hard to be a decent parent when the child hardly spoke. He was real big on single-word answers, but downright allergic to complete sentences. And it seemed as if he was way too comfortable disobeying Laura when she was home alone with him. They'd actually had to take the studs away from the kid after the school principal had called Laura at the animal shelter to tell her that Alfred had arrived in his classroom with the line of steel balls back in his ear. And twice Alfred had ignored Terry's edict that the cruiser was off-limits unless he was present, taking the keys off his dresser and climbing inside. There was a Remington 870 in the trunk, a weapon with a twenty-inch rifle-sighted barrel, and the last thing he wanted was for the lad to discover that little piece of hardware.

He shuddered when he thought about the lyrics to the songs the kid listened to on his headset, or the fact that he played the music so loud they could hear the low rumble three and four feet away.

Still, Alfred wasn't violent, Terry reminded himself, and that was helpful. The caseworker had said some kids were—and everyone in the state knew about the teenage boy who'd shot his foster dad dead despite living under the same roof with the man for three years. During the summer before Alfred had arrived, Terry had in fact feared that because he was a state trooper they'd give them a real problem child. If they'd wanted to, of course, they certainly could have found one for Laura and him. A fire starter, maybe. Perhaps a kid who tortured animals.

If they'd wanted to, they could have sent the two of them a real curve by giving them a teenage girl. Those kids were an accusation of sexual assault just waiting to happen. Don't sit on the bed with her when you two are talking. Those were the exact words in one of the manuals they'd received. Or: When the two of you are alone in a room, always keep the door open. This way your intentions will not be misconstrued.

He sighed. Maybe he was too hard on Alfred. The boy wasn't particularly trusting, but as far as anyone knew he wasn't a delinquent, either. He'd done time in a group home when he was five, but that was only because the kid had clammed up so badly—apparently it had been a hell of a lot worse than the mere quiet that marked his behavior right now—after his foster father was diagnosed with pancreatic cancer and he'd been moved someplace else.

He glanced at his watch and saw it was only a quarter to eight. The general store was open another fifteen minutes. If he left now, he could be there before the place closed for the night and call the house. Talk to Laura and Alfred. Tell them he was looking forward to coming home tomorrow, with or without a deer, and for sure he'd be back by supper.

He stood without folding the newspaper and told the men at the card table that he was going to the store to use the pay phone to call his family, and he wanted to get there before the place closed.

Oh, please, Russell said, without looking up from the cards in his hands. The phone's outside the front door.

So?

Store doesn't have to be open to use it.

Well, I want to call before it's too late, he said, but he knew exactly what his brother was suggesting. He figured Phoebe would be there, and he wanted to see her again before he left.

It's your life, Russell said.

He ignored his brother because he didn't plan on anything other than a little general-store banter with the woman by the cash register. Harmless stuff, completely harmless. Besides, he reminded himself as he zipped up his coat, the real reason he was going was to call his wife and the boy.

Nothing wrong with that.

He realized he wanted to brush his teeth, but he knew he didn't dare. Surely his cousins or Russell would say something to him if he went anywhere near his toothbrush. Fortunately, he was almost certain he'd seen a tin of Altoids on the front seat of his cousin's moldering Blazer, and he figured he could grab a handful on the way to his truck.

"It had finally stopped raining and so I went to the river to wash our clothes. I knew how high the water was before we got there, because I could hear it. It sounded like there was a waterfall nearby, but there wasn't. It was just the river. And then I heard the guns, and I knew the men were coming back and they were in trouble."

VERONICA ROWE (FORMERLY POPPING TREES),

WPA INTERVIEW,

MARCH 1938

The Heberts

Even before she had opened her eyes, she knew he wasn't in the bed with her. It wasn't that she couldn't hear him snoring, or she couldn't smell the cream he sometimes put on his shoulder at night—that smell, after all, lingered long after he'd left the room. It was the way the quilt felt heavy upon her. When he was in bed, the quilt rose high off her body, more like a tent than a blanket, because of the way he slept on his back with his knees bent into triangles.

She reached for the little clock and brought it close to her eyes so she could read the numbers. The roman numerals were supposed to glow in the dark, and they still did, more or less, but the hands for the hours and minutes were just too close in length, in her mind. She'd bought it at a yard sale over Labor Day Weekend to replace the digital clock that had to be reset every time they lost power. It drove her crazy in the winter, because they seemed to lose power for a minute or two at least three or four times a week. One good wind, the lights would flicker, and she'd be resetting the digital clock that was plugged into the wall—a clock with digits that somehow managed to move forward at a pace that was downright geologic until they approached the hour and minute she was looking for. Then they'd speed up, explode forward like a rocket ship, and force her to start the process all over again.

This clock was a little better both because it ran on batteries and because she could set the time with a knob on the back she could control, but it was far from perfect. If only the minute hand were maybe a quarter of an inch longer.

She figured at four in the morning that Paul was up for the day. The man had never farmed a day in his life, but now that he was in his mid-sixties, he was starting to act as if he had eighty-five Holsteins to milk. He just didn't sleep anymore.

She decided she might as well get up, too, and join him downstairs for breakfast.

I hope I didn't wake you, he said when he saw her in the kitchen doorway. He was reading what looked like a magazine at the pumpkin pine table, and when he looked up at her she was struck, as she was often, by the way his head had grown rounder and his skin had grown smoother with age. His hair, as thin and fine now as an infant's, was whiter than table salt, and it covered his skull like a bathing cap. He was eating cold cereal from a glass salad bowl while he read, and she saw that he had poured orange juice on the flakes instead of milk. She found herself wondering, as she did every morning when she saw the orange and brown mixture, how he could eat it that way. She remembered the first time he'd done it, about two years ago, she had feared it was the onset of Alzheimer's: The poor man was pouring juice instead of milk on his bran flakes, completely oblivious to convention. No doubt he'd start getting lost in the bathroom any day now.

But then he had reassured her that he was fine, and explained that his doctor had suggested the juice was merely another way he could cut back on his cholesterol.

You didn't wake me, she said now. Did you sleep well?

For about four hours.

She opened the canister with the coffee and spooned some into the percolator. She asked him what he was reading.

One of those touristy history texts we got on the road, he said with disdain. She'd worked as a docent and gallery manager at a small folk life museum in the village of Middlebury once the youngest of their children had started high school, and he knew she would share his scorn for the piece.

Which one?

The Pony Express.

Someday they'll have one for e-mail, she said. A little e-mail museum.

When he removed his fingers from the magazine, the pages flipped shut. Too virtual, he said. No bricks and mortar to celebrate.

She plugged in the coffeepot and then sat across from him. Though he'd been old enough to retire for close to half a decade, this was the first semester that he hadn't been in the classroom, his first autumn away from the college. It was clear to them both how much he was going to miss teaching and being around young people, and so they'd taken a road trip to make the transition easier. They'd tuned up their ancient Volvo wagon and driven all the way to the Little Big Horn and back. The plan had been to drive to Illinois, visit her mother's ancestral homestead in Rockford, and then continue west so he could see firsthand the actual places he'd talked about for so many years in his classes. The Corn Palace. Wall Drug. Wounded Knee. He'd taught American Studies at Middlebury and concocted courses that his peers on the faculty considered interdisciplinary nightmares: a muddle of popular culture, American myths (and misperceptions), and irresponsible history. One time, he devoted a whole semester to the iconography of Route 66. Another year he had students read nothing but romance novels that featured white women with men of color: Savages. Slaves. A Chinese immigrant who was helping to build the transcontinental railroad. The students had loved it, and he believed they had learned.

The two of them were having so much fun on their trip, however, and covering so much ground so quickly, that they decided to head south as well, and wound up making a loop that stretched from Vermont to Montana to New Mexico. They came home via Route 66, driving east along a road that was known best as a route west to California, an irony which struck Emily as eminently logical given who her husband was. Altogether, they made love in seven Best Westerns and four Quality Inns, and had sex in nine states. Emily thought this was mighty impressive for a couple whose combined age was 129.

By the time they returned to Vermont, they had spent six and a half weeks on the road—forty-five days and forty-four nights—and amassed seventy-seven small bars of wax-paper-wrapped motel soap.

There's a light on at Terry and Laura's, Paul said, pushing aside the nearly empty cereal bowl.

In the boy's room again?

Uh-huh.

I still say it may just be that he sleeps with a light on.

This time I saw it go on. One minute the room was dark, then it was light.

What time was this?

I came down here about three-fifteen. He got up a few minutes after that.

You know for sure it's the boy's room?

I do. First night, I saw him pull up the shade and look out the window. There he was.

He see you?

Doubt it.

She listened to the baseboards in the kitchen tinkling as the hot water coursed through the thin pipes behind the metal. Below her the furnace rumbled.

Maybe the lad wakes up, sees it's dark, and turns the light on. Then he goes back to sleep, she said.

Maybe.

Maybe? There's no maybe to it, in my opinion. Unlike us, that boy has a body that still needs some sleep.

Paul wiped his eyeglasses on his bathrobe and instantly regretted his decision. The flannel only made the smudges worse.

I saw Laura yesterday, she said. Did I tell you?

Don't think so.

She really doesn't seem a whole lot different than before the child arrived.

It's an adjustment.

She still seems so frail. You almost want to speak in whispers around her.

And she might always be frail. Imagine how you'd be if something like that happened to Nick or Catherine or Andy—or if something like that happened to all three of them. God almighty, imagine how I'd be.

This week's the anniversary of the flood.

I know. You see the boy, too? he asked.

Briefly.

He seem happy?

Not particularly.

He say anything?

Not really.

I saw him walking up the hill to the cemetery, Paul said. He likes his hat. Don't know if he's opened his book. But he likes his hat.

I'd expect so. He wearing it backward? That seems to be the way the kids do it these days. Have you noticed? They buy a cap with a sun bill and then wear it backward so the visor is worthless.

I don't know. Yesterday he was wearing it correctly. Of course there was no sun . . .

Meaning?

There was nothing to rebel against by wearing it backward.

She nodded. All those years in the classroom had really paid off. Few people she knew understood the mind of a child or a teenager as well as her husband.

———

"What makes them think fraternization is even an issue? There is a better chance we will find ourselves befriended by the Comanches and Mexicans than we will by the white settlers we're here to protect."

———

SERGEANT GEORGE ROWE,
TENTH REGIMENT, UNITED STATES CAVALRY,
UNDATED LETTER TO HIS BROTHER
IN PHILADELPHIA

———

Alfred

In the night he heard Laura crying. He'd woken up, as he had most
nights in this house where he just couldn't seem to get comfortable,
and he'd heard her quiet sobs in the bedroom down the hall. At first he had
thought he was hearing some wild animal outside the house—a coyote
maybe—and then he imagined it was some local dog that had wandered
away from the village. For a brief moment he had even wondered if he was
hearing a ghost. One of those little girls, perhaps the one in whose bed he
was sleeping and whose presence he was sure he sometimes felt.

But then he understood it was only Laura, and he grew embarrassed for
her. Nevertheless, he climbed from his bed—astonished by how cold the
wooden floor was on the soles of his feet—and tiptoed across his room to
turn on the lamp on the bureau beside the window. He chose not to
switch on the floor light near the bedroom door, because that one had a
hundred-watt bulb in it and was much brighter: It would be more likely
to toss a throw rug of light through the slit underneath the shut door, and alert
Laura to the fact that he, too, was awake and had therefore heard her weeping.
Then he jumped back into bed and pulled the quilt up over his shoulders.

He'd never before heard her cry, and he was sure it had something to do
with her daughters. Her children. He wished he knew how to ask her to tell
him about them—not because he thought she needed someone to talk to or
because he believed he was capable of offering her comfort by listening, but
simply because he was interested. How could he not be? When he was alone
in his dark room at night, he had the sense that someone was with him—a
sense that wouldn't go away until he'd turned a lamp on.

He realized he didn't even know what the girls had looked like: In no room in the house had he come across photos of them either hung on the walls or resting on bureaus.

Unfortunately, he couldn't imagine how to initiate a conversation about her children, or what he would do if she actually told him any details. And so all he knew for sure was that they had been twins and they had died in the flood some years earlier. But that was about it. He thought they might have been in the third or the fourth grade when they'd died—just a little younger than he was—but he wasn't positive.

He decided he would have liked to have known at the very least where they had been when they drowned, because it hadn't been on the Sheldons' property. That was clear. The house was too high on the hill, and there wasn't any water.

He assumed that they'd been at the river in the village. He'd been living up in Burlington at the time of the flood, but he remembered hearing that rivers all over this part of the state had poured over their banks. He guessed it was possible that they'd just been washed away. But he also knew that the people who had the dairy farm on the other side of the trees had a small pond, and he wondered if they had died there. Maybe the pond had stretched beyond its banks, and they'd fallen in and drowned.

He was also curious about where Laura and Terry had been at the time. Had they been close enough to try to save the girls—perhaps even seen them go under—or had the kids died alone with no one nearby?

Then again, it may not even have happened here. Maybe the girls had been at a friend's house in another town. Or at a grandparent's house.

Now, there was a thought: What would it be like to be a child who had grandparents as well as parents? Perhaps even two sets of grandparents?

No, he decided, it had happened here in Cornish. He had met Laura's parents and Terry's mother—it had been a pretty typical meet-the-foster-kid show, where everyone gathers at the foster parents' house and tries to be polite, but no one has the slightest idea what to say—and all those old people would have been a lot more screwed up if their grandchildren had died on their watch.

He realized he was thinking too much. Making too much up. The fact was, he hadn't a clue where the girls had died. It could have been anywhere.

He was glad for the woman that Terry was coming home the next day. She might not have been the happiest person on the planet, ever, but at least she didn't wake up in the night and start crying when Terry was home. Terry didn't respect him the way Laura did, of course, and he had a feeling the man didn't especially care for him. He didn't let him get away with nearly as much as Laura did. But it was still pretty clear that Laura was better off when he was there.

Alfred turned over the pillow and fluffed it. Maybe, he thought, when Terry was back he could figure out a way to ask him about the girls. He wasn't sure how—the subject would most likely make them both pretty uncomfortable—but at least it would give the two of them something to talk about for a couple of minutes. He might even be able to use that somehow with the man. Make him believe they were friends.

Outside his window, the clouds in the sky were breaking up and the moon was starting to appear. It would emerge for a couple of long seconds and make the clouds around it look like gray smoke. He thought it was full.

He considered going downstairs and seeing if one or both of the cats wanted to sleep in his bed. He'd had the idea before, but the animals seemed pretty set in their ways and he'd never tried bringing them upstairs to his room. They slept, as far as he knew, near the woodstove in the den, in what was actually a dog bed Laura had ordered by mail. Because they'd been together their whole lives, they slept almost in a single ball, so at first glance it was hard to tell where one cat ended and the other began.

He didn't go downstairs, however, because he knew Laura would hear him. Instead he remained under his quilt and tried to take comfort in the notion that he was warm and fed, and these two people—Laura and Terry—didn't seem to drink and had never once hit him. He glanced briefly around the room, surveying the unfamiliar toys and clothes that had been amassed for him by these grown-ups, and the new paper they'd put on the walls just before he arrived. It was yellow with thin blue and white stripes, and he had a feeling that if he peeled away a corner, he'd see something underneath that was flowery and pink. He knew this room had belonged to one of those girls—maybe even to both. It seemed big enough for two people.

But the house had a third bedroom that Terry and Laura called the guest bedroom, and that one had recently been redone, too. Maybe it had belonged to one of the twins.

For a moment he savored the fact that this was the second place in a row where he'd had his own room. Sometimes he couldn't believe his luck in that regard.

New wallpaper. What he guessed were new curtains. A new throw rug. These people were generous, no doubt about that.

Still, they'd had girls their whole lives and it was clear they weren't quite sure what to get a boy his age. Laura, anyway. But then, she always seemed to be the one who felt like opening up her wallet.

He hadn't told them he was too old for Legos, but he guessed they'd figured it out since he hadn't gone near the box they'd given him. Same with those odd plastic cars that you could twist and turn into robots and bugs and reptilian-looking monsters.

He decided a BB gun might have been fun: After all, Terry sure had his share of guns in that case down the hall. There were two rifles locked in there most of the time, the one with which he liked to hunt and the one that had belonged to his father that he never used. Only Terry's father's gun was in there right now, since Terry had brought his own rifle with him to deer camp.

And then there was Terry's sidearm. A 40-caliber Smith & Wesson Sig Sauer with a bullet in the chamber and twelve more in the magazine in the handle. Now, that was a cool-looking gun. He'd seen rifles before, but never a pistol. One time Terry took out the bullet and the magazine and let him hold it. They were having breakfast and Terry was in his uniform, and he took Alfred's request to see the gun seriously. Led him outside into the back-yard, where he unsnapped his holster, pulled the magazine from the weapon, and worked the slide—locking it open and ejecting the chambered round into his hand.

This is not a toy, he had said, his voice even. It's a tool. About the most dangerous tool you'll ever see. Do you understand? He then handed him the unloaded gun.

Laura had been watching from the back door, and she got so upset that Alfred feared she might have a stroke right there in the kitchen. She couldn't believe what her husband had done—and neither could Alfred. Not then, and not now.

He wasn't sure what had surprised him more: the idea that Terry had let him touch his sidearm, or how much that sidearm had weighed. He hadn't realized a real pistol would be so heavy.

He thought some more about what sorts of things he really wanted, and decided that one of those pocket-size computer games would be nice. And, perhaps, a pair of in-line skates—though he wasn't going to ask for a pair of those. There was no place to use them out here. Same with a skateboard.

He'd had a chance to steal a skateboard that spring when he was living with the Patterson family in Burlington. He and Tien, both. They'd wandered into the shop on Cherry Street around ten-thirty in the morning, and the place was empty because every other kid in the city was in school—or supposed to be, anyway. They could hear the young guy with the tattoos and the tongue stud in the bathroom peeing, and he and Tien had the same thought at the same time. Grab boards and run. The guy would never know they'd been in the store. It might be days before he or the owner even realized two boards were gone.

But they hadn't taken anything. It was only when they were both back on Church Street with the cigarettes they'd bummed off the salesperson after he emerged from the bathroom that they even shared the fact with each other that they'd both considered swiping a skateboard.

A few times Alfred had taken packs of cigarettes and candy bars from stores, and the studs he'd worn in his ears were stolen—but it was that kid named Maurice who'd actually ripped them off the black canvas display rack when no one was looking, before deciding he didn't really like them. Once he and Digger had lifted a couple of videos from a shop in the mall, but he'd done that more to impress the older boy than because he wanted the movies. And for a while—three or four weeks, maybe—he'd taken dog food from the Hannaford's supermarket for that pathetic animal the Fletchers kept tied to a clothesline yet hardly ever bothered to feed.

He wasn't proud of the list, but he told himself it really wasn't all that long and he'd never been caught.

The truth was he'd never owned very much, or cared a whole lot for whatever he had. His CD player, maybe, and some of his CDs. But there was no future in things, because things didn't go with you.

Most things, anyway. You took what you could in a couple of plastic garbage bags and a suitcase—unlike a lot of kids, he actually had one—and that was pretty much the rule. He'd been with the Sheldons since Labor Day Weekend, and he didn't think he'd collected more than two or three things he'd take with him when he left. He'd take some of the new clothes, of course, but he'd leave behind the shirts and the pants he was getting too big for. He'd take his buffalo soldier cap, that was cool. And he'd take the football.

Was there anything else? Some food, maybe. Laura hadn't noticed, but in the back of his closet he'd been building up his small store of provisions. That was one of the first things you learned: Always have rations handy in case they move you out fast, because there's no telling what kind of food will be waiting for you at the next stop. So far he'd amassed Twinkies, canned peaches (along with one of the two can openers Laura had in a drawer that was positively overflowing with kitchen utensils), and four of those single-serve boxes of cereal. If you only took one or two things a week, the grown-ups rarely figured out that you were building up a stash.

Maybe, he decided, there would be more possessions he'd want after Christmas—especially if he asked Laura and Terry for one of those hand-held computer games—and he figured there was a good chance he'd be here through the holidays if he kept out of trouble.

If. Like it was really up to him, and he had any say. Maybe if he wanted out, all he had to do was take another hike up to Burlington. Or give Terry some lip. But he knew he had no control if he actually wanted to stay. As soon as things changed or those two got tired of having a stranger under their roof, he'd be out the door.

He wondered if he would care when that happened (or how much); he wished he knew what he wanted.

He closed his eyes. With the light on in the bedroom and the assurance that he was completely alone, he figured he would fall back to sleep quickly, and he did.

ONCE WHEN HE was sitting on the stairs petting one of the cats, he and the creature quiet but for the animal's small purring, he had overheard Laura telling Terry that she was concerned about the effect his uniform might have on the boy. The sort of memories it might evoke.

Alfred had rolled his eyes, even though no one could see him.

You need to come with me, son.

Laura needn't have worried. Terry wore khaki and green. The uniforms that moved him around—that kept him on his toes on the street, that watched him warily when he'd walk from a store with stolen cigarettes or a stolen candy bar, that years and years ago now had appeared in his life when his mother first started to choose her rock and her men over him—had always been blue.

ALFRED'S BUS WAS small: The two columns of seats stretched back a mere four rows, and it actually looked more like a van than a school bus. Still, it could seat sixteen children, though he was one of only a dozen kids who were riding it this year. The bus made a big loop out by the Cousinos' and the cemetery, and, as Alfred knew well, there just weren't many houses in that direction. Moreover, he was the only kid on the bus beyond the third grade. Apparently if he'd been on the bus last year, there would have been three sixth-graders, but the group—two girls and a boy—were old enough now to attend the union high school in Durham.

Alfred saw Tim Acker walking down the sidewalk adjacent to the front of the elementary school as his bus was pulling into the parking lot, his red hair an almost neon beacon at fifty or sixty yards.

In the past Alfred had always walked to school, and after two and a half months he still wasn't used to the bus. The fact that he was at least two years older than everybody else on the route didn't help, but he also found the notion of a schedule confining and the idea of the bus itself a constant reminder that he lived in the middle of nowhere. He was jealous of Tim and Schuyler and Joe Langford because they lived in the village and could walk to and from school—the way he had when he'd lived in Burlington.

Tim was alone today, which meant the boy might wait for him when he got off the bus. When Tim was with other kids, Alfred had noticed, the whole group usually went pounding on ahead together, and Alfred wouldn't catch up with them until they all met in the coatroom just inside their classroom.

Hey, Tim said to him, once the small horde of first-, second-, and third-graders had raced off the bus, squealing today about cartoon stickers and gummy fruit snacks. Alfred could see the shape of the other boy's in-line skates pressing against the inside of his nylon backpack.

Hey.

Can you stick around after school today? Tim asked. My mom says she could drive you home.

They started up the cement steps, the crisp November air on their backs. The rain had come and gone in the night and the sun was up now. It was going to be unnaturally warm by mid-morning.

Alfred tried to think if there was any reason why he couldn't stay after school with Tim, and he couldn't come up with one. At some point he'd need to phone the animal shelter and make sure it was okay with Laura—or, at the very least, leave a message on the answering machine at the house. Then, when Laura returned, she'd listen to it and figure out where he was.

I'll have to call Laura, he said, still unsure whether that meant at the Humane Society or their home. As soon as he'd spoken, however, he figured it would be easier for everyone if he just left a message at the house. He'd probably get Laura's voice mail at work, anyway.

Terry got a deer yet? Tim asked.

Hadn't as of last night. And he's coming home today.

My dad hasn't got one yet, either. But my brother did. A button buck. Sixty-eight pounds.

Cool, Alfred murmured, guessing that sixty-eight pounds must be pretty good if Tim was boasting about his brother's kill. He wondered what a button buck was.

When they reached the classroom, they saw Schuyler Jackman and Joe Langford by the classroom aquarium, and without taking off his jacket Tim went to join them. Alfred started to follow, but he had the sense that he shouldn't. Once before he'd accompanied Tim to the group when they'd arrived at the classroom together, and it had been awkward. The other boys lived within blocks of each other in the small village, and had known each other practically since the day they'd been born. The only reason Tim didn't walk to school with them every day was because it was slightly quicker for him to cut across the athletic field and the playground from where he lived. Usually when Alfred saw him alone, it meant that he was running a few minutes late.

Alfred took off his blue-jeans jacket and draped it over a hook, and hung up his backpack beside it. Then he unzipped the top compartment and reached inside for his loose-leaf notebook. He noticed that he had inadvertently allowed the notebook to mash the visor on the cavalry cap the Heberts had given him, and a part of him wished that he had worn it to school today—if only so the bill wouldn't have been crushed. When he was filling his backpack earlier that morning, however, he decided at the last minute not to wear it. Kids might ask him who the buffalo soldiers were, and he'd have to tell them the little he knew—which meant driving home the point, one more time, that he was black and they weren't.

By the aquarium the three boys started to laugh at something Schuyler had said, and though Alfred didn't believe it had anything to do with him— at least that's what he assumed—the laughter hurt him if only because he wasn't a part of it.

HE KNEW HE was the only black kid in the fifth grade, and he was almost as positive that he was the only black kid in the school. Certainly he'd never seen any others. In the entire village he'd never seen any other black people, children or grown-ups.

The school had a single class for each grade, and during an assembly one morning he heard the principal say there were 119 students in the school, including the morning kindergarten class. The assembly was held in the gym because the school didn't have an auditorium, and so the kids sat on the polished wood floor under the basketball hoops.

One time when he was standing in the lunch line at the cafeteria with Tim, a first-grader who rode his little bus had asked him why his skin was so dark. The inquiry wasn't meant to be hurtful, but it had made him self-conscious: He was embarrassed because the question was asked in front of Tim and slightly angry because he knew nobody would ever think to ask this six-year-old boy why his hair was so blond.

Burlington, of course, had had a couple of black kids, as well as a black teacher. Burlington had even had Chinese kids and Japanese kids and kids whose parents had come from Vietnam.

Briefly he wondered how his friend Tien was doing, and what she was up to right that second. He guessed she, too, was in school, but you could never be sure with Tien. He wondered where she was living.

Alfred knew a little history, just enough to sense that no one here discriminated against him because he was black. No one called him names, no one wanted him to have less of anything. No one expected him to use a different water fountain. It wasn't like those pictures from the South they'd looked at in Ms. Huntoon's class when he was in the third grade in Burlington.

But he also felt as if the people here, teachers, too, were always staring at him when he was on the playground or in the lunchroom, and that may have been because he was black—although it may also have been because he was a foster child. A person just dropped into a school filled with kids who'd been together since the very first day of kindergarten.

Either way, some of the kids still kept a certain distance, even now when he was involved in one of their games. He was part of the group that was playing Capture the Flag during recess. Immediately after lunch the teachers had herded everyone outside because it was so warm for November and the sun was out. Schuyler Jackman had made sure that Alfred was on his team, which had made him feel better than if he'd wound up as a spectator with his back to the brick wall of the building—something that had happened twice before. But he still found that he could reach the opposing team's flag almost at will, as if the other kids didn't want to tag him. His team had won both games so far, because with a minimal amount of darting and ducking he had raced through the defense and grabbed the red art smock that was serving as their flag.

He couldn't figure out whether they were being nice to him, or whether it was something else entirely. No one, he could not help but notice, had clapped him on the back or asked for a high five when he'd crossed back onto Schuyler's team's side with the smock—not even Tim. That had certainly been a part of the victory celebration in the games he had witnessed from the sideline. In his case, however, both times there had been a few small cheers and a few kids had pumped their fists into the air, but then he had simply been expected to hand the jersey back to the losers so they could begin a new game.

Certainly Peter Wolcott should have held up his palm and offered some skin. Both times Peter had been the teammate nearest him when he'd returned, victorious, with the opposing team's flag. Instead Peter had ignored him.

He wondered what would happen if he just gave them back the jersey and walked back inside the building to his classroom. A teacher would probably stop him—probably his own teacher, Ms. Logan—but there was no way one of the kids would make the effort. He felt himself growing angry, but he couldn't stop himself and he didn't care. Would it have been so hard for Peter or Schuyler or anyone to ask him for five? For Tim? Of course it wouldn't.

It wasn't his fault that his mother had gone AWOL on him when she had another child, and that no one seemed to know who his dad was.

And so after racing around Liam Freeland and a pair of girls who were offering next to no defense of the flag, he swiped the red smock from their goal, sprinted back to his side of the field, and then thwacked the cloth hard against Peter Wolcott's fat back. The boy yelled, more in surprise than in pain, and when he turned Alfred thwacked him again. This one got him on the side of his head, and would probably redden that pale, pale ear in a matter of seconds. Alfred apologized—he knew how much an ear could hurt—and was about to say something more because he really hadn't meant to nail the kid there, but he saw one of the teachers walking purposefully across the playground field toward him and he realized there wasn't a thing more he could say at this point that would do him a bit of good.

———

"I informed Sergeant Rowe of the order I'd received that henceforth the company would be kept fifteen yards from the white soldiers during inspection and would no longer march in review. He replied that they could live with inferior mounts (though not happily) and would continue to wait patiently for adequate Spencer carbines, but argued respectfully that they could not be separated during inspection and excluded from their place in review. It was clear he was prepared for disciplinary action, and was surprised when none was forthcoming and I agreed to speak on the troopers' behalf."

———

CAPTAIN ANDREW HITCHENS,
TENTH REGIMENT, UNITED STATES CAVALRY,
REPORT TO THE POST ADJUTANT,
AUGUST 18, 1869

———

Terry

He didn't go back into the woods in the morning, but decided to leave the camp at first light and go home. Not straight home. He planned to stop at the barracks first and grab a shower. He would tell Melissa, their dispatcher, and any troopers who happened to be there that he still reeked of the woods and didn't want to smell too earthy when he walked in the door of his house and was greeted by Laura.

Still, he doubted Laura would smell anything on him, even if he didn't go by the barracks. After all, he'd showered at Phoebe's friend's trailer.

There had been something a little pathetic about the arrangement. Phoebe hadn't wanted to bring him back to her father's house, and so they had gone to some woman friend's trailer instead. Phoebe had made a phone call from the bar in Newport where they'd gone from her store, and the friend had left a key under a flat rock by the front steps and then gone someplace else for a couple of hours. He had a feeling the friend was going to drive into Newport herself, perhaps to hang out in this very bar.

Nevertheless, he took pride in the simple fact that he had managed to seduce this attractive woman who clearly, at first, had not wanted to get involved with a married man. Moreover, the sex had been good, even if it had been on a twin bed in a room likely to induce claustrophobia in anyone who hadn't once worked in a submarine. He hadn't been with a woman other than his wife since he started dating Laura years earlier, and the novelty of another woman's smell alone had been appealing in ways he hadn't expected. And Phoebe's body was so very different from Laura's, even though the two women were probably about the same size.

63

He wondered what it was that he'd done or said that had pushed her over the edge, and changed her mind about him. Getting her to the bar had been easy: He figured she simply expected she would lead him on a bit, tease him. Make sure he understood exactly what it was that he wasn't going to get. And for at least their first fifteen minutes at the bar, she really did little more than abuse him. She made fun of his small mustache, and how closely the regulations demanded he trim it. She teased him about the gray in his temples, and told him that she'd never had a drink before with a man so old who wasn't a friend of her mom and dad's.

I would wager that I am less than a decade older than you are, he'd said defensively, and then added, and you are young and beautiful.

At some point, however, the fact that he was a father came up. They never discussed Laura, but he did mention he had a foster boy living under his roof and they did talk about the girls. Everything changed when he told her they'd died. Suddenly his interest in her seemed to grow less sordid in her mind, and it became almost explicable. It wasn't that tragedy justified adultery. But it did make certain needs more comprehensible.

Still, Terry was absolutely positive that he had not told her the girls were gone because he thought he could use it, he was quite sure of that. Indeed, he had almost left after telling her what had occurred. (How many words had he needed? A dozen? A dozen and a half? You couldn't use more, because if you did, he knew, you started to cry.)

He was less sure, however, why he had then gone on to mention that the anniversary of his children's death was the day after tomorrow. Wednesday, in fact. He hadn't needed to add that little tidbit. But he had. He had looked into the beer foam that ringed the inside edge of his mug after speaking, because he knew he couldn't meet Phoebe's eyes.

Later that night when he was lacing his boots and the two of them were preparing to leave the trailer in their separate vehicles, Phoebe asked him if he ever got to Montpelier.

Sometimes Barre, he answered, referring to the city five miles south of Montpelier. Two or three times there have been changes of venue and I've had to testify in the courthouse in Barre.

You do that a lot?

Testify? Yes and no. Sometimes when I'm an arresting officer I have to testify. But the truth is, the better the affidavit, the less likely I'll wind up in court. Whether it's a speeding ticket or a B and E, you want it to be pretty darn cut and dried. And usually I'm not in Washington County, anyway. I'm in Addison. But you know what? Our headquarters are just north of Montpelier in Waterbury. I actually get there every once in a while.

She nodded and looked at the cowboy boot in her hand as if she didn't recognize it.

Why do you ask? he said.

She was wearing a pair of heavy wool tights, and it seemed to take a great effort to slip her foot—even though it had seemed so small and petite to him no more than an hour ago—into the boot.

Well, she said finally, I was going to suggest you drop by when you're in the area. But I'm not altogether sure that would be a good idea.

Probably not, he agreed. But the moment he'd said it he wondered if his ready assent might have hurt her feelings. He'd never done anything like this before—and he vowed that he never would again—but maybe there was an etiquette here he didn't fully understand. Maybe he was supposed to pretend this was more than it was, try to elevate it into something less tawdry than a roll in a twin bed in some stranger's trailer. And so he waved his arm at the two of them and then at the narrow room with the fake wood paneling in which they were getting dressed and said, You know something, Phoebe? This whole evening wasn't a good idea. But I'm glad we did it.

Oh, I am, too, she said. Really. I am, too. But don't do it. Don't come see me when I move back to Montpelier.

He considered asking her why she was so firm in her resolution, but he was pretty sure it was simply the fact that he was married. Still, when he thought back on their conversation and her admission only a moment ago that she had almost suggested he drop by when he was in the county someday, he realized there might be something more: He was a state trooper. Someone who was supposed to be righteous and upstanding, someone who was supposed to uphold the law. Someone who was actually a bit of a hero once in a while.

Perhaps when he had mentioned the idea of testifying in Barre, he had reminded her of what he did for a living.

———

IN THE SHOWER in the barracks he started to cry. This time he didn't make a sound, it wasn't like those afternoons in his cruiser, and he stared straight up into the cascading water with his eyes shut tight so the tears would roll down his body and disappear down the drain with the water.

The girls—the word alone could unhinge him sometimes, the plural especially, because of the seraphic memories it conjured—had been named after their grandmothers.

HE WAS ALREADY nearing the massive blue silos at one edge of the Cousinos' dairy farm when he decided to turn around. He drove back along the two-lane road linking Cornish with Durham until he reached the Durham town commons, and then he parked in one of the diagonal spaces in front of the gazebo. There was sun today, lots of it, more than there had been in almost a week, and the side walls of the gazebo—repainted that summer for the first time in at least a decade and a half—looked whiter than milk and too shiny for wood.

He went first to the florist, because he knew what he wanted to get Laura. He asked the woman who worked there to prepare for him the most colorful bouquet of cut flowers she could manage.

Make it cheerful, please, he said to Carol. Very cheerful.

I think we can arrange that, Carol said, and she went to the refrigerator with the tall glass doors. Larkspur, she murmured, more to herself than to him. I love purple flowers. And some yellow lilies. Laura likes yellow, yes?

Yes.

And, let's see . . . iris. Blue irises.

What are those? he asked, pointing at a collection of flowers in a gray bucket on the bottom shelf.

Oh, good choice. Gerbera daisies. Some hot pinks would be nice.

And roses, too, he said. A couple red roses.

Red means love, she said, and she added four sweetheart roses to the assemblage of flowers she was preparing.

After he had paid for the flowers, he put them in the passenger seat of his pickup and went to the big drugstore next to the supermarket. It was the closest thing the town had to a variety store, and he thought he might be able to find something there for the boy.

HE GOT HOME before lunch—hours before Laura would return from the animal shelter and Alfred would return from school. If he wanted, he knew, he could shower yet again. Three showers, he figured, and not even a bloodhound would be able to detect a trace of Phoebe Danvers on his skin. But a third shower seemed more than a little paranoid, even if the cats seemed more interested in him than usual, and so he didn't bother to bathe yet again.

He considered placing the wrapped flowers in the refrigerator, but Laura wouldn't be back until somewhere around two-thirty. That meant they'd have to sit there for three solid hours. And so although he'd only put flowers in a vase a handful of times in his entire life, he did now. The arrangement wasn't pretty—somehow the irises and the lilies kept hiding the daisies, and the roses kept sagging to the side—but at least this way the flowers would be alive when Laura got home, and she would know how to fix them.

He'd bought Alfred a football kicking tee and a magazine about the NASCAR circuit. He didn't know if the kid liked auto racing, but it was clear the boy was interested in his cruiser, and the glossy pictures of the race cars were pretty hot.

And Alfred did enjoy football. It was, as far as Terry could tell, one of the few obvious things they had in common. The boy didn't like shooting baskets with him, but they'd tossed a football together three or four times that autumn and watched a couple of Patriot games on TV.

He grew a little annoyed at Alfred when he listened to the answering machine in the den. The kid had simply left a message announcing that he was going to stay in town after school and play with that Acker kid. The child's mother would drive him home. The part that irritated Terry was the fact that Alfred had left the message on the machine here, instead of calling Laura at the shelter. Now she'd be racing home as usual to greet the boy when he got off the school bus, when maybe she would have done something else if she'd known she didn't have to come straight home.

Sometimes the boy just didn't think. The girls would never have shown so little common sense.

The girls. He found it interesting that since they had died he always viewed them as a pair, as if they had lacked individual personalities or were incomplete when they were apart. In reality, when they were alive they had done many things separately, and Laura hadn't dressed them alike since they were toddlers. They wouldn't have stood for it.

The truth was they had very different interests, and you could see it in the "Try-It" badges that had monopolized so much of their lives during their last years. Both children had been Brownies and then Girl Scouts, and it would have been so much easier if they'd ever been interested in getting the same badges at the same time. But of course that hadn't happened. Megan had been obsessed with the ones that seemed to demand hours outdoors, while Hillary always focused on those badges that involved cooking and clothing and manners.

And yet it had been Hillary who was the jock. She was the one who'd played youth soccer and T-ball and Little League. Not Megan. No interest in sports at all. She liked to be outside all right, but it was always so she could look for birds' nests and mole holes. Fairy houses, when she'd been younger. There had been a period when he and Laura hadn't dared move a stone or a twig in their yard, because it might have had totemic importance for one of Megan's secret, make-believe sprites.

He liked to hike—along with hunting and pickup basketball one night a week, it was about the closest thing he had to a hobby—and the summer before the girls died, the family had gone on some nice, long hikes together. Hillary had seemed to enjoy them because of the effort the walks demanded, while Megan had derived her pleasure from the wonders—real and imagined—that she would insist lived beneath every leaf.

About twenty to three, he poured himself a glass of apple cider. The cider was pungent and thick, and reminded him of the day that autumn when he and Laura had taken Alfred to the orchard. The boy had never been to one before, despite living almost his entire life in Vermont. It had been a perfectly fine day until it was time to leave, and the boy refused. Just wouldn't budge. Then, when they thought he'd finally agreed to return with them to the car, he disappeared the moment they'd turned their backs. One moment he'd been a dozen steps behind them, and the next he was gone. It had taken them twenty minutes to find him, and Laura had grown so frightened that she started to cry. The orchard bordered Lake Champlain, and the kid had wandered all the way down to the shore, where he was looking at the boats and throwing rotten apples as far as he could into the lake.

He said he missed the water. Said he used to hang out by the waterfront sometimes when he lived in Burlington.

Just after Terry had poured the glass of cider, Laura pulled into the driveway. He heard the car and went to the front steps to greet her. As she emerged from her little gray Taurus, a massive wave of guilt rushed over him: Here she was, the woman he'd fallen in love with and married. Here by the carriage barn they used as their garage was his wife. Her hair was held in place by the thinnest of headbands, and it was blowing in all directions as she walked up the bluestone toward the front door. He saw wisps of animal fur on one of the sleeves of her jacket, fluff from the white coat of some very big dog.

She smiled and waved, and pulled the strap of the wicker tote bag she used as a purse up over her shoulder. She was, he decided, as fragile as she was beautiful, and she must never, ever know what he had done the night before. Never. And so in case he was wrong about Phoebe Danvers—in case the scent of her perfume or her skin or that woman friend's trailer had indeed come home with him, despite two showers in half a day's time—he took the glass of apple cider he was holding and spilled it down the front of his red-check flannel shirt.

———

"And so I have begun to post rules for my men. Rule number one: They have to care for their horses as well as they care for themselves, since a good horse can mean the difference between life and death out here, and a mount's best days are probably behind it by the time it reaches us."

———

SERGEANT GEORGE ROWE,
TENTH REGIMENT, UNITED STATES CAVALRY,
LETTER TO HIS BROTHER IN PHILADELPHIA,
NOVEMBER 18, 1873

———

Phoebe

In September there were the mannered strangers from Connecticut and New Jersey who bought maple syrup, sometimes two and three half-gallons at a time, and in October there were the busloads of elderly from New York. They bought maple syrup, too, but almost always in pints. They were also likely to buy a good many postcards.

In November the hunters arrived, joining the local boys, and they were some of the biggest spenders the store would see in the course of the year. They viewed the place as a small supermarket, and planned to fill their refrigerators and coolers with provisions for a weekend or a week. They didn't seem to mind paying an extra dollar for a can of coffee, or an extra seventy-five cents for a jar of peanut butter. They were happy to pay for bologna as if it were roast beef, either because in their minds they were now on vacation or because their wives usually did the shopping and they didn't have the slightest idea what things really cost.

In December the skiers would start coming in with some frequency. At least that's what Frank and Jeannine told her. She hadn't worked at the store yet in December. But Frank and Jeannine had owned the place for almost two decades, and they said the store could expect to sell a lot of wine in the heart of the winter, and easily a case of lip balm a day. They didn't get as many skiers, of course, as the towns closer to Burke and Jay Peak, but they still had their share. The store was located about a half-hour from one of the mountains, and forty-five minutes from the other.

And, always, the store depended to a large extent on cigarettes and beer. Pepsi and chips were big, too, and Phoebe thought there were some mornings when she sold literally gallons of coffee, but nothing could compare with cigarettes and beer.

She put the sandwiches she'd made for two unfamiliar hunters in a brown bag, along with the rest of their lunch. They sipped their coffee as they watched her ring up the sale, and she barely heard what they were saying. It was still early—the sky was only now lightening to the east—and she'd been behind the counter barely fifteen minutes.

When they were gone and she was briefly alone, she found herself staring at the front door and wondering if Terry would stop in before either disappearing into the forest or leaving town. She knew he was definitely going home that day (at least that was what he had said), but he'd implied he might first make one last foray into the woods. She wasn't sure what she would say to him if she saw him. She wasn't exactly ashamed of what she had done— what they had done. Shame was too strong a feeling. After all, they had done nothing irrevocable, they had caused no one irreparable harm. Yes, she had slept with a married man, but she'd made it clear to him afterward that she regretted that decision, and under no circumstances should he mistake their tumble for an episode with a future.

At least while he was married.

Still, she wasn't proud of herself.

She told him that if someday he showed up in Montpelier separated or divorced, then maybe they could have a beer together and see where things went. But she also told him that she wasn't sure she would think very highly of a man who left a woman who'd lost both her daughters.

When he first told her about them, she remembered the newspaper story. A couple of kids can't drown in Vermont without it being news, the state's just too small. She thought there might have been a third child—Terry's daughters and one of their friends—but she wasn't absolutely sure. Maybe that third child had simply been with the two girls but hadn't washed away.

She liked to believe that she'd only slept with him because of those girls, but she knew there was more to it than that. It had been a long time, and he was handsome in a military policeman sort of way. His cheeks were slightly hollow, but she imagined that was due to the grief he had shouldered for two years. If he hadn't been a state trooper, she would have guessed he was a career man in the Air Force. Maybe one of those veteran F-16 fighter pilots stationed at the airport in Burlington.

Of all the hunters she'd seen that first weekend of deer season, he was the only one who had bothered to shave every day.

She heard the cowbell on the front door ring when someone pushed it open, and she saw the man Terry had said was his brother. Beside him were the cousins. All three men were wearing their green-and-brown camouflage clothes and orange vests, and she knew it was day four in those duds for each of them. She shuddered when she thought about the socks they were wearing.

There was no sign of Terry, and she concluded that he was now on his way home to Cornish. She was more disappointed than she'd thought she would be.

Quickly she turned and walked back toward the deli section in the store, and tried to busy herself slicing sandwich meat. She knew she'd have to wait on the group soon enough, but this way she thought she might minimize the need for conversation.

She remembered that Terry said Russell spent his life flirting with trouble. Not big trouble, at least not yet, but the sort of stupid things that embarrassed the state trooper. He had a DWI on his record. A misdemeanor conviction for marijuana possession. And though it hadn't led to an arrest, Terry said his brother had once shot a deer near a highway rest area in September, a maneuver that could have gotten him busted for reckless endangerment and fined for taking a buck out of season.

Out of the corner of her eye she saw Russell pausing now before the Polaroid she'd taken of him yesterday with his buck, and she saw the other two men grabbing bags of potato chips off a metal rack.

Biggest damn one-hundred-and-fifty-pounder I ever lifted, Russell said, loud enough for his cousins to hear him.

Give it a rest, would you, Russell? one of the cousins said, and she saw he was smiling at his brother at Russell's expense.

I will. It's just . . . that animal was one heavy son of a bitch for a hundred and fifty, he said, shaking his head. He turned away from the picture and strolled back toward the deli section, and Phoebe knew a little morning chitchat was imminent. She considered getting it off on exactly the wrong foot by asking the man why he had bothered to climb one more time into his camouflage clothes. He had his deer, and the limit was one in the two-week rifle season. But there was no reason to torment Russell just because his brother was sleeping around on his wife.

Or, at least, had slept with somebody else a single time. For better or worse, she'd really believed Terry when he said he hadn't been with a woman other than his wife since they'd been married.

Good morning, Russell said cheerfully.

She looked up and offered him a small smile.

How are you today? he asked.

Oh, fine.

I'll bet.

Was this a confirmation that he knew where, more or less, Terry had been the night before? Had Terry actually said something to him? Or was she reading too much into his two-word response? She wasn't sure, and decided to ignore the inference. She asked him what he'd like.

I'd say I'll have a little of what my brother had, but I'm afraid someone might misconstrue my meaning and I'd wind up getting slapped.

I don't recall what your brother had, she said simply. I've made you boys lots of sandwiches over the last couple of days.

Hmmmm, he said, curling his lips over his teeth as he looked down at the meats and cheeses in the refrigerator case. She realized he was staring at her hips and waist through the glass. There's a lot there I like.

Uh-huh.

But unlike my brother—you do remember my brother, I bet—I'm comfortable having the same thing day after day. I'm just a one-sandwich man, I guess.

He looked up at her and tried to offer what he must have thought was a playfully sanctimonious gaze. But the choirboy eyes didn't fit with the scruffy red beard that had grown on his cheeks and chin over the past couple of days.

Turkey? she asked.

Is that a guess?

No, it's an assumption, she said. I believe we are what we eat.

She held his stare—her eyes wide—until he looked away and murmured, hoping to save face, Turkey will be just fine, thank you very much.

ALMOST AS SOON as she'd made Terry's brother and his cousins their sandwiches and the men had left for the woods, another group of hunters arrived at the store. And then, just before seven-thirty, Frank got there, and Frank and Phoebe together managed the minor crush that descended upon them every day at exactly this time and lasted until about a quarter past eight. There were the men on their way to the day shift at the furniture mill, and the women who worked at the hospital. There would be the people who drove into Newport to work, and at least a dozen different mothers: mothers who brought their children to the bus stop thirty yards from the store, and mothers who for one reason or another drove their children to school. There was always something they needed, even if it was just information about a neighbor. There was nothing that Frank didn't know and wouldn't share if someone asked.

By eight-thirty the traffic had slowed, and would remain a quiet trickle till lunch. Phoebe sat down on the squat bar stool beside the register and watched Frank put in his order with the bread salesman who'd been waiting patiently beside his dolly while they finished with the last flurry of customers.

She kept thinking of the state trooper she'd slept with, and comparing him to the few state troopers she knew. They weren't a single breed, that was for sure, but they all shared one thing: They were control freaks. That wasn't a bad thing—in fact, it was probably a pretty good thing professionally—but it seemed to be something they shared.

They were control freaks and they were decisive.

In an instant she had a vision in her mind of Terry Sheldon sitting in the front seat of his idling green cruiser somewhere on Route 22A, with a silver BMW he has stopped just before him. He was making a flatlander from New York City wait an extra minute or two—stew behind the wheel while his wife and kids watched him, or looked uncomfortably out the window at the woods—before he was issued his ticket, because the New Yorker had the temerity to ask if it was possible that Terry's radar was in error.

Terry probably did such things all the time. They all did. He said there were few things that annoyed him more than someone handling three or four thousand pounds of metal recklessly. Speed and metal were a bad combination, especially in a state in which there were still many more miles of dirt roads than paved ones, and there was a whopping 375 miles of four-lane interstate. The rest of the paved roads were two lanes: picturesque, yes, but also twisting and narrow and filled with people frustrated by the notion that they were expected to drive between thirty-five and fifty miles an hour.

She didn't ask, but she figured Terry had seen some pretty nasty car accidents in his time. She figured he'd seen a lot of nasty things, on and off the roads. Theft. Assault. Women whose men had just beaten the living hell out of them.

Domestic abuse, she knew, was Vermont's dirtiest little secret. The state had only ten or fifteen murders a year, but the vast majority of the time the victim knew the assailant. And though a batterer wasn't likely, in the end, to actually kill the poor woman he had under his thumb, she'd heard far too many tales of wives and girlfriends who'd had their heads rammed so hard into walls there were permanent indentations in the Sheetrock, or who had been bludgeoned with wrenches and shovels and two-by-four pieces of wood.

All that blood and violence and gore. The injuries and the death. It had to affect how the man grieved.

Of course, even when the violence was of the more random sort that plagued less rural states, it had its own twinge of rustic excess. Not too long ago, a lunatic in central Vermont had allowed his grudge with the town clerk to fester, and then decided to shoot the fellow and the town treasurer—a young mother who'd had the misfortune of being in the town clerk's office at the wrong time. Then he grabbed some guy on the road crew who stopped by the office to take a pee, and lit out. Quickly there were troopers on his tail, and after a looping forty-minute car chase along both back roads and the interstate, he holed up inside his cabin and held off the state police there for almost six hours. Supposedly he'd had an arsenal inside with him that would have impressed some Third World nations, and he had ringed the perimeter of his property with bombs.

She knew this had happened somewhere near Hancock, a town not too far from Cornish and Durham.

You had to be impressed with what the troopers had accomplished that day. Somehow they'd convinced the man to walk out the front door without anyone firing another shot, and the fellow from the road crew had dinner that night with his family.

She figured there was a good chance that Terry had been involved. This had happened in his county—in what amounted to his backyard—and by the end of the standoff there were dozens of troopers there. Literally, dozens. She'd seen the pictures on TV.

It seemed to her that you probably wanted someone decisive in charge when there was a madman with a hostage and an armory in his house. Most of the time, all anyone figured the state police did was assist motorists who'd slid off the road, stop people from speeding, and catch unruly kids who were drunk. But there was a lot more to the job than that, and perhaps she could forgive Terry one marital indiscretion.

At least she would try to if their paths ever crossed again. She'd forgive him and she'd forgive herself. But she also wouldn't go out of her way to wind up naked with the man in her friend Rose's trailer.

———

*"I saw them from the top of the ridge, and I knew
they couldn't cross back over the river. What do you do?
Do you take your children and run so they, too, won't
see? Or do you go to your husband? Maybe some people
would have run, but I didn't. I couldn't. I stayed."*

———

VERONICA ROWE (FORMERLY POPPING TREES),
WPA INTERVIEW,
MARCH 1938

———

Laura

There had been a period in the nineteenth century when the headstones for the children who died were shaped like sleeping lambs. At least that had been the fashion in northern Vermont. One epidemic in 1857 had resulted in whole clusters of the small granite and marble animals in the Cornish cemetery.

Laura's girls' headstones were more conventional—each was an arch—though she had insisted on the whitest marble that could be found, and each had a slightly abstract carving of an angel chiseled into it: an angel's shape and an angel's wings, but no features or face.

She found the two-year anniversary easier than the first, though that by no means meant it was easy. But this year she and Terry went alone, they weren't accompanied by her parents from Massachusetts—her fine, dignified parents, he a senior officer on the verge of retirement after a distinguished career with the Federal Reserve in Boston, she his regal wife, the perfect complement to an upper-echelon financial manager—Terry's mother, or his sister and brother. They had been joined by this considerable group last year, a reenactment in too many ways of the massive funeral that had packed the small church a few days after Hillary and Megan died, and then everyone had gone back to the house, where they'd looked at pictures of the girls and tried to be cheerful. A year ago, she and Terry had taken the day off from work.

This year they hadn't. As soon as Terry had reminded Alfred not to act up at recess and the boy had climbed onto the school bus, they had walked together up the hill to the cemetery, holding in their hands two of the lilies

Terry had brought home the day before, as well as a few of the gerbera daisies. They'd made two bouquets they could leave on the plots.

The girls were buried in the newest section of the cemetery, at least two or three acres away from the 1857 sheep. Laura wasn't positive, but she believed Alfred never visited this section when he wandered up here alone. It wasn't as interesting as the older parts, nor was it as panoramic. But although you couldn't see Mount Ellen or Abraham from the girls' spot, there was a nice view of the hills that rolled south into the state forest. Sometimes both Terry and Laura wished there was a tad more shade, but that wasn't a big deal and they both knew why there weren't more trees nearby: In the days after the girls' death—days in which most decisions were made with little or no thought—Laura had said something to someone about wanting the location to be sunny. And so it was.

When they arrived at the twin tombstones, Laura knelt and placed the flowers on the ground and allowed herself to cry freely. She was about to get up when she felt Terry crouching behind her, one of his hands on her shoulder, and she decided to stay where she was. The earth was still soft and spongy from the warm front that had arrived on Tuesday, but she didn't mind.

Before leaving, she brought her fingers to her lips and then pressed them for a long time against each of the slick and solid marble slabs.

SHE CHOSE A black-and-white Border collie with fur that was thick and soft, and walked into the cement pen with the animal. Then, almost in a single motion, she rotated the collar around the animal's neck so the metal loop was at the back and clipped the collar to the clasp at the end of a long canvas leash.

She runs and she barks, but she's very gentle, Laura said to Alfred as the animal pulled her out of the cage. Trust me, she's a real sweetheart.

She handed the leash to the boy and watched as the good-sized dog yanked the boy's arm so it was almost parallel to the ground. The dog really wasn't all that big, but then neither was the boy. Sometimes when he'd move in a certain way and she'd see the shape of his knee or the width of his thigh in his blue jeans, she'd realize just how baggy the pants were on him and how thin his legs really were. One time at dinner she noticed his wrists, and they were so small that she feared he could probably have worn a napkin ring like a bracelet.

And I should take her up the dirt road in the back? he asked as the dog pulled him down the hall toward the door.

That's where most people walk them, she answered, but take her wherever you'd like. Then the boy and the dog were off. They raced out the shelter's back door, and the moment they were out of sight she experienced the slight tremor she always felt when the child was in her care and she couldn't see exactly where he was. Something would happen, and she would be powerless to stop it. To save him.

She stood there until the sensation had passed, and then she went back upstairs to her office. It was the Monday before Thanksgiving, and the schools were closed for the week. She hadn't been sure what she would do with Alfred, and she'd considered taking the week off herself. She had no meetings of consequence over the next couple of days, and there was nothing critical she couldn't accomplish from home. But today, at least, Alfred had wanted her to go to work and he had wanted to go with her. He'd been to the shelter before that fall, but never for more than half an hour at a time.

The county shelter was built into the side of a hill, and only the first floor was visible to any cars that happened to pass by. It had two and a half undeveloped acres around it, and around that was the road on one side and forest on the three others. In the back there was a dirt road—what had once been a logging trace—that went into the woods, and it was here where the volunteers usually walked the dogs.

Upstairs, a mother with a baby in her arms and a seven- or eight-year-old girl beside her were still looking at the cats. The baby's nose had been running so long, there was a crust above his lips the color of melon, but he didn't seem unhappy. They'd been there for almost an hour, and had probably considered at least a dozen of the animals so far. Briefly Laura wondered if they had no intention of adopting an animal but were simply here as an outing. Perhaps they needed someplace to go with the schools on vacation, and Mom had decided the shelter was about as close to the zoo as you were going to get if you didn't want to drive all the way to Quebec.

The girl looked nothing at all like Laura's own daughters, and she was glad.

For a moment she joined the group and watched as Caitlin, one of the women who worked at the shelter for Laura, took a massive gray cat from a cage and gently placed it on the floor beside the little girl.

The cat was named Rikki, and Laura knew it wouldn't be a good fit with this family. It was an ottoman and it was old. If this family really wanted anything, they wanted an animal that would chase string and jump after moths. Something cute. Rikki was eight, unfortunately, and pretty set in her ways. She'd been at the shelter close to three months now, and Laura knew she wouldn't be there much longer: Either a miracle would occur and she would be adopted, or they would have to put her down. No animal should have to live that long in a cage.

Nevertheless, she thought she should put in a good word for Rikki before returning to her office. She knelt on the floor and ran two fingers along the top of the cat's head, and said to the mother, Rikki's very good with small children. Sometimes the feistier cats will scratch a little one by mistake, but not Rikki. She is incredibly serene—perfect for a house with a little baby.

The girl joined Laura on the floor and started to stroke the cat. The animal stretched out a paw and then glanced up at the child with a look of complete indifference on her face.

LAURA FIGURED ALFRED would spend about ten or fifteen minutes with the Border collie before returning. She figured the next dog she would give him would be the sheltie, and after that it would be Gilligan—a mutt that was part black lab and part something considerably smaller. Gilligan looked a bit like a dwarf.

If Alfred wanted to walk still more dogs after Gilligan, she'd have to give the subject a little more thought. The other seven dogs at the shelter that day included German shepherds, Gordon setters, and a couple of mongrel strays. The dogs were generally sweet-tempered and happy to be around people, but they were big and unused to being walked on a leash. And though Alfred was strong for his size, he was still only ten and he had never been around dogs this large in his life.

One of his homes had had some breed of small dog, but it didn't sound as if he was ever walked. Alfred said they only had him for a couple of months. The owners would tie the dog to a clothesline in the backyard in the morning and then bring him in at night. When Alfred and an older child who lived at the house came home from school, the dog would start barking, but the kids weren't allowed to bring him inside the house. Until it got too cold, on occasion Alfred would go outside and play with the animal. But the dog wasn't trained, and it didn't sound as if Alfred spent much time with him. There wasn't much you could do with a dog on a clothesline. Alfred was too young to have serious homework then, but an older child—a girl, Laura believed—said the dog's yapping made it impossible to study. The neighbors complained constantly of the noise, and eventually the owners grew tired of the protests and got rid of the animal. Alfred had no idea what that meant. And so although Laura could only hope that what she was saying was true, she told the boy the owners had probably returned the dog to their nearby animal shelter, where the creature had, with any luck, found a good home.

She wondered if the boy made any parallels between himself and these dogs. She hoped not, and they certainly hadn't discussed it. Still, the boy could read, and each animal had a clipboard on the front of its pen that listed, among other salient details, why it had been brought to the shelter. Most of the time the staff simply wrote, "My owner couldn't keep me," their all-purpose explanation for a litany of reasons that usually had everything to do with the owner and nothing to do with the canine. Often people moved and the dog was no longer convenient, or they had a child and the dog abruptly became too much work. Sometimes the dog wasn't belligerent enough for the sort of young tough who would return his animal to the shelter in the back of his pickup, or it was too aggressive for a home with young children—it wouldn't tolerate the poking, prodding, and handling that even a well-meaning three-year-old will inflict upon a dog. Nine times out of ten, she guessed, the animals in the building had done absolutely nothing wrong to wind up in their four-by-seven pens. They'd simply been dogs.

It was odd, but one of the first things she and Terry had discussed when SRS told them there was a ten-year-old boy in Burlington in need of immediate placement was the possibility that the child would want to bring home a dog from the shelter. They had both liked that vision very much—a boy and his dog—and had even said something to that effect to the woman from the state who had brought them the news. But then she reminded the couple that they should only get a dog for the boy if they themselves wanted the animal, because the boy obviously would not be taking it with him if—and Laura couldn't tell for sure, but she thought that the woman had almost said *when*—the child was placed somewhere else.

My owner couldn't keep me. Suddenly Laura disliked their umbrella expression, and she worried about Alfred. She turned her attention to the handwritten messages on her desk, wondering if there were one or two there that could be dealt with in the time the child would be with the Border collie—anything to take her mind off those words. There really wasn't, and so she carefully read the final draft of the shelter's end-of-the-year fund-raising letter, and penciled in a pair of small changes she wanted as director. Then she placed a yellow Post-it note on the top of the draft with her approval.

As she was about to start down the stairs to greet Alfred, her personal line rang. Instantly she knew it was Terry. She wasn't sure how she knew, or why she was so sure. But she was. It was her husband. Ever since he returned from deer camp last week, he had been unusually solicitous and kind. Not that he had ever been unkind. But he had never before been this attentive, he had never before been so interested in the inconsequential nothings that comprised a life. He had never before seemed to listen so carefully to every single thing that she said.

The bouquet he'd brought home the other day had been the first flowers he'd given her since the one-year anniversary of the girls' deaths.

She picked up the phone before her voice mail kicked in, and sure enough it was Terry. Off and on over the past week there had been something in his voice that she found troubling, and she heard that something loud and clear now.

How's your day going? he asked.

Where are you? she asked in return, a reflex, before realizing that she hadn't answered his question.

Just south of Shoreham, near the county line. You and Alfred having fun?

Yup, we're fine, she said, and instantly she understood why she'd asked a question before responding to his. It was as if she had suddenly stopped trusting him. These days, wasn't she always asking him where he was the moment he called?

What's he doing?

Right now he's walking a Border collie. A girl named Rascal.

Can he handle her?

Yup.

You need me to bring anything home for dinner? Pick something up in Middlebury, maybe?

Dinner's taken care of, she said, and a moment or two later they said good-bye and hung up. When the phone was back in the cradle, she stood for a moment next to her desk. Outside the window she saw the dog leading Alfred back to the shelter, the leash between them as taut as a tightrope. They were walking into the sun, and Alfred was wearing the cap with the cavalry insignia the Heberts had given him.

She wondered if there was a way she could ask Terry's brother if something had happened at deer camp. She didn't think there was, but that didn't stop her from pondering the idea.

THE THINGS PEOPLE said to her about Alfred only drew her further away from the rest of the world, and closer to the boy—regardless of whether he talked or what he said when he did.

You know, Laura, you can hardly tell he's an African-American—he might just be a boy with a very dark tan! So said Abby Rousch that afternoon at the supermarket, when Laura realized that dinner was not completely taken care of, after all, and so she and Alfred had stopped at the grocery store on their way home from the animal shelter. Alfred had been twenty-five or thirty feet further down the aisle, looking at the brightly colored cereal boxes, and so he hadn't heard Abby—her long, pale, elderly finger resting on the side of her age-speckled jaw as she spoke—when she offered Laura the words that she presumed would be comforting.

Laura nodded, wondering if she would ever get used to these remarks, and then said, He's a beautiful boy, Abby, and brown is a beautiful color. I wouldn't want him to be anything but what he is.

Of course you wouldn't, Abby said, as if she knew something that Laura did not, and she took that long finger of hers with the nail yellowed by age and tapped it gently on Laura's wrist.

Laura guessed that people said this sort of thing to her weekly, even people who she thought should know better. People like the boy's teacher, a woman who couldn't have been more than thirty-five. I am completely color-blind, she had said proudly the first day Laura brought Alfred to the school, I treat all my students as if they were white.

The fact that the teacher had felt the need to say such a thing—and to phrase it so badly—discouraged Laura. One day some weeks later when she drove Alfred to school, her fears were confirmed. The buses hadn't arrived yet, and so they were alone but for his teacher and a little girl whose name, she believed, was Kathleen. She watched Alfred boot up one of the two classroom computers, and saw he was having trouble finding his folder amidst the icons that appeared on the monitor screen. She realized, however, that she was at a loss as to how to help him. She looked to the teacher, but she was busy tacking posters about the rain forest to a corkboard, and seemed oblivious to the notion that one of her students might need some assistance. Yet a moment later when Kathleen merely glanced with raised eyebrows at the woman—before she had even opened her mouth—almost instantly the teacher put the posters down and was kneeling by the girl's side, explaining to her exactly how to access her folder. Her heart sank when Alfred looked into his lap and then shut down the computer, and she wished she knew how to convey to the woman that the boy—*her boy*—needed help, too, without making a scene and antagonizing the child's teacher.

Even at church they weren't exempt from well-meaning but ill-advised pronouncements. Their first Sunday, one of the deacons bent at the waist and stooped his ancient shoulders so that he was almost Alfred's height, and with one hand on the boy's arm informed him, God loves all children. Black. Yellow. Whatever. It's good to have you here, son.

During the moment that Sunday morning when the congregation greeted one another, she noticed that there were people around them who practically fell into her lap trying to shake Alfred's hand and people who did all that they could to avoid the child beside her.

Her own parents—no, anyone's parents but hers—might have risen to the occasion and become surrogate grandparents, but they chose instead to remain almost predictably remote. They came north to meet the boy in the first days of autumn and then retreated south. They were going to come again at Christmas, but their plan was to stay a single night and then leave.

Here, in their minds, was one more example of their daughter's incorrigible lunacy. Going to college in Vermont, of all places, instead of to any of the more reasonable choices in the Berkshires, New Haven, or even right there in Boston. Marrying (and there was no distinction here) a policeman. Choosing to work at an animal shelter with all that noise and those smells, and trying to find homes for tick-heavy mongrels. Now agreeing to house this strange black child.

Most of the time Laura wasn't completely sure how much Alfred heard or understood, but she feared that he grasped a very great deal, and that only made her all the more determined to view the woods and the farm that separated their house from the village as a buffer zone—a barrier—that would keep all that meanness and hurt at a distance.

———

"Indians had been raiding the more outlying ranches for weeks, stealing horses and mules, and we knew they had murdered five settlers. It was with this knowledge that Sergeant Rowe's detachment began its pursuit of the marauders."

———

CAPTAIN ANDREW HITCHENS,
TENTH REGIMENT, UNITED STATES CAVALRY,
REPORT TO THE POST ADJUTANT,
MAY 11, 1876

———

The Heberts

A horse?

A horse, he said. I've wanted one ever since we sold Archie and Rex and moved out here. You know that.

It had snowed earlier that week, but the day was warm for Thanksgiving and the snow had largely melted. At that moment the sun was as high as it would climb that day, and so the old couple had chosen not to don hats or gloves or their winter coats before venturing outside. They didn't need them. They were able to stand comfortably on the edge of their lawn and discuss his idea wearing instead the matching Route 66 warm-up jackets they had bought that autumn in Tucumcari, New Mexico. Each jacket was black with a big red convertible patch on the back, and the old highway's number presented in turquoise beading over the heart. They had cost—like so much other merchandise in the shop—sixty-six dollars apiece.

You haven't ridden a horse in ten years, Paul.

Eight. Barely.

When Paul was a boy, he had actually ridden fairly well. His family had lived in southern Vermont, and they'd always had horses. Then when their own daughter, Catherine, had grown interested in riding as a little girl, they'd gotten a pair of cob horses cheap from a friend, and their children—and Paul—had ridden them daily for over a decade. When their youngest child, Andy, had gone off to college, however, they'd decided to move to a small house with slightly less land, and that had meant selling the two animals. They were a lot of work, and Emily had never shared her husband's or her children's interest in them: They were big and smelly, and you could read a newspaper article in the time it took one to pee.

You'll probably fall off the damn thing and break your hip, she said. And I will have an invalid for a husband.

Nah.

And the animal will outlive us both, you realize.

He nodded, and a response passed through his head that he kept to himself: Then I'll get an old one, he thought. But he didn't say that because it would have been merely glib—and untrue. He was not going to get an old horse. He might not get a young one, either . . . but he was definitely not going to bring home an animal as geriatric as he was, that was for sure. With a pair of living antiques in the house, they didn't need a third one in the meadow that was about to become a paddock.

I spoke to Chip Pearson. He's actually finishing up a project at the Goodyears right now and can give us a little time next week. Squeeze in three days, maybe, which he says is about all he should need to get the side of the barn ready for a horse.

That barn hasn't had anything in it but automobiles since we've lived here! It'll take more than three or four days to get the stalls ready—

A stall, he said, emphasizing the word *A.* I'm not getting a herd. I'm getting a single animal.

The barn is a disaster, she went on.

It's not. Chip looked at it last week. Three days, and it'll be a dandy home for a horse. Warm and cozy. Downright palatial.

You had Chip here last week?

Yup.

So you've been thinking about this awhile.

I have. Got the idea when we saw those horses in Junction City.

Kansas? she asked, meaning, in essence, *You've been considering this since we were in Kansas?*

That's right.

She shook her head. Can't this wait until spring?

It could. But that would mean giving up between one-tenth and one-twentieth of the riding longevity that remains to me. I am most decidedly not prepared to do that.

You're going to ride in the winter?

When it's not too cold, yes. We used to do it all the time, remember?

You've thought this through.

I have. I can have the posts and the electric fencing here Monday morning if I want. And so long as the ground doesn't freeze, even an old fart like me can handle the props for electric fencing.

In his mind, he knew exactly the design of the paddock—the shape of that fencing if viewed from the sky—and where the horse would graze. The animal would have just under two acres of space in the day, and a warm barn to sleep in at night. There would be patches of trees: the maple and ash, which would offer plenty of shade, and the line of pine, which would screen the worst of the wind. And though the horse probably wouldn't care, the views of the mountains would not be shabby—even at night. When there was sufficient moon and few clouds in the sky, a man could see clearly the silhouette of Mount Abraham, a profile that had always looked to Paul a bit like a toppled, though gargantuan, pear. Once that great mass of granite and dirt had been called Potato Hill, an oddly diminutive designation for so much earth, but not inappropriate given the number of hardscrabble farmers who used to plant and dig potatoes easily two thousand feet up the mountain's sloping sides.

He glanced at the barn, noting the slight bow along the north and south walls—the walls parallel to the structure's steep pitch. He liked the notion that once again there would be hay in that loft, as well as heavy bags of grain.

You're lucky the ground hasn't frozen already, Emily murmured.

I am. People younger than us worry about global climate change. When you're our age, it's a blessing.

She sighed. Couldn't you just take up golf? Isn't that what most old men do?

I could. And we could both move to a condominium in Florida. Start walking the malls in our tennis sneakers, and elbowing the other codgers in the buffet lines at the early-bird suppers. But that's not who I am. And it's not who you are, either.

They were quiet for a moment, and then almost at the exact same time they looked at their wristwatches, pulling back the thick, elasticized cotton at the cuffs of their jackets. They were due at their daughter's house for Thanksgiving in just about two hours. If they left right away, they would only be a few minutes late.

"Rule number two: They are to think. This sounds obvious, but out here you'd be amazed how easy it is not to."

SERGEANT GEORGE ROWE,
TENTH REGIMENT, UNITED STATES CAVALRY,
LETTER TO HIS BROTHER IN PHILADELPHIA,
NOVEMBER 18, 1873

Alfred

He sat on the very bottom of the basement steps and watched Terry fire staples into the edges of the last of the new insulation in the ceiling. The man had spent Thanksgiving morning repairing the sections that had begun to sag like stalactites, making easily half the basement resemble a cave. Alfred had helped him where he could, but he wasn't tall enough to hold the long pieces of insulation in place between the joists, and Terry didn't want him unrolling the great hay bales of fiberglass or slicing the pieces off once he had determined a length: He said he feared the boy would cut his small fingers. Mostly, therefore, Alfred handed Terry the utility knife and the staple gun when he needed them, and found the tape measure when it disappeared under the debris.

He figured he would actually have been happier upstairs watching the parade on television (though he still didn't understand why the town didn't have cable or why these people wouldn't get a dish so there would be something decent on the tube), and he didn't believe Terry would in reality have cared if he jumped ship on what he had heard Laura refer to with a smile as their "male-bonding project." But he knew Laura would be disappointed if he left Terry alone, and he decided everyone would be happier in the long run if he feigned interest in insulation.

Still, he thought to himself, this is why people smoke cigarettes. He imagined the pleasure of having a cigarette right that moment, and then snuffing the butt in the mud floor just beyond the cement pad at the base of the steps.

Almost abruptly Terry sat beside him, his staple gun still in his hands, and stretched out his legs. We did it, he said.

Well, you did.

The man nodded. I guess. He surveyed the ceiling, and the crisp, tight strips of fiberglass that rolled to the very top of the cement and stone walls. In a corner, there was a large pyramid of the insulation he had removed, and it looked to Alfred like a pile of wet, muddy sheep's wool.

So, Terry asked suddenly, you like it here? The question caught Alfred completely by surprise. He had been asked it by other foster parents, but neither Terry nor Laura had ever brought the subject up. Moreover, if anyone was going to ask whether he was content here in Cornish, he would have guessed it would have been Laura.

Yeah, sure, he answered, his mind briefly spinning. Was now the time to bring up the girls? he wondered. Ask Terry where they had died? Or should he take advantage of this moment to address a secret—and perhaps easily satiated—want? A Game Boy, perhaps. That BB gun, maybe.

He realized he would have loved to tell Terry that sometimes he wished they lived in town—or, at least, a place where there were sidewalks, other children, and noise—but he didn't dare. After all, what could they do about that? Nothing.

Who are your friends? Terry went on. He reached for a mug on the step behind them and drained the last sip of his cold coffee. I know sometimes you pal around with Tim Acker.

Alfred shrugged. Was the man asking this because he was curious, or was there more to it than that? He thought he heard concern in Terry's voice, as if he was either worried about him or about his choice in friends. Foster parents, it seemed, were either way too interested in who you hung out with or completely uninterested. There didn't seem to be an appropriate middle ground.

He decided that if he chose to answer truthfully (or, at least, completely), he would tell Terry that he was pretty sure Tim Acker filled out the list. Tim was about as good as it got. Maybe he could add Schuyler Jackman's name, though he'd never spent any time playing with Schuyler alone. He only knew what the boy's house looked like because Tim had pointed it out to him when they passed it as they walked down the street.

One time he'd had lunch in the cafeteria with Joe Langford, when Joe's real friends, including Schuyler, were all home with the flu. And once he'd climbed that massive old maple tree at the edge of the schoolyard with John Patchett.

You can invite kids over here, you know, Terry continued when he didn't say anything in response to his question.

Alfred thought about that, too. Never in his life had he ever brought a friend home to wherever it was he was living. It had simply never crossed his mind. Why would it? The Ryans' apartment over the bus station was tiny and always seemed to smell of gas fumes, and the Fletchers' house, while big enough, was a pigsty. Loralee Fletcher sure as heck never cleaned up, and the one time he and Isabel had gotten out the vacuum, their foster mother took it as a personal affront and grounded them both for two days.

They'd both snuck out, of course, because Loralee never kept close tabs on any of the kids in her care. Still, it had been a pretty nasty scene.

He was about to say something to Terry. Thank you, maybe. Perhaps even admit that he might decide to invite kids over after all. Before he could speak, however, Terry was on his feet, and so he stood quickly, too. Then the man started up the stairs, observing that they could clean up the mess on the floor after getting a breath of fresh air. In a moment, he was through the door that led into the kitchen, and Alfred could hear him rinsing out his coffee cup in the sink.

He followed him, wishing that he'd spoken sooner—allowed some words to escape reflexively from his mouth for a change. He wasn't sure, but he had a feeling he had inadvertently irritated the man with his silence.

BEFORE THEY LEFT for Terry's mother's house for Thanksgiving dinner, he went to the room in which he slept, took out his small photo album from the back of the closet where he kept it, and sat down on the foot of his bed. In the album were pictures of most (though not all) of the places where he had lived, and many of the people who had raised him—or had been, for better or worse, a part of his life. The first photograph was an image of a woman with skin considerably lighter than his—cinnamon-colored, though in truth it was shinier than that. Renee, his mother, had straightened her hair and pulled it back into what looked like a painfully tight bun the day the picture was taken, despite the fact that she couldn't have been more than twenty-two or twenty-three years old. She was standing before a brick building somewhere in Philadelphia, wearing a raincoat that was almost fire-engine red. Her hands were in her coat pockets and she was smiling, but her eyes—almost Asian, he decided years later, after he had befriended Tien—were sad.

On the next page was the second of the two photos he had of his mother, and in this one she was sitting on a couch in an orange-colored T-shirt, with a newborn baby on her lap. The baby was sound asleep, its eyes slits between a cap and the small puff balls that passed for cheeks. The baby, he knew, was him. His mother looked exhausted and scared, and the apartment was a mess. Empty Burger King bags lay discarded beneath the table in front of the couch, along with the greasy wrappers that once held the food. Magazines and newspapers and a *TV Guide* were piled on a second table to Renee's right, next to a baby bottle that sat on its side like a torpedo.

The album held one four-by-six picture per page, and it was fat now with photos. Almost full. He flipped past the Howards and the Ryans and the Fletchers, pausing longest on the Christmas card that Mrs. Howard—he'd called her Elizabeth, hadn't he, the name she used when she signed the card?—had sent him a few months after he was sent away, explaining in it that Richard was sick but they were praying hard that he might get better. He glanced at the images of the different children he'd lived with, the foster kids who moved around like he did, as well as the regular kids with their regular parents. He realized that Isabel, one of the children he'd lived with at Loralee Fletcher's house, was probably sixteen years old now. Maybe even seventeen, if they ever straightened out her birthday. She might even have her own place.

He spent a few extra seconds studying the picture of Tien, a pretty girl his age sitting on a bench on Church Street in downtown Burlington. If he were to pick a couple of people he would like to see again, Tien would be on the list. Maybe he'd ask Louise, the new social worker who looked in on him once in a while, to hook the two of them up again. After the incident when he hitchhiked to the city alone earlier that fall, he didn't dare try to do it himself. But Louise worked for the state, she had access to kids' records, so maybe she could figure the whole thing out.

He realized his door was open, and he hopped off his bed to shut it—closing it quietly so that neither Terry nor Laura would venture upstairs to see if he was up to something. Then he slowly removed his discovery from the back pocket of his blue jeans, where it had sat since he placed it there that morning while briefly watching the parade on TV in the den. He had figured out why there were no pictures of the two girls on display any-where in the house—or, at least, where a heck of a lot of them were stored. He'd come across a pile of photo albums in a cabinet in a bookshelf against the far wall, and they were filled with pictures of the two kids. There was a picture, it seemed, from every imaginable holiday—Easter and Christ-mas and Halloween—and a photo of the girls in every single dress or shirt they must have owned. There were pictures taken outside and inside and in places he couldn't begin to recognize. Florida, maybe. A place with a beach. What he guessed was the ocean, though he had never been to the seashore.

He stared again at the snapshot of the girls who had once lived in this house, the girls who he suspected were with him when the bedroom was dark in the night, and he reassured himself that no one would care that he'd taken the picture. Probably no one would even miss it, there were so many. Then he slipped the photograph into one of the few remaining clear plastic sleeves at the back of his thick little book and returned it to its hiding place in the back of the closet.

ON THEIR WAY to Terry's mother's house they passed a group of a half-dozen boys playing three-on-three soccer in the wide side yard of a home he didn't recognize. But he did spot Tim and Schuyler and Joe Langford in the group.

Oh, look, Laura murmured from the front seat of the car, there's your friend Tim.

One of the boys he didn't know, a goalie, caught an attempt at a score and punted the round ball away as if it were a football. Despite the sound of the car's engine and heater and the fact that the windows were closed, he could hear the kids screaming as they ran in the opposite direction, and he won-dered how long they'd been out there. He imagined they'd been kicking the ball around while he was sitting in the basement with Terry. For a brief moment he began to wish that someone had called and asked him to join them, but he pushed that thought away as fast as he could. Besides, the game would probably be breaking up pretty soon anyway, and then the kids would scatter to their own homes for their Thanksgiving suppers with their families. He hadn't missed much, he told himself.

You know the kid in the Giants cap, Alfred? Terry asked.

No.

I don't, either. Must be a cousin or something.

Neither of the grown-ups said anything for a long time after that, and the silence made even him uneasy. He had the sense that Terry and Laura wished they hadn't passed this group of fifth-graders, and suddenly he grew embarrassed that no one had asked him to play.

HE SANK DEEP into what he viewed as an old person's armchair—massive and comfortable, though the fabric had pilled and grown coarse—and allowed himself to be dwarfed by the faded cushions. He tried to watch the football game on television, but he could feel Terry's brother and Terry's brother's new girlfriend observing him. The two were on the couch off to the side of the armchair—slightly behind it, actually—and so they could see him though he couldn't see them. Still, he sensed that they weren't watching the game the way he was. They were a little drunk, and he could hear the sounds of small kisses and whispers behind him.

In the dining room most of the adults were still talking and drinking coffee, but a few were in the kitchen sealing up the uneaten food and beginning to clean the mountains of plates and buckets of silverware they had used. Terry, he knew, was carving the remains of the turkeys—Terry's mother had roasted a pair of medium-sized birds instead of one big one, so the men would have four drumsticks to fight over instead of two—and Laura was cleaning the roasting pans.

Alfred had been surprised when he discovered that he was the only kid who was going to be there. He had always assumed that real Thanksgiving gatherings had plenty of children present. But not this one.

Russell, no, he heard the girl murmur, a small giggle separating the two words in her short sentence.

Terry had two younger siblings: the brother in the living room with him, and a sister who was at that moment in the kitchen. Terry's sister had married the year before, but she and her husband hadn't had children yet. And Russell . . . well, even Alfred didn't think Russell was ready for marriage or fatherhood. He drove a truck for a cola company, delivering soda to supermarkets and general stores in this corner of the state.

Including Terry's two aunts and uncles and Terry's mother, Alfred had counted eleven other people squeezed around the dining-room table. And *squeezed* was indeed the right word, because although this aging house and everything inside it was huge, including that table, some of the adults who were sitting around it—especially the older ones—seemed awfully big, too. The only exceptions were Laura and Russell's new girlfriend, Nicole.

It was hard to believe that the youngest person in the house, other than him, was Nicole.

Finally, when he heard her once more whisper Stop it! to Russell, Alfred got up to leave. Nicole's voice had been playful, but the pawing behind him was making him uncomfortable. He figured he'd wander around outside. There wasn't much of a yard because the house was smack in the middle of Saint Johnsbury, but maybe there was a tree or something he could climb.

Hey, Nicole said, and he knew instantly she was talking to him, you don't have to go.

I know.

Don't you like football?

He looked at the television set. It's okay, he answered.

We were going to go for a walk anyway, she went on. Weren't we, Russell? It's a gorgeous afternoon, and it won't be dark for at least another half-hour. Want to come with us?

Russell didn't say anything, but Alfred could see he was annoyed by his girlfriend's suggestion. He guessed Nicole was in her early twenties, a good five or six years younger than Russell. He knew she was a nurse at the local hospital, and he was pretty sure this was her very first job—real job, that is. That was a distinction that had seemed to matter to her when she talked about it at the dining-room table, and so he assumed she had had other jobs before going to nursing school.

Come with us, Nicole said. It will be fun.

He might have gone if Russell had felt like going for a walk, too, but it was clear even to Alfred that the man didn't want to. And so he said simply, No, thank you.

But then he wasn't sure what to do with himself, because he couldn't go outside now, not if this pair was going that way. It might make them mad that he hadn't been willing to go for a walk with them. He was considering the kitchen when Russell spoke.

You don't say much, do you? he asked.

Alfred knew from Russell's tone that he wasn't going to like where this conversation was headed. The girl was standing with the fingers of one hand draped lazily on Russell's shoulder, but the man was still collapsed on the couch with a leg dangling over the armrest.

I guess I don't, he admitted.

Russell, no ten-year-old kid says much, Nicole said, especially when he's in a weird house.

This is not a weird house.

Strange house, she said. Pardon me: Strange house.

There's a difference. I grew up in this house, you know, and there was nothing weird about it.

I know, she answered, and she sounded annoyed.

Me? he went on, and he stared straight at Alfred. I'm a big talker. That's my deal. I probably talk way too much. You think so?

I don't know.

Well, I do, Nicole said. And at the moment, at least, you're talking when we should be outside. I think you could use a little more air and a little less beer.

Russell let his leg drop to the floor, and his foot made a large stomping sound even though he'd taken his boots off when he arrived and was now wearing only heavy wool socks on his feet.

You want a cigarette?

Russell!

Come on, I wouldn't really give him one. But I bet he'd smoke one if I did. That right?

He shrugged, knowing he shouldn't tell this man the truth, but unsure he could pull off a convincing lie.

Seriously, son, you always this quiet?

I guess.

See, here's the thing: When a man doesn't talk, you don't know what he's thinking. And when you don't know what a man's thinking, you can't trust him. At least not completely. You follow?

Alfred looked at Russell and felt himself growing flushed.

I follow, he answered.

Russell reached for the open beer on the table beside him, and the little cloth doily—it had probably been white once but was now the color of oatmeal—stuck to the bottom of the can. The woman reached for the doily, but Russell misunderstood the gesture and thought she was trying to stop him from taking another sip of his beer.

Don't touch my beer, he snapped, whipping the can away from her, but then added, please. Please do not touch my beer when I am about to drink from it. Okay?

I wasn't going to touch your precious beer. I was only getting the coaster, she said. Okay? When she said *okay,* she was mimicking him.

So, Al . . . I can call you Al, right?

I like Alfred better, he said, and he tried not to fidget though he knew that he was.

Alfred's an old man's name. Al is the proper name for a tough kid like you, right? I mean, my God, Alfred makes you sound like somebody's servant. And it seems to me that would be the very last thing you'd want. Am I right? You are nobody's servant. No way. Right?

Russell, lay off him, okay? Just stop.

He looked toward Nicole and glowered for a long second, and then turned back to Alfred.

How do you like my brother? Pretty slick, huh? Especially when he's all dolled up in his uniform?

Alfred could see the woman was leaving. She had turned on her heels and was heading back across the front hall and into the dining room or, maybe, the kitchen.

I like him fine.

I do, too. Most of the time. What about Laura?

What about her?

You like her, too?

Sure.

She's pretty, isn't she?

Alfred knew now he needed to leave the room, too. There was no telling what Russell might say next. And so he started to walk past the man, careful to walk toward the far side of the couch, since Russell wouldn't dare lunge across the cushions for him.

He was wrong. Although the man never actually rose to his feet, he bounded across the sofa and stretched his free arm over the far side of the couch, and wrapped it around Alfred's waist. Alfred started to pull away—

he was aware that the beer can was now on its side on one of the cushions, but he couldn't tell if there was enough left that some was spilling out onto the thick pillow—but Russell held him tight and looped his fingers through one of the belt loops on the side of his jeans.

I am sort of like your uncle, you know, he said. There's no call to be rude. I like you.

In the hallway Terry and Nicole were approaching, and then Alfred saw them both jog the final half-dozen steps into the room. Instantly Russell released him.

What the hell do you think you're doing, Russell? Terry asked, and he seemed to tower over his brother. What the hell do you think you're doing now?

Russell stood, but he was no bigger than Terry and he lacked the trooper's posture.

Oh, we were just talking. Getting to know each other.

Nicole looked down at the swirls on the carpet, and she seemed to be shaking her head just the tiniest bit. Then she noticed the beer can on the couch and grabbed it.

That's not what I hear, Terry said.

I don't know what you heard, but—

Or what I just saw.

Hey, you're no saint, either, Russell said, raising his voice, and for a split second Alfred thought the man was going to cry. But the second passed, and he realized that Russell's voice simply grew high when he got mad. You are no saint, he said again to his brother.

The other adults started streaming in slowly from the dining room and the kitchen, and congregated in the hallway behind Terry and Nicole. When Laura saw Alfred by the side of the couch—only feet from where the brothers looked like they might square off—she went to him and put her hands on his shoulders. Her hands were damp, and she was still wearing the red apron she had put on when she volunteered to tackle the greasy, cast-iron roasting pans.

I've never claimed to be a saint, Terry said, his voice even but clearly annoyed.

You always take that tone with me, Russell said.

Not always. Only when you've had too much to drink.

You are such a hypocrite! So smug and self-righteous! Well, I got news for you: I know what you were doing at deer camp! We all did, we all knew exactly where you went!

Alfred didn't dare turn around to look up at Laura. He wanted to, he wanted to desperately, but he didn't dare. He had a feeling if he did it would be a violation somehow, like the time he had heard her crying when Terry was gone, and he had made certain that she never knew he was awake that night. He wasn't sure what Russell had meant just now, but it was clear it involved something bad, something Laura knew nothing about. And he sensed that if he turned his head the slightest bit in Laura's direction, then she would know that he—and, therefore, every single person in the room—understood that Terry was hiding something from her.

And so instead he kept his eyes on Terry. The look on the man's face suggested he was merely disappointed in his younger brother—vexed by this adult man's childishness—but his hands were balled into fists. Everyone remained silent, frozen in place, until their mother emerged from the crowd of older people in the hallway and said, forcing a small, unsure laugh from her lips as she spoke, You two will never grow up, will you? You're having the same squabbles you had when you were children.

She patted Terry, and Alfred saw his fingers unclench. She was not a frail woman, but Alfred had overheard enough to know that she was neither as confident nor as hearty as she had been before her husband died. Her hair was curly and short, and dyed a blond that looked a bit like the camel's hair coat Laura sometimes wore. She was the only woman in the house who was wearing a dress.

Alfred, Laura said, why don't you join us in the kitchen? I could use some help drying the pans. There was an unfamiliar quiver in her voice: It wasn't the tremor he'd noticed the few times her daughters had come up, or the tiny shudder that gave her words a slight waffle when she was worried about him. It was an inflection he'd never heard from her before, but one that had peppered the sentences of a previous foster mother—a woman whose husband would disappear less than two months after Alfred had arrived at their apartment in the building by the bus station.

It was, he was quite sure, the sound of a person whose feelings have just been badly injured.

"*There were no boulders on their side of the river, and no brush at all. And so they shot the horses and used them as cover. Then they fired at the soldiers until they had no bullets left.*"

VERONICA ROWE (FORMERLY POPPING TREES),
WPA INTERVIEW,
MARCH 1938

Phoebe

Of course she couldn't be pregnant. He'd worn a condom.

But they'd made love twice, and they hadn't showered in between. It was possible that . . . no, it wasn't possible. She didn't believe he'd ever been inside her without wearing a rubber.

She reminded herself that she was a grand total of five days late. Five days, that was it. No biggie. Surely she'd been five days late before in her life. In fact, she'd probably been that late often in high school. It was really only over the last two or three years, as she'd begun to near thirty, that she had become as regular as a navy clock.

Yet she kept replaying in her mind their time together in Rose's bed, trying to recall in minute and chronological detail exactly what they had done. And, unfortunately, each time she could find a moment when his penis might have grazed her vagina during foreplay, or when either of their hands might have moved too swiftly between his genitals and hers. Each time she could see in her head pearl-colored semen—real or imagined—on the outer edge of the condom.

Moreover, it was always possible that one of the rubbers had been defective. Maybe one had had a small tear.

Upstairs she heard her father turn off the television set in his bedroom, and in a second, she knew, she would hear him turn on the radio. Since her mother had died, he fell asleep listening to talk radio.

The farmhouse wasn't small, but sound carried through the small rooms, and usually you knew what everyone else was doing. When she was growing up, she had always heard her brothers talking before they fell asleep, and before her parents had sold the herd—when she was a small girl—she had always heard her father and oldest brother tiptoeing down the stairs at five in the morning for the first milking.

She realized that she hadn't comprehended a word in the magazine before her. She had merely been flipping the glossy pages, only vaguely aware of the photos and articles and the ads for lingerie, cigarettes, and perfume.

Outside the back door she heard her father's dog on the steps, and she rose from the table to let the animal in. She felt very tired when she stood up and decided that this, too, was proof that she was pregnant.

IN THE MORNING, she knew, she would open the small general store for Frank and Jeannine. She would arrive there a little before seven A.M., brew a couple pots of coffee, and chat with the regular customers—some of whom, of course, she'd known her whole life because she had gone to school with them or they were friends or acquaintances of her family. There would be fewer people than usual, however, because it was the day after Thanksgiving and some folks would have the day off. Moreover, with the schools closed she didn't expect she would see any of the moms who either dropped their kids off at the nearby bus stop in the morning or drove them to school.

She wondered briefly if her father had any plans for tomorrow, but she couldn't imagine he did. Most days he didn't go anywhere, and she really wasn't sure how he passed the time. In all fairness, he had gone hunting this year, but it didn't seem as if his heart was in it. Sometimes he went for drives, and sometimes he went as far as Littleton, New Hampshire, to visit her brother Wallace, the second oldest of the small brood. Wallace now sold insurance from a little office on Main Street. Twice that autumn he had even stayed overnight with Wallace and Veronica and the grandchildren.

Most days, however, he seemed to stay home.

Wallace and his family had been back in Vermont that day for Thanksgiving, and Phoebe thought that was nice. A couple of kids running around the house and the yard, some other adults in the dark farmhouse for a change.

Wallace and Veronica had both told her in the kitchen that they thought it was time for her to move back to Montpelier and resume crunching numbers for the state. Dad was doing fine now, they said, and it was clear that she had no life here: few friends, no boyfriend, and a job that could only be called inappropriate for a girl who had a two-year degree in accounting from a college in Burlington.

She'd smiled and agreed with them when they said she'd done her good deed.

She didn't tell them that sometimes she fantasized about leaving Vermont. Perhaps even New England. She had a roommate from college who'd moved all the way to Santa Fe when she married an engineer who was going to work at the lab in Los Alamos. Imagine, New Mexico. Endless blue skies, hot and dry summers. Something completely different from all that she knew. Shauna, her friend, had mailed her photographs of her family's townhouse, and of the glorious-looking day-care center where their toddler son spent most weekday mornings.

Still, she loved her father and it was hard for her to picture him alone in this house in the nights as well as the days. Here was a man who had lived in these rooms for decades with a wife, four kids, and—when the herd was at its biggest—a hired man. What would it be like for him to be so completely alone? Even the cows were long gone.

And what of her? Really, she'd just—well, maybe not *just,* but not even four months ago now—watched her mother die. Of all the siblings, she was the one who was there those last weeks, she was the one who helped her father adjust the oxygen prongs in her mother's nose and, near the end, administered the morphine. She was the one who heard her mother's occasional odd, incomprehensible murmurings when the painkillers kicked in, and listened in silence for signs of life from her grieving father. Yes, she had only done what many grown children did. But that didn't make it easy.

She rolled over in her bed—the very same bed in which she had slept as a child and a teenager—and inside her she felt something move. Intellectually she knew it was impossible. After all, even if she was pregnant (and she tried to reassure herself once again that she wasn't), it would be months before she would feel something move.

Assuming, of course, that she kept the baby.

She told herself she was thinking way too much: It didn't make sense to start weighing motherhood and abortion on some scale in her head. At least not yet.

She tried not to hear the low rumble of the men talking on the radio in her father's bedroom, but the noise was inescapable, and so, as she did some nights, she propped herself against the fluffiest pillow and tried listening carefully instead. Anything, she decided, was better than lying in your bed attempting to convince yourself that you weren't pregnant, when you knew in your heart that you were.

"We killed two warriors and sustained no casualties ourselves. Two other warriors drowned in the river when they tried to flee."

SERGEANT GEORGE ROWE,

TENTH REGIMENT,

UNITED STATES CAVALRY,

REPORT TO CAPTAIN ANDREW HITCHENS

AFTER THE ENGAGEMENT AT CANYON CREEK,

MAY 9, 1876

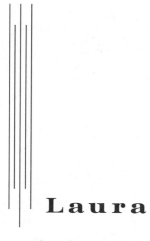

Laura

They drove home in the dark, though it wasn't even six-thirty when they left her mother-in-law's house. The drive from Saint Johnsbury to Cornish was a solid two hours, but still she found herself wishing it was longer: She needed time to think. It didn't matter that she was confined with him right now in the Taurus, because the vehicle was dark and they were listening to country music on the radio. They didn't have to speak—though Terry had made easily a half-dozen overtures when they first left, trying to assess the damage. Finally he'd gotten the message that she wasn't talking.

A few times the notion that her marriage might be over crossed her mind, but the thought made her a tiny bit nauseous and she would try to remember how loving he'd been lately. Yes, that kindness had made her slightly wary, but it also suggested that whatever Terry had done or was planning to do, it did not involve leaving her.

She figured she would confront him once Alfred was asleep, and he would either deny that something had happened and offer an explanation—perhaps fabricate some lesser transgression—or confess.

She realized that she wasn't sure she wanted him to confess. Would it be to a one-night stand? A weekend? Or would it be to something more profound? A long-running affair, perhaps? She wasn't convinced that she wanted to know.

A question occurred to her: How in the name of God did one have an affair at deer camp? The place was a dump, and the men degenerated into wild beasts when they were there. They rarely shaved or bathed, and they spent their days tromping around the woods.

Maybe that meant nothing had happened. Maybe Russell was just being Russell at her mother-in-law's tonight: Difficult and argumentative. A troublemaker.

And after losing as much as she had, was it even possible that she could lose her husband, too? Would she really be expected to endure that as well?

She wondered what would happen to Alfred if she kicked Terry out—or he left on his own. Right now the two of them had care of the boy, but there would be something called a case review in two or three months. Probably February, Louise said, and definitely no later than March. If their home was perceived as unstable—if she was suddenly a single mother—would she lose the boy?

Certainly she could not allow that to happen. It wouldn't be fair to Alfred, and it wouldn't be fair to her. She had no idea if the two of them had made any real progress in their relationship, but she was sure that eventually they would. Positive. It was only a matter of time.

She turned around, expecting to see a small boy asleep in the backseat of the car. She already had the picture in her head: seat belt still snug around his waist, but his body on its side on the couch, his feet drawn up onto the long cushion. She was smiling at the image. Instead, however, when she turned she saw Alfred upright and awake. At some point he had put on his CD headset, oblivious to the music on the car radio, and started listening to something else. He was staring straight at her, his face completely impassive. For a second the surprise caused her smile to wilt, and she had to will it back for the benefit of the boy.

WHEN THEY APPROACHED the turnoff for Cornish, Terry veered up and off the main road, planning to drive the final four miles via the notch way instead. It took a couple of minutes longer to loop home along this route because a part of the road wasn't paved, but it also meant that they wouldn't have to drive past the spot where their daughters' bodies had been recovered from the river. In the days after the flood, this hadn't been an issue: The River Road had had such yawning chasms that it was closed for months while it was rebuilt, and they couldn't have driven past the spot even if they'd wanted to. Soon, however, this alternate route had become a habit, a way home so ingrained in the muscle memory in their hands that most of the time neither of them even thought about why they were spinning the steering wheel to the left as they approached the notch, carefully avoiding a long stretch of the River Road.

Most of the time. Not all of the time. That night Laura thought about how she hadn't driven home along the River Road—the road she'd always taken prior to the girls' death, and the road most people used to reach Cornish—more than a half-dozen times in two years. She knew the dam was long gone, and the place where the battered bodies had lodged with the riverbank flotsam looked like nothing more than another bend in the river, but she understood also that in a heartbeat she could locate the exact spot where a pile of sepulchral debris had briefly entombed both her daughters.

She thought of Hillary and Megan's friend, Alicia Montgomery, and tried to conjure a picture in her mind of the little girl—what she looked like now. She was in the sixth grade. The family had moved to Rutland soon after the flood, and she hadn't seen any of the Montgomerys in well over a year. She knew that Alicia had been badly shaken by her friends' deaths, and had endured sweat-causing nightmares for months after the flood. Supposedly, that was why the family had moved. They wanted to get Alicia away from the sound and the smell and the sight of the nearby Gale River.

Yet sometimes Laura felt they'd moved also so they wouldn't have to run into either Terry or her at the supermarket in Durham. Those encounters grew unpleasant after the flood: Alicia's mother, Colleen, was convinced that Laura and Terry blamed her—or, in some way, perhaps even Alicia—for the deaths of their little girls. One day five weeks after the river had raged over its banks, Laura's friend Karen actually got Laura dressed and out the door to do some Christmas shopping for Terry. They only went as far as Durham, but still this struck both women as enormous progress. There, however, at the small bookstore in the village, they ran into Alicia's mother, and it was clear to Laura that something had happened since Colleen Montgomery was at her house after the funeral. She wasn't cold, but she was formal. Not curt, but reticent. They talked for less than five minutes, and even Colleen's parting embrace struck Laura as more obligatory than genuine: It seemed to Laura as if the other woman was actually careful to preserve a narrow alley of air between their two bodies when they hugged—no small feat since both women were wearing heavy parkas.

On their way back to Cornish in Karen's car, Laura asked her friend if she'd noticed it, too, and Karen admitted she had.

Survivor guilt, she offered Laura as an explanation, because Alicia had gotten off the bridge in time.

But that night in December Terry had suggested another motivation, a rationale for Colleen's desire to get away from Laura that he said didn't mean Colleen wasn't experiencing survivor guilt—he, too, believed she probably was—but that may not have been the only reason she'd been distant.

When I was in Fran's office last week, he'd said, referring to the woman who was the county's state's attorney, there was a deposition going on. It involved that fellow who was drunk when he plowed into the minivan full of kids.

Laura remembered the event well, though she hadn't thought about it since her own daughters had died. A drunken driver had tried passing a slow-moving pickup and slammed head-on into a minivan with four Cub Scouts aboard. One of the boys had died, and another had spent three weeks in the hospital. This had occurred in September, before the flood washed her daughters from her life, and Laura recalled thinking at the time that she couldn't imagine how she would have coped if she had been the mother of the little boy who died.

The man's been charged with manslaughter, Terry had continued. And after the trial, there will be a civil suit—or at least talk of one to get to a settlement. You can bet on it.

Instantly Laura understood what Terry was suggesting, and what he concluded Colleen Montgomery had been thinking—or fearing.

We're not going to sue them! she had said.

No, Terry agreed, of course we're not. But I've heard through the courthouse grapevine that the Montgomerys have spoken to David Tenney, just in case. She knew that Tenney was considered one of the very best lawyers in the county.

A few months later the Montgomery family moved, and though it may have taken yet more time after that for their fears of a civil suit to dissipate, at least they didn't have to worry about running into Terry or Laura in either Cornish or Durham.

She and Terry had talked about leaving Cornish after the flood, too, but for completely different reasons and never realistically. In the months after her children died, it had demanded a monumental effort for Laura to simply get out of bed, and there were a good many days when she didn't achieve even that. Drained by the loss of her daughters, she had lacked the energy to seriously contemplate the notion of leaving, much less finding a new house and packing a decade and a half of their lives into supermarket cartons and moving.

Besides, the lieutenant in Terry's barracks would be retiring in a few years, and Terry was a strong candidate for the promotion if they stayed in the county.

And as that first winter gave way to spring, she realized that both she and Terry were probably as happy in Cornish as they would be anywhere else. She liked her house. She realized she liked the solitude it offered. And she liked her proximity to the cemetery where her girls' bodies were buried: She took small comfort in the idea that she was near them.

You're at the shelter tomorrow, right? she heard Terry asking her now as they continued home from his mother's. His voice sounded strangely far-away, and she found herself turning toward him, her ear pressing against the headrest, as they motored up through the heavily wooded notch.

I am, she murmured.

Alfred, anything special you feel like doing tomorrow? You want to hang out with me? Terry asked. No basement insulation, I promise.

When there was no noise from the backseat, Laura turned. Perhaps he'd fallen asleep at some point, after all. Instead she saw he'd hardly moved in forty-five minutes. He was still sitting upright, now gazing ahead at the two of them.

Alfred? she said, wondering if he had heard Terry with his headset on.

Almost imperceptibly he shrugged his shoulders and said, Sure. Whatever.

Yup, you and I will do something tomorrow, Terry said. We'll do something interesting.

She realized she didn't know quite what that shrug had meant, or for whose benefit it was intended. Terry's? Hers? She couldn't tell what he really thought of a day with her husband, and, as she did often, she found herself wishing that the boy would just talk more.

BY ELEVEN O'CLOCK she was sure that Alfred was asleep, and so she put the book she was reading on her nightstand and said to Terry, Are you awake?

Without turning toward her or even moving, he answered he was.

I want to talk to you, she said.

I expected as much.

I want to know what Russell was talking about.

When my brother drinks too much, he doesn't know what he's talking about.

Are you going to look at me?

She heard a deep inhalation and then a long sigh, and the quilt on his side rose up like a small boat on a wave. Finally he rolled over and sat up. Yes, he said, I am going to look at you.

What happened?

I had a drink with a woman in a bar. I was bored at the camp, and I had a drink with—

She put her hand on the front of his face and covered his mouth—she felt the stubble on his cheeks—and started to squeeze her fingers and her thumb together. She wasn't sure what she was trying to do; she couldn't tell whether this was like a slap and she was trying to hurt him, or whether she was simply trying to stop him from speaking. From confessing. She felt his teeth through his face, through the thick slabs of flesh that were his cheeks, and she knew her eyes were growing wet, but he didn't stop her or make any effort to remove her hand.

Finally she took her fingers away. His cheeks had deep red marks where her hand had been.

Who was this woman?

Nothing happened, he said. Nothing physical, nothing emotional. Nothing.

I asked you a question.

Her name, I believe, is Phoebe. She works at the store near the camp.

You *believe* you know her name? I'm supposed to believe you had a drink with some woman you picked up in a bar, and you don't know her name? Come on!

It wasn't like that, I didn't pick her up.

Then what was it like? Tell me.

I went to the store to call you—

When was this?

Monday night, I believe.

A week ago Monday?

Yes. If you'll recall, we spoke on the phone a little before eight. Remember? Well, the store was closing when we were talking and the woman was leaving, and we waved at each other. Just being polite, because we knew each other a bit since Russell and me and the boys had been shopping there so much over the weekend. Then you and I said good night, and I hung up. I was planning to go straight back to the camp, but I really had next to no desire to play cards till eleven or twelve at night, and listen to Russell's dirty jokes. And so I went to a bar in Newport and sat down at the counter and had a beer. It was—it is—completely innocent.

Innocent?

Innocent.

Except for the fact you picked up some woman. God, Terry, what do you take me for?

I didn't pick up anyone. That woman—Phoebe—was there, too. I didn't see her at first, I didn't even say hi. But she came over to me after I'd been there awhile, and sat down on the stool next to me. And, yes, we talked.

That's it?

Well, no. I did pay for her beer. It seemed like the courteous thing to do.

Did she try and pick you up?

Yes, as a matter of fact, she did. Until I told her I was happily married. And then we just talked.

What did you talk about?

We talked about Alfred. We talked about you. We talked about the girls.

With two fingers he wiped away a tear at the edge of her eyes, and then took the cuff of his cotton jersey—he was sleeping tonight in sweatpants and a T-shirt with long sleeves—folded it over his thumb, and gently dabbed at both of her cheeks.

How long were you there?

I don't know.

An hour?

Maybe a little longer.

Two?

Laura, you're treating me like I'm a hostile witness. Usually it's only the public defenders who interrogate me like this.

How long do you think you were at the bar? Tell me.

I don't think I like this tone. I told you: Nothing happened.

You went to a bar with a—

No, stop that. I went to a bar alone. I can swear under oath that I drove to that bar alone. Under oath. Understand?

You had a drink with a woman in a bar. How long?

I'm guessing. Okay? I'm guessing. Ninety minutes, if you have to have a number.

So you were back at the camp by nine-thirty.

No.

Then when?

Why are you doing this?

Why am I doing what? Asking where the fuck my husband—

Why are you getting like this? Why are you using words like—

Fuck? Why am I using words like *fuck?* Well, maybe because my husband is taking other women out for drinks when I think he's with the boys at deer camp! Maybe because two days before the anniversary of our daughters'—

Don't go there, you're—

I will go anyplace I please!

Do you want to wake Alfred? Look, I made a mistake. I shouldn't have bought her a beer, and I'm sorry. Really: I'm sorry. But I couldn't face Russell, I couldn't face my cousins, I couldn't face one more hand of hearts. Okay? I couldn't face any of that macho deer camp bullshit. And you know what? It felt good to talk about the girls. It felt good to talk about Alfred. It felt good to talk about you and us and our—

You told this woman about me? About us? What exactly did you tell her about me? I can't wait to hear this, she heard herself saying. It was odd, but just when she thought she was calming down, just when she thought this was going to be okay, he would say something and set her off again. Was this what he was trying to do, she wondered, was this by design? Or was he trying to defuse the situation, and the task was just proving beyond him?

We talked about the girls, yes. Maybe it was exactly because Wednesday was coming. And it really did feel good. Let's face it, there are some things we can't talk about anymore. Maybe we never could. My God, look at us. I love you, Laura, I absolutely adore you. You know that. But look at me, look at you. Look—

Me? Don't you dare try and say it's my fault that you went to some bar with some woman.

I'm not!

Then what?

We're not . . . we're not the same as we were before the flood. I love you, I love our marriage. But we don't talk about the same things, we don't make love like we used to. We go through these phases. And I'm saying *we*. I'm not blaming this on you. We. Me, too. And if I was in a court of law, I'd probably have to confess that I enjoyed talking to Phoebe in that bar. But I went there alone, and I left there alone. Okay?

She had a sense that they were at a stage in the fight where she had complete control to either end it right now and minimize the damage, or allow it to continue and risk serious escalation. If she wanted to believe him, then his worst crime had been withholding from her the fact that he had a beer with this person named Phoebe—which meant he did feel guilty about something, but that something may have been the simple notion that he had been at a bar with another woman. But he hadn't slept with her.

She thought she could forgive him that. Not right that moment. But with the passage of a little time—especially if they used this revelation (she couldn't call it a confession, because he was only telling her now because of his brother) to shore up their marriage and try to address whatever emptiness had led Terry to open up to another woman in the first place.

If she doubted him, however, then now was the time to force the issue. Let him know that she hadn't lost what was for her an important—perhaps the most important—thread in their squabble: If he had only been with this Phoebe at the bar for ninety minutes, then why, by his own admission, was he not back at deer camp by nine-thirty? He still hadn't answered that question for her.

She stared at him for what felt like a long time but she guessed in reality was no more than ten or fifteen seconds. He looked to her a bit like a sleepy little boy, despite his mustache and the small flecks of gray in his sideburns: His hair was already mussed by the pillow, and his eyes were small and tired. She half-expected him to rub them with his hands balled into fists.

Okay? he asked again.

She opened her mouth, unsure what was going to come out, and then she heard the word, and if she wasn't completely okay, she thought she would be soon enough. There was much more that they had to discuss—and she resolved that they would—but for now she was . . . okay.

Okay, she said one more time, her voice now soft as a whisper, and already he was falling forward and resting his head on her chest.

———

"Any white man who believes the colored troops are any good must be living with a dusky companion himself, and expressing her opinion. He must be like a renegade or a colored himself: Doesn't care what color a woman is, as long as she's female."

———

ANONYMOUS LETTER SIGNED "11TH INFANTRY," *ARMY AND NAVY JOURNAL*, MAY 19, 1876

———

Alfred

He'd heard other grown-ups use the word *fuck,* but never Laura. He wasn't sure he'd ever heard her use any swear word before. Not even *damn.*

He climbed back into his blue jeans and left his pajama bottoms on the edge of his bed. There was a New England Patriots sweatshirt on the floor in the corner of his room, and he slipped that on over his pajama top. He considered filling his knapsack with the food in his closet—and maybe adding something more from the kitchen, just in case—but his plan certainly wasn't to leave. He hoped he wasn't going anywhere. He just needed to get out and wander around for a couple of hours. Like he did in Burlington. And so all he took with him was his CD player.

His boots and his jacket were by the front door, and when there was only silence in Terry and Laura's room, he tiptoed down the stairs to put them on, too. The house was darker than he would have liked, but he didn't dare turn on the hall light.

Outside, the branches on the cat spruce near the edge of the driveway moved like sleepy fingers in the breeze.

He had expected a direction would occur to him once he was outdoors, but now he was there and he still didn't have a clue where he might walk. This place wasn't like Burlington: There weren't lights on every corner, and rows of apartment houses filled with college students who were still wide awake. There weren't bars and restaurants open well past midnight some days. He was actually rather scared of the dark, and the only street lamp out here was at the bend in the road near the Cousinos' dairy farm—and that was at least a quarter of a mile away, on the other side of the patch of woods that bordered the street. The other direction led up the hill toward the cemetery, and although he liked the graveyard a good deal during the day, there was no way he was going to go there right now.

He considered listening to some music, but he decided he should be able to hear the strange noises that seemed to mark the night here in the middle of nowhere, and so he kept the headset draped around his neck like a horseshoe.

The cement steps before the house were stone cold, but he sat down on them anyway and stared across the street at the old people's place. He saw there were rooms in the house that were lit, despite the fact it was late and most everyone else in Cornish was probably sound asleep. He wondered if they also slept with lights on, or whether one or both of them were awake right now, too.

He thought of Terry and Laura in their big bed in their room. Once before he had been living in a home when the grown-ups decided to get a divorce. He'd been five and a half, and he hadn't been there all that long. It had been the Ryans, those two people who lived in the apartment by the bus station. The man left, and soon after that he was shuttled to the north end of the city to live with two older foster kids—a boy and a girl—at the Fletchers', where he would sleep for close to three years on the pullout bed in the living room and wear the older boy's clothes when he outgrew them. Mrs. Fletcher was a soap opera fiend. She was also a hard drinker, and she used to whale on Isabel, the oldest child in the house and the only girl. But she never touched the boys, and only rarely did she ever stop any of the kids from roaming around Burlington.

He feared that if Terry left—if Laura kicked him out—he'd be sent back to the group home until they could find another placement. The group home was the world of the real losers. Bed wetters. Kids who'd do really weird shit, like set things on fire. One girl there had once carried all her foster dad's pants and shirts and underwear into the backyard, soaked them with the gasoline the family had in the garage for the lawn mower, and burned them up. Made a big bonfire out of them. A neighbor called the fire department, but the girl had the blaze under control and knew exactly what she was doing.

There was a rumor that the man might have touched her, but no one ever said anything for sure.

Although at first he had figured Cornish was just a temporary placement at best, he was pretty sure now that Louise—his latest caseworker—thought she'd found the promised land with Terry and Laura. Louise had lots of studs and rings in her ears—even more than he'd had the previous summer, when he and Tien convinced Digger to do their ears in the bathroom in the basement of the shopping mall. He had a sense that Louise viewed Terry and Laura as the perfect family for him. Tough cop for a dad, sweet lady for a mom. Home nowhere near the city. Maybe she was right. Maybe it didn't get any better than this. But if it didn't—

If it didn't, he didn't know what to think. Sure, they didn't scream at each other (though Laura had seemed pretty close to yelling tonight), and they didn't hit him. They gave him clothes and toys and he had his very own bedroom. But they sure as shit weren't happy, and every minute he felt like he was walking on glass. You moved slow in this house, as if everything—and that included the people—was just about ready to break.

He guessed it hadn't been like that when the girls were alive. When he was supposed to have been watching the Macy's parade and had gone through the family pictures instead, he'd learned that the house had been a different world then. Terry and Laura had looked younger—which, of course, they were. But they had looked a *lot* younger. More than just a couple of years. And the family had always seemed to be doing things. Several pictures stuck in his mind: Terry and a group of girls, including one of his daughters, playing T-ball at the Little League field. Terry was wearing shorts, and showing the kid how to hold a bat.

He wouldn't have believed that uptight cop had ever owned shorts. And he was smiling. That was pretty rare for Terry, too.

Another picture he liked showed the T-ball twin's sister using a spoon to sprinkle glitter on what looked like a foot-tall teepee made of twigs. She was probably six or seven, and her hair was down to her waist. It was taken in the house's front yard, and he thought it was spring because there was the green of some flowers just starting to emerge through the pine bark in the garden.

The picture he found most intriguing, however, was a shot of the four of them taken at the peak of some little mountain, with little more than blue sky behind them. The girls were in blue jeans and windbreakers, and each one was sitting on top of a parent's shoulders, their legs dangling like they were Halloween straw men. He guessed they were about five. What fascinated him was that everyone was not merely smiling in the photograph, they were laughing—laughing hysterically, it seemed, as if whoever was snapping the picture was the funniest person on the planet. They were all so happy, it was like they were stoned.

He'd considered taking that one, but he was afraid it would be obvious it was missing. And so instead he'd taken a photograph of the two girls dressed up as brides, one of about seven or eight pictures that had been snapped the same day and stored in the photo album. But it wasn't merely the fact that there were many similar shots that had made the picture such a find: It was one of the few images on which someone—Laura, he guessed—had bothered to scrawl the girls' names on the back:

Hillary and Megan, planning their weddings. Second grade.

Across the street Alfred saw the front door opening, and he saw the old man emerge on the porch. For a second he thought the man was wearing a dress under his winter coat, and he was about to race back inside Terry and Laura's house. But then he realized that what he thought was a dress was merely the bottom half of the man's flannel bathrobe. The guy had simply put his parka on over his robe.

With his hands in his pockets, the man shuffled across the street and up the walkway. Alfred watched his breath rise up into the night air like cigarette smoke. When he reached the Sheldons' house, he sat down on the steps beside him.

Evening, Alfred, he said, without looking his way. He stared straight ahead at his own place.

Hi.

I've always suspected that you, too, are a night person. I don't sleep much either these days.

I've seen your light on at night, Alfred said.

And I have seen yours. Of course, I have an excuse for not sleeping well: I'm old. You're a growing boy. Your body is supposed to be hungry for sleep. Just crave it.

Alfred thought for a moment. Not mine, he said finally.

Well, all bodies are different, the man said. Some people just don't need much sleep. He stretched his legs straight before him, and Alfred realized the man was wearing black rubber galoshes into which he had tucked his pajamas.

Your feet must be cold, he said. He envisioned the man's feet were bare in the rubber.

Not too bad.

You wearing socks?

Nope.

Me, either. But at least I put on winter boots.

You're a wise lad, he said, and then—as if they'd been talking about animals all along and his inquiry didn't reflect a change in the subject— continued in the same placid tone, You like horses?

I don't know. I guess. I've never seen one, except from the road.

Well, I'm getting a horse. If you want, I'll teach you to ride. It's not difficult.

Where are you going to keep it?

The man pointed at the meadow next to his house. The fencing will be here on Monday, he added. You can help me put that in, too—but only if you want to. And you don't have any homework. Homework has to come first, you know.

They don't give you much homework, Alfred said, a half-truth. In actuality he received lengthier assignments here than he had in Burlington, but on those days he felt like doing it, he could knock the work off in half an hour.

That's too bad. They should. They should give you mountains of home-work. A daily avalanche. If you'd like, I can talk to your teacher. Tell her to give you some real work.

Oh, you don't need to do that.

Well, you tell me if you change your mind, he said, and then he went on about his horse. The animal will probably have a name by the time I get it— which is too bad. I kind of think a person should name his own pony. Might help them bond.

Alfred tried to imagine the old man on a horse, and he kept seeing him astride an animal while wearing galoshes. Have you ever ridden a horse before? he asked.

You sound like my wife.

Just asking.

I have. Thank you for your concern.

It must have been a long time ago.

He felt the man staring at him, and he found he had to struggle hard not to smile.

I know what I'm doing, the man said evenly.

So this is like, what, a toy? A hobby?

You really have spoken to my wife.

I haven't. I'm just asking.

I guess it's between a toy and a whim—though I probably shouldn't use either of those words, given the fact that a horse is a living, breathing thing with a fine brain. It must be respected, and it will demand a lot of work.

I once lived in a place that had a dog. That didn't demand much work. They just kept it tied to a clothesline. Alfred knew that a horse and a dog were very different animals, and he knew that the dog on the rope had been unfairly ignored. But he discovered that he liked tormenting this old professor with his feigned naïveté.

This will demand considerably more effort than a dog on a line. Trust me.

And you want one, anyway.

I certainly do. Very much. Suddenly they're popping up in my reading all the time. Every book I open, it seems, has a horse in it. I figure that's a sign. Don't you?

Maybe, Alfred said, and then asked what he meant as a serious question: Is that how you got so interested in the buffalo soldiers?

Through their horses? No, not at all. To be honest, the buffalo soldiers only interest me because of the larger historical context in which they lived. Let me rephrase that: I'm interested in the buffalo soldiers because they were successful black men in a white army that would have been very happy to see them fall flat on their faces. They just happened to ride horses because that's what we had to work with in the nineteenth century.

Alfred thought of the image on the front of the cap the man had given him. They never rode buffalos, he said.

No.

I didn't think so.

A buffalo wouldn't take kindly to carting around one hundred and forty pounds of human flesh on his back.

He nodded to himself and then put forth the inquiry that had troubled him off and on for almost a month. Then tell me something, he began. How come they were called buffalo soldiers?

It's not in that book we gave you?

Suddenly he felt stupid. Of course it was in that book somewhere, it was just that the volume was thick and the type was small and there really weren't very many photographs. Briefly he considered lying—saying he didn't remember, or he was only on page seventeen, anything—but he knew he'd get caught, and he realized at that moment that the answer was more important to him than his pride.

Maybe if it was a video or a DVD I would have watched it, he said finally.

Haven't gotten to it yet, eh?

I guess not.

The old man sat up a little straighter and fixed the collar on his parka. He cleared his throat. The name, he said, was probably given to the troopers by the Comanches. Do you know who the Comanches were?

Indians.

Right. Native Americans. They lived on the Great Plains, Wyoming to Texas. They had seen white troopers for years, but not many black ones. Then in the 1860s they started to see hundreds of them. Whole regiments. They were the ones who christened them buffalo soldiers.

But why?

Why the name? Their hair, probably. Their woolly hair reminded them of the buffalo.

Alfred shook his head when he heard. It was even worse than he expected, because it was the Indians—and not the white men—who had given the soldiers the name. I figured it was all about hair, he said.

You sound annoyed.

It's always about what people look like. Their hair, their skin. Always has been, always will be.

It was a term of respect.

How you figure?

The buffalo was a sacred animal to the American Indians. Revered. It was smart, strong. Dedicated to its herd. Good family values, you might say. The Indians depended upon the buffalo for an awful lot of life's little necessities. Food. Clothing. Shelter. There's no way they would have called the black soldiers buffalo soldiers if they didn't respect them.

Alfred wanted to believe him, but he wasn't willing to give himself up to such a fantasy just yet.

And think about this, the man went on: The black troopers in the Ninth and Tenth Cavalries liked the term. They knew it was meant respectfully, and so they commandeered it for their insignias—like the emblem on that hat of yours. They knew they weren't being insulted.

The hat was upstairs in Alfred's room. He wished he had it with him right now so he could look at it.

No, the old man remarked, being called a buffalo soldier was nothing to be ashamed of. They were a very proud bunch.

I didn't really believe they rode buffalos, you know, Alfred said.

I didn't think you did.

When will you get your horse?

Next week, with any luck. You want to come with me? I'm going to see a former student of mine. She's got two animals, and there's one she thought I might be interested in.

I have school next week.

We'll go after school. She only lives about thirty minutes from here.

I'll have to ask Laura.

You do that. And I'll ask Emily.

You need your wife's permission?

He stood up, and so Alfred stood with him. He watched the man shake out his leg as if it were stiff from sitting. *Permission* isn't exactly the right word, the man said. *Tolerance* might be more accurate. I need her tolerance. And on that note, my friend, I'm going to go home. Good evening.

Then he gave Alfred a small salute and rambled down the walkway toward the street. When he reached the road, he stopped and called back in a stage whisper—loud enough for Alfred to hear, but not loud enough to wake Terry and Laura—Give that book we gave you a chance. I'm telling you, you won't regret it.

He nodded and waited for the man to reach his house. Then, once Paul was inside, he quietly opened the front door behind him and decided he, too, would return to his bed for the night.

PART TWO

Advent

"I saw Night Bird and Moon of the Big Leaves die. I saw Red Sands and Lone Bear dive into the water. Did Lone Bear see us, too? Is that why he tried to cross the river? I hope not, but I believe that's what happened. He saw us and dove into the river, and then Red Sands followed him because Red Sands always followed my husband."

VERONICA ROWE (FORMERLY POPPING TREES),
WPA INTERVIEW,
MARCH 1938

Terry

He had turned his cruiser around even before the dispatcher finished her cool, evenhanded recitation of the facts, and switched on his siren and lights. It never ceased to astonish him that the news, no matter how bad, was always presented this way.

He guessed he would beat the ambulance to the scene, because the accident had occurred in Leicester, on a strip of Route 7 a few miles south of Middlebury. The ambulance would have to wind its way through the college and the village and then the traffic that, inevitably, stalled near the commons this time of the day. The very beginning of rush hour. Dusk. He, on the other hand, was already south of the town, and no more than five or six miles separated him from the construction site where the accident had occurred. Other than a couple of dairy farms and a long stretch of forest, there was little between him and some wretched construction worker who'd managed to get himself impaled on a line of rebar spikes.

The red taillights of the vehicles ahead of him moved to the right, and the white headlights of the oncoming ones edged to his left. He could have driven smack in the middle of the road if he'd wanted, he could have aimed his car straight ahead atop a pair of solid yellow lines.

Apparently the guy was still alive when the 911 was called in, but Terry couldn't imagine he would be by the time he arrived. He hadn't fallen far—no more than a couple of floors, it sounded like—but he had landed smack on top of a row of six-foot-high, inch-thick metal spikes. According to the site foreman, his body was hanging, skewered, three or four feet off the ground.

The building wasn't going to be very big by most city standards, but it was for Addison County: three stories, and roughly twenty-two thousand square feet of space. It was going to be some kind of elegant executive retreat and small-business conference center, and so the developer had been able to get the zoning approvals and building permits he needed.

When he reached the site, he parked as close as he could to the big hole at the bottom of the steel skeleton, pulling in between a pickup and a cement mixer. He saw people were shining lights down into the hole because the daylight, fading fast aboveground, was almost gone down there, and he saw the body—part of it, anyway—right away. He couldn't see the man's face and chest because two other workers were cradling the body like it was a huge piece of timber they were trying to carry. They had wrapped their arms around him as if they feared the body might slip down the spikes if they let it go.

He climbed down a ladder into the pit and ran across the fresh cement to the two men and the victim. There were easily a dozen construction workers in what would eventually be the building's basement with the small group, and—like the cars on Route 7—they gave way the moment they saw him. Before he even glimpsed the fellow's face, he had a sinking feeling that the poor son of a bitch was still breathing—worse, he was still conscious—because he could hear one of the men who was holding the body murmuring, You're gonna live, man, I wouldn't shit you. I'm telling you, you're gonna make it.

The victim was no more than nineteen or twenty, and his skin had gone as white as vanilla ice cream. His lips were blue. He was on his side on the bars, and his hands were wrapped tightly around the rebar that seemed to have speared him through his chest. It looked like he was holding himself up on it, as if this was some kind of gymnastic feat. A second rebar had stabbed him through his thigh and a third had pierced his abdomen. Because of the jeans jacket and sweatshirt he'd been wearing while he worked, Terry couldn't tell how badly the man—*kid,* Terry thought to himself, *kid*—was bleeding. But the outer jacket didn't look wet, and neither did the kid's jeans. The thing was, the spike in his leg looked pretty damn close to a femoral artery, and the one in the chest had to be near the guy's heart and the complex knot of blood vessels that surrounded it. They must have just missed them somehow. He wondered if the spikes had rammed through him so clean and fast that they were actually stanching the bleeding.

Quickly Terry turned to look the kid squarely in the face, both because he could no longer bear to look at where the barbs entered and exited his body, and so that the young construction worker wouldn't gaze at them, either. He was a redhead, gray eyes and lots of freckles, and despite the cold, his hair was matted with sweat. Terry said who he was and then figured the best thing to do was to lie.

We'll have you off there before you know it, son, he said, keeping his voice as even as he could. If you listen, you'll hear the ambulance.

See? one of the men holding him said. We're in agreement here.

What's your name? Terry asked him.

The young man moved his lips but nothing came out, and one of the workers nearby said his name was Kevin. Kevin McKay.

You can hear me, right, Kevin?

The kid looked at Terry and nodded, and then rasped that he was about to puke.

You go and do that, Terry said, and he held the young man's head in his hands. When he was through, Terry walked away and wiped his hands on his pants, and took his radio off his belt and asked the dispatcher to send a fire truck, too, if one wasn't already on the way. He had a sense that they couldn't possibly saw through the bars while the kid was still breathing, because the jostling alone would kill him. That meant that they'd have to use an acetylene torch to slice through the rods, but if they didn't do it right, the steel spikes would conduct the heat from the flame up into the body. Cook the kid from the inside, like he was a baking potato rammed through with a metal tine. And so they'd have to keep a stream of cold water on the bars above the torch to keep them cool, and that was where he anticipated the fire department would come in.

He recognized the crew from the rescue squad that was arriving, and briefly watched Kristin Engels, a volunteer like the vast majority of EMTs in the state, take the kid's vitals while he hung on the spikes. Then he saw Henry Labarge climbing down the ladder into the hole, too. Henry was not simply one of his troopers, he was the man who'd driven all the way out to deer camp some two years earlier to tell him his daughters had died. Briefly—for a month, maybe—Terry had been unable to have this younger man in his presence, not exactly hating him for being the messenger, but unwilling to be reminded whenever he saw him of the moment he'd learned what had occurred back in Cornish. Like so much else that brought back images of Hillary and Megan, however—school buses and bridges and the sight of a group of kids playing T-ball—eventually the connection faded, and he grew to like Henry once again.

Sounds pretty gruesome, Henry said.

It is. I guess the poor kid just slipped and fell.

He gonna die?

I presume. Help me find someone who's got a torch.

A light?

No, a torch. An acetylene torch. These people are building a building, so somewhere around here there's got to be one. Let's face it, we sure as hell can't use a saw to get him down. A thought crossed his mind, and he asked, Anyone doing traffic up there?

Yeah, a pair of volunteer firefighters from East Middlebury.

Soon there were more men and women in uniforms in the pit—the khaki and green ones that Terry and Henry wore, the blue and gray of the officers from the county sheriff's department, the yellow bunker coats the firefighters were wearing—than there were construction workers, and everyone stood in a tight sickle moon around the two men holding Kevin McKay. Though it seemed to take hours for the site foreman to bring a torch and a tank with some fuel, Terry guessed in reality it hadn't taken more than two or three minutes. The foreman held the torch in his hands and asked, You want me to do it? I've at least got some experience with one of these.

What's your name?

Ed Whittemore.

Terry looked him over. He was in his mid-forties maybe, and he looked pretty trim. Competent. He pulled aside Kristin Engels and the paramedic from the hospital, some young buck named Brent who right now looked a sick shade of green, and said, Seems to me old Ed Whittemore here is as qualified as any of us to cut the kid down. You okay with that?

I'm in no hurry to do it, Kristin said.

Brent?

Hey, I've never even held one of those things, he said, his voice weaker than Terry had heard it the three or four times their paths had crossed since Brent started working at the hospital.

Okay, then. Ed Whittemore's our man.

Henry ushered in a pair of firefighters, and he was relieved to see they'd brought in a small booster hose instead of one of the massive attack lines: The last thing Kevin McKay needed right now was to experience 250 pounds of water pressure sprayed through a hose with a two-and-a-half-inch diameter. Someone up at the truck turned on the water, and briefly they all felt the cold spray as it bounced suddenly up and off the cement ground, before slowing to the trickle they wanted.

We'll feather the valve, Terry heard one of the firefighters saying as he turned toward Ed Whittemore.

You know what you're doing, right? he asked him.

Fuck, no! Whittemore snapped. This isn't something they teach you. But at least I know how to use the torch.

That's a start.

I mean, I guess I should keep the flame as low on the rebar as I can. I can probably run it along the metal three or four feet below him.

Think three feet. Not four. I don't want us getting the kid up to the ambulance only to find out he won't fit through the back doors because he's still got so much pipe coming out both sides.

Eighteen inches above the ground? Whittemore suggested.

Okay, Terry said, and he led him back to the bars. On the way, he grabbed another volunteer firefighter he recognized—he believed his last name was Mikkelson—and told him to clutch each spike above where Whittemore was running the torch and let them know if he felt it getting hot.

A part of him hoped that McKay had died while they were tracking down a torch so his suffering would be over, but the fact that he wasn't dead yet was beginning to give Terry some small measure of hope that they might actually manage to save the guy's life. Wasn't likely, of course. But stranger things happened, and he grew excited at the prospect that the young man might live.

He looked straight into McKay's eyes—for better or worse, the kid was still very much alive—and said, We're about to cut through the bars. At the same time, these firefighters here are going to dribble water on them. Your job? Tell us if you feel any warmth, okay? You feel some heat, any at all, you tell us to stop. Can you do that?

The kid moved his lips and seemed to say yes, but—as when he'd first tried to tell Terry his name—he didn't make any sound.

I'm serious, he told McKay. You make noise if you feel something new. He motioned toward Mikkelson and added, This gentleman is going to tell us if he feels anything, too. Just in case. But don't you be shy now, okay?

Then he stepped back and was about to tell Whittemore to go ahead when one more thought crossed his mind. Are there going to be any sparks? he asked him.

It's a goddamn torch! Of course there will be sparks!

And so he turned to one of the firefighters and said, See if you can drape a wet bunker coat around that kid—and the two guys holding him. Let's try not to compound our problems here by setting someone on fire.

WHILE ED WHITTEMORE held the torch against the individual rebar spikes, Terry and Kristin Engels stood like baseball umpires in front of McKay's face—their bodies bent slightly over, their hands on their knees—watching for any sign in the young man's eyes or any movement on his lips that he could feel the rods heating up. Terry was moderately impressed with the number of people he had wedged around the wall of steel rods, and downright amazed than none of the rescuers had bumped the kid yet and inadvertently killed him. Still, he didn't see how they could get the fellow down with fewer people.

Occasionally Terry glanced up at the two guys who were holding McKay to make sure they were ready for the extra weight: Before starting he'd reminded them that as each of the rebars was cut away, McKay would get a bit heavier, until—he hoped—the only thing holding the man off the ground would be their arms. He guessed McKay didn't weigh more than one-forty, one forty-five, and so he figured a couple of construction workers could hold him like that for the split second it would take for Brent and the EMTs to rotate the kid onto the backboard once Whittemore had sliced through the final rebar.

At one point while they were burning through the second of the three spikes, McKay closed his eyes for fifteen or twenty seconds, and both Terry and Kristin thought he had died. But then Whittemore finished with the middle rebar and the young man grimaced in pain, opening his eyes as if he'd just been slapped. The spike had moved inside him a bit, and clearly it had hurt like hell. If he could have spoken, he probably would have screamed.

THE THIRD REBAR was the most difficult to burn through, both because it was the one that went through McKay's chest and because everyone knew that once it was severed, there would be nothing supporting the young construction worker but the two men. Still, Whittemore managed to cut through it without setting anyone's clothing on fire, and, apparently, without causing the section of the spike inside McKay to slice through anything especially critical. The kid was still breathing and awake when he was carried on his side on the backboard to a plywood pile a few yards away, and Brent started him on a series of IVs.

Terry saw that while they'd worked to get McKay down from the bars, a group of construction workers had built a ramp with wooden beams and bricks that led up and out of the hole. It was wide enough for the EMTs to carry McKay up to street level, and while he watched them bring the kid out, he felt a moment of great satisfaction, greater than anything he had felt in a very long time. He was confident now that McKay would get to the hospital, where the surgeons were waiting, and there they would extricate the spikes from inside him. They would do this without ripping apart anything that couldn't be sewn back together.

Terry was vaguely aware that Henry Labarge was standing beside him, his arms folded across his chest, and he allowed himself to take pride in what they had accomplished. Somehow they'd gotten the kid off the spikes. Three of them. Unbelievable, he thought. Unbelievable. The sensation didn't last long, however, because in the headlights from the cars parked around the top of the hole he saw the litter bearers abruptly stop, and he saw Brent and Kristin suddenly checking McKay's vitals. He could see by the way their faces were changing—alarm, then panic, then, quickly, frustration—that something had happened. Cardiac arrest, maybe. A seizure. Maybe McKay had simply stopped breathing.

Then he watched the group disappear into the back of the ambulance, and he knew they would work on McKay in the ER, perhaps drag him into the OR since it was most certainly prepped and ready. But the kid was already dead. If Terry had any hope left, it evaporated completely when he heard Henry murmur, What was that just now? Heart attack?

Your guess is as good as mine, he said.

I'd say heart attack.

You're probably right.

Well. That sucks.

Yes, it does, Terry agreed.

I didn't get the sense he was married.

No. I didn't notice a ring. And he was pretty young.

So at least there aren't any kids involved. At least not likely.

Nope, probably no kids. But his parents are still alive, I'd imagine, and I doubt they're a hell of a lot older than I am. And if you want to know the real meaning of the word *heartbreak,* my man, outlive your children.

He realized he'd said more than he'd meant to, and—perhaps too energetically—he hit Henry on the back and said, We better get up there and see what the traffic looks like. Maybe give those volunteer firefighters a break.

AT DINNER THAT night Laura talked about a new litter of puppies the shelter had, a mix of Great Dane and German shepherd, and how massive she imagined the animals would be when they grew up. She mentioned that they were starting to receive the checks that came in every December from people who needed their tax deductions by the end of the calendar year, and even though many of the checks were only fifteen and twenty dollars, it all helped.

Briefly she and Alfred talked a bit about Kwanzaa, and she told the boy that she thought it would be fun to celebrate the holiday this year.

Terry gazed across the table at her, and he knew they'd been together long enough that she would understand from the vacant look on his face not to ask him how his day was. Maybe she would in bed. But not now. For now she would provide all the talking the table demanded, and allow him to sit and eat and listen.

In the morning, he knew, he would be fine.

———

". . . and so although a lack of water was usually the most complicating aspect of our marches and either the capture or dispersal of the hostiles, this time the Pecos River was our greatest ally."

———

SERGEANT GEORGE ROWE,
TENTH REGIMENT, UNITED STATES CAVALRY,
REPORT TO CAPTAIN ANDREW HITCHENS
AFTER THE ENGAGEMENT AT CANYON CREEK,
MAY 9, 1876

———

The Heberts

The boy could look straight up into the horse's great nostrils if he wanted. He stood before it, separated from the animal only by the thin wooden rails of the fence and a cord of rusted barbed wire, and ran his fingers down the Morgan's slender nose. Quickly the animal curled her lip upward, momentarily trapping the boy's smell inside her so she could study it more carefully.

The horse seemed happy enough with strange people, Paul thought, but you couldn't be sure until you'd spent some time with the animal. Still, Paul was reasonably convinced this was a horse that he wanted. She stood fifteen and a half hands tall, and the two large coal-colored spots on her hide seemed to shimmer in the afternoon sun. Her mane was black, and her body—those spots and a pair of white stockings on her rear legs notwithstanding—was a deep auburn. The color of the hills on the day the leaves have just started to turn.

Pet her all you want, Ruth said to Alfred. Let her get used to your smell, your voice. You'll see she's very gentle.

Ruth had taken three classes with Paul that he could remember, including one of his senior seminars: History 441, or "Ugly Vermont." That was the course's actual name in the catalog. In it they had studied, among other tawdry secrets one never discussed in regard to the Green Mountains, the state's aggressive eugenics project in the 1920s and 1930s. Ruth had been a fine student, and managed to approach the material with irony instead of the merely politically correct earnestness that marked the work of most of the seniors.

Now Ruth was in her late twenties, and pregnant with her second child. She had a two-and-a-half-year-old boy napping back at the house, and a baby in her tummy who was pressing hard against her blue parka. The young woman's hair was braided and fell down her back, and her eyeglasses fogged in the cold.

When she was in his class, her hair had been short and he couldn't recall her wearing eyeglasses. Maybe she'd worn contact lenses then. Maybe he just didn't remember. Either way, he decided, she'd grown from a pretty girl into an attractive woman, and the memory reminded him of how much he missed being around . . . children.

That was, after all, how he'd viewed his students for the last decade and a half he'd been in the classroom. Once he was more than twice their age— and then three times the age of the freshmen—they weren't adults to him anymore. They were kids. He could refer to them as teenagers, young people, even young adults, but the fact remained, for him they were children. They were a hell of a lot closer to Alfred's age than to his.

You won't miss her? he asked Ruth, referring to the horse, and he stroked the animal's cheek lightly when the animal was done chewing the handful of pony nuts the boy had just given her.

I will, she said. But I know I won't be able to care for two horses and two children. We think we can handle one of the animals, but not both. Something tells me someone is going to wind up neglected.

For a moment all three people watched the other horse, a majestic gray Percheron, nuzzling the circle of thick Styrofoam Ruth's husband had cut and set in the water bucket to help prevent a layer of ice from forming in the night. The Percheron had been with Ruth for more than six years—longer than the woman had been married, and twice the time she had been a mother. The Morgan had been with the family barely eighteen months, and so although Ruth loved both horses, she felt a greater loyalty to the gray one.

Paul bent down to examine the animal's forelegs through the fence, and realized that unless the horse was grotesquely splay-footed or knock-kneed, he wouldn't have the slightest idea whether the animal's conformation was solid. But he didn't notice any glaring deformities, at least, he didn't see anything specific that might make the horse prone to lameness.

If anyone was going to come up lame, he decided, it was probably him. His knees cracked when he stood back up, and all too often they ached.

Can I ride her? the boy asked suddenly, his voice surprising both of the grown-ups. He hadn't spoken more than a word or two since they'd arrived.

Why don't you brush her first? Ruth suggested, and she reached into her coat pocket and pulled out a rubber curry comb. She showed the boy how to slip his fingers through the buckle in the back, and then she gently guided him through the gate and into the paddock. Paul followed the pair, noting the small pyramids of light brown manure that dotted the field near the fence. Certainly their garden would benefit from the presence of the horse.

Mesa just loves to be brushed, Ruth said as the boy ran the comb over the big animal's side. After Alfred had been brushing the horse for a minute or two, she took his free hand and placed it on a spot just between the horse's shoulder and neck.

Feel that? It's something special.

I feel a hole, he said.

You, too, Professor Hebert, she said. Right here. Put your hand here.

Paul, he said to her. At this stage in our lives, it's Paul. Then he put his fingers where she had told him, and he felt an indentation that reminded him of his underarm.

A prophet's thumb? he asked.

Yup.

I don't know if I've ever felt one before, he said. Of course, I haven't been around a horse in a serious way in over eight years.

What's a prophet's thumb? the boy asked, and he seemed to be directing his question at Ruth.

It's supposed to be good luck, she said. It means that the animal might be descended from one of Muhammad's horses.

Muhammad?

He was a prophet, Ruth explained.

Of course, Paul said, what it probably means is that when she was a foal in her mother's stomach, her hind foot was resting on her neck and the muscle atrophied. Let's face it: Morgans weren't real common in the Middle East in 600 A.D.

Still, Mesa's a great horse, Ruth said. Even if she isn't sacred.

Agreed, Paul said.

Can I ride her now? Alfred asked.

You're really dying to, aren't you? Ruth said.

Alfred nodded, but the gesture was muted, as if he feared he had over-stepped some important boundary with his enthusiasm.

Tell you what, she said. Let me get a lead, and then you can walk her a bit. Once you've led her around, you can sit on her. Okay?

Sure.

When Ruth had left the paddock and was no longer within earshot, Paul asked—his voice a conspiratorial whisper—Think I should buy her?

Yes.

Me, too.

Will she cost a lot of money?

Some.

I hope I get to ride her.

I can tell, Paul said, and he realized that the boy was actually anticipating something with pleasure. He tried to recall if he'd ever seen that in the short time that he'd known the child, and he didn't believe that he had.

IN THE CAR on the way home, Alfred readily agreed to everything Paul suggested. Alfred would help him muck out the stable, check the bedding daily, and feed and groom the horse when he came home from school. He— Paul—would handle the morning routine, but he would expect Alfred to assist him in the afternoon.

I'll make a chart, he said aloud as he drove, his eyes on the road. That'll help because some afternoons I might not be there.

Where will you be?

Good question. Damned if I know. But together the chores will probably take us an hour. Alone, give yourself an hour and a half. I'll pay you four dollars a day, and I'll expect you to keep up with your homework. And, of course, all this depends upon Terry and Laura's permission.

Four dollars?

Four dollars, he repeated, unable to tell from the boy's tone whether he was pleased with the sum or disappointed. It had seemed like a reasonable wage to Paul when he'd verbalized the amount, but he understood that because he was in his mid-sixties, there were times when he still expected things to cost what they had in the administrations of Presidents who'd been dead longer than this lad had been alive.

And I can ride her?

When I'm there.

A buffalo soldier was supposed to exercise his horse every single day—when he wasn't already out scouting, anyway.

You started that book?

Finished it.

Good man, he said, at once pleased and impressed.

A lot of buffalo soldiers weren't much older than I am, you know. You only had to be sixteen to sign up.

You're ten.

I just want you to know I can help exercise your horse for you, too.

When I'm around, you can ride her plenty. When I'm not, don't even think about it, he said, and then added quickly, Please.

The boy was quiet, and Paul assumed his silence signaled his agreement. You did a nice job with Mesa, he said. I think she likes you.

I like her, too. And I liked sitting on her.

What did you like about it?

I liked being tall, that's for sure.

Yes, I always liked that, too.

Abruptly he felt the boy poking him in the shoulder, and when he turned toward him Alfred was smiling. You looked funny up there, he said.

Me?

You looked like an old army general, except you couldn't believe you were on a horse. You looked like you were scared to death.

Oh, not to death. That would be an exaggeration. But it did dawn on me when I was up there just how hard the ground is right now, and just how much havoc it would wreak on an old man's hip if I fell.

You won't fall. Ruth said you had good form.

It's a bit like riding a bicycle: The muscles don't forget. Of course, they also don't forgive. I'm going to be sore as hell tomorrow.

From riding a horse?

You, too, my friend. Mark my words.

Not me. I just sat on her.

We'll see.

As they rolled through the village, Paul glanced at the bridge and he thought of the Sheldon girls. The sight of the bridge didn't usually make him think of them, but it did now because he had Alfred with him. He assumed it would always remind Terry and Laura of their children, and he knew that Laura saw the bridge every Sunday morning because it was no more than a hundred yards from the church where she worshiped every week. Terry, on the other hand, only attended church on the major holidays, but Paul didn't believe that had anything to do with the deaths of his children. He'd gone to church only two or three times a year even when his girls were alive. The boy, it seemed, usually accompanied Laura, but Paul had observed as well that at least once or twice he had stayed home with Terry.

It would take more than a few minutes on Mesa to do me in, the boy was saying.

He nodded and smiled, but he didn't stop thinking about Alfred's foster parents. He wondered if the girls' deaths had been easier—marginally easier—for Terry because his job demanded he witness so much unpleasantness on such a regular basis. As the trooper had once remarked to him, Let's face it. I seldom see people at their best. And though Terry had never shared many details of his work, Paul understood that the younger man saw regularly the battered women in their homes and the dying teenagers in their cars who frequently filled the small and large type in the local section of the daily newspaper. For all he knew, Terry might even have been with the young construction worker who'd died in Middlebury the other day after falling onto a line of the rebar spikes used to reinforce concrete walls.

How are you getting on with Terry and Laura? he asked the boy now.

Okay, he said.

Okay? Is that good-okay or bad-okay?

The child continued to stare out the window, silent now, the bridge and the church growing small in the distance. Paul realized that inadvertently he had brought the two of them back into the world of the one-sentence answer, and he quickly scoured his mind for a bit of historical minutia about the buffalo soldiers—clearly a more congenial topic—to pull the boy back from his shell.

"Rule number three: They have to try to learn how to read. They don't have to succeed, but at the very least they have to try."

SERGEANT GEORGE ROWE,
TENTH REGIMENT, UNITED STATES CAVALRY,
LETTER TO HIS BROTHER IN PHILADELPHIA,
NOVEMBER 18, 1873

Terry

Christmas was less than two weeks away, and once again there was absolutely no snow on the ground. He guessed it had snowed three or four times so far that winter, but never more than two or three inches at once. And, each time, the snow had been gone a couple of days later.

When people talked about the winter, either they murmured in rueful tones about global climate change or they shook their heads unconcernedly and observed that they would all have to pay for this warm and snowless December after the first of the year. Winter would simply be dragged out on the other side, and, in the end, they would get their annual hundred-plus inches of snow. It was inevitable.

Snow or no snow, it was time to get a Christmas tree, and so Sunday afternoon, exactly twelve days before Christmas, he took Laura and Alfred into the spit of woods between their property and the Cousinos' to begin the search for an evergreen. He'd been working hard at being both a husband and a dad for a month now—especially since Thanksgiving—and he wanted Christmas to be perfect. Laura hadn't brought up Phoebe once since that night in their bed, and even his occasionally problematic younger brother hadn't alluded to the woman when he'd seen him at their mother's last week. He hoped this one stupid mistake was behind him, and he'd never have to speak of it again.

As Laura and Alfred returned home from their separate Sunday-school classes, the three of them piled into his pickup and drove six hundred yards down the road. There he backed the truck up onto the brown earth at the

147

edge of the forest, and they started their short hike through the trees. Alfred carried the bow saw, the metal blade effulgent as silver though Terry had brought it home when the twins were mere toddlers.

Most years they'd taken a balsam from a cluster that grew perhaps a quarter of a mile in, but Laura had said she wanted a change of pace this Christmas, and so he had his eye out for a good cat spruce. Sunlight fell like flashlight beams along part of the path, and they clomped carefully through the wet leaves, because underneath were ones that were iced.

When Alfred started walking further ahead of them, he took Laura's hand in his. She was wearing mittens, and the wool felt soft against his palm.

How was Sunday school? he asked her.

A little wild. The kids are pretty wired with Christmas coming.

I'll bet, he said, and he thought about the things Alfred wanted for Christmas. He had been surprised by how short the list was. The girls had always had lists that seemed endless, whether there was a list for Santa or, by their last Christmas, separate lists for their parents and the guy in the heavy red suit. Their last Christmas, when they were eight, neither he nor Laura had been able to tell whether the girls truly believed in Santa Claus or were simply pretending to because it was hard to give up such a fundamental cornerstone of their childhood.

Laura had said that she found the boy's few wants a bit disconcerting. It wasn't the brevity of the list—the only items that Terry could recall were a backpack, a handheld computer game, and some CDs by groups whose music made them both deeply uncomfortable—it was her sense that everything they'd picked out for the boy when he first arrived had been wrong. They were toys for a boy who was younger. Less mature. Terry had noticed this, too, but he reminded her that, in all fairness, they'd never shopped for a boy before Alfred or thought about what a ten-year-old boy might want to play with these days.

He wondered if maybe the child would like something to do with horses. They'd bought him a helmet by that point so Paul could teach him how to ride, but little else. They hadn't been sure how long his interest would last.

I found one, Alfred called back, and he pointed at a thick and nicely shaped balsam that stood about nine feet.

That's a balsam, he half-said and half-yelled. Laura was thinking she wanted something—

It's perfect, Laura shouted, and he felt her squeezing his fingers in her hand.

The boy looked back at them, and Terry could tell he was trying to read from their faces whether this was indeed a fine tree or whether he'd made a mistake of some kind.

That's the one, all right, he tried to reassure Alfred, that's definitely the one. He jogged up to the boy to show him how to use the bow saw, and perhaps make the first cut in the tree so that it would be easier for the kid to keep the blade in the groove. He realized he was smiling: He never expected he'd have the privilege of showing a boy how to use a bow saw in the woods, and he was surprised by how lavish the small moment was with its pleasure.

THAT NIGHT HE and Laura made love, and it was like the years before the girls had died. There was no desperation to the act, as if they were depending upon sex to compensate for a loss too big to be counterbalanced, and it was clear that neither of them were merely going through the motions. It didn't even seem to him as if they were afflicted anymore by what had become their monumental "what if": What if Laura hadn't had her tubes tied? What might sperm and egg be doing now?

Instead there had just been the two of them, their togetherness and their orgasms, and it all felt the way it once had.

At least, he thought, it had been that way for him.

He recalled Phoebe, but not as a fantasy or because he wanted someone other than Laura. A vision of their one night together crept into his head simply because he had been with this other person only a month before, and it was inevitable that for a time an intimacy so pronounced would come back to him.

No, he reassured himself, Phoebe was an aberration. He had a wife. He had a boy. He had a life with some promise.

THE NEXT DAY, Monday, his stomach jumped when he stopped by the barracks to eat his lunch and Melissa, their dispatcher, told him that some woman was trying to reach him. He'd spent a good part of the morning with an elderly couple in Orwell whose carriage barn had been burglarized in the night. Their grandchildren's bicycles, two camping tents, and a chest of antique toy soldiers from the First World War had been stolen. The sense of violation coupled with the loss of their grandchildren's bicycles had left the pair nearly hysterical. Then, on his first attempt to return to the barracks mid-morning, some idiot had tried passing one of the town's sand trucks out in Shoreham, only to discover another car heading straight at him in the oncoming lane. He was actually pretty lucky. He'd wound up wrapping his uninspected Ford Escort around a tree, but the rescue squad figured he was going to get off with a couple of broken ribs and a concussion, and neither of the other two drivers had been hurt. Terry had expected a lot more gore when the radio call first came in and he'd spun his cruiser around, flipped on his strobes, and hightailed it southeast along the winding road that passed for a major artery in this corner of the county.

She in my voice mail? he asked Melissa, referring to the woman who'd phoned.

Nope. Didn't want to leave a message. She said she'd call back.

And she called twice?

Yup. Nine forty-five and eleven-twelve.

And she didn't leave a name.

Right.

That's odd.

Maybe.

Was she in trouble?

No, this wasn't an emergency call. I asked her. And she called on the regular line.

He tried to look perplexed. She say why she was calling?

Nope.

She say who she was?

A friend of yours.

A friend of mine?

Well, you know, a friend of yours and Laura's.

He nodded. Had he told Phoebe Laura's name? Probably.

Melissa put a manila folder into a tray behind her, and the diamond in her engagement ring flashed briefly when it was caught by the overhead light. She was twenty-two, and she was going to be married in May. I mean, she went on without looking at him, I assume she was Laura's friend, too. She sounded like a friend of the family to me.

He realized they were the only two people in the barracks at that moment, and he was glad. He wouldn't have wanted anyone to overhear this conversation.

Sounds like a stalker to me, he said offhandedly, trying to make a joke of the fact that a woman had called him at work—called him twice—and not left her name.

That's right, Terry, it was a stalker. There's a woman out there who has a creepy thing for state troopers. She smiled at him to let him know she was teasing, and the woman who'd called hadn't struck her as someone he should worry about.

Well, I'll be here for another half-hour if she should call again.

Good enough.

He went to the large office he shared with the two other shift supervisors, reached for a small sheaf of open case files and complaints, and sat down at his desk with the coffee and sandwich he'd brought back from the diner in Middlebury. When he was settled in his chair, it became plain to him just how badly his heart was racing.

———

"My children were two and three years old, they were almost babies. How could we run? And I was only sixteen. At first the soldiers thought I was my babies' big sister."

———

VERONICA ROWE (FORMERLY POPPING TREES),
WPA INTERVIEW,
MARCH 1938

———

Phoebe

It seemed to Phoebe as if the whole world was pregnant. At the store that Monday that was all anyone wanted to talk about. Holly Sheahan had just found out that she was going to have a baby, and, of course, Eliza Gailmor was due any day now—certainly she wouldn't last until Christmas. She was huge, and the due date was the eighteenth. Even the cover of the *People* magazines the store had received that morning featured four actresses who were pregnant.

She had opened the small market that day, and so she was able to go home by three in the afternoon. But she decided to drive south to Saint Johnsbury to do some Christmas shopping instead and see what she could find for her father and her niece and nephew—Wallace and Veronica's two kids. She didn't want to feel rushed, and so she told her father that she wouldn't be back for dinner.

There were even fewer cars than usual on the interstate this time of the day, and she was able to drive for as long as half a minute without seeing another vehicle. There was still over an hour of daylight left when she started off, but already the sky was growing dark over the White Mountains to the east.

One time she pulled into a rest area to pee, and—given the kind of day that she'd had—she was only mildly surprised when she found even here evidence that the world was a very fertile place: Badly buried at the top of the trash can by the sink in the ladies' room was an empty box from a home pregnancy test kit—though, clearly, this one hadn't been used at home.

Instantly she envisioned some poor high-school girl driving here alone, or perhaps with her best girlfriend, to confirm her worst fears. Maybe the

153

kid had sat in the very same stall she had, and then waited there, staring at the damp little stick in her hands.

Imagine, she thought, being so frightened that you wouldn't do the test in your own home because you feared you couldn't hide the garbage well enough, and so you went and tested yourself in the highway rest stop after school.

She looked at herself in the mirror by the sink, shaking the water off her hands, and allowed herself a small smile: She'd actually taken the box and the instructions from her kit and tossed them into her dad's woodstove. She'd then stood beside it for a good twenty seconds and watched the reinvigorated fire through the glass window, as if she needed reassurance that the evidence had disappeared completely into atmosphere and ash.

When she got to Saint Johnsbury, she considered trying Terry once again from the pay phone in the Chinese restaurant. It was the most private place she could think of in the town, and there wouldn't be a soul in the dining room at four-fifteen in the afternoon. It probably wouldn't even be open for dinner yet, but the pay phone was in an anteroom that was accessible from the street.

But then she wondered, as she had off and on that whole day, why she was even planning to tell Terry she was pregnant. Twice she'd failed to reach him that morning, and each time she hung up the phone, a part of her had been glad that he hadn't been there. After all, what good could possibly come from his knowing? What did she really expect would happen? She didn't want him to leave his wife for her, at least in part because she honestly didn't want this other woman's life to be any worse than it already was. She didn't want to inflict any more pain on her—Was the woman's name Laura? She believed that it was—than she must already be having to endure. Moreover, as much fun as it might be to fantasize about a very different life from the one she was living, the reality was that she and the trooper had spent about five hours together. She certainly wasn't prepared to break up a marriage because one night in November she'd allowed her better judgment to go south and she'd wound up in bed with a stranger—a nice enough guy, yes, but still a virtual stranger.

Nevertheless she did dial Terry's number once more, deciding in the end that even if they never saw each other again, he had a right to know. He was, after all, the father.

She leaned against the dark paneling on the wall by the pay phone and looked down at her black-and-white cowboy boots. She wondered if her feet would get too big for them soon. The toes were pointy and they'd always been a tight fit, and she recalled hearing somewhere that the feet of pregnant women often swelled. Or was it the ankles?

Either way, she might soon have to give up the boots.

At least she would if she decided to keep the baby.

State police.

The sound of the dispatcher's voice instantly pulled her away from her boots.

Hi. Is Sergeant Sheldon in, please?

I'm sorry, he's not. Would you like to speak with another trooper?

No, that's okay. This isn't an emergency.

May I take a message? Or would you like his voice mail?

No, thank you, she said, and quickly hung up. She considered whether her call had been traced—automatically, perhaps—as she had worried both times she phoned earlier, but she didn't think she'd ever been on the line long enough. And when she thought about it, she decided that the worst that would happen is that they would trace one or both of those first two calls to the general store where she worked, tell Terry, and he'd know that she was trying to reach him.

Hell, he probably knew now! What other woman was calling him and not leaving her name?

A thought crossed her mind and she wished that it hadn't. Maybe Laura wanted out of the marriage. It was possible. If Terry was so unhappy that he'd come on to some woman in the general store near the family deer camp, maybe Laura was miserable, too. Terry certainly hadn't made his wife out to be a real joy to be around. Not a bad person. Probably a very good one, in fact. Just not a particularly happy one. Maybe, Phoebe thought, she'd be doing everyone a colossal favor if she broke up that marriage.

She didn't seriously believe that for a second, and she scolded herself for even allowing such a notion to enter her head. It was one thing to make a mistake one night; it was quite another to allow that mistake to become life-changing.

But hadn't it become life-changing already? She was pregnant, for God's sake, she was—and the words hit her with scatological clarity—knocked up!

Back outside in the crisp air, she decided to head up the street to the sporting goods store. Her brother was giving his kids snowmobiles for Christmas, a pair of small Z-120s. They didn't go very fast and they didn't make much noise—they were designed for children—but they still looked like crafts from a George Lucas movie: sharp and sleek and low to the ground. They were both green, and her sister-in-law had christened them "the twin iguanas." Phoebe was hoping to find some snowmobile accessories for the children at the store. A Tek vest, maybe. Perhaps some special gloves.

A part of her couldn't believe that she was tacitly condoning the notion that her eight-year-old niece and her six-year-old nephew were about to start riding snowmobiles. Lord knew she would never allow this child of hers to climb onto a snowmobile in elementary school—at least not when the child was in the first or third grade. Sixth grade, maybe. But not until then.

What in the name of heaven was Wallace thinking?

She tried to remember how old her brothers were when they first started riding, and she guessed they'd been in junior high school.

The salesperson at the store was another woman her age, and she held up the orange safety vests against her own chest so Phoebe could see how small and cute they were—as if she were showing her customer a knit sweater for a toddler. Phoebe was surprised by how little each vest was: The protective shoulder pads looked tiny.

She could see clearly now that everything was going to remind her of the fact that she was pregnant and there was something inside her that was alive. She wondered if there was a purpose here—whether it was all just a series of flukes, or whether it was a signal of some consequence that she was meant now to become a mother.

THE BAKERY IN Montpelier was busy even though the real lunch rush was still an hour away. It was popular because it was known for offering its sandwiches on homemade flatbread, and it took Phoebe a moment to find Terry in the maze of crowded tables and the small crush at the counter. When she saw him he smiled, but he didn't stand. She figured he didn't want to draw any more attention to himself than was necessary. He'd taken a table in the rear of the restaurant, by the doorway that led to a corridor with a bathroom at the far end.

Oh, good, she said, you got us a table near the bathroom. Pregnant women like that.

She'd meant the remark to be funny, but instantly his face grew stern and she saw how tired he was. She'd given him the news that she was pregnant over the telephone the day before, and she found herself wondering just how much sleep he had gotten last night.

A joke, she said quickly, draping her parka over the chair as she sat down.

Ah.

You have bags under your eyes. How are you?

I should be asking you that, he said. He was wearing his uniform, and it was perfectly pressed: Even the green pants had a precise, daggerlike crease.

Oh, I'm fine. It's still so early, I haven't even had morning sickness yet.

There was a porcelain mug on the table with a dark brown ring at the bottom.

You've been here awhile, haven't you? she said.

Not too long. What would you like?

Maybe some tea, she said.

You should eat something, too.

Surprise me.

She watched him stand to go to the counter, his eyes scanning the room as if he wanted to make sure there wasn't a soul in the place who he knew, and then she noticed something she found interesting: When he got to the glass counter, everyone around him gave him a little extra space, as if his body exuded a bubble. She wondered if it was because of his gun or his uniform or both. This was a pretty crunchy crowd in here—a lot of women in sandals and thick socks, a good number of the men sporting small earrings—and so it may just have been a general distaste for authority.

She decided he looked cute in his uniform, a bit like a little boy playing dress-up. She understood the handgun was real, but his badge and his boots and those pants—spinach green with yellow piping up the side—struck her as the sort of thing a toy store might sell to a ten-year-old who wanted to masquerade as a soldier. Even his necktie was green, and she wondered if there was any other organization or business on the planet that would make a green necktie a mandatory part of a uniform. Maybe the Royal Order of Leprechauns, if there was such a thing, and she found herself smiling at the idea.

When he returned to the table, he brought with him a couple of warm scones on glass plates, and a handful of single-serve packs of butter and jelly. Then he went back for her tea.

This should work for eleven A.M., he said when he finally sat down.

When she smelled the food, she realized how hungry she was and eagerly began to butter the scone.

So, he said, doing the same. A baby.

She nodded. I almost didn't call you, you know.

Uh-huh, he said, and he rolled his eyes in a way that she thought was meant to be good-natured. But then you got past it, and tried me at least four times—at least four times that I know of.

One time I hung up before anyone answered, she admitted. So I guess the grand total was five. But I really did give serious thought to never telling you. Even now I'm not completely sure why I did and we're talking right now.

Well, maybe because you figure I'm the father. Isn't that reason enough?

I don't *figure* you're the father. I *know* you're the father. I told you that on the phone.

I understand that.

But you doubt me?

Matter of fact, I don't. I believe you.

God. What kind of a person must you think I am? she said, her voice little more than a mumble. Why would I—

Phoebe, I just said I believe you. Okay?

Okay. Thank you. The thing is, I almost wish I hadn't called you. Your knowing would make some sense if we were . . . involved. But we're not. The reality is that we had a night together in a trailer. And while it was very pleasant, it's not exactly a solid foundation for a . . . a long-term relationship. We barely know each other, right? I mean, I don't even know if I'm going to keep this child. I still haven't decided if that's a real option.

He reached for his mug, forgetting for a moment that it was empty. I am sick about this, you know, he said. You understand that, don't you?

I do.

Aren't you? His eyes looked almost pleading. Suddenly she wanted to reach across the table and take one of his hands in hers, but she didn't dare.

I was. When I first realized I might be pregnant, I assumed I'd get an abortion and no one would ever be the wiser. I'd even made up my mind to use the Planned Parenthood down in Hanover, where there wasn't a prayer in hell I'd be recognized.

And then?

Well, to be honest, I started to think I might make a good mom and I could afford to raise this little person inside me. At least I think I can.

You sound like you've already made up your mind.

Not completely. All I meant is that I went from thinking I'd get an abortion, to not getting an abortion because I realized I might actually want this baby.

Imagine that—wanting a baby.

You know what I mean.

Certainly I do.

But if I do decide to become a mom—and it's true that I am leaning that way right this second—I want you to understand that you don't ever have to be involved in any way, shape, or form. I don't ever have to see you again, no one would ever have to know who the father was. You didn't ask for this—

Neither did you.

No, of course not. But it just might be something I want.

And if I wanted to be involved? What then? This is, after all, my son or daughter, too.

She washed down a bite of her scone with a long sip of her tea. Maybe that's why I phoned, she said. I don't know. But I do think it's the same part of me that might want this baby that led me to call you.

He nodded, and then said in a tone that was so controlled it was almost hurtful, Understand that involvement would never mean leaving my wife. Is that clear?

I don't expect you to leave her, she said, and she hoped she didn't sound defensive. She was surprised by how much his two short sentences had wounded her. I thought I'd made that clear.

She's fragile, he went on, his voice softening. This is a woman who lost both her children. You simply cannot know how awful something like that is until you've lived through it. That's a fact. It's been two years, and it's only now that she's beginning to come out of it.

I appreciate that, she said. And I know it hasn't been easy for you, either.

He took a deep breath that seemed to signal his agreement, but he didn't say a word.

So, my sense is, I should finish my scone and move on, she said. And I'm okay with that, Terry. Honest. I'm okay.

I didn't say I didn't want to see you again, he said, and he sounded slightly exasperated. I didn't say I wanted you and this baby out of my life. I simply said I'm not going to leave Laura, and I need for you to understand that.

Another one of those unattractive thoughts crossed her mind: In truth I am here because some maternal instinct inside me wants to do whatever I can to ensure that this baby has a father. I'm here because I want to make this man leave this bakery with me. Isn't that why I was so careful with my lipstick this morning, and why I spent so much time brushing my hair? Isn't that why I wore a skirt and a tight denim blouse with a few buttons I could leave undone?

Her tummy was still flat, and she knew it would remain so for at least another month or two.

I don't want you to do anything you don't want to do, she said. I want you to be happy. I want your wife to be happy. I want your foster kid to be happy.

Alfred. The boy's name is Alfred.

I'm sorry. Alfred. I want you all to be happy, that's all I meant.

Thank you.

And that's all I would want for this baby, too. I simply want it to be happy. To make other people happy, to have a good life. A joyful life. That's all. I don't know about the rest, I don't have any specifics.

He stretched his legs straight out to the side of the table and folded his arms across his chest, the bottom of his badge disappearing behind his balled fist. When do you think you'll know?

About what, the baby?

About whether you're going to keep it.

Well, you tell me, Terry: What do you want me to do? What would you prefer happened?

I'm going to give you an unfair answer—and understand that I know it's unfair. Okay?

She shrugged. She knew she'd asked her question more out of curiosity than anything else. She wanted to see how he'd respond.

I think you should keep it, he said. Sometimes . . . sometimes you don't know how precious something is to you until it's disappeared and you can't get it back.

She was surprised and moved by his answer. In some ways her life would have been easier if he'd said she should get an abortion. Then she could have told him, yes, she probably would, leave him at the bakery, and do whatever she liked.

Do you believe that even if it means I have to raise this child completely on my own? she asked.

Even then. But it won't come to that.

An absurd thought crossed her mind, and she started to giggle. Well, if you're not going to leave your wife, she said, then I just guess that means you're about to go Mormon on me!

He looked at her, momentarily perplexed, but then he understood the reference. I don't believe polygamy is legal even in Utah, he said. And it sure as hell isn't legal in Vermont.

A little commune action, then, she said, and she could tell that her giggles were going to grow. She tried to rein them in, but it was clear her emotions were beyond her control. We'll churn a little butter, we'll drink a little Chianti. Spend all kinds of time naked. There used to be hippie communes all over my corner of the Northeast Kingdom, you know—before I was born, of course, she added, but he couldn't possibly have understood the last part of her sentence because of the way her great gulps of laughter were swallowing her words. She was laughing loudly, embarrassingly loud, but she couldn't stop herself. People at the tables around them were starting to turn toward her, their faces transforming quickly from benign curiosity to concern when they saw the wrought-up, vaguely insane cast to her face. She felt her eyes starting to water and she wiped the sleeve of her shirt across her cheeks, shaking her head all the while. When she opened her eyes, she could see that Terry was red, and staring down into his empty glass plate. He'd brought his legs back in under the table.

I've never even met your wife, she said, and her voice, muddled by laughter and tears, sounded to her like a toddler's in the midst of a tantrum. What do you think, Terry, would we get along?

He looked up at her. Phoebe, come on.

Seriously, me and Laura? How would we do?

Phoebe . . .

She sniffed deeply, and a tiny squeal of a hiccup was the last sound that she made. Suddenly the place seemed eerily silent to her.

Let's get out of here, he said, his voice barely above a whisper.

Yup, let's, she agreed, and they stood up together, put on their coats, and started toward the bakery's front door. As they were walking through the small restaurant, she wondered where they would go once they were outside in the crisp December air, and she realized that she hadn't a clue.

"In addition, the detachment returned with three Indian children. Apparently, their father was among the marauders."

————

CAPTAIN ANDREW HITCHENS,
TENTH REGIMENT, UNITED STATES CAVALRY,
REPORT TO THE POST ADJUTANT,
MAY 11, 1876

————

Alfred

He awoke and tried hard to resist the urge to climb out from under the heavy quilt Terry's mother had made and switch on either the lamp by the window or the one by the door. It was quarter to twelve, and for a brief moment he thought that Terry or Laura might still be awake. The idea offered him comfort: He wasn't afraid in the dark when those two were reading or watching TV. But as he listened carefully, he decided the house was completely still and the grown-ups were sound asleep. He was alone.

No, he wasn't alone—and that was the problem. At least he didn't believe that he was. He opened his eyes, his body otherwise still, and scanned the bedroom. He was on his side, his back to the window, his vision the door and the closet and the desk. He half-expected to see there one—or both—of the girls. He half-expected one of the girls to ask him what he was doing in her bed.

But he saw no one there in the dark, and once again he shut his eyes. For a brief moment he imagined he was buffalo soldier George Rowe, half-asleep somewhere in West Texas, confident even though it was night and his detachment was far from its fort. Rowe was disciplined and sharp; he didn't care that he was an outsider. He'd won a medal. He was Alfred's favorite of the black men he'd met in the book.

In his mind, he traced the outlines of the boulders and scrub pine that might have surrounded Rowe's camp, and then slowly watched as those shapes were transformed into the more familiar contours of the furniture in his room and the objects that sat upon them. He burrowed into the closet, envisioning exactly what was there on the floor. His backpack. The photo album. Food.

He wondered if the girls were mad at him for stealing their picture, or whether they cared. Whether they knew.

When he opened his eyes again, he saw the half-circle silhouette made by his riding helmet, and for a split second he thought it was the head of a person crouching by the desk. It wasn't and he knew that, but the notion alone was so frightening that he pushed off the covers and lunged for the bureau with the light. For a long moment he stood there in the bright room, his fingers still within inches of the lamp shade. He was surprised that he hadn't bounded back into bed yet. Normally he would have by now.

Then he knew why. He was uneasy, still not completely convinced he was alone, and he needed to open the closet door and make absolutely sure that no one—no thing—was in there. And so he moved slowly across the wide wooden floorboards, a gunmetal gray, and then over the thick throw rug. He opened the door, pausing for just the barest second with his fingers on the knob, and sighed—he hadn't even realized until that moment that he'd been holding his breath—when he saw there was nothing to fear in the closet, either. Nothing. He reached in for his album, brought it back with him to bed, and flipped the pages until he reached the one with the photograph of the twin girls.

Without thinking about what he was doing, he ran his fingers over the plastic that protected their image from thumbprints and smears. What was it about them, he wondered, that once had made Terry and Laura so happy? They were pretty girls, but was that alone enough to make grown-ups smile? Maybe strangers. He'd seen the way rich strangers would smile at pretty kids all the time as they walked briskly in the mall or down Church Street in Burlington. He knew the way his teacher treated some kids in the class better than others. The handsome boys, the pretty girls. But parents probably weren't like that. Not real parents, anyway. Real parents probably wanted their kids to look good, but loved them regardless.

Of course, his mom had been a real parent, and she'd clearly been capable of not loving him—or, at least, of not loving him enough.

Adults, especially parents, were a code that he couldn't begin to decipher. And though Terry and Laura had indeed seemed happier lately, he realized he didn't understand why. He didn't think it had anything to do with him, mainly because he was spending so much time these days with Mesa and Paul—unless that was in fact the reason for their contentment: The foster kid was no longer underfoot, and was now less demanding. Less time-consuming. And so life had improved.

He didn't really believe that either, he decided. His first instinct had been the correct one. If the pair was more content these days, it had nothing to do with him.

Through the window on the east side of his room he could see the Heberts' house and he could see the barn where Mesa lived. He had never told Paul this, but he believed on some level that the horse liked him so much—and he liked the horse—because they were the same. They'd both been shuffled around, they'd both lived in a lot of places. When Ruth had decided to unburden herself of a horse, wasn't it Mesa she chose to unload? Yes, indeed. The truth was, Mesa had had a home before living with Ruth, and she'd have a home after Paul Hebert got too old to handle her. That's just how it was. She'd be sent somewhere else.

Outside he heard the wind press the storm window against its metal guides, a heavy click, and then the glass shuddered for a long second.

He wondered how well Paul had known the two girls, and whether there was anything he could share. Maybe he knew what made them so special. It would be a heck of a lot easier to ask him about them than either Terry or Laura, that was for sure.

He rolled onto his side—once more unwilling to leave his back to the door—and fell asleep with the light on and the album open to his picture of Hillary and Megan Sheldon.

A CANADIAN WIND had blown in overnight and it was freezing that afternoon, but there still wasn't much snow on the ground. You could see it in the far distance on the top of the mountain, and that snow glowed white against a cerulean blue sky. But not here. Here there was largely hoarfrost and ice, despite the fact that Christmas was only eight days away.

Alfred was careful to keep Mesa on the pavement or, once they left the road, on the long stretches of brown earth. Paul insisted on this. He told Alfred that he didn't want him to tumble off the horse if the animal momentarily lost her footing on one of the nearly invisible patches of black ice that veined the sides of the street—runoff a few days before, now slippery as slate and solid as stone—or that dotted the fields on both sides like miniature frozen ponds.

Heels down, the man was saying to him now as he walked briskly beside him and the horse. Ride on the balls of your feet. And relax a bit—let her bounce you up. If you're too tense, the animal will feel it and get spooked—or, worse, your back will hurt like hell in the morning.

He tugged at his ear where the chin strap for his helmet dug into the scar from the infection he'd had there that summer. Even wearing a glove, he could feel the shape of the skin, still slightly mottled both from the studs and the scarring, and he wished he'd remembered to bring along a piece of cotton as a cushion. He decided it was too bad he wasn't allowed to ride in his Tenth Cavalry cap. What better time was there to wear it than when he was atop this fine horse?

He bounced toward the wrought-iron entrance to the old portion of the cemetery, the sensation of riding always reminding him of the afternoon he'd gone swimming at North Beach in Burlington, and a rainstorm had rolled in and built whitecaps along the surface of the lake. He'd swum in those waves, and they'd carried him. This horse was like that.

He watched Paul pull up the clasp that kept the heavy gates closed, and then push one of the waist-high doors forward. He was surprised by how much it squeaked in the cold, and so was the horse. She froze for a moment at the new sound, her ears pointing like arrowheads at the noise.

Come on ahead, the man said to him.

He drew back on the leather reins with his left hand, pushed his heels into Mesa's sides, and then watched in astonishment as the horse followed his lead. He'd been riding her daily for almost two weeks now, but he was still surprised that he could control an animal this big with such ease. Yet there as she turned were those great nostrils, the pewter-colored bit, and one of those massive, deep eyes. It was hard for Alfred to believe that anything could, as Paul put it, spook eyes such as those. It was difficult for him to imagine this big creature scared.

Once they were inside the graveyard, Alfred halted the animal, moved slightly in his saddle, and motioned toward the Granger family's memorial and the massive hydrangea beside it. He didn't tell Paul that earlier that autumn he used to go there all the time, but he made sure the older man was aware of the monument. It was beautiful to look at, and through the tapestry of clawlike twigs he could see the spot where he'd once gone for half an hour or an hour at a time.

Paul nodded at the sand-colored obelisk as big as a closet, and then said, The Sheldon plots are in the new section. Far side of the new section. Not a lot of landscaping yet, you'll see, but sunny. When there is sun. Guide her around the outer edge of the tombstones, okay? No sense in you two having to traverse an obstacle course.

From high up on the horse the graveyard appeared very different. The lines of the markers looked more definite, more pronounced, even while the headstones that were on the verge of collapse—blackened fungus on aged marble, a rusted metal rebar support exposed like old bone through dead skin—grew more apparent. The columns of antique markers stretched to the end of the hill, not a single one younger than a century. He counted seven G.A.R. stars and guessed there were more.

From atop Mesa, even a tremendous tombstone such as the Grangers' looked less like a marble skyscraper. In the distance he realized he could see the steeple for the church in the village, and the first cluster of houses on the far side of the Cousinos' dairy farm. The Sheldons' home remained invisible, however, because of the way it was nestled behind the near hill.

As they approached the new section, the headstones grew more diverse in color and shape—there was black marble dappled with white, clusters of ivory granite, and a few markers that had the blush of old bricks—and nearby there were more likely to be signs of visitation. Fresh flowers. Plastic flowers, sometimes in a plastic vase. A photograph housed inside a block of glass. The quiescent brown grass flattened by footsteps or, in a few cases, the tire tracks of a truck or a car.

Over there, Paul said, and he pointed to a section Alfred had never bothered to visit. Too new to be interesting. Not a single star or American flag in sight.

They descended down a path with no markers on either side, and the horse moved carefully, as if she knew how easy it would be to slip among the patches of snow, baseball-sized rocks, and hard ground. Then they wandered down the wide, unpaved road—a pair of tire ruts actually, that were cut by the repeated passage of vehicles through the grass—that sliced the new section in two. They passed a fresh grave, the dirt and the flowers still moist, probably one of the last to be dug in the earth without the help of a backhoe till spring.

Dorothy Cammin, Paul said. Nice woman. Had a nice service. Short.

Was there a service for those girls? Alfred asked.

The Sheldon girls? Of course.

Kids come?

Whole school, it seemed. The church was packed. They had to set up monitors in the basement and two of the Sunday-school classrooms so the overflow could watch it on TV. Can you imagine?

He nodded as he rode. He could imagine that many people gathered together in a single spot, but he couldn't envision that many caring enough to come to a funeral. He figured if he drowned, there'd be a handful of people at his service at best—and he couldn't say for sure who any of them would be.

Those arch shapes over there, Paul said. That's what you're looking for.

He stared at them for a moment, and thought back on how easy it had been for him to verbalize the question once he'd decided to ask it. Yesterday afternoon, the two of them together in the barn. Paul had been rinsing the bit in a bucket of water, while he was sitting on the stool with the heavy saddle in his lap. Rubbing it down with the soft, chamois leather rag. The sound of Mesa, nosing in the new hay in the trough just behind them. And the words had come out in a quick stream, more casual in tone than in intent, but it didn't matter because Paul always seemed to listen carefully to every word that he said. He'd asked, very simply, where Terry and Laura's children were buried. Drying the bit, not looking up, Paul said if he wanted he could show him tomorrow. That was it. No big deal. They probably would have gone that very day, but the sun had just about set.

He tapped his feet against Mesa's sides and turned the horse in toward the lengthy file with the graves, careful to keep her moving straight between the rows—rows that seemed, very suddenly, to be as thin as an escalator and every bit as difficult to traverse with a horse.

After the funeral, a lot of the church came here, too, Paul was saying as he walked on the grass on the other side of the markers, his arms folded against his down jacket and his gloved hands buried deep in his underarms. The horse breathed out another wispy column of steam, and Alfred reached forward and softly patted the wide plate of her cheek. He sat up straight and commanded the animal to halt—with his words and by pulling back on the reins—because Paul had stopped walking. Then, with his usual great effort, he swung his right leg over the massif-sized back of the Morgan and jumped to the ground, pausing when he realized there was no place where he could hitch the horse.

Here, Paul said, and he took the reins like a lead line and held them loosely. Almost immediately Mesa leaned over as if she thought she might start trying to pull clumps of frozen grass from the earth with her teeth, but Paul remembered the bit in her mouth and gently lifted up her head with his hands.

Alfred studied the two graves before approaching them. They were identical but for the names of the girls. White as brand-new piano keys, and just as slick to the eye. On each was what he had assumed at first was a carving of a fairy but then realized was an angel. Wings extended like capes. Faceless but haloed. Floating.

I know practically every person in this section, Paul said, and it sounded to Alfred as if this revelation disturbed him. Quickly Alfred glanced at the tombstones on either side of the Sheldon girls, checking the dates to see when these people were born and when they had died, and he saw they were old people who'd passed away within a few years of the twins.

Finally he walked up to the headstones and then took off his gloves before kneeling to touch one. Hillary's. It was slippery and solid. Thick. The rock-hard ice that coated Lake Champlain by the middle of January. He glanced to his right at Megan's tombstone, and then crabbed over there to touch that one, too.

I heard somewhere she was named after her grandmother.

She was.

Hillary, too?

Hillary, too, Paul said. You would have liked them, I think. Assuming you can abide girls. I presume you do. When I was ten, I didn't. But I understand that things are different now.

I liked Tien, he answered, unsure exactly what he meant when he used the word *like*. At the same time, he knew, he had enjoyed living in the same house with Isabel, but that had been very different from his affection for Tien. Isabel was older, and everything about her was sexual. Tien was just . . . Tien. A rail of a girl who would go where he went when they'd wander around Burlington, the two of them sometimes trailing Digger and sometimes not.

Yes, things are different, Paul murmured. Childhood lasts about a month these days. My granddaughters outgrew their Barbies before second grade.

When he looked at their monuments, he wished the months had been carved there as well as the years. He wanted to know exactly how old the twins were when they died, because months mattered greatly when you were nine—their age when they'd drowned.

Their toys are all gone, Alfred told Paul. Barbies, whatever. I haven't seen a girls' toy in the whole house.

I'm not surprised, Paul said.

They act like twins?

What do you mean? Did they act the same?

I guess. I've never met any twins.

The horse craned her long neck and stared for a moment up the hill at the trees, at a sound she must have heard there. A gust of wind rattling the leafless branches, maybe. Perhaps only the wind itself. The man thought about his response and then said, First of all, they weren't identical twins. You know that, right?

Uh-huh.

Not that identical twins act identically. Because of course they don't. And those two acted liked sisters. Not friends, sisters.

Because they loved each other so much?

Paul laughed briefly, but it was loud and enthusiastic. A human horse snort. Because they were happy to fight like hell with each other, he said, and because they knew exactly how to get under each other's skin. They were sisters, first, Alfred, twins, second. I don't know what Laura or Terry has told you, but trust me—

They haven't told me a thing, Alfred said.

No, I guess they wouldn't, Paul agreed, nodding, not those two. Then, as if he had never been interrupted, he continued, They were little girls, that's what they were, they were younger than you when they died. They did little-girl things. For reasons I'll never completely know, I always associated Hillary with her dad and Megan with her mom. I have this picture in my head of Hillary being carted everywhere on Terry's shoulders until she must have been in the second grade. But I'm sure he carried Megan that way, too.

Maybe it's just the sports. Hillary loved baseball—even T-ball—and soccer, and Megan didn't. And Terry would help out with the coaching.

I saw a photo, Alfred said.

Sometimes they'd come over to our yard to go exploring. Especially in the barn. Terry and Laura have that little carriage barn, of course, but the girls seemed to like the size of our hay barn more. It's bigger, more to it. The loft alone made it more interesting to them.

Alfred wandered behind the headstones and looked out at the hills that rolled up into the forest. This was the vista that would spread out before the girls if they could sit up and see the view. What were they looking for? he asked.

Oh, lots of things. It would change. Leprechauns. Tomtens. Elves. Who knows? Some days they'd just play hide-and-seek in there. Once they brought over their stuffed animals and set up all these teddy bears and such in the hay from the Eisenhower administration.

Eisenhower . . .

A President from a long time ago. I just meant that the hay was very old. Not like the new stuff we're feeding Mesa.

In the woods in the distance a group of blackbirds was lifting. Six, ten. A couple dozen. The geese were long south now, Alfred knew, even the ones that had to come down from Canada. He looked at the grass before him, intensely aware that he was within feet of the girls—or, at least, of their bodies. Beneath him was lawn, dirt, then the shiny wood and brass of their coffins. Their remains. Here they were. He was sleeping in the room that had once belonged to one of them, probably in that little girl's very bed.

Suddenly he thought he might cry, a sensation he hadn't had in years, and only before, he believed, when he had hurt himself badly—or been badly hurt. But it took a lot of pain for him to cry, that he knew well: He'd barely flinched when Digger did his ears, or when he'd fallen off those rocks at the lake in Burlington, or when Mr. Patterson had whaled on him for taking cigarettes off his wife's nightstand. He watched the horse to take his mind off his proximity to the bodies, and allowed the moment to pass over him. In a minute he was fine. He was a buffalo soldier. He wasn't going to cry.

He took the reins from Paul, inhaled, and climbed atop Mesa's back. He considered himself bigger and stronger when he was in the saddle, more in command. It wasn't simply the height the horse offered him, or the power of the animal beneath him. It wasn't even the pictures he had in his head of the proud cavalry troopers. It was the simple reality that he felt—and it was a feeling he rarely had—as if there was something important in his life that he controlled.

Time to head home? Paul asked.

He nodded, and they started back through the columns of graves.

How did they die? he asked the man as they walked, his eyes focused before him on the hill they were approaching and soon would ascend.

They drowned, Paul answered.

I know that. I want to know how.

The details.

Uh-huh. I want to know everything you do, he said. He glanced to his side and saw that Paul hadn't been looking at him, either.

Okay, the man said, and he nodded. Then he put his hands into the wide pockets of his parka, and as they walked home through the graveyard, he told the boy all that he could.

"Rule number four: They are to obey orders, but they are to remember they belong to no one but themselves. There is a difference between a good soldier and a slave."

SERGEANT GEORGE ROWE,
TENTH REGIMENT, UNITED STATES CAVALRY,
LETTER TO HIS BROTHER IN PHILADELPHIA,
NOVEMBER 18, 1873

Laura

Some businesses closed on Christmas Eve, but Laura knew animal shelters could not be among them. There were still cages to clean, quarantined cats to observe, dogs to feed and walk, and—if, somehow, there was time—a variety of animals in need of any momentary act of kindness.

Consequently, Laura went to work on Christmas Eve, and got home a little later than usual because she'd had a small party for the employees and volunteers—dog walkers and fund-raisers mostly, but a pair of board members who had stopped by to help as well—who actually had to be at the shelter that day. It was close to four by the time she passed the Cousinos' silos, and the sun had almost set. She didn't expect Terry until somewhere between seven and seven-thirty. If everyone felt up to it, she was hoping they'd go to the midnight service at the church.

When she neared her house, she saw instantly that something wasn't right. She would have expected no lights on at all if Alfred were still across the street tending to Mesa, or a single light on in the living room if he had finished early and gone home to watch television. Maybe a light on upstairs if he had gone to his bedroom. Though it was a Thursday, the schools were closed because it was the day before Christmas, and Alfred was supposed to have spent the morning with Tim Acker, and then the afternoon—as if it were just another weekday—with Paul and the horse.

Instead, however, it looked like every single light on the first floor was on, including the outside porch light over the front doors. A part of her thought the house looked rather festive, as if she and Terry were having a holiday cocktail party or open house. Her parents were driving up from Boston tomorrow and spending the night, and she could only hope the house would look that nice to them. A gold ribbon was laced through the swag on the wreath on the front door, and it sparkled for a brief second when it was caught by her headlights as she turned into her driveway.

Then she noticed that the electric candles in the windows hadn't been plugged in, however, and instantly the illusion of a party vanished. Moreover, Terry's cruiser wasn't here, and so her husband hadn't come home early to surprise her.

She felt a pang of fear—any parent's natural instinct, but inflated beyond reason by the reality that she had lived through any parent's worst nightmare—and started fighting with her seat belt and her keys to escape the car. For a long second she forgot how to unbuckle the shoulder harness, and it felt to her like she was trapped. She heard herself swear once, just before the mechanism clicked and she was released.

When she reached the front door, she found it was unlocked, and the house was quiet.

Alfred, she called, Alfred?

In here, someone said, but it wasn't the boy and it wasn't her husband. It was Paul Hebert. Without putting her bag down or taking off her boots, she ran through the kitchen and down the hallway into the den, toward the source of the voice, and there on the couch she saw the professor and Alfred—the child with what looked like a wadded dish towel against the far side of his forehead—watching, of all things, the Christmas Eve service from Saint Peter's Basilica on a French-Canadian television station. The cantor was singing in Latin just outside the cathedral, and she could tell from the waves of umbrellas that it was raining in Rome.

Alfred? she said, and she half-sat and half-leaned on the arm of the couch beside him, and gently pulled away the towel. She realized the cloth was filled with ice cubes, and he offered her a small smile.

It really doesn't hurt anymore, he said.

Now watch this, Paul said, as if she hadn't just entered the room—or, perhaps, as if she'd been there all along. We're about to see the woman who's going to present the Mass in sign. See there, in that corner: That's her. Incredible, what this woman does. Incredible! Not only does this character speak Latin and French and Italian, but she's about to take all these different languages, translate them instantly in her head, and then present them in sign for the hearing impaired. Unbelievable!

What happened? she asked.

I fell off Mesa, Alfred said, a trace of an apology in his voice—as if he felt guilty, somehow, or feared he had done something wrong.

My God, she murmured, trying not to panic and frighten the boy. So brave, she added quickly. Her mind began conjuring the worst: spinal injuries that would cripple the child for life, a concussion or brain injury that would become manifest any moment. She tried to remember the signs of a concussion, and the ones that came back to her were dizziness and nausea. She had a vague sense that she should look at his pupils, but she figured they would have to be dilated to the size of dimes before she could be sure anything was wrong.

How do you feel? she asked simply.

Really, okay.

You don't feel a little woozy or queasy?

Nope. My hand and my wrist hurt a lot more than my head.

She noticed then the gauze that was held tight to the palm of his left hand by the white hospital tape they kept in a drawer in the bathroom on the first floor.

Okay, the Pope is about to switch from the zucchetto to the miter. I hope they show it. You watching? If we had pomp like that in this country—

Paul, how did this happen? she said, lifting Alfred's arm and trying to imagine the cuts on the inside of his hand. She realized his wrist was swollen and bruised.

The professor turned to her and shook his head. Well, as Alfred said, he fell off the horse.

I understand that! she snapped.

Forgive me. These are the salient details. We were near the Cousinos', in a meadow maybe fifty yards in from the road. We were just out hacking, really, giving Mesa some exercise, and—who knows exactly how these things happen—one minute the boy was in the saddle, and the next he was on the ground.

I thought you were just walking the horse, Laura said.

A little trotting, Paul admitted.

Since when?

Monday.

Go on, Laura said.

There's really nothing more to tell. Maybe Alfred encouraged Mesa at the exact moment she hit a patch of ice under the snow. Maybe the horse just slipped—it all took about a second, a second and a half—and your boy here went head over teacup. Or whatever that expression is.

You should see my glove. It looks like an animal ripped it apart.

The professor shook his head. It doesn't look that bad. But it is pretty useless now.

I think we should go to the doctor, she said.

If it would make you feel better, Paul agreed. But we did call and speak to the nurse, and she didn't see any cause for alarm. The boy doesn't need stitches, and his wrist isn't broken or sprained.

How do you know that?

Well, I don't. At least not for a certainty. But the swelling isn't huge and he can move it pretty well. Right?

Right.

And his head? Laura asked.

The nurse said to keep ice on it for a bit. So far he doesn't have any signs it's going to be more serious than a goose egg.

Was he wearing his helmet? She didn't like how angry she sounded, but she couldn't help herself.

I was, Alfred said, although the question had been directed at Paul.

And you still conked your head?

Might have been considerably more troublesome if he hadn't had the helmet on, Paul said.

When did this happen?

About an hour ago.

An hour! She thought to herself how an hour ago, the moment when Alfred had fallen from the horse, she was holding a plastic cup of punch in one hand, and a twelve-year-old terrier named Lucky in the other. Lucky had been brought in earlier that week after his elderly owner died and the woman's only son proved allergic to dogs. He came with a red dog sweater the woman had knit, and he was wearing it that afternoon to the party.

Laura, Paul said, and it was clear this word was going to be the first of a series of small, soothing waves, in the last hour we have walked the horse back up the hill and put her back in the paddock. We have spoken at length to the nurse at your doctor's office, and taken the appropriate medical action. And we have polished off easily a dozen of those chocolate-chip cookies we found in the tin by the toaster.

They're good, Alfred added.

On the television the announcer abruptly stopped speaking and the choir started to sing. Laura watched the boy and the man turn their attention from her to the screen, as if the spectacle before them were a football game.

I always wanted to do a course on cultural pomp, Paul said. I love it. Not simply religious pomp, since religious pomp is all cultural, in my opinion. But, rather, all kinds of pomp. Religious pomp. Movie pomp. Rodeo pomp.

Rodeo pomp? Alfred asked.

You just fell off a horse. Depending upon the event and the severity of your fall, all kinds of wonderful ritual might have surrounded the moment had it occurred in a rodeo. Ever heard of a rodeo clown?

No.

They distract the animal, so a cowboy in the dirt can get out of the ring— or, if he's out like a light, be extricated by somebody else from the ring.

She started to say something—a rebuke or a chastisement, perhaps, a plea to behave like a responsible grown-up and a responsible fifth-grader and to listen to her words—but she stopped herself. She was afraid she would sound hysterical. Then she wondered if she should prohibit the child from climbing on top of that horse ever again, or at least until he had had some lessons. Real lessons. Not the teaching and ministrations of an old man who hadn't ridden in eight or nine years himself.

Instead, however, she found herself gazing for a long moment at the pair and she knew she wouldn't do that. She couldn't do that.

When Paul saw her looking at him, he said, So, you plan on taking your coat off and staying through Christmas?

She felt the corners of her mouth quivering, and then forming into a small smile. I have to go put sheets on the bed in the guest room, she said, and she stood. My parents are coming tomorrow. She glanced down once more at Alfred's forehead and carefully pulled aside his hand with the towel full of ice. He was lucky, she decided when she looked at the small bump that had formed. It could have been worse, so very much worse.

I didn't know how you'd be feeling when you got home and saw the boy here had done a header off a horse, and so—if you want—you're welcome to come over to our house for dinner, Paul said. I spoke to Emily, and it's fine.

That sounds very nice, she said, but Terry won't be home until seven. She realized that she hadn't set foot in the Heberts' house since before the older couple had taken their Western road trip that autumn. She and Terry and Alfred had had ice cream there one night in early September, about a week and a half after the boy arrived in their lives. Likewise, as far as she could recall, Paul and Emily had only been here in her home one time since they'd returned, and that was when they dropped by unexpectedly with the gifts of what they called the bad-for-you food they'd bought on the road—St. Louis barbecue sauce, Santa Fe bean dip—and such odd trinkets as that cavalry cap Alfred seemed to like.

In a way, of course, Laura understood that this was exactly how her relationship with the Heberts had been for over two years. Since her daughters had died. In truth, Paul and Emily had been here any number of times in the last twenty-five months, but in each case it was on an errand of mercy. Bringing flowers and food in the days and weeks after the flood. Bringing more food during the holidays in the two years that followed, cookies and cakes and homemade breads. Bringing the family souvenirs from their trips—T-shirts, gaudy dish towels, and the magnets that clung to their refrigerator.

In that case, why don't you go do the bed and then come watch the Vatican Mass with us, Paul said. We can all go over and join Emily for supper when it's over.

She considered the idea. On the shelf above Alfred she saw the black, red, and green Kwanzaa mat she had started to make with the boy, using the pot holder loom they'd found at the craft store. It was one square—perhaps an hour's work—from completion. If she stayed with the two of them, she could probably finish the mat now.

What's with the hat? Alfred asked, referring to the Pope's miter. Why is it shaped like that?

A fine question. It goes back to pomp. Symbolism and pomp and the whole notion that in the ancient world heaven was a place in the sky, Paul began, clearly savoring the small classroom he had created for the boy. As he spoke, explaining to Alfred the meaning of the staff of Peter and the different liturgical vestments, that part of Laura that was a mother wanted nothing more than to stay and watch Alfred sitting so contentedly with this much older man.

But the pair seemed exactly that: A pair. A duo. A couple of mates. They were complete without her right now, and she didn't want to risk disturbing that chemistry—a sacrifice she was willing to make because she understood that this, too, was a part of being a mother. And so she lightly kissed the gauze in the palm of Alfred's hand, and interrupted Paul to tell him that she was going to go across the street to help Emily make their dinner.

WE WERE GOING to have a ham, Emily was saying, pausing briefly as she broke an egg into a bowl of creamed margarine. But I figured we'd have something more cheery after Alfred took that tumble.

What if we weren't coming? Laura asked. The two women were working side by side along the stretch of kitchen counter next to the sink. One by one Laura was dredging pork chops in a mixture of bread crumbs and shortening and milk, and then placing them on a cookie sheet. Eventually, when Terry returned home, the pork chops would be dropped in Emily's two massive cast-iron skillets and browned.

Cheery for Paul and me, in that case.

At first Laura hadn't understood why Emily deemed pork chops more cheerful than a ham, but then Emily had gotten down a blue denim looseleaf binder from a bookshelf full of cookbooks and removed the lined sheet of paper with the handwritten recipe. This was Peggy Noe's pork chop recipe, and Emily had gotten it from Peggy herself when she and her husband stopped for lunch that fall at Peggy's Joplin, Missouri, eatery, the Ozark Café. It was the best pork chop recipe Emily had ever tried. Likewise, this was Peggy's recipe for oatmeal and brown-sugar cake that Emily was preparing beside her.

There were windows over the sink, and outside them the women could see the horse in her stall in the light from the barn. The door was still open. In a few minutes Paul and Alfred would be over to feed and bed the animal down for the night. The horse looked monstrously big to Laura, especially when she envisioned Alfred tumbling from the creature's back to the ground.

I know lots about cats and dogs, Laura said, but next to nothing about horses. Is Mesa as big as she looks—for a horse, that is?

She's a Morgan, not a draft horse. A Percheron or a Belgian would be a lot bigger. Stronger, stockier. Still, people ride those horses, too. But I know what you mean. An hour hasn't gone by since Paul brought that animal home when I haven't wondered if a year from now he'll be flat on his back and out like a light, because he's just had both of his hips replaced.

I had a very grim thought walking over here: What if Alfred had broken his arm when he fell?

Emily was wearing a red apron with the words *Pop Hicks' Celebrity Diner* written in white cursive letters across the front—another memento, no doubt, from their road trip that fall. She turned to Laura and said, Grim? A broken arm can be an annoyance and it can hurt, my dear, but I wouldn't call such a thing grim. Not when you're ten, anyway. Don't think like that.

I can't help it. If he'd broken his arm, we would have taken him to the hospital right away, and SRS might have immediately assumed the worst. Child abuse. His evil foster parents had broken his arm.

If he'd broken his arm, it wouldn't have been you taking him to the emergency room. It would have been my vaguely capricious and mildly irresponsible husband.

I'm not sure that would have been a whole lot better. Then SRS would have discovered that I'm allowing a ten-year-old boy to go horseback riding without any training or lessons when he comes home from school—and, today, while I was away at work.

Paul is always with him.

Paul's a wonderful man. But he's not exactly an Olympic equestrian. And if I lost Alfred because I'd allowed him to ride a horse . . . She allowed her sentence to trail off, because she wasn't exactly sure how she wanted to finish it. She honestly didn't know what she would do if Alfred was taken away from her.

Do you want us to keep him off the horse, Laura? He could still work with the animal. Feed her, groom her. You know, take care of her.

I'm not sure I could do that to Alfred. He loves riding her, that's so clear.

She had finished breading the pork chops, and so she rinsed what felt like plaster of Paris off her fingers. Maybe there's a stable nearby where he could get some basic lessons, Laura continued. Do you think Paul's feelings would be hurt?

Paul? Lord, no. I'd encourage him to take them as well.

Because I can't lose Alfred, she said again. Really, I can't.

Of course you can't. And you won't. Why would you?

She shook her head. Outside in the barn the horse stood contentedly inside her stall, only occasionally bothering to nuzzle the empty manger for the remaining oats or soaked sugar beets she might have missed earlier that day.

LATER THAT NIGHT, she knew, she would open the door to his bedroom and she would watch him sleep in the bed that had once belonged to Megan. She would stand in the frame first for a long moment to make sure that he was indeed asleep, and then she would walk softly to the side of the bed and she would gaze for whole minutes at the gentle roundness of his cheek as he lay on his side, and the way he seemed to sleep with a half-smile on his face. His breathing would be even and slow and serene. He might wake at three or four in the morning—periodically she had heard him stirring in the middle of the night, sometimes turning on the lamp on the bureau before climbing back into bed—but he seemed to sleep deeply until then.

She had watched both her girls this way. Sometimes she would begin in Hillary's room, and sometimes in Megan's. Sometimes Terry had been with her, but even then this had usually been a ritual that belonged only to her. She alone would tuck in the girls' sheets and pull their quilts up to their chins. She alone would move out of the way the stuffed animals that were hogging the pillows and might interfere with her children's sleep at some point in the night. She alone would close the book that might still be open atop Megan's bed.

In Alfred's room there would be no stuffed animals to move, but there would still be blankets to pull tight and a second pillow to fluff. There would still be a shade to draw closed. There would always be something to do that would give her an extra moment to stand by his bed and simply smell the soap on his skin from his bath or watch the quilt rise an incremental quarter-inch with each silent inhalation.

"Apparently, we were very close to the village. If the marauders had been even three-quarters of a mile upriver they would have crossed and we would have followed, and I hate to think of the surprise that would have greeted us in another few minutes of riding. Incidentally, we learned today that the older girl is actually the mother of the two young ones, and not their sister."

SERGEANT GEORGE ROWE,
TENTH REGIMENT, UNITED STATES CAVALRY,
LETTER TO HIS BROTHER IN PHILADELPHIA,
MAY 17, 1876

Terry

He told her about the cans of Ensure, not surprised that this was the first memory he recalled when Phoebe asked him about his father's death, but the first he was willing to offer in return for what she had shared about her own mother's passing that summer.

I used to play golf, he began, and Russell used to play softball. Still does, really. He's good. But I haven't picked up a golf club in over two years. The bag just sits in the far corner of the laundry room. Anyway, the night after the funeral, once Mom had gone up to bed, Russell and I were standing in her kitchen. We each had a beer, and we both saw the Ensure at the same time. Two cases on the floor beside the old refrigerator, and at least another ten or twelve cans on the counter. Leah—

Your sister?

My sister. She wasn't married yet, and I don't believe she had even met Rick back then. She was upstairs in bed, too.

Where was Laura? And your girls? They must have been in, what, first grade?

They'd just finished kindergarten. Young things. Laura took them home after the reception, and Russell and Leah and I stayed with Mom in Saint J. That was our plan. The three of us kids would spend the night at Mom's house so we'd all be there when she went to bed, and we could all have breakfast together the next morning. Then we'd all go our own separate ways. Now it was pretty late. Somewhere between midnight and twelve-thirty, I guess, because Russell and I didn't get to the golf course until quarter

185

to one in the morning. We parked in the lot right by the pro shop and the old caddy shack, and then we each took a case and as many singles as we could carry and walked out to the second hole. Par five, four hundred and ninety yards. Nice long fairway—not that we needed it. We had my dad's ancient clubs, and we'd slipped an old baseball bat we found in the basement into the bag. In truth, it was all a lot of effort for a couple moments of pleasure. But it was very satisfying.

She leaned forward and punched him lightly on the arm. Kind of like sex, she said, smiling broadly. Lots of foreplay to get what you really want.

It wasn't that good. Trust me. But it was fun. We teed the little eight-ounce cans up one at a time, and found we could whack one, oh, forty yards with the driver, and maybe thirty with an iron.

No tests with the putter?

Absolutely not. This was good old-fashioned, testosterone violence. Tee 'em up and swing. Blast 'em. These were the cans of protein shakes our father used to vomit up, after all, and so nothing said cancer to us like Ensure. Nothing. I mean the stuff doesn't taste half-bad—I actually like the chocolate—and it's very smooth. But . . . well, we were angry.

My mom used to drink strawberry, Phoebe said. Ensure Plus Strawberry. Extra calories, extra protein. Yum.

The worst thing to watch was how much it hurt him when he threw up. The radiation had burned the living shit—pardon me—out of his esophagus, and so it was pure agony for him when the stuff would come back. We'd hear him gag, and then he'd spray this watery brown gruel into the toilet, or the lobster pot he kept by the couch. But some days that was the only thing he had even a prayer in hell of keeping down. The only thing.

Anyone hear you?

On the golf course? Oh, I doubt it. One time Russell screamed Fore! but I reminded him that people might frown on our little activity, and after that we weren't quite so hysterical. We were laughing pretty good, but at least we weren't screaming down the fairways.

You stayed on the second hole?

Yup. I tossed him a couple lobs from the ladies' tee so he could get a few good rips in with the baseball bat. But mostly we used our dad's golf clubs. It felt good. Juvenile, but worth every whack. Sometimes we'd hear the cans pop when we cracked 'em open, and the shake would spray like a Fizzie as it zoomed off the tee.

Funny, I don't recall what we did with the cans we never used. I guess we donated them somewhere. Maybe to the hospice or the local food shelf. Wallace took care of that sort of thing for Dad. He got rid of all the signs of Mom's illness.

We did that, too. Leah and me.

On the street outside the coffee shop where they had met for a late lunch the crowds were starting to thin. Because it was Christmas Eve most of the stores would be closing soon—some had even locked their doors an hour earlier, at three P.M.—and most of the other people in the restaurant had left. There was another couple at another booth, great bags of presents in the aisle beside them, but otherwise the dining room was empty and quiet.

What did your dad do? she asked him.

He was the manager of the lamp factory in Saint J. It wasn't glamorous but it was lucrative.

The brass lamps?

Right. He always wanted to buy it—or at least a piece of it—so he could own a business himself, but the Bowen family never wanted to sell. Over the years he worked himself up from an eighteen-year-old guy on the line to the man in charge of the whole operation. Even did a little selling—got the lamps into a couple of very big hotel chains. Owning the company seemed the natural next step. But it never happened.

She sipped the last of her tea and then asked, Will you and Laura and Alfred be going to church tonight?

In all likelihood.

Me, too. My dad and I will eat dinner as soon as I walk in the door, and then go to the early service so he can go to bed. He doesn't sleep a whole lot, but he likes to be in his bed with the radio on by nine-thirty or ten.

We used to go to the early service because there was always a pageant the girls would be in. They'd be sheep or angels. One year Megan was a shepherd. But after they died Laura couldn't bear to see all their friends together like that in the church, so ever since we've gone to the late service. The thing is, I think she'd be okay with the pageant these days. After all, she teaches Sunday school. But now the late service is a habit.

She nodded and he realized she was about to leave. He guessed her drive home was about ninety minutes. Maybe more. They could have had this whole conversation—the important part, anyway, the part where she told him that she'd decided she was definitely going to keep the baby—over the telephone. But they had both, it seemed, felt the need to see each other, and so they had tiptoed gingerly around the possibility of meeting in person and settled on the idea of coming back here to Montpelier: a city, albeit a small one, but still a place where they could be anonymous. They hadn't seen each other since they met nine days earlier at the bakery barely a block from where they sat now, and then wandered in the brisk air around the edge of Hubbard Park—the hilly patch of forest preserved just west of the state's gold-domed capitol building. He'd wrapped his arms around her when she cried and held her hand when the more dense clusters of hemlock and tamarack trees had shielded them from the nearby houses. They'd stayed on the sidewalk and never ventured inside the forest, and not simply because the inner paths would be slippery and cold: He feared they would kiss if they went there, and he did not want to repeat the mistake he had made at deer camp.

I hope before too long we'll see each other again, he said, surprised at the small current of neediness he'd detected in his voice. He hoped she hadn't heard it. This was the third time they'd been together, and he realized that as he'd gotten to know her, he'd grown to enjoy her company—her odd sense of humor, the surprising number of things they'd discovered they had in common—more with each visit. He realized that he wanted them to remain friends (nothing more, that could not happen again, he reminded himself), and not simply because she carried within her his child—their child, the baby they'd made together—but because he liked her. It was really that simple. She made him happy.

Oh, I'm sure we will, she said. After the New Year we should probably talk—but seriously, Terry, only if you want to.

I understand.

No pressure.

None felt.

Still, I have to ask. Why?

Why do I want to see you?

Uh-huh, she said. Is this just about being responsible?

He saw that she was reaching for her purse and the wallet inside, and so he motioned for her to put it away. Let me get this, he insisted, happy to have something to do with his hands as he stood and thought about what he wanted to say.

HE'D TOLD LAURA he wouldn't be home until seven because he hadn't known what would happen with Phoebe. How long they would be together. Where they might go. Laura knew he was using a few hours of personal leave time to take the afternoon off, but he had hinted strongly to her that he was planning to go Christmas shopping. In truth his shopping was done, and since Montpelier was only about an hour from Cornish, he could be home by five-thirty if he wanted.

But he didn't want that, and this reality disturbed him. He realized he didn't know what he wanted, and for a long time he simply sat in his cruiser in the large parking lot behind the hotel on Main Street. At that moment he guessed Alfred was finishing up with the horse and Laura was leaving the shelter. Maybe helping to clean up the plastic cups and spilled punch from the party.

The trouble was that once again that day he had imagined all too precisely what would have greeted him at his home if a season of rain and a single wave on a river hadn't undone his life. In his mind he had projected the images, from the minute he pulled into his driveway and he heard—and sound, suddenly, was everything—his girls' voices when he opened the front door of his house, to that moment a little later when he'd hear the whine of the bureau drawers and closet hinges (it was the bureau in Megan's room that made so much noise, but it was Hillary's closet that squeaked) as they picked out their clothing for the Christmas Eve service at the church. He saw the four of them eating dinner together, and he heard Megan's high voice—higher than Hillary's, anyway—making fun of his belt as he passed her the mashed potatoes. She always made fun of his uniform, especially his regulation belt, because it looked as black and wide as a strip of new highway, and that, in her opinion, was a very bad fashion statement.

Nothing would be like that now, even though they had a child inside their house once again.

Yet he reminded himself that the only changes that should trouble him—there was nothing, after all, to be done about the fact that his daughters were gone and would never be back—were the changes that were looming outside his house. If he was going to focus on anything, he should stew about what he had done (*was doing,* he told himself quickly, *was doing*) away from the world of his wife and the boy.

He tried to consider a way out, but he didn't like the shape of those words in his head, with their disturbing ring of culpability and guilt, and corrected himself quickly: He tried to imagine what would happen next. What he would decide. And surely something would happen now that Phoebe was committed to keeping the child, even if he himself did absolutely nothing. How could it not? In this case, doing nothing was doing something. Neglect. Desertion. Becoming, in essence if not in the literal-mindedness of the law, one of the deadbeat dads who drove him wild.

But that was one of his options. He could ignore his real child—the one who would be born, he guessed, late the following summer—and, yes, this woman who was that real child's mom. This other woman who wasn't scarred like his wife, and who told jokes and made him laugh. He could do that, it was a legitimate choice. She'd made that clear.

Or he could leave Alfred and Laura. He could abandon a boy who had already been abandoned who knew how many times in his life, and a woman who'd lost both her daughters. That, too, was an alternative.

Or—and he shook his head at the absurdity of the thought—he could juggle two families. Never tell Laura about Phoebe, but continue to be an element in this other woman's life. A part-time husband and father and, yes, breadwinner.

Terry allowed his forehead to rest against his steering wheel. His salary—and Laura's—supported their household nicely, but a sergeant with the state police certainly couldn't afford to keep a second household in diapers and milk.

It was a ridiculous notion, anyway. He knew the very last thing Phoebe wanted from him was money. The truth was, he wasn't sure she wanted anything from him at all. Maybe that was why he'd never given serious credence to the idea that the baby might not really be his.

Besides, he'd seen enough liars in his life to single them out, and he knew Phoebe wasn't that kind of person.

The words *real child* came back to him. It wasn't lost on him that he was perceiving a microscopic blob of cells in Phoebe's womb as a real child, while viewing the ten-year-old boy living under his roof as something else. Something impermanent. Something not his.

He sat back in his seat and started the cruiser. It was Christmas Eve and he had a wife and a child—real or not, what did it matter now?—at his home, and still he didn't have the slightest idea where he was going to drive. He knew only that he wasn't yet ready to head back to Cornish.

IF THERE HAD been a tack shop still open, he might have stopped and gotten another small gift for the boy. One of those horse combs or something. Maybe some special riding gloves. The child's big Christmas present, of course, were the cowboy boots Laura had found at a leather store up in Burlington: They were a brownish red that reminded him a bit of his own leather wallet, and they looked nothing at all like Phoebe's black-and-white boots. Even the toe was different—less pointed. Almost blunt. But, still, he couldn't help but think of Phoebe's boots when he saw what Laura wanted to buy for the boy, and then—therefore—of Phoebe herself.

He considered driving to the mall in Berlin Corners, guessing even now there might be stores open there. He was no more than fifteen minutes away, and he figured the mall would stay open till five or five-thirty at least. He might even find something more for Laura as well. A new sweater vest, maybe. Or perhaps one of those bulky knit cardigans she was so fond of when it was cold.

But he couldn't bring himself to steer the cruiser onto the road that led south to Barre and Berlin, and turned instead up into the hills full of stately old homes just behind the capitol building. He drove down the white-pine-and maple-lined streets, reminded a bit of Saint Johnsbury and his mother's house—his house, too, of course, because it would always be the house in which he'd grown up. These houses would be noisy tomorrow morning. Christmas. They'd be like his house had been when he was a child, and like his current home in the hills over the mountain when his girls were alive.

He wondered what Alfred would be like tomorrow—just after he woke up. He couldn't imagine the child getting up early to race downstairs to scope out the loot the way his daughters always had. It was so clear he was unfamiliar with the notion of generosity on any kind of scale—certainly not on the scale Terry's daughters had known and, in fact, taken for granted.

Still, the house would be noisier tomorrow than it had been in the recent past, and that would be a welcome change. Most mornings were eerily quiet. That was, perhaps, the most disconcerting of the myriad small ways their lives had changed since the girls died. The house had become almost too quiet to bear, and Alfred's presence had done little to change that.

He didn't know how Laura stood the place when she came home from the shelter. There was no Hillary taking the steps two at a time, pounding up the stairs like a sprinter. There were no wooden clogs—Megan's shoe of choice—scraping against the soft pine in the kitchen and the hall as she shuffled along in her own little world. There were no giggles, no fights, no squeals. No television. No CD player blaring the latest pop hit from that week's teen queen sensation.

The girls made noise, and that noise, he understood now, was testimony to the fact that their house was alive and vital and well. His marriage to Laura, too: His children's vitality was one small barometer of that fact.

He drove back into the business district and decided that what he wanted more than anything was a beer, but he was still in his uniform and so a bar was out of the question. So he decided that he would settle instead for companionship (not friendship, not really, because both he and Laura knew well that a parent's friends start disappearing about two or three months after a child has died, if only because the grown-ups now have nothing in common and it's unbearable to sit and talk only about the children who no longer are there) and drop in at the headquarters in Waterbury. He hadn't been to Waterbury in months, and a visit—regardless of who was there the day before Christmas—would kill at least another half-hour to an hour before he would have to head home.

As he merged with the traffic on the interstate, a memory struck him with clarity. He wasn't exactly sure how he had arrived at it, but he believed it had to have something to do with the noise that had once filled his house, and, specifically, the music: It was an image of Laura and the girls dancing together in their nightgowns when Hillary and Megan were eight. He had missed dinner that night because of a B and E out in Waltham, and when he got home it was almost eight-thirty. And there were his girls—all three of them, really—prancing and capering in the den like go-go dancers to the energetic love songs of some rock and roll heartthrob.

And then, trailing the memory by no more than a second, was a realization: If he ever told Laura the truth about Phoebe, his marriage was over. It was that simple. It wasn't a question of whether he could or would leave her for this other woman—because, most assuredly, he would not. The reality was that Laura would leave him first if she knew this Phoebe Danvers carried within her the child she herself could no longer have.

*"I expect soon enough the three of them will be sent
to Fort Sill. After all, they're prisoners."*

SERGEANT GEORGE ROWE,
TENTH REGIMENT, UNITED STATES CAVALRY,
LETTER TO HIS BROTHER IN PHILADELPHIA,
MAY 24, 1876

Phoebe

She watched her eight-year-old niece put the Tek safety vest on over her sweater, and her nephew—younger than Crystal by close to two years, but, still, almost as tall—pound the girl's shoulder pads with the pillowy flesh at the bottoms of his fists. His hands looked to her like a pair of small baking potatoes.

Stop it! the girl said, but it was clear that she wasn't all that annoyed. She liked the present, and she liked the proof that the shoulder pads cushioned the blows.

Her brother and sister-in-law's living room was still layered with the crinkled wrapping paper that the family had deposited there earlier that morning. Whole sections of the rug were hidden beneath crumpled red foil, some of which her brother had balled up and placed in a corner by the couch when she and their father arrived, but had since been reanimated into a pile that dwarfed the coffee table beside it. The tree in the bay window was massive, it must have been just inches short of ten feet: Someone had placed the star against the tip of the tree, rather than upon it, because the tip was almost touching the ceiling. She noticed there were far more ornaments along the bottom of the evergreen than the top, and she assumed this was because her nephew and niece had done most of the decorating.

We're supposed to get some snow tonight, maybe as much as six or seven inches, her sister-in-law was saying to the children. Tomorrow should be much better.

Apparently, earlier that morning her brother and sister-in-law had put the miniature snowmobiles in the back of the truck and tried to find a patch of ground outside of the town with enough snow to try the machines out, but they'd failed. There were long patches of rock-hard ice and the ground was pretty solid, but there just wasn't a lot of powder. The kids had been disappointed, and so their parents mollified them by reminding them every chance they got that the forecast included snow.

Her brother and sister-in-law lived in a stately brick house just up the hill from Main Street in Littleton. It always amazed her how well Wallace had done for himself—selling insurance, of all things. Veronica, his wife, had grown up just south of Littleton in a village called Sugar Hill, and came from ski money—her grandfather had helped open one of the resorts near Echo Lake—but Wallace took pride in the fact that they had bought this house entirely with the income they'd earned from his insurance company and Veronica's interior design business. In reality, of course, most of Veronica's clients were friends of her parents and grandparents in Franconia, Bethlehem, and Sugar Hill. No matter. It was still income instead of interest. Not a penny had come from a trust fund.

You're sure you wouldn't like a glass of wine or some eggnog? Veronica was asking her. Maybe a beer?

She knew she shouldn't have wine or beer because of the baby, and so she considered asking whether there was any rum in the eggnog. But she had never shied away from booze of any kind before, and she assumed that Veronica would figure out instantly why she was wondering—or at least want to know more. Besides, Wallace and Veronica always put rum in the eggnog, so why bother asking?

Coffee is really what I'm in the mood for today, she answered.

Decaf?

Yeah, that would be great.

She wasn't sure when she would tell her family she was pregnant. She had already called Nancy Fleming, her ob-gyn, but she hadn't decided how she would tell her father. Or, for that matter, her brothers. They'd all think she was insane. Irresponsible and insane. And what of her resolve to keep the name of the father a secret? They'd be annoyed by what they would interpret as a self-imposed martyrdom.

But that wasn't it, that wasn't it at all. As she watched her niece and her nephew running around the living room with their safety vests on, she didn't feel a bit like a martyr: She felt joyful and, truly, expectant. The world was filled with single mothers, and somehow they got by. And most of those single mothers wouldn't have the support that she had. She imagined her father baby-sitting the child some days, weekends at her brother Wallace's fine house with her little one and these energetic, older cousins. Maybe when she got her old job back with Developmental and Mental Health Services, she'd rent a nice place in Montpelier. Her old apartment certainly would have been big enough. She saw herself walking into the bakery just off Main Street with a toddler—in her imagination, a little girl—and buying the child one of the long biscotti that sat in the glass jar, and watching her daughter gnaw at the cookie as if it were zwieback.

In her mind the girl had Terry's gray eyes, but otherwise looked like her.

Her father glanced up from his grandchildren at the same moment that she found herself looking at him. He moved slowly these days and his back was stooped from his years with the cows—milking would always take a toll on a man's back, even when the task had been handed over to a mechanical pump and a hose—but when he was seated, as he was now, he was still a powerful figure. He actually had thicker hair, and more of it, than either of his sons, and his shoulders had remained broad.

Your mother would have loved to have seen the kids in those outfits, he said to her, referring to the Tek vests the children were wearing. She would have thought they looked mighty cute.

They do, Phoebe agreed. She wanted to ask him how he was feeling now that they were at Wallace and Veronica's. He had been depressed before they left the house, saddened by the reality that he was enduring a Christmas without his wife—her mother. He seemed better now, but it was hard to tell with her father.

Mom would have worried they're too young to have snowmobiles, Wallace said.

And she would have been right, Phoebe added, but she meant it good-naturedly and she kept her voice light.

Those rigs? Nah. They're practically Matchbox cars, Wallace said. They're made for kids.

From the kitchen everyone heard the oven timer, and Veronica stood, reaching reflexively for the dish towel that she must have brought with her and kept hidden in her lap like a handkerchief. That would be the pie, she said. Dinner's about five minutes away.

Smells like apple pie, Phoebe said to her sister-in-law.

Apple and sour cream. Even better. Veronica turned toward her children before leaving, and said to them, You two: Wash your hands, please.

I need to— Crystal started, but her father cut her off.

You don't *need* to do anything, he said, except listen to your mother and wash your hands right this minute. Now go. Scoot. Chop-chop.

Without taking their vests off, they started down the hallway to what Veronica referred to as the powder room, and Phoebe realized she was alone with her father and her brother, and this was probably about as good as it was going to get. If her other two siblings had been there, she decided, the moment would have been perfect for dropping her bombshell, but Scottie was with his wife's family in Massachusetts, and Mary was having her own Christmas celebration in Burlington. Still, the moment was good enough. She hadn't planned it this way, and she understood on some level that she might regret what she was about to do.

Of course, that might have been exactly why she was doing it—because she might regret it, at least at first. What was it her old boss used to say? Breakthroughs begin with breakdowns. She'd tell her father and her brother her big news right now—perhaps begin by pointing out to them that she was drinking decaf coffee today instead of wine or eggnog or beer—which would give them a chance to get used to the idea long before the baby was born. This way they'd be there for her when she needed them most.

Besides, if she told them on Christmas Day, they would have to be charitable.

She opened her mouth and started to speak, but quickly stopped herself. She realized that she wanted Veronica present. Her sister-in-law would be an ally if she were among the small group that was told first; she would help ensure that the men were appropriately . . . supportive. And so she quickly decided that she would wait, after all, until they were finishing dinner, when her niece and nephew would have been excused to go play with their presents. Then she would tell her father and Wallace and Veronica.

Her brother and her father were looking at her. What were you about to say, Phoebe? Wallace asked.

I lost my train of thought, she said. Sorry.

You get that from your mother, her father told her.

If it's important, it will come back to you, her brother added.

She sipped her coffee and smiled, and rested one open palm on her stomach.

IT STRUCK HER as funny, but her mouth felt parched. The kids were gone from the table, and any moment now Veronica was going to stand up, start carting the dessert plates into the kitchen, and suggest that they all take their coffee into the living room. Despite the large water glass that she'd drained, her tongue felt like a massive dry sponge and her throat had grown raw. Almost out of desperation, therefore, she took the spoon—unused—and tapped it against the rim of the goblet, as if she were at a wedding or an anniversary party. If she didn't get their attention that very instant, the moment would pass and it would be weeks or months before she would tell them.

The three other grown-ups in the room looked at her—Veronica actually paused while dabbing at her lips with her napkin, holding the linen there as if she were trying to clot the blood from a small cut—their eyebrows raised and their eyes wide. What, their faces asked, was Phoebe up to now? Her brother and her sister-in-law, she could see, were expecting . . . mirth.

Well, she thought, this won't be mirth, but it will sure as hell give them something to talk about. Dad, too.

You look like you have something important to announce, Wallace said, as his wife carefully pulled her napkin from her face, rolled it into a tube, and slid it through the pewter ring by her place mat.

She nodded and reached across the table for his water glass because it was still half-full, and took a long swallow. Then she said, I do indeed have some news. Some good news.

You have a boyfriend, Wallace said. Hallelujah! It's about time—

No, I can't say that I do. I have something better.

Her father folded his arms across his chest and leaned back in his chair. His face changed before her from one of expectation to one of annoyance. Suddenly, if only because he couldn't guess at the surprise and it wasn't as innocuous as a new boyfriend, he had grown wary. It was as if he knew this surprise, whatever it was, whatever she was about to say, was going to displease him. And that made her just a little bit angry, because he had no right to be displeased about anything she said or did. She'd come home before her mother had died and been with him ever since. She'd been working at the general store, for God's sake, to be with him. Given up a pretty good job, and something that at least resembled a social life.

And that is? Wallace asked.

She looked from her father to her brother and reined in her resentment. Maybe her father feared that she was about to announce she was leaving his house, and her return to Montpelier was imminent. Or maybe his face and his arms and his pose meant nothing. Absolutely nothing. For all she knew, he was sitting that way to stretch out his spine or relieve an ache in his back.

I'd ask if you were sitting down, she said, giving herself one more brief second when the news was hers and hers alone, but of course you all are— which is probably good. So, here it is, Phoebe's Christmas Day bombshell. Guess what? I'm going to have a baby.

There were a pair of lit candles on the table in glass holders, and in the absolute silence that followed her announcement the flames barely moved. Her family was quiet and the air was still, and the trim fires at the tips of the wax were as upright and straight as the slender candles below them. Finally Wallace spoke. Didn't you just tell us you don't have a boyfriend? he said, and his voice was so even that she couldn't tell what he was thinking.

Nope, there's no boyfriend, she said.

A fiancé? he asked, and then his voice brightened just the tiniest bit. It was clear that in his opinion, a fiancé was a whole lot better than a boyfriend when his sister had gotten herself knocked up.

No, I don't have one of those either, she said, and out of the corner of her eye she caught the silver serving tray with the pieces of turkey her father had carved, and the combination of the meat and the subject matter at hand made her think of turkey basters—that was how that gay mother she knew in her office had gotten pregnant—and she feared she was going to have another attack of the giggles. She'd been having them all the time lately: uncontrollable, nearly hysterical fits of laughter, beginning almost two weeks earlier when she met Terry at the bakery in Montpelier.

Then how? Wallace asked her.

She knew he meant who or why, but his choice of words—*How?*, as if he were interested solely in the manner or the technique—put her over the edge, and she started to laugh.

Don't worry, brother, I didn't use a turkey baster, she said, and she snorted in a manner so unattractive that the sound made her laugh even harder. She saw her father glance at her brother, and it was evident that he didn't have the slightest idea what she was talking about. She wasn't sure that her brother did, either. Both men looked confused, cautious, concerned. They actually looked a bit like Terry did when something would set her off, and her giggles would grow into nearly frenzied peals of laughter.

Veronica's mouth was hanging open a tiny bit, but not in horror, it seemed, so much as in interest. She wanted to say something, but she was going to wait for her sister-in-law to regain her composure. Finally, with her hands folded into a teepee, her nails impeccable cuts of pink salmon, she said over the last, small ripples of Phoebe's chuckles, Do we know the father? Have we met him?

She shook her head. Doubt it.

Veronica nodded. Will we get to meet him . . . soon?

I don't think so, because—

Jesus Christ, Phoebe, do you even know who the hell the father is? her brother asked, unable or unwilling to conceal his incredulity and aggravation. Do you?

Wallace, please, Veronica said. Of course Phoebe knows—

Before her sister-in-law could finish speaking, however, her father stood up and angrily threw his napkin into his chair, snapping his wrist as if there were cow shit on it he had to get off. He shook his head and murmured, If your mother were alive . . .

But he didn't finish the sentence, and then he left the dining room for the mudroom just off the front hall, where they heard him putting on his boots and his coat and opening the door to the street.

———

"Having committed theft and murder upon govern-ment employees within the reservation and upon civil-ians outside it, the hostile factions within the Comanche tribe have given us no choice but to draw a line. In order that we may be able to distinguish between the hostile and friendly groups, henceforth all friendly Indians must set their camps east of the river, and only at points selected and approved by the Agent."

———

GENERAL ORDER NO. 57,
LIEUTENANT COLONEL KENNETH OATES,
TENTH REGIMENT, UNITED STATES CAVALRY

———

Alfred

The morning after Christmas was the first day of Kwanzaa, a holiday they seemed to talk about often in school—Cornish as well as Burlington—and one his teachers always presumed he understood. This was the first time, however, that he'd actually lived in a house that was acknowledging the celebration. Together he and Laura—Laura mostly, in truth—had produced a small Kwanzaa mat from, of all things, a plastic machine that was meant to make pot holders, and placed upon it the symbols from the book she had given him about the holiday: Seven candles in seven holders, each representing a particular value. A clay goblet she had bought from a potter at a pre-Christmas craft show. Three ears of dried corn from the supermarket she had saved through the fall, and a variety of squash from their garden that remained in the basement. Acorn. Butternut. Spaghetti.

They built the display in the middle of the dining-room table, and Alfred liked the way you could see the Christmas tree he had picked out in the living room behind it. It looked like a mountain in the distance.

That night, Laura had said, when Terry returned home from work, they would celebrate the first night of Kwanzaa—what Laura had called the *ingathering*.

Ingathering? he asked as he flipped through the Kwanzaa book in search of the definition. It was only nine o'clock in the morning, but already Laura's parents were gone. They'd left before eight, hoping to be far to the south before the storm hit in earnest and the roads grew slick with snow. He had to admit, he was relieved they hadn't stayed longer, and he had the sense that Laura was, too. Laura's mother was wheezing constantly from the animal fur that suddenly he and Terry and especially Laura were discovering every-where, and Laura's father was clearly uncomfortable with the drafts in the house. They both kept bringing up small homes, all charming, one or the other had seen for sale in Dedham and Newton and Wellesley. While the two women prepared dinner, the men—including Alfred—parked themselves in front of the television to watch a basketball game, and Alfred didn't believe any of them said a word.

Laura centered one of the candles and then sat in the ladder-back chair beside him. She was still wearing her red flannel nightgown and he was still in the navy blue pajamas that Laura's parents had given him. Terry had left the house while the older couple were having their breakfast, and had already been at work for ninety minutes. I'm sure the book will explain it better, Laura said as she adjusted her headband, but I believe it has to do with building bonds between people and getting together. Family, maybe. Parents and children. She smiled and shrugged, and then added, You might say the ritual began yesterday with Christmas, though it's pretty evident that some parts of this family are more comfortable with the notion of gathering together than others.

He reached for the acorn squash nearest him and held it in his hand like a softball. He'd never really grown anything in his life; he wasn't sure he had ever even worked in a garden. By the time he arrived here, Laura was already putting her vegetable garden to bed for the winter, and harvesting the final zucchini and squash. The gourd he was balancing that moment in his palm might have been among the very last vegetables she had brought into the house. He wondered if other kids—regular kids—gardened, and without thinking about whether this was a smart subject to broach, he asked Laura, Your girls like to garden?

The smile instantly evaporated from her face and he regretted the question. Only a split second before it had seemed to him both an innocuous inquiry about a hobby and, perhaps, a safe way to begin to understand the children who had come before him and whose memory had such a hold on these grown-ups with whom he lived. A phrase Laura had just used echoed in his mind: parents and children. That was, she had said herself, a part of the ingathering. So why not bring up the girls? Wasn't it time?

For a long moment she sat there, saying nothing, and quickly he focused his attention entirely on the page that was open in the book. The words, the

English as well as the Swahili—*umoja, ujima, ujamaa*—became a blur, and he stared at the image of a slim wooden statue of an African man. Finally he heard a small noise from her mouth, a sound so soft it could have been made by one of the cats, and then she answered him.

Hillary wasn't especially interested in gardening—not vegetables or flowers—but Megan was. A little bit. She didn't like the weeding and planting parts, but she liked to be out there with me sometimes. She'd look for wildlife. Chipmunks. Toads. Bluebirds. Come March or April, you'll see that we actually get a couple families of bluebirds in those birdhouses Terry put up in the side yard. She—and before you laugh at this, remember that she was younger than you are now—also liked to look for fairies. She claimed they lived under the largest leaves, like the ones on the pumpkin plants.

As Laura spoke he glanced up from the book, and he saw that she was watching him. Her hands were perfectly still in her lap, and the corners of her mouth were upturned once again into a very slight grin.

Megan didn't contribute a heck of a lot to the final harvest, she continued, but she was great fun to have with me. Always.

Hillary, too?

Hillary, too. But Hillary was usually on the same planet with the rest of us. That wasn't always true of Megan. Megan sometimes seemed to exist in her own little world. Megan-Ville, we used to call it. Especially when she'd be off on one of her searches for goblins or elves.

What else did they like to do? Both girls?

You mean when Megan wasn't pawing through the pumpkin patch in search of make-believe creatures?

Uh-huh.

Oh, I could go on for hours, Alfred. I could show you pictures, I could take you to the attic and we could unpack cartons and cartons . . . their whole lives are up there. Well, not their whole lives. We gave a lot away. But we kept a lot, too. There are some things I couldn't part with, even if I couldn't bear to have them around where I could see them every day.

Clothes and toys?

Some. I know there's a box of Barbies up there, and the books I couldn't bring myself to give to the library. There's even a couple pieces of furniture. But mostly it's schoolwork and projects and the sorts of things they would do in art class. Things they drew or made with their own hands. Paintings. Little clay sculptures. Their stories and essays.

But not their photos, he said, and he thought about the albums of pictures he'd studied in the den, and the one image he had taken for himself. They're not in the attic.

No, not their photos. You've seen them?

He nodded, and he could feel his face flushing with guilt.

A day doesn't go by when I don't look at them, she said. I can't have them up on the kitchen refrigerator or in a frame in the bedroom—I just can't do it, I just can't run into them casually when I'm supposed to be doing something else—but I also can't last a day without seeing them. Visiting with them when I'm alone in the house.

He thought about this, wondering what it must be like to lose someone you cared about. Really cared about. Especially if you weren't used to such a thing. Is it as hard now as it was a couple years ago? he asked. When it happened?

No, she said, the single syllable drawn out a tiny bit by her sigh. In truth, it isn't. But it will never, ever be easy.

You still miss them?

One of the cats jumped into her lap, surprising them both, and she pulled the animal into her arms and against her chest. She raised her eyebrows into a tawny pyramid and looked at something in the distance far beyond Alfred, and murmured softly into the cat's ear, Oh, I think I will miss them forever.

"They issued an order to try and help them know who was hostile and who wasn't. They used the river as the dividing line. I knew then I would never see my people again."

VERONICA ROWE (FORMERLY POPPING TREES),
WPA INTERVIEW,
MARCH 1938

Terry

It would start to snow any minute, you could feel it in the crisp, moist air. Because Christmas had fallen on a Friday this year, the roads now—the day after Christmas—were particularly empty. Few people were going to work. Few people were going anywhere.

Still, it was clear it was going to be one of those days when virtually every car or truck that he saw was going to be speeding. First of all, there was the imminent arrival of the storm. Second, a person could drive for long moments without seeing another vehicle, and that led almost everyone who didn't have cruise control to press the pedal just a little bit harder. He did that himself on occasion.

And third, and perhaps most important, he could just tell he was going to have a bad day. Whether it was because he, of all people, had conceived a child out of wedlock with Phoebe Danvers, or (worse, in so many ways, worse) because it had been little more than a day and a half since he was with the woman at the coffee shop and already he wanted to see her again, or whether it was simply because he felt an ill wind blowing in from the west, he couldn't say. Sometimes you simply had bad days, mornings or afternoons when every driver on the road was handling his car like a moron and endangering you as well as himself.

And, of course, he thought this just might have had something to do with the girls. His girls. Christmas was hard without them. Maybe Alfred had helped Laura, but as much as he hated to admit it even to himself, the sad truth was he wanted his own children. Not some kid somebody else had deserted. He wanted something that was linked to him by genes and blood and the shape of a chin. The tint of the child's hair in the sun. Somehow he had held himself together for Laura for over two years—kept both his anguish and his fury in check—but he had a sense that now, finally, his control was beginning to lessen, if only because his wife needed him less. At least it seemed that she did.

Bottom line? The despair was starting to leach from that corner of his soul where he had managed to contain it for (he knew the number exactly) twenty-five and a half months, and he was angry.

And so even though he'd only been running the roads for forty-five minutes, already he'd stopped four cars and issued four tickets—including one to a nice enough lawyer from Burlington, a guy who was on his way to Albany to see his brother and sister-in-law and their kids. Normally he gave out a warning for every traffic complaint, but not today.

But it's Christmas weekend! one woman—an attractive skier in a Saab who had maybe a year or two on him—had insisted, but even she didn't have a prayer. Any other day she would have only gotten a warning, especially since she hadn't a single prior and she was going just nine miles over the limit—fifty-nine in a fifty-mile zone—but not now. He was feeling ornery this morning, and though he understood why, there wasn't a thing he could do to restrain himself.

Ahead of him, coming north on Route 22A as he was motoring south, he saw an old Subaru station wagon, and even before he heard the radar's audio start to whine—shrill, small, and annoying after a time, a noise that he had always associated with a mechanical monkey—he could tell the car was moving pretty damn fast. Instantly he froze the oncoming speed on the box just above his dashboard—the digital numbers showed seventy-one—and twirled the radar antenna around to see if the guy had bothered to slow down. A bit, but not a whole lot. Still rockin' and rollin' above sixty-five. And so Terry spun his cruiser and turned on his strobe lights. Though they were in the midst of relatively flat farmland, he'd had to travel a few hundred yards farther south before he found a spot level enough to whirl the Impala 180 degrees. That meant, he guessed, that unless the guy had slowed some more when he saw the trooper's vehicle in the distance behind him, it would take him a good half a minute to catch up.

He gunned the car, and was exceeding sixty, seventy, then eighty in seconds. Soon he saw the station wagon before him, a rusted-out piece of shit, dirty white with orange flecking and streaks, now motoring along a mere fifteen miles above the speed limit. It was exactly the sort of junk heap that Terry just knew was going to have registration and inspection tags that were out of date. No doubt a blinker or a light would be gone, too. And now this idiot thought he was going to see if he could feign ignorance: *Gee, Officer, was I speeding? Oh, I'm sorry, I didn't see you behind me.*

He was about to turn on his siren, perhaps even use the two-tone to command the guy to pull over, when the station wagon slowed dramatically and coasted to a stop at the side of the road. Terry noticed that the brake lights had worked, but the driver hadn't used his directional, so he decided he would have the guy test it while he was stopped. Just in case. Just to be a pain in the ass.

He saw they were in a houseless stretch in the midst of two dormant cornfields, the earth this time of the year a series of waves of solid brown curds. He called in the stop, including the numbers on the car's tag, and told dispatch his location. Then he pulled his baton from the floor at the side of his seat and pushed his campaign hat further up on his head so whoever was driving could see his eyes. It was always good to remind the person behind the wheel that you were a human being, too—just in case. He noticed that the first specks of snow were starting to fall, small white crystals that grew into droplets the moment they hit the warm windshield on the front of the car.

He kept his baton flat against his left leg as he approached the driver. He had never once been attacked while issuing a traffic complaint, but that didn't make the moment any less stressful. He knew what could happen. As soon as he reached the driver's window, however, he relaxed a tiny bit. The guy looked annoyed, but he had his hands on the wheel at ten and two o'clock, with what looked like his license and car registration pressed between his thumb and the wheel. The fellow was heavy—more fat than muscle—and he had a closely trimmed beard that rounded his face like the fuzz on a tennis ball. Terry guessed he was in his mid-thirties, which might also have been the rough age of the badly battered parka that hung off him like a quilt. He saw a cigarette was burning in the ashtray.

I was speeding, I know it, he said, shaking his head, but he didn't move a muscle in his arms. Was clearly not going to hand over the small rectangles of paper until he was asked, as if . . . as if he'd been busted before. Initially Terry had assumed the fellow would simply prove to have a couple of points on his license, and that was why he was so familiar with the drill: both hands in clear sight on the wheel, license and registration out. Now, however, Terry began to wonder if there might be more to it than that, and he felt himself tightening his grip on his baton. The notion crossed his mind that it hadn't been simple stupidity or arrogance that led the man before him to continue cruising over seventy, even after observing a state trooper in the oncoming lane.

Any reason you didn't slow down then when you saw me?

I didn't see you, he said.

Terry nodded, and he scanned the passenger seat, the floor, and the back of the car. He wasn't looking for anything specific—drug paraphernalia, a weapon maybe, even something as simple as a computer or CD player that didn't look as though it had come from underneath a Christmas tree. He thought he smelled beer on the guy's breath, but he couldn't be sure because the stench of tobacco was strong.

When he saw nothing more incriminating than some candy bar wrappers and a carton of cigarettes, he asked for the man's license, registration, and proof of insurance, and started back toward his car. He could feel the chill wind on his face, and thought the sky looked almost as white as the ground would in a couple of hours.

For a long moment he simply watched the fellow smoke a cigarette in his seat, reassured now that the guy was harmless. He might have been irritated because he'd been pulled over, but that made him no less pathetic. In the end he didn't even have the balls to ask what the radar had just shown— although that was never the way they phrased the question. Never. Instead they asked, *Gee, Officer, how fast was I going?* As if they didn't know, which was, of course, ridiculous. The first thing a person did when he saw a trooper behind him or before him was brake, followed almost instantaneously by a glance at the speedometer. And so what that question—a universal, really— actually meant was, *How fast was I going according to your radar? Just how badly fucked am I?* No, Terry decided, when he finally got around to calling dispatch about the guy, he would discover only that the man had a good many points on his license and perhaps a couple of warnings to boot. That was the only reason he knew to have his hands on the wheel and his papers handy when a trooper approached.

Nevertheless, Terry continued to sit in his seat, immobile and watching, waiting, he realized, for nothing more than another car to pass so the fellow's humiliation would be complete: There he'd be, off to the side of the road, the first crystals of snow sticking to his windshield and hood, while his license was checked, and the complaint—coupled with a nice, hefty fine— was written. Finally Terry saw another vehicle approaching over a small ridge perhaps a mile distant. He thought there might even be a second one behind it. In something less than sixty seconds—maybe seventy if the first one slowed to a crawl because its driver saw the flashing lights up ahead— the loser before him would have his moment in the pillory. Head and arms through the stocks.

At last he pulled the radio from the dashboard and called in the license of one Francis B. Hammond, requesting as well a list of any prior convictions or involvements. He watched the two cars pass, slowing both because of the blue lights on his cruiser and the opportunity to gawk at the individual inside the beaten-up station wagon. Soon he heard the low, static-covered voice with the information he had requested: Hammond had no priors and no points on his license. Not even a warning. Terry was both surprised and dis- appointed. He had been positive that the fellow would have a solid number of points, and there was even an outside chance that the ticket he was about to issue would cost Hammond his right to drive for ten days. After all, ten points in two years and you were out for a week and a half.

No such luck, however, the guy was clean. Completely clean. A Boy Scout.

He took the metal notebook in which he kept his pad with the complaint forms and a pen and wrote out a ticket. Even on a good day he doubted he would have issued a warning, given the fact that he'd clocked the car going twenty-one miles over the limit and Hammond hadn't slowed till he had to. But he didn't believe he would have been as angry as he was now. He left the cruiser, the complaint in his hand, and marched up to the Subaru.

Any reason you were going twenty-one miles over the speed limit? he asked.

Not a good one.

Try me.

I have to pee. Badly. And my home's all the way up in Burlington.

Terry remembered the slight odor of alcohol he thought he might have detected on the man's breath.

Have you been drinking?

What?

Terry realized he had misjudged Hammond: This man had some spine after all. Please don't answer my questions with questions of your own, okay, Mr. Hammond? he said. Now, let's try this again: Have you been drinking?

It's not even nine A.M.!

Are you telling me no?

He ran his hands through his hair, aggravated. He wasn't wearing gloves, and Terry could see what he guessed were permanent ink stains on the man's palms and under his nails. He probably ran a press at one of the printers in the city.

I didn't have anything this morning, but I drank a few beers last night.

How many?

Oh, I don't know. Two. Maybe three.

When did you have the last one?

About four-thirty.

In the morning? He'd asked it reflexively. He realized now that Hammond had most certainly meant in the morning.

Yup.

What time did you start?

Drinking? I don't remember.

Terry guessed he had had a hell of a lot more than two or three beers. You slept? he asked.

Oh, a bit, Hammond answered. But if you think you smell beer, I have to believe it's because my brother spilled some on my coat. On the sleeve.

Uh-huh. Please step out of your car.

What?

I will ask you one more time politely: Exit your car. Please.

Hammond shook his head, but he swung his legs—baggy blue jeans the color of moonstone, leather work boots that looked as worn as an old baseball glove—onto the ground.

Now recite the alphabet for me, Terry said.

In English or in French?

You're asking me questions again, Mr. Hammond. Please—

You really think I'm drunk? I can't believe this!

You were going seventy-one miles per hour in a fifty-mile zone. And you have acknowledged to me that you were drinking almost till sunrise. That's all I think.

Seventy-one?

Seventy-one.

Fine, he said. We'll start in English. Then I'll be happy to—

Mr. Hammond, I am very happy you can speak French, but you are making your life a lot more difficult than you need to. Okay?

May I sing it?

I am going to presume that question was not meant to be flip, because I have been asked it before. Yes, you may.

He nodded, buried his hands in the pockets of his parka, and proceeded to sing the alphabet accurately and with a slight Quebecois accent.

Thank you, Mr. Hammond. That wasn't so hard now, was it? Now I would like you to raise one foot slowly, keeping it parallel to the surface of the road. You are to keep your hands at your sides, focus your eyes on the toe of your boot, and count rapidly to thirty.

Then can I go into the field and pee?

Terry glared at him, and a small part of him was relieved that this time he had left his baton in the cruiser. Given how he was feeling today, this last question might have put him over the edge.

I am not interested in the state of your bladder, Mr. Hammond, he said, enunciating each word slowly. And if I hear one more thing about it, I am going to put you in the cruiser and you are going to be using the bathroom at the county jail.

Hammond smiled, placed his hands at his sides, and looked down at his boot. He lifted his right leg and he counted quickly to thirty. When he was done, Terry checked the inspection tag on the front windshield of the Subaru and saw the car wasn't due until March.

Let me see your directional now, please, he said to Hammond.

I promise you, my directional hasn't been drinking, Hammond told him, but he opened his car door, turned on the ignition, and flipped the directional to the right and the left. Both worked, and Terry signaled for him to shut off his engine.

I'm only going to issue you a speeding ticket this morning, Mr. Hammond, he said, handing him the paper and returning to him his license and registration. I believe you have had more than two beers, but I also believe you are not impaired and are fully capable of controlling your vehicle. I believe—

Spare me your speeches. I was speeding, first time ever, and you're treating me like a criminal. Making me stand by the road, recite the alphabet. Ordering me to act like an ostrich. What's the deal with that?

I urge you to watch yourself, sir—

And all this *sir* shit. Please. It's the creepiest sarcasm I've ever heard, and I've heard some pretty creepy sarcasm in my life. He then turned away from Terry and started to duck back into his car without signing the traffic complaint.

We're not done here, Terry heard himself saying, his voice losing the controlled edge he had cultivated over the years—he sounded almost whiny—and he reached for the man's shoulder, planning to turn him back toward him or at least regain his attention. Instantly Hammond wheeled around, a movement as balletic as it was violent, complete and utter reflex, no thought, and his elbow hit Terry's stomach like a punch. It doubled the trooper over and momentarily caused him to lose his breath. But it was just a moment, and when Terry looked up Hammond was staring at him in horror: He couldn't believe what he had just done. Accidentally or on purpose, it no longer mattered, he had just knocked the wind out of a state trooper, and Terry could see in his deer-in-the-headlights dark eyes that Hammond knew instantly the magnitude of the mistake he had made.

He drew his sidearm—astonished that he had climbed so quickly the ladder of force, but convinced he hadn't a choice because his baton was back in his cruiser—and with his free hand threw Hammond against the back door of his Subaru. He was furious—furious that he had been challenged, furious that he had been caught off-guard and humiliated, furious that he had allowed a minor speeding violation to escalate into this—and there was a long second where he was tempted to swing Hammond's head into the edge of the open front door. Crack open the son of a bitch's skull.

In the distance he heard a rumble, however, and out of the corner of his eye he saw a massive eighteen-wheel milk tanker approaching from the south. This reminder of the rest of the world—the world other than he and Francis B. Hammond, an overweight pressman who had allowed a chip on his shoulder to get himself slammed against the side of his car but whose body was now as limp as a marionette—settled him just enough that he understood this was at least as much his fault as it was Hammond's. He should never have allowed this to go this far. That didn't mean, of course, that he didn't have every right to bust Hammond: He did. Oh, for sure he did. But he realized he wasn't about to.

You just assaulted a police officer, he said as he slid his sidearm back into its holster. You should be under arrest.

His head was pounding, and he could feel his pulse thrumming in his neck and his ears.

I'm not going to arrest you, however, because . . . because it's the day after Christmas. Let's leave it at that.

The milk tanker slowed, the driver turned to watch the spectacle at the side of the road, and then it was past. The pavement was still trembling beneath its weight when Terry released Hammond and backed away, and told him there would be a gas station open in Vergennes if his bladder could make it another ten or fifteen minutes, but otherwise he should just go and use the woods. Then he retreated to his cruiser and watched Hammond drive away, only then realizing he hadn't gotten the man's signature on the traffic complaint.

WHEN HE FINALLY returned to the barracks, he couldn't bear to begin the paperwork he found waiting for him on his desk, and so he decided he would phone his mother instead. He'd been meaning to call her all morning. Yesterday when he'd spoken to his family—his mother and Leah and Russell had all gotten on the phone for at least a moment—Russell had sounded pretty hammered. He wanted to be sure now that his brother hadn't gotten into any trouble.

He was surprised when Russell answered the phone, but also a little relieved: It meant the man had had the common sense to understand he was too drunk to drive, and had spent the night at their mom's.

I am mighty impressed to find you in Saint J., he said. What kept you from trying to weave your way home?

You want me to say it was good judgment, Russell said, his voice low and tired.

That would be nice. Unexpected but nice.

His brother yawned. I just fell asleep and no one bothered to wake me.

Passed out, eh?

No, I fell asleep. There's a difference.

Where?

In my truck, he said, and he laughed. Leah and Rick found me, and carted me back inside. It seems I couldn't find my keys in my pocket, and I never made it down the damn driveway.

You are one very lucky son of a bitch. You could have killed someone, you know, you could have—

I have a headache, Sergeant Sheldon. Spare me this morning's lecture.

This is serious.

You think everything is serious.

He rubbed his eyes: He still had his headache, too. You working today? he asked Russell.

I was supposed to. Soda and the mail, people got to have it.

You call in sick?

Do I have two moms? Is that what I got for Christmas? A second mom?

Is that yes?

Yes, I called in sick. You can sleep easy.

Look, would you rather I didn't worry about you?

I'm fine, okay? I had too much to drink yesterday, but I won't do it today. Okay? I'm clean, my truck's clean.

He shuddered at his brother's use of the word *clean,* since he thought they were only talking about beer. He realized Russell was protesting too much, and if he was pulled over for speeding or even something as simple as a broken taillight, he'd probably wind up busted once again for possession.

Good, he said, but he was unable to muster the enthusiasm he imagined his brother wanted to hear.

You sound like you've had a pretty bad morning yourself.

You've got that right.

The two of us should take a day off together next month and go to the Outdoor Show, Russell suggested.

Maybe.

Not maybe, definitely! We'll go to Saint Albans and spend the day ogling camping gear and guns. I know you need a new hunting jacket.

We'll see. Mom around?

Is indeed, Russell said, and while his brother called their mother to the phone, he stared at the photos on his desk of Laura and the girls, and worried that a better man would have brought in a picture of Alfred by now.

———

"[They lack] habits of thrift, economy, or . . . respon-sibility, and they are, with few exceptions, thieves and liars."

———

———

Laura

The boy sat beside her on the couch, and she told him all that she could remember about any picture he chose. He balanced each photo album on his knees, and when they had finished with one, he would place it gently on the floor and she would hand him another. Once she got up to get a cup of hot tea, and once he rose off the couch to go to the bathroom, but otherwise they never left the small room with the woodstove. Though it was nearly lunchtime, neither of them had bothered to get dressed yet. And when they were through—when they had flipped through the acetate-covered pages of five photo albums—he asked if there were more.

Outside it had been snowing for well over two hours, and the ground was a down comforter of white.

There are, she answered, but all the pictures in them were taken before the girls were born. They're photos of Terry and me, and the different cats we've had over the years. I'm afraid they'd be pretty boring. She reached over and stroked the back of his neck and his head for a long moment, quite certain that she had not derived pleasure like this from these photos—from anything—in a very long time. She wasn't exactly sure why that was, but she thought it was because she was sharing these memories with a person who'd never met Hillary and Megan before, and so she was almost telling their stories from scratch. She was reciting the anecdotes as if they were fresh and new, and she was sharing them with a person who was not listening just for her sake. Alfred was there beside her, hanging on her every description, because he was interested in her children. He wanted to know who they were, and if she didn't understand completely his reasons, that didn't matter. He wasn't treating her like she was an emotional invalid, and he wasn't doing her a favor.

She took back her hand and he looked at her and started to smile.

What's funny? she asked.

Your hair, he said.

My hair?

It's been a mess ever since you took out your headband. It looks like it did in that picture Terry took when you just woke up. The time the girls brought you breakfast in bed. Mother's Day, right?

And that's funny? My hair amuses you?

No, but you were just rubbing and rubbing my head, and I bet my hair looks the same as before you started. Neat and tidy. Same as when I wake up in the morning. See, my hair always looks fine. It looks fine when I go to bed at night, and it looks fine when I wake up in the morning. I never looked at it that way before. But yours? Yours is—

A rat's nest, I know, she said, trying her best to keep a straight face.

Just not neat.

And you like that.

I just think it's funny.

You do, do you? she asked in mock outrage, and then she placed both her hands on his head and—despite his squeals that she was tickling him and she had to stop—used her fingers like scalp massagers and did her very best to mess up his hair.

AFTER LUNCH ALFRED wanted to visit the horse, and Laura went with him. She tried to convince herself that she wasn't joining him because she wanted reassurance that the animal wasn't some wild beast with froth at the mouth, but as they tromped through the snow, she knew that was among the reasons she was going. Though the lump on his head had gone down a bit and his wrist was feeling a little better, she remembered well the image of the boy with the ice pack on his head. Nevertheless, she knew that Alfred had no plans to ride today, despite his desire to try out his new boots: There were already nine or ten inches of snow on the ground and the storm was showing no signs of slowing. Laura had heard on the weather that the storm would drop perhaps half a foot on their corner of the state at the most, but it was clear now that the earlier prediction was considerably wide of the mark. The moment she opened their front door, she could see that the air was thick with flakes the size and shape of small sprigs of parsley.

Briefly she thought of Terry, and she experienced a sharp pang of worry when she imagined him out in the storm. There would be cars in ditches by now, and cars colliding with trees and telephone poles and other vehicles. There would be fender benders and serious accidents, and it was likely there were already people who'd been rushed to area hospitals. And Terry, no doubt, already had been by the side of motorists whose cars were at best lodged in drifts and at worst had become the sort of twisted wrecks— shattered windshields, flattened roofs—that gave her the shivers when she saw them at body shops or on the backs of flatbed trailers.

Sometimes when she expressed her concerns to him he would point out that while snow certainly sent a great many cars off the road, it didn't always lead to the bloodiest crashes. Speed did, and even those idiots slowed a bit in a snowstorm. He would also remind her that he was about as good as it got when it came to driving in snow, if only, he said, from years of practice.

The horse nickered when she saw Alfred, and leaned over the front of the stall. She watched the boy feed the animal the baby carrots he'd begun buying weekly for Mesa with his own money, sometimes stroking her nose when she was done chewing. Soon he opened the stall door and led the horse out, and she was impressed by the way he effortlessly slipped what he called the noseband over the great creature's muzzle and was capable of buckling the halter so close to one of the animal's eyes. The horse seemed far more interested in her, she decided, than in the leather straps Alfred was placing around her head, or in the fact that she was tied now to a post in the center of the barn.

Here, he said, and he took her hand, still in its mitten, and placed it against the small indentation between Mesa's shoulder and neck, and told her what he knew about the prophet's thumb.

She noticed for the first time the wide ribbons of white that looked almost like stockings between the horse's rear hooves and hocks, and the way her head sometimes seemed to move in slow motion. The mare seemed gentle and inquisitive, but she also seemed huge: bigger and healthier than the horses she occasionally saw, since most of those animals were neglected and starving and abused. A horse in their county had to be in a pretty sorry state before it came to the attention of the animal shelter.

They'd been there a short while when both Paul and Emily joined them. The wind was not loud—there was really very little wind at all—but the snow had muffled the sound of the older couple's footsteps as they trudged from the house to the barn, and Laura jumped when she saw them suddenly beside her. Alfred had already shoveled out the stall and was bent over using a metal pick to remove manure from Mesa's hooves when they arrived. She had noticed that her body tensed whenever he stood or walked or crouched anywhere near the animal's hind legs: She worried that the horse was going to kick back and crush the boy's skull or, if he was lucky, merely smash in his jaw.

Emily was wearing a long parka with a cotton scarf over her ears and what might have been the ugliest cowboy hat Laura had ever seen on her head. The straw was dyed green and the pink band along it was, essentially, an ad for a restaurant in Texas that specialized in something appalling called the ladies' choice thirty-two-ounce steak.

We didn't mean to scare you, Emily said.

You didn't. Your hat did.

It's from Amarillo, Emily said, laughing. They do like their beef there.

Apparently.

Paul strolled over to Alfred, looked briefly at the hoof he was working on, and complimented the child on his work.

Merry day after Christmas, my friend. I'm sorry we won't be riding today.

Alfred shrugged, not unhappily, let the hoof fall back to the ground, and patted the side of the big animal.

Did you call to see about lessons yet? Emily asked her.

I made a few calls. Most places were closed today, but I did find a couple that still picked up the phone. It sounds like the nearest place with an indoor ring will be up in Burlington. Are you still interested? she asked Paul.

Of course he is, Emily answered for him. He'll be happy to drive the two of them there and back for as long as the lessons last. Right, Paul?

Absolutely. There's nothing I want more than to have some nineteen-year-old kid teach me exactly what I already know.

When she saw that Alfred was returning the hoof pick to a toolbox on a shelf along the side of the barn, she ventured up to the horse and ran her hand slowly along the long slope of her nose.

She won't bite you, Paul said. She might try and nuzzle you to death, but she doesn't bite. Trust me, Laura, she's a very good-natured horse. You don't have to worry.

I will always worry. I worry about . . . everything.

Well. If you can find a way to keep Mesa off the list, you'll be doing you both a favor.

She took her hand from her mitten and ran her fingers over the winter coat that was growing fast now all along the animal's body. It reminded her of the solid, bristlelike fur on a German shepherd or a husky.

When is Terry due back? Emily asked. It had come up on Christmas Eve that he would be on duty the day after Christmas.

Late afternoon, early evening. His shift ends at four, but with weather like this I'd be surprised if he gets home before six or six-thirty.

Did your parents have a nice visit?

As nice as they ever have here, I guess. They left early—in theory to beat the snow.

And you?

She could tell by the earnestness with which Emily had invested those two words that the woman wasn't asking to be polite, but with Alfred nearby she decided she would answer the question as if it were a mere conversational pleasantry.

Yes, she said. Very nice.

Emily nodded and looked at her carefully, then stamped her feet against the cold. Would you like a cup of tea? she asked, without ever lowering her gaze or taking her eyes off Laura. Inside, maybe, where it's warm?

Okay, she agreed. She didn't know what Emily wanted to discuss, but it was evident that she didn't want Paul or Alfred around, and so for the second time in three days she joined Emily in the kitchen that looked out upon the barn.

SHE SIPPED TEA from a mug that proclaimed Gallup, New Mexico, was the Pride of the Land of Turquoise Jewelry, and talked about the photographs she had shared that morning with Alfred—and, what was really the point of her story, how much she had enjoyed just being with the boy. It was warm in the kitchen, as warm as it had been in her own den earlier that day, and she found she was, once again, happy to relive her memories of her children.

How are he and Terry getting along?

The question felt sudden to her, but she told herself it had come to Emily because she herself had brought up Terry so often in her recollections. Terry taking the girls out for Halloween, each child a witch. Terry planting annuals in the garden while the girls stood beside him, supervising. A photo of Terry and her and the children—both girls in bonnets—was in the living room barely twenty feet away, a picture Paul had taken one Easter when the twins were in kindergarten.

I think fine.

Emily drizzled honey with a wand into her own tea, and seemed to be scrutinizing the translucent stream as she spoke. He struck me as a bit out of sorts on Christmas Eve. Maybe it was just me. But he seemed tired, and he almost never seems tired. Is he?

Tired? Oh, he may be. It's not easy to be a parent when you've lost the rhythm.

Alfred is pretty self-sufficient. He might be the most low-maintenance child I've ever seen.

She glanced out the window at the barn, but she couldn't see either the man or the boy through the snow. She was wondering why Emily was disagreeing with her, and where this conversation was going. She couldn't help but think of Terry's admission that he had had a drink with some woman in a bar up in Newport in November, and she had to reassure herself that there couldn't possibly be a connection.

He is now, she said, referring to Alfred. But September and October were difficult. You know that. There was some adjustment. I told you about the time he just up and left for Burlington one Saturday morning. Terry and I were frantic. And then there was that day when he disappeared at the orchard. One afternoon we went to an apple orchard on the lake out in Addison, and Alfred just vanished on us. One minute we were walking back to our car and he was right behind us, and the next he was gone. He just hadn't felt like leaving yet, so he didn't. Went back to the lake to throw apples. You can imagine how much that little escapade endeared him to Terry.

So that's all it is, then? Terry's tired?

She tried to make light of Emily's questions, but it was impossible not to wonder what Emily knew that she didn't—and whether, perhaps, there was more to Terry's indiscretion than a beer after all, and everyone in the town but her knew. God, this really is about Terry, isn't it? she said. I thought for sure you wanted to tell me something about Alfred. Maybe something had happened when he was with Paul.

I think Alfred is doing just fine.

You're not trying to keep something from me?

You mean like a tumble?

She nodded. Or acting up, maybe.

Nope. No more tumbles. No acting up.

And he hasn't said something?

About?

I don't know. About his past, maybe.

If he has, Paul hasn't told me. Really, Laura, I think the child is doing very, very well.

Me, too. He's spending Monday with Louise—the girl can't be more than twenty-five or twenty-six years old, but she's been his caseworker most of the fall—and I think she's going to be thrilled with his progress.

Good.

Don't you?

Yes, but I don't think you should worry about pleasing some twenty-five- or twenty-six-year-old social worker.

I want her to know Alfred's happy.

I think he is. I think you are.

She waited for Emily to add, *I think Terry is,* but Emily brought her mug to her lips and it became clear that this—*this*—was the reason she had brought her inside her house. It wasn't meant as a warning or—as Laura might have viewed it had she been feeling more despairing—an indictment. It was merely an observation. She considered adding that final sentence herself, because Terry certainly had seemed happy through most of November. Yes, he had been preoccupied over the last couple of weeks, but he was entitled. After all the two of them had endured, wasn't he allowed to be a bit moody?

Would you like more tea? Emily asked after a moment.

No, thanks. I think I'll go see how Alfred's doing.

I hope I didn't offend you, Laura. I'm so sorry if I did.

I'm not offended. You're concerned about my husband. I—

Abruptly she cut herself off, unwilling to finish the sentence. If she had, she realized, she would have said, *I am, too,* and she told herself once again that she had no reason to be. She reminded herself that he had every right— every right in the world—to be a bit temperamental, and the worst thing she could do was not grant him that prerogative.

"We stayed at the fort with the moacs and the brunettes—the buffalo soldiers—and I wouldn't speak at first, except to my children. I wouldn't even talk to the scouts who could speak my language. What would you expect? These people had fired the bullets that drove my husband into the river where he died."

VERONICA ROWE (FORMERLY POPPING TREES),
WPA INTERVIEW,
MARCH 1938

Phoebe

By Sunday afternoon the snow had stopped and the roads were cleared, and she went to the discount department store in Saint Johnsbury to look at baby clothing and cribs. She was playing, really, because it was still so very early, but she told herself the coming year was all about education and preparation, and it couldn't hurt to begin to familiarize herself with the latch mechanisms on cribs (learning, of course, which would be the easiest to operate with one hand), and to start thinking about the sorts of mobiles she would hang in the nursery (though where that nursery would be and what it would look like were still unknown and almost unimaginable). When an older woman in one of the store's blue smocks asked her if she needed any assistance, she grew slightly uncomfortable because she realized she was wearing neither a wedding band nor an engagement ring, but she didn't need any help and the salesperson didn't stay long.

When she left the store it was barely two o'clock, and the low winter sun was beginning to break through the clouds. There were even small patches of blue starting to appear in the west.

She knew that Terry's mother lived in this town, and she remembered that he'd mentioned she lived near the courthouse and the Fairbanks Museum. Church Street, she thought he had said. She pulled the map from the glove compartment of her tired little Corolla and found the street easily. If she could be sure that all the sidewalks had been shoveled by now, she would have walked there, but the city must have gotten sixteen or seventeen inches of snow altogether, and so she decided she'd be better off driving. She had no real plan—she didn't even know what color the house was—but this was the street on which the father of her child had grown up. The street the baby's grandmother lived on even now. Driving slowly down the road would be a bit like looking at cribs: innocuous fun that was also, in some way, educational. She'd learn a bit more about the background of the child inside her. Its roots, so to speak. She considered whether her behavior might also be viewed as a distant cousin of stalking, but she knew she was pretty harmless. In reality, she decided, she was just killing time on a Sunday afternoon.

She drove carefully around the trailer-sized drifts of snow in the parking lot and started up the hill toward the mannered section of the city. Since Terry had grown up near the courthouse and the museum, he'd probably lived in one of those stately Victorian behemoths. Some were more run-down than others, and some were downright ramshackle, but once they had all been very elegant.

Church Street looked a bit like a Christmas card from the 1940s, because everyone had pulled their cars into their driveways, garages, and little carriage barns so the plows could get through. The maples and hemlocks that lined the residential street were heavy with snow, further reinforcing in her mind the idea that the road was a place out of time. She noted that the two- and three-story houses sat close to the road and didn't have a whole lot of land, but some had wrought-iron fences and each seemed a bit like a private enclave. She saw that a few of the properties still carried themselves with the grandeur of their early days.

It was clear to her instantly which houses were most likely to have children, because those were the ones that already had snowmen and snow forts in the front or the side yards, and sleds, toboggans, or cross-country skis lined up along the porch.

She slowed when she heard children laughing, and she rolled down her window to listen. There, at the end of the street, a snowball fight was in progress, and there must have been eight or nine children involved, none older than eleven or twelve. In their parkas and hoods it was hard to tell which were the boys and which were the girls, but she had brothers and she guessed by the way the combatants were hurling the snow that most of the group was male.

She paused, her motor idling, the only car on the road. She envisioned Terry throwing snowballs on this street. Russell, too. Maybe in the very section where the small war was occurring right now. She imagined Russell surrounding a small rock of ice with snow, and then claiming innocence when he gave someone a black eye or bruised cheek. She imagined Terry trying to whip the lad into shape, and then just giving up.

There was one house in particular that showed no signs of small children and looked slightly weary: It was gray but the paint was peeling, and the clapboards along the porches were in desperate need of repair. She decided this was probably the home of a widow. Perhaps even Terry's mom. She parked her car against the sidewalk before it, pulling up smack against the snow that had been pushed off the road, and watched it for a long moment. She looked at the windows, trying to guess which was Terry's bedroom—assuming, of course, this was even the correct home—and she was surprised when a vision crept into her head: She was sitting on a sofa inside that house with her little baby in her lap, and placing the infant's minuscule fingers into its grandmother's hand. She wondered if she was concocting this fantasy—if she was on this street, in fact—because her own family had been so monumentally unsupportive on Christmas Day.

The door of the house opened and an older woman with curly sand-colored hair—dyed, she decided—ventured out onto the porch. She stood in her cardigan sweater, her arms wrapped around her chest, and seemed to be studying the car to see if she recognized it or knew the driver.

Her instinct was to slam the car into drive and pull away fast, but she didn't want to frighten the woman. Maybe this really was Terry's mom, maybe not. Either way, she didn't want to scare her. And so she left the motor running and climbed from the seat and called out, I'm looking for the best way back to the interstate. I think I've gotten a little lost.

The woman nodded and smiled, and started down the walk to the car.

WHEN SHE TOLD her ob-gyn she was pregnant, the woman made sure that Phoebe knew what to eat and how to take care of herself, but she said that she didn't really need to come in for an examination until she was a little further along. They scheduled an appointment for the middle of February, when she would be just about through the first trimester.

Though she figured she knew the basics—no more long-necks at the bar, plenty of spinach, lots of rest—she concluded that it couldn't hurt to do a little more research, and so on Monday afternoon after work she drove directly from the general store to a bookshop in Newport. There she picked out a pair of books that offered both practical advice and time lines that chronicled how the baby inside her would grow and her body would change.

Her father was still barely speaking to her, and so at dinner that night she told him she was seriously considering having the baby at home. In her bedroom. She wasn't, but she wanted to get a rise out of him, and she did. He picked up his plate with the beef stew she had made the day before after returning from Saint Johnsbury, and he went into the living room to eat his dinner in front of the television news.

In truth she might have had her baby at home if she had a husband and her very own house. But she had neither, and so in her mind a home birth wasn't an option.

When she was alone she reached into the shopping bag, opened one of her two books on the kitchen table, and started to read as she ate.

THE NEXT MORNING she threw up for the first time. Somehow she got to the general store and managed to open its doors and sell the first customers their coffee and cigarettes, but as soon as Frank arrived—about a quarter to eight that day—she disappeared into the small bathroom in the back of the shop. When she emerged she told Frank she wasn't feeling well and had to go home, and even in the dim light of the store in the dead of winter she must have looked green, because Frank asked her if she'd gotten a flu shot that autumn.

She tried to keep down the saltines she had placed in the front seat of her car for exactly this sort of emergency, but she hadn't a prayer and she threw up again on the road halfway back to her father's house. She kicked snow—brown now from car exhaust and the sand the plows sprinkled—onto the vomit before climbing back behind the driver's seat and soldiering on.

Mid-morning she felt a little better. A little less nauseous. But even in her bed with the door closed she could feel her father's contempt. He certainly didn't want her to get an abortion, but he couldn't understand how in the world she could have gotten herself into this situation in the first place.

On the nightstand by her bed was another letter from her college friend Shauna, her old roommate who had moved to Santa Fe. She reread the letter to take her mind off her father, and lost herself in her friend's pictures of the desert, Anasazi ruins, and her young son creating a soap bubble the size of a beanbag chair at the local children's museum.

She put the photos back in the envelope and found herself wishing that she'd never told Terry she was pregnant, because then she would not have seen him again. Each time they'd been together, she'd found herself more attracted to him—and this, she knew, was not a good thing. Not a good thing at all. What was it they'd said to each other on Christmas Eve, right after they discovered that they both liked to hike? She'd asked, half-kidding, Are we getting to know each other? and he'd answered, Yes, I think we are, and the realization had made them both sit quite still for a long quiet moment.

She hoped wherever he was that morning he was happy and well. She knew she shouldn't see him again, but that didn't stop her from thinking about him.

"Rule number five: They are to look white soldiers and white civilians in the eyes when they speak to them. They are to stand tall."

———

SERGEANT GEORGE ROWE,
TENTH REGIMENT, UNITED STATES CAVALRY,
LETTER TO HIS BROTHER IN PHILADELPHIA,
NOVEMBER 18, 1873

———

Alfred

He sat on the bed before breakfast with his headset over his ears and a new CD in the small player on the mattress beside him. He thumbed slowly through the pages of one of Terry and Laura's photo albums, and thought how different the bed felt to him now that he knew it had been Megan's and this room had once belonged to her. Hillary, Laura had said, had slept in the other room—the room that he heard referred to now as the guest room. They'd chosen this room for him, she'd added, because it was sunnier.

It was the Monday after Christmas and he hadn't heard from Schuyler Jackman or Joe Langford since school closed for the Christmas holiday. He'd spent part of Thursday with Tim and he'd thought there was a chance he might have heard from him at some point over the weekend, but Tim hadn't called, either. He knew Tim was in town—he was pretty sure Schuyler and Joe were around, too, for that matter—and he didn't believe his schoolmate had any cousins visiting who might be monopolizing his time.

In truth, of course, he hadn't taken the initiative and phoned any of the children he knew from his class, either. Once he'd come close to calling Tim, but it was a Sunday and Tim's father might answer, and the two times he'd run into the man, he came away feeling bad about himself. The man worked for a bank up in Burlington, and the first time they'd met he was working on some kind of paperwork at the kitchen table, and Mr. Acker—tall, wiry, but, like Terry, in pretty good shape for a grown-up—quickly turned the documents over when he wandered into the room to get a drink of water. The other time, while waiting for Laura to pick him up to bring him home, Alfred noticed that Mr. Acker's hunting rifle was gone from the cabinet in the front hall where it was usually kept. Deer season hadn't begun yet, and, only mildly curious at best, he asked Tim where the gun was. The other boy grew uncomfortable and said something about his dad moving it whenever kids came over to play. He could tell instantly that Tim was lying: The boy's father only removed the weapon when one certain kid came over to play, and that child was clearly the foster kid living up at the Sheldons. The black foster kid.

He wanted to tell Tim to tell his father that he shouldn't waste his time hiding his gun. If he wanted, he had an armory at his disposal: Terry was a state trooper, remember? But he'd kept his mouth shut, because it didn't make sense at the time to anger the closest thing he had to a friend in this town.

He told himself it was possible that Tim and the other boys had all gone snowboarding at one of the ski resorts today, and he'd hear from them tomorrow or the next day. If that was the case, it made sense that no one had called, because he didn't have a snowboard and had never even been to a ski mountain. Besides, he was supposed to stick around this afternoon because Louise was going to drop by sometime around lunch. He hadn't seen her since early November, and so she'd offered to take him into Durham or Middlebury for pizza. Maybe they'd even go to a movie. He'd said that was fine, though he didn't really care. He knew that basically she just wanted some time alone with him so she could see how he was doing and what he thought of Terry and Laura. When she got to Cornish, he figured he'd see if she'd prefer doing what he really wanted, which was simply to have a grilled cheese and a cup of canned tomato soup with Laura, and then the two of them would go see the horse. They could have all the privacy they wanted in the Heberts' barn while he groomed Mesa, and she could ask him all the questions she liked.

He placed the photo album on the foot of his bed, clipped his CD player to his belt, and went to the closet to get his very own pictures. He'd almost shared them with Laura the day after Christmas, but decided he wasn't quite ready yet. He wasn't sure whether he should remind her that he'd once been friends with Tien, because then she'd remember the time he'd gotten so lonely and bored that he decided to thumb his way up to Burlington. That was stupid, and he thought of Sergeant Rowe's rules for his men.

Rule number two: Think. Use your head. Moreover, he knew that Laura despised Digger, and didn't understand at all the way the older boy had looked out for him, or that he'd been able to trust Digger the way he could no adult. He imagined himself showing the pictures to Laura someday soon, however, and telling her all about the different kids—and, yes, grown-ups— he'd met and lived with in his life.

His photo album was hidden in the back of his closet, with the food he had stored through the autumn and early winter, underneath a small pile of bedding and a quilt that Laura kept there. He hadn't checked his cache in over two weeks, and he figured he should familiarize himself with what he had—just in case. He didn't believe there were any plans to move him someplace else soon, but the fact that Louise was coming for one of her visits was a disturbing reminder of the itinerant nature of his life.

And so he lined up the food in rows on the floor between the closet and the bed, squatted before it like a baseball catcher, and surveyed what was there. It took up as much space as a throw rug, and he was pleased with what he saw. He actually had more than he could ever get out of the house when the time came, so he began to prioritize what he would take. The small bags of popcorn, the packages of Twinkies, and the canned peaches were defi- nitely keepers. The cereal, on the other hand, would stay here because he didn't really like cereal dry and you could never be sure that the next house would have whole milk or even two percent. If you went to a place where the grown-ups were older, you had to expect skim, and he had never enjoyed that watery, tasteless, almost translucent blue milk.

Suddenly he felt a hand on his shoulder and he jumped forward, falling to his knees on the wrapped sponge cakes and corn chips. He turned and saw Terry in his uniform—complete with his winter parka, campaign hat, and gloves—towering above him. He realized he hadn't heard the door open because he was listening to his music.

He reached up to take off his earphones, and as he did Terry bent over and ripped the cord from his hands—detaching it from the CD player on his belt—and flung the headset across the room. It bounced against the bureau with his riding helmet, and fell onto the floor beside the wastebasket.

You want to tell me what you're doing with all this? he asked, his voice angrier than Alfred had heard it since well before Halloween—since, he guessed, the day he'd wandered off at the orchard.

He looked at the food and the few utensils he'd taken—a can opener, a spoon, a pretty dull knife—and wasn't sure what he could say that might make this explicable or calm the man down. He tried to think, wondering what Terry would say if he explained that he always had a small stash—lots of kids did—just in case they moved you on without a whole lot of notice, and he was about to start talking when Terry spoke first.

You were planning on leaving, weren't you? You were planning to up and go. That's it, isn't it?

No!

You were going to run away again, weren't you?

Again? I—

Do you have any idea how lucky you are? Do you have any idea how much Laura cares about you, or how hurt she'd be if you ran away?

I wasn't going to run away. I just—

You just took enough food to keep your stomach from growling for four or five days. Empty your pockets.

What?

He quietly pushed the bedroom door shut so Laura couldn't hear them, and then sat on the bed and faced him.

I told you to empty your pockets, Terry said.

There's nothing in my pockets!

Good, then you have nothing to hide.

He considered standing perfectly still, wondering if Terry was mad enough to hit him. He'd never paddled him before, but there was always a first time.

I can't wait all morning, I have to get to work. You can either turn your pockets inside out or I can do it for you.

He reached into his blue jeans and pulled out the white cotton pockets so Terry could see they were empty. Not even a used tissue or a piece of wrapped chewing gum.

Thank you. Now turn around.

He did, and then he felt Terry's hands on his bottom and for a brief moment he feared the man was going to try and touch him there—he knew other kids, boys as well as girls, who regularly had to give it up for the men in their homes—but then he understood Terry was just making sure he had nothing in his back pockets, either.

Now, I'm not about to tear apart your bedding because I don't have the time, and I don't want Laura to know about this. You understand? She would be devastated, and that woman does not need another disappointment. Not now, not ever. So I want you to look me in the eye and tell me: Have you taken any money?

No, sir.

Sir? Since when do you call me sir?

He stood there and tried to figure out what he should say. After all, he'd only called him sir because he was trying to be respectful, he was trying to settle the man down.

I call people *sir,* Terry said. I do that.

He swallowed and blinked, because he had begun to fear he might cry. And he wouldn't do that, not now, that was for sure. The worst thing was that he understood his eyes weren't close to welling with tears because he was scared of Terry, or because the grown-up had misunderstood completely why he'd taken a little food. Rather, he realized with a pang that almost made him shudder, this might mean he wouldn't get to stay here much longer. And unlike most places where he'd lived, here was a spot where—despite the quiet or his lack of friends or what people like Tim's dad may have thought of him— he wouldn't mind staying. He didn't want to leave Laura or Paul or the horse.

Still, he wouldn't cry, he wouldn't do it. He straightened his back and stood as tall as he could and looked Terry squarely in the eye.

When a moment had passed and he hadn't opened his mouth—Really, what was he supposed to say in response to Terry's apparent outburst over the fact that he'd called him *sir?* What *could* he say?—Terry shook his head. You think you are one tough hombre, he said, and you can hide behind those tight lips of yours. Well, I promise you, young man, I am tougher. Now, I am going to trust that you are telling the truth and you haven't taken one penny from Laura and me. Okay?

Okay.

I am not going to search this place. But when I come home from work, I will expect that every single crumb of food is back in the kitchen, and that Laura is not one tiny bit the wiser. You got that?

Yes.

Spoons and knives, too, please.

Okay.

And tonight, maybe, you and I will have a little talk. I honestly don't know what it is that you think you want, but I'm telling you: You have found Shangri-la here. Right here. It doesn't get any better than this, let me assure you, but it does get a lot worse. You know that, son, I know you do.

Yes.

The man pushed himself off the bed and picked the headset up off the floor. He handed it to him on his way to the bedroom door and then paused with his fingers on the knob. Now go on downstairs and eat your breakfast with Laura, he said. And do me one favor: Don't bring that headset with you, okay? It's just not polite.

He then pounded quickly down the steps to the first floor, told Laura that he was off—his voice surprisingly normal, Alfred thought from the top of the stairs—and closed the front door behind him.

"I didn't want to go. You know that expression, the devil you know? And so I finally started to talk, and I told them I was only at the river to wash clothes. I guess that's why they made me a laundress."

VERONICA ROWE (FORMERLY POPPING TREES),
WPA INTERVIEW,
MARCH 1938

The Heberts

She watched Paul place the black phone back in the cradle and then sit down in the chair in their library on his side of their massive partners desk. She stood before him with her arms crossed because she'd been listening—standing still in the frame of the doorway, watching him pace in the room as he spoke—and she had the sense from the half of the conversation she could hear that something had happened that involved the boy.

So? she asked finally, when Paul didn't immediately tell her what the phone call had been about.

Without looking at her he said, So, I think Terry's been working too hard.

He did seem preoccupied on Christmas Eve.

He didn't seem preoccupied. He seemed angry. Edgy. Ticked off at the world.

I was being kind. That was Terry just now?

He nodded, his hands clasped behind his neck. He was wearing the heavy Irish fisherman's sweater their daughter had given him for Christmas—a bulky gray cardigan—and he looked surprisingly elegant to her: the college professor once more. She had assumed he would be wearing the sweatshirt he'd bought at a seaside lobster shack that summer when they were in Maine. It had a cartoon on the front of a lobster in a leotard in the midst of a somersault, and was captioned with the words *Lobster Roll*. She'd seen him take it out of his armoire earlier that morning when she was lying in bed.

It was.

It sounded like he was calling about the boy. Has something happened?

On their desk were frames with pictures of their children and grand-children. He unfolded his arms and turned one so that it was at a better angle for him to see it, and then picked it up and held it in his hand. It was a photograph of their daughter on the day she graduated from college.

I don't know. But he thinks the boy might be planning to run away. Maybe use Mesa.

Well, that would make him harder to find. Little black kid on a big horse in Vermont? No one would ever notice that.

Terry thought the boy might believe he could cover more ground if he stole the horse. Go further.

Why does he think Alfred wants to leave in the first place? Did the boy say something? Did they have a fight?

He caught the boy getting ready to pack.

Getting ready to pack: What does that mean?

He said Alfred had been stealing things from them, and Terry walked in on him when he had the stuff laid out on his carpet.

What kind of stuff? Clothing? Money? Food?

I don't know. I guess.

That's awful. Laura must be crushed.

She doesn't know. And Terry doesn't want her to find out.

She probably should know . . .

Probably. But it's not our place to tell her. The main thing is—the reason he called—Terry doesn't want me to leave the boy alone with the horse. He doesn't want Alfred grooming her, for instance, when I'm not around.

Because he thinks they might take off . . .

Right.

That's too bad.

He returned the picture of their daughter to the desk, and she watched him rock back in his chair and stretch his legs before him. You know, he said, it would be if I took the idea seriously. But I don't. Really, I don't.

You don't think the boy's going anywhere.

Nope. Something else may be going on, but I don't think Alfred has any plans to run away. After lunch he's bringing some social worker over to see the horse, and I have absolutely no intention of baby-sitting the two of them.

I trust him. I'm going to head up to Burlington and do some errands just like I'd planned.

You're not concerned.

If I'm concerned about anyone, I'm concerned about Terry.

Me, too.

But, no, I'm not worried about Alfred, he said, and then shrugged. I don't know, maybe I'll talk to him—Alfred. See if there's something he wants to bring up. But I doubt he will. There's no quicker way to make that lad grow quiet than to bring up Terry or Laura.

Behind her in the living room a log in the woodstove collapsed, and she looked around at the sound to make sure the fire was still under control. It was.

I assume he was calling from work.

He was. Abruptly he turned toward her, swiveling his whole body at the waist and sitting forward. You read about these foster kids—teenagers, really—who run away from their foster homes and get themselves into real trouble. You see their pictures in the newspaper, their faces on the TV news. They wind up as prostitutes in New York or Montreal. They wind up in jail for selling drugs. I imagine at one time that could have been Alfred in a couple more years, but we both know it won't be now. At least it won't be if Terry and Laura don't screw this up. The kid is too . . .

She stood there quietly, giving him a moment to frame his thought.

He's too smart and he's too responsible. Here's a ten-year-old kid who hasn't once in the last month—not one time—tried to get out of his chores with the horse or even shown up late. How many other children could you say that about?

She nodded. She took pride in her own family, but when she thought back on the reality of the work their horses had demanded when Nick and Catherine and Andy were young, she knew that often it had taken a sizable effort on her part to get even one of them out to the barn once a day.

If something's going on over there, he said, motioning with his head and his shoulders toward the Sheldons' house, I think it has a whole lot more to do with Terry than with Alfred. Really. I do.

"In that they are children, even the one called Popping Trees, they pose no threat either to the company's safety or to its morale. Perhaps I would think differently if the two smaller ones were boys who might grow into warriors, but the fact is they, too, are girls. It seems to me that if Colonel Grierson can bake Army bread for the Indians, we can perform this small act of kindness."

CAPTAIN ANDREW HITCHENS,
TENTH REGIMENT, UNITED STATES CAVALRY,
REPORT TO THE POST ADJUTANT,
JUNE 19, 1876

Alfred

He saw that Louise was careful to keep her distance from the horse, especially after he'd suggested that she not stand behind the animal. He wondered if he had grown a bit in the seven weeks since he last saw her, because this woman—merely short in early November—now seemed tiny to him. Not slight, but squat. She wasn't more than a couple of inches taller than he was, and he had never had the sense that he was tall for his age. She was a little plump and so her face was round and full, and this—along with her height—reinforced the idea in his mind that she was almost too young to have the job of a grown-up.

Still, he respected her. She was smart and nice, and clearly very hip. Her hair was brown, but she did something to it to give it a reddish tint, and she even let it get a little spiky at the front. She claimed to listen to the same music that he did, and she dressed like one of the teenagers who hung out on the streets back in Burlington. A lot of leather and fake leather, and nice lines of silver in both ears.

And you can get up there all by yourself? she was asking, motioning at the top of Mesa's back.

Yup. Sometimes Paul helps and sometimes I use a block. But when I have to or want to, I can. The hardest part is getting the saddle on her and tightening the girth.

Why is that?

With the hand in which he was holding the curry comb, he pointed at the saddle on the wall. Lift it, he said.

She did, and he could see that she was surprised by how heavy it was. She dropped it back on the two slender rods that extended from the wall like the front of a forklift. Okay, I'm impressed, she said.

He nodded and considered asking her if she wanted to try brushing Mesa with him, but it was clear she was nervous around the horse and he thought she might make the animal skittish. Maybe in a little while, he decided. He wished he could take the mare out for a short ride so she could see how well he handled her, but he wasn't allowed to ride without Paul.

Laura said you were going to start taking lessons. When's that?

January, I guess. They'll be after school.

Are you looking forward to them?

He shrugged. I think I ride okay. But I guess a few lessons wouldn't hurt.

You can always get better.

Maybe.

Laura showed me your report card. Nice. I mean there's still plenty of room for improvement, but I saw a lot of B's on there. Keep it up. Don't let the lessons keep you from your homework.

They won't.

Seriously, why do you think your grades improved? Is it the school? Your teacher? Or are you just working more?

It isn't my teacher, that's for sure.

No?

No.

Why's that?

Maybe I'm working more, he said, not exactly answering Louise's question. I don't know. It's not like there's a lot to do out here. Until Paul got the horse, most days I just went straight from the bus to Terry and Laura's house.

Home.

He looked at her, understanding that the word, in her mind, was both a clarification and a desire. She had wished he'd called that house home. Without giving it serious thought, he figured he could oblige. Home, he said, repeating the word for her.

It seemed to work: She smiled. Do you like your new friends? Laura tells me you've made some.

I guess. But the kids here have known each other forever. They've been hanging around together since they were, like, two.

Is that why you'd just go straight home after school?

Mostly.

You still think you stand out like a sore thumb?

He scooted under the line that linked the horse to the post, returned the comb to the toolbox, and got out one of the dish towels that Paul had him use to polish the animal. Because it was cold outside he hadn't moistened the towel the way he normally did, but he did scrunch it into a ball as if he had, and then he started wiping it gently along Mesa's sides.

Yup. This was something they'd discussed when she came by in November, and they'd gone into Durham for doughnuts and hot apple cider.

You're a smart kid—and handsome. That's a rare combination. Trust me, I know.

I know what I am.

I understand. But sometimes I think you think about being different more than other people do.

Yeah, right.

The horse like that? she asked, watching him as he rubbed her down.

Yup.

Can I try?

Briefly he considered the request, still concerned that her nervousness around the animal might get her in trouble, but in the end he handed her the dish towel. She was, after all, an adult. Just don't be jumpy around her, he said. She's big, but she's a kitten. She won't hurt you.

Okay, she said as she mimicked his motions. I hear you're celebrating Kwanzaa this year.

Just one more way I can be different.

Laura said you're having a good time.

Sure I am. But I probably like Christmas more.

Of course you do. You get presents.

I've gotten some stuff for Kwanzaa. I get a present a day from Laura.

Laura and Terry, you mean?

Uh-huh.

Good stuff?

Good enough. So far I've gotten a book that explains what Kwanzaa is, and a shirt with a lot of black and red in it. Those are the Kwanzaa colors. It's only been two days. I'll get something else at dinner tonight.

Doesn't sound shabby to me.

No. It's just a weird holiday.

Why is that?

Well, he said, it doesn't make sense for me. Yeah, I'm black, but that's about all I have in common with the values Laura and that book talk about. I've never been to Africa, and I probably never will get there.

Maybe you will. And even I know there's more to Kwanzaa than that.

Right: Family. Community. Getting all the people together. What's that got to do with me? What people do I have? What family? He realized he was talking too much and quickly quieted down.

Don't you view Laura and Terry as family?

I don't know.

When Louise didn't say anything for a few moments, he realized that inadvertently he had brought them to the *serious* part of her visit. There was always a serious part to these get-togethers, and over the years he'd come to recognize when the caseworker—Louise now, and Cliff and Sarah before her—wanted to shift gears and discuss what Cliff had always called *the heavy stuff*. What he thought of his current home, his foster parents. Whether he was listening to their words, and they, in turn, were doing right by him. Whether he was happy.

It was always a pretty complex dance because you didn't want to say something that might somehow get back to your foster parents and cause them to make things even harder, or get you moved someplace really awful. And, he knew, there was always someplace worse than where you were. It was inevitable. He knew what some foster parents were like, and what they would do. And he certainly hadn't been happy inside the group home.

But sometimes it was also just time to move on, and either you or your foster parents or the caseworker figured it out.

Of course, it wasn't as if he himself had any real control. Not really. He could watch his words and try to act as if he had some say in what was going to happen, but in reality he didn't. He knew that. The grown-ups would do whatever they wanted, anyway; when they no longer had any need for you, or they just got tired out, they moved you on. It didn't matter whether you liked a place. All that mattered was whether they liked you or they needed the money they got from the state.

Here was a perfect example. He wanted to stay in Cornish, but it was pretty obvious that Terry didn't like him and eventually he'd be gone. He'd pissed Terry off too much in the fall, and now the guy had gotten the idea into his head that he was stealing and planned to run away. It probably wouldn't matter that Laura liked him or the Heberts liked him or this big old horse liked him. It didn't matter that he liked all of them.

An odd idea crossed his mind: Maybe he should tell Louise what had happened that morning, and the way Terry had misunderstood what he was doing. Maybe she could fix things. Quickly he pushed the notion aside: Terry had told him he didn't want Laura to know anything about it, so Louise couldn't talk to her. And if she tried to discuss it with Terry directly, the trooper would be furious because he would know that Alfred had snitched. Still . . .

Family is complicated, Louise was saying. These days, there are lots of different kinds. It doesn't have to be Mom and Dad and the two-point-four babies they had. You know that.

I guess.

You like Laura? I like her very much.

I do, too.

Good, good. Because she certainly seems to like you.

When she had finished rubbing Mesa down, the horse turned her long head toward her—her nose almost in the woman's face—and snorted, and he could see Louise flinch. She handed him the dish towel and he draped it over a wooden brace by the toolbox to let it air out. Later he'd fold it and put it away.

She's been through a lot, Louise went on, referring to Laura. You understand that, right?

Yup.

What about Terry?

What about him?

How are you two getting on? she asked, and he watched the lashlike, gray-blue fog of her exhalation rise up toward the loft in the barn and then disappear.

Okay.

He seems like a nice guy. Sometimes state troopers—all cops, actually—give me the creeps. All that paramilitary stuff. The uniform, the strut. The handcuffs and the baton. But he seems pretty down to earth. Is that true?

He decided once and for all that he couldn't tell Louise about Terry—not what Terry thought of him or, likewise, what he thought of the trooper.

He wanted to stay in Cornish at least a little longer, if he could—with Laura and Paul and the horse—and that meant keeping quiet. Keeping his opinions, and what had occurred that morning, to himself. Besides, why should he tell her, anyway? She was just a social worker who understood *family* so well because she probably had one. A real one. She was just another adult who was paid to appear in his life every once in a while.

Alfred?

Yeah, he's a nice guy, he said finally.

You don't sound convinced.

He's busy, he works a lot. We get along fine.

Okay.

Now you think something's going on, but nothing is.

She nodded and pulled the bridle and reins off the broad circle peg on the wall.

Be careful that doesn't get tangled, he said.

These are the reins, I gather?

And that's the martingale.

I've never heard of such a thing.

It's a strap that goes around the horse's neck. It gives a beginner something else to hang on to.

How have you learned all this?

Paul. He's a good teacher. He used to be a teacher.

So I hear, she said as she looped the leather lines back on the wall.

He used to have horses. When he was a kid, and when he had kids of his own.

She smiled and leaned over, resting her gloved hands on the stored saddle. What exactly is the deal with you two?

No deal.

You like him?

Sometimes he cracks me up. You should see him on Mesa. Goes about a mile an hour. Babies crawl faster than he rides that horse.

Well, he is pretty old.

Not that old. I heard him say the other day he's only sixty-five.

So you do like him . . .

I like him fine.

I understand he's paying you to help care for the horse.

Four dollars a day. I've already made almost a hundred dollars!

You've got almost a hundred dollars?

Not anymore, because I spent some on Christmas presents for Laura and Terry, and I even got little gifts for the Heberts: I got Paul some saddle soap and Emily some blueberry jam. But I still have over forty-five dollars, he said, and excited by the size of his savings, he went on without thinking, See, that was the dumbest thing about what Terry said this morning! I don't have to steal any money. I got plenty. I—

Instantly he stopped talking when he realized what he'd just told her. Louise's face was impassive, a mask he couldn't read, but he knew now he would have to tell her everything that had happened that day—everything, in fact, that was probably wrong with his relationship with Terry Sheldon.

———

"At first, it was two Negro brothers named Edmonds who taught me English. They had not been with the soldiers who chased down my husband, and that made it easier. They were from Mississippi, a word that always sounded like the wind in my ear."

———

VERONICA ROWE (FORMERLY POPPING TREES),

WPA INTERVIEW,

MARCH 1938

———

Terry

Monday afternoon he switched on his lights and his siren and pressed hard on the accelerator, savoring the fact that he was on the long straightaway just north of New Haven Junction on 7 and the snow and the ice had been cleared from the road. He would be at sixty-five, seventy miles an hour in an instant, and he glanced briefly down at his speedometer to watch the angular digits climb higher. The snow in the fields on both sides of the two-lane road was still pretty fresh, and the world around him became a white blur: He was going too fast to take note of the few houses and antique stores on this stretch, or the odd motel that dotted the landscape.

He didn't think the accident would be bad, because the dispatcher had said everyone was outside of their vehicles. But half the equation was a tractor-trailer—its cab was nose-down in the snow in a ditch, and the mass of the truck was blocking most of both lanes—so he wouldn't know for sure until he got to the scene. The other half of the equation was a county van that took seniors grocery shopping. Fortunately, the driver had just dropped the group off when he and the truck had their run-in, so he didn't have any passengers, frail or otherwise, in the van with him.

The accident was in Ferrisburgh. Six miles north, and still he'd be there in five minutes—five and a half if some self-absorbed moron didn't pull over in time and he had to slow down.

He came up over a ridge, and in the valley before him he saw the water tower and the opera house that marked Vergennes, once the self-proclaimed smallest city in the country, and Lake Champlain just to the

253

west. Not frozen yet. Maybe never this year, because every cold snap seemed to be followed by a warm spell. The ground sloped steeply below him, and in the distance at the base of the hill he saw a neon blue SUV coming south and a small conga line—a pickup, an Escort, a UPS truck—heading north, and gingerly they all pulled over into the plowed muck on their separate sides of the road. They heard him, they saw him, and the waves were starting to part.

FORTUNATELY, ALL HE would have to do with this mess was conduct a few roadside interviews, fill out some accident report forms—granted they would include both the long form he loathed and a commercial vehicle supplement—and stand in the cold directing traffic. But no one was hurt, and neither driver was even badly shaken up. The van had hit a patch of black ice and careened across the yellow line, dinging the side of the tractor-trailer before skidding off the road forty yards further south. The tractor-trailer, trying to avoid the van, had slid away into the ditch.

And so while the tow truck pulled the van from the snowdrifts and they waited for a heavy-duty wrecker from Bridport to hoist the tractor-trailer back onto the road, he stood on the pavement and helped the cars snake their way through the thin strip of asphalt that remained between the rear of the truck and the piles of snow off to the side. At this stage in his career the work demanded only minimal concentration, and—as usual—his mind wandered. It wandered first to Sunday night, the day after his in-laws had left, and how Laura—sweet, sweet Laura—had tried like hell to draw him out during dinner, and though there was nothing he needed more than to be drawn out, he couldn't do it. He just couldn't bring himself to reach back across that divide—no chasm, this, the divide was really no wider than the kitchen table—and accept her offer. All she wanted to do was listen, all he needed to do was talk. But he couldn't do it. He loved her, he would not forget that, he loved her. But at that moment, he knew, he wanted something—someone—else.

He realized he was thinking about Phoebe more than was healthy or right, and he wished he could go back in time to the evening he went to her store and they wound up at her friend's trailer. No, that wasn't exactly true. If he could go back in time, he decided, he needed to go back further than that: A full two years and two months was more like what was required, so he could stay home from deer camp and prevent his little girls from going anywhere near the bridge on the day of the flood. After all, if he wanted anything back, it was his life then: When he had Hillary and Megan and he wasn't married to someone who had been, for the better part of two years, an emotional wreck. When he himself wasn't crying alone in his cruiser or sobbing like a madman in the shower. When he wasn't picking up young— younger, anyway—things at deer camp.

In a way, he realized, the last thing he wanted was to go back a mere two or three months. Was he any worse off now than he was, say, on Halloween? Arguably, he wasn't. If he didn't want to, he never had to see Phoebe again. That was pretty clear. On the other hand, if he desired such a thing, there was a beautiful woman just waiting for him to leave his wife, a woman who was already carrying his child: his second chance at a family. There inside Phoebe was the baby he could help to raise right, as he had his own daughters, not some kid who was so screwed up by the time he was brought into his and Laura's life that he was incapable of communicating properly with his foster parents but quite willing to steal from them. Unbelievable. He hated to imagine what else the kid might try, especially if he ever had a gun and a horse at his disposal.

He made a mental note to ask Paul what was in that book about the buffalo soldiers he and Emily had given the boy, and that had now grown to interest him so. Certainly it was meant as a harmless gift, but he knew nothing about what the buffalo soldiers actually did, and the last thing the boy needed right now was to have all kinds of renegade ideas put into his head.

He waved for an oncoming pickup to slow down to a crawl, and decided the woman behind the wheel looked a bit like Laura had when they first met. Slightly darker hair, he decided when the truck got close enough for him to see, but she was even wearing the sort of beret that his sister had given her one Christmas soon after they got married, and Laura had worn for a couple of years when the weather was right.

Leaving Laura, of course, was just a dark fantasy: He didn't think he ever would or could do such a thing. He didn't believe he was capable of that kind of cruelty.

But if she left him? Well, that was another story. He knew he wasn't always an easy person to live with, especially right now, and one just never knew.

No, if he could go back in time, it would have to be two-plus years, not merely two months. There was still no doubt in his mind that what he had done with Phoebe was wrong, absolutely wrong. But he decided he no longer regretted it.

HE STOOD BEFORE the pay phone at the general store in the center of Orwell, wavering. He knew he shouldn't touch it. He should just return to his cruiser and resume running the roads. But there was an odd symmetry here, and that alone caused him to remain: It was, after all, the pay phone at another general store—hours and hours to the northeast—that had first brought him to Phoebe. And so he did reach for the receiver, and then like a teenager he hung it up. Then he grabbed it again. He wasn't sure how many times he had done this—three, four, did it matter?—when he finally kept it in his gloved hand and called her. He heard her move with the cordless phone away from the cash register when she heard it was him, and he could tell that she wasn't alone in the store. There was someone else working with her, a man, bantering with the customers as they arrived and paid for their groceries.

For a few minutes they talked about their lives—she told him she had broken the news to her family that she was pregnant, he told her his in-laws had come and gone—and then, unsure how she would respond to his honesty, he told her he wanted to see her.

She was quiet for a moment, before murmuring, That wouldn't be a good idea. He was just about to agree and hang up—perhaps that would be that— but she continued, Of course, I remember you telling me once that none of this was a good idea. Montpelier, again?

That was indeed what he had pictured. But when he envisioned his cruiser parked once more in the parking lot behind the hotel on Main Street, as it had been on Christmas Eve afternoon, he knew instantly he didn't like that image very much. The thing was, a state police cruiser stood out like a palm tree in Vermont. Especially one in a hotel parking lot. He'd gotten away with it before, and he could probably get away with it again. But why test fate? Why go anyplace in Montpelier? The reality was that anyplace he parked outside of his district could become a problem if someone—a storekeeper, a building owner, or (worst of all) another police officer or trooper—asked him why he was there. Or made a phone call to see why a cruiser was parked on the street.

The truth was, if they were going to meet again, they should find a location that was not merely equidistant but appropriate. Logical. One that made sense. He wished it were the middle of March, when he was scheduled to be teaching for two days in Pittsford at the academy. He could spend the night away from home, and maybe . . .

He pulled the thought back. Just because he didn't regret what he'd done didn't mean that he was prepared to do it again.

How about Waterbury? he offered instead. I worry about what people think when they see a cruiser in a new spot.

Waterbury?

Headquarters are there. Someone from the barracks is going to need to visit the quartermaster in the next week or so, anyway, to pick up a couple new uniforms and some campaign hats. They may be ready right now, for all I know. I'll offer to go.

He heard her laugh on the phone. Well, I can't think of a better place for us to have a clandestine little conversation than the headquarters for the Vermont State Police.

We won't talk there.

Oh, we'll only have sex?

I didn't mean that, I—

She giggled. I know what you meant. We'll just meet there and go someplace else. In my car, I suppose?

If you don't mind.

Hell, I don't care. I kind of like the idea of having a state trooper trapped in my car beside me. Will you keep your hat on?

Excuse me?

In a mock whisper, she said, Can't let anyone see I have Smokey Bear in the passenger seat, now can I? Every trucker in the state will get reckless if they know I have you otherwise engaged in my car.

I see. He smiled and suddenly, without warning, gave out a little puff of laughter, a tiny yelp of percolating happiness. Yes, I will take my hat off.

And anything else I request?

We can talk about—

I'm teasing you, Terry. This is not a clothes-optional rendezvous.

I agree.

They decided they'd meet Wednesday and have lunch at one of the restaurants in the town.

You know, I used to work in Waterbury, she said.

I remember.

Aren't you worried we'll run into someone I know?

I guess. Maybe we'll have to head up 100. Find a restaurant in Stowe, instead.

All these logistics for a little lunch, Sergeant Sheldon. You must really want to see me.

A couple of teenagers emerged from the Orwell store and eyed him nervously—most people did—and then climbed into a blue pickup with some major dents on one side, and the massive off-road tires he despised. He knew the kids were going to try to keep the car quiet when they turned over the ignition, and he knew also it was going to roar like a jet.

He sighed. Yes, I do, Phoebe Danvers. I want to see you very much.

"Rule number six: They have to exercise themselves as well as their horses."

SERGEANT GEORGE ROWE,
TENTH REGIMENT, UNITED STATES CAVALRY,
LETTER TO HIS BROTHER IN PHILADELPHIA,
NOVEMBER 18, 1873

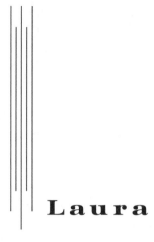

Laura

Here was this woman named Louise before her once again, this time at her kitchen table, the ladder-back chair between them filled by her little boy—the little boy in her care, she corrected herself quickly; she shouldn't be so bold as to consider him hers, especially since it was clear that this social worker was in her house now because something was amiss (perhaps even troubling her) and she wanted to discuss it. The three of them were sipping hot chocolate (real hot chocolate, made from real milk, not the weak stuff that was concocted from warm tap water and a mix that came in a foil packet), and she knew this amiable conversation was going nowhere good.

In so many ways, things had been going well, so very, very well. She should have known it couldn't last.

The young social worker (too young, Laura decided, to be knowledgeable or experienced or familiar with pain on a personal level) was saying something about how the horse had come right up to the stall guard (she said she had learned that term from Alfred) the instant they opened the barn door and he said her name. She was saying she thought the horse was a very good thing for Alfred, and asking Alfred if he agreed.

He nodded, but he looked nervous to Laura as he stared down at the marshmallows that floated at the top of his mug.

Anyway, I was hoping I could come back later this week and watch him ride, since I didn't get to today. Maybe have dinner with the three of you, she went on.

The three of us, Laura said, and for a very brief moment she wondered if Louise actually meant that she wanted to have dinner with her and the boy and the horse. But then she understood that Louise was including Terry in the group—she wanted to have dinner with her husband and her and the boy—and almost reflexively she added, Terry and Alfred and me.

Yes. If that would be all right. Forgive me, Ms. Sheldon, I don't usually invite myself places for dinner, but I just think it would be so much fun to see Alfred up on that animal, and then get the chance to, I don't know, just connect with you and Sergeant Sheldon.

When?

When? Oh, I was thinking Wednesday, maybe. I'll be in this part of the county early that afternoon, anyway, and I could rearrange my evening easily enough and drop in here—that is, if it's okay with you.

It's fine, she said.

And you wouldn't mind my dropping in again, right, Alfred?

He shrugged—no, he wouldn't mind—without looking up from his hot chocolate, and she could see that his fingers were wrapped tightly around the mug.

If it was all right with you, I'd arrive here about three-thirty, maybe quarter to four, and that would give me a chance to see Alfred up on the horse before the sun sets.

And then we'd have an early dinner, Laura said.

Well, we can eat whenever you normally would—whenever Sergeant Sheldon gets home.

I believe he'll be home his normal time Wednesday night. We can probably eat around six-thirty or seven.

Good. Let me bring some bread or something from that nice bakery in Durham. I could do that, at least.

You could, but you needn't, Laura said. It's our pleasure to have you.

Well, thank you. In the meantime, there was something I was hoping you could . . . help me with. Maybe help me smooth over.

Here comes the hammer blow, Laura thought to herself, here comes the beginning of the hurt. The first piece of news that something is wrong, direly wrong, and I have managed to miss all the signs. No, it will be worse than that: I will have seen the indications and I will have to live with the reality that I saw them and chose to ignore them. She wondered if it would have something to do with the horse and her willingness to allow the boy to ride without formal lessons—maybe that fall and the bump on his head—but then she decided it wouldn't be that because Louise seemed so pleased with Alfred's involvement with Mesa. The hurt would begin someplace else.

Yes? she asked simply when the woman paused, waiting for her to say something.

Louise turned to the boy as he was putting down his mug of hot chocolate on the place mat and said, I think Alfred wants to tell you about it.

Clearly this was the last thing in the world that Alfred wanted to do, and he sat there without saying a word.

Alfred? Laura asked, but he ignored her as he had ignored Louise, and stared out the window at the sky and the skeletal-looking branches on the trees near their house.

Remember what we agreed, Louise said. You need to be a grown-up here, you need to take some responsibility. I can help, but you need to get the ball rolling.

She could almost see the conflict on the boy's face: There was something he wanted desperately to tell her, but there was something even more powerful that was compelling him to remain silent. He wouldn't look at either of the women, and he wouldn't look away from the window.

Go ahead, Alfred, Laura said to him at last. You know the last thing I want is for us to have secrets.

Slowly he turned to meet her eyes, and for a second she thought he was going to open up and explain to her what was troubling him—what was troubling Louise—but then he pressed his palms flat on the armrests on the chair, pushed himself to his feet, and walked right past her and the social worker, across the kitchen floor, and then up the stairs to his room.

Laura started to stand up to go after him, but Louise shook her head, and so—despite her faith that she knew what was best for the boy and that meant going to him that very moment—she sat back in her chair and waited for this other woman to speak.

WHEN HE HAD shut the door and it had been completely quiet upstairs for easily a minute or a minute and a half, she asked Louise, What is it you want him to tell me? What's happened?

The younger woman widened her eyes and started to push her dark hair back behind her ears, her thumbs bouncing over the silver balls there like they were a line of speed bumps on the road. Well, it's your husband. I need to get in the middle of this, and I'm not happy about that, but not getting in the middle would be worse. It would—

What's happened?

This morning, it seems, Sergeant Sheldon—

Terry, please. Call him Terry, and call me Laura.

You know, I do that with Alfred. Around Alfred, you're both just Terry and Laura. I mean that as a compliment.

Go on.

This morning, before he left for work, Terry and Alfred had a bit of a misunderstanding. You don't know this about Alfred, but he's a bit of a food hoarder.

A what?

A food hoarder. He hoards food. You know, hides it. A lot of foster kids do, it's actually pretty common. It usually only happens the first time a child leaves his biologic home, especially when there's been some serious privation. But there are also the kids like Alfred, kids who've had some real bad luck over the years and been shuttled around more than anyone deserves. They squirrel away snacks, too, so when they have to go someplace new, they have some comfort food with them to help them get through the first couple of days.

A few times this fall I thought things had disappeared, but I assumed it was just me, she heard herself saying, and she remembered vividly opening the box of Twinkies one morning in October when she was making Alfred his lunch before school, and seeing there was only one wrapped cake remaining when she was quite sure that the night before there'd been two or even three. And then there was the afternoon she'd spent easily ten or fifteen minutes in search of the can opener with the white handle—the one she reserved solely for cat food cans—before finally giving up and deciding it wasn't a big deal if the family used the same can opener for refried beans and pineapple slices that they used for the seafood supper she fed to the cats.

It's never a lot, Louise continued. But Alfred has taken a little. You know, things like Hostess cupcakes. Canned peaches, I think he said. And the only reason it's a problem—

You can't believe either Terry or I would care if he took some canned peaches!

No, of course not. But there was a misunderstanding. This morning Alfred had the small things he'd procured (she smiled for Laura when she used the word) spread out on the floor in his bedroom when Sergeant Shel—Terry—walked in. And Terry saw the food and Alfred's backpack, and he suspected the worst.

The worst? What exactly would that be?

He thought Alfred was going to run away.

She nodded, and allowed the notion to seep in.

He said he wasn't, and I believe him, Louise went on. He has no history of running away.

Except that Saturday a couple months ago when he just upped and went to Burlington to see that little Vietnamese girl.

No, that wasn't running away, and I think you know that. That was just a . . . a badly planned and executed play date or visit.

How did you hear about this? Was it Alfred who said something, or did Terry call you this morning?

Your husband? He didn't call me. He and Alfred had an exchange, and—

And Alfred told you about it.

Yes.

And not me.

It isn't like that, there were—there are—circumstances.

She resolved that she would not sink into that place where she wanted (no, needed, there'd been a time when she'd needed) to curl up in her night-gown in bed, unmoving, the sheets around her pulled up to her face and her ears. But it was getting harder. Everyone around her these days had infor-mation for her: her husband with his news that he had had a drink with some tramp in a bar, Emily with her belief that something was bothering Terry, and now this social worker with the reconnaissance that something was going on between Terry and Alfred, and neither had chosen to tell her. If only the world could be just her and the boy—no, she didn't mean that, she loved Terry and didn't want to lose him—if only the world could be just her and the boy and her husband and the time they spent alone as a family. She and Alfred looking at photos. Using a dime-store loom to make a Kwanzaa mat. All three of them getting the Christmas tree that still stood in the den.

The thing is, Louise was explaining, and she turned her attention as best she could back to the younger woman, Terry thinks you're fragile. That's pretty clear. He made Alfred swear not to tell you what happened. That's why neither of the men in your life mentioned their squabble this morning.

Squabble. I can't tell whether you're trying to make this more or less of an issue with that word. Tell me, please, exactly what Alfred told you.

Okay, Louise said, and the caseworker proceeded to construct for Laura a short motion picture, beginning with the instant when Terry surprised Alfred in his bedroom, to the moment when he had the boy empty his pockets and accused him of stealing money. She tried to sit perfectly still as Louise spoke, unmoving, afraid if she did more than breathe, the reality of what she was hearing would cause her to flinch and then she would be undone. And she would not allow that to happen, not in front of this person who worked for the state. So long as she merely listened, however, not even nodding, she knew she could remain poised and concerned: A good foster mother. A good mom.

Anyway, Louise said as she finished, I don't believe Alfred would have told me if Terry hadn't thought he'd been taking dollar bills from your purse and whatever cookie jar you keep in this kitchen. The only reason the story even slipped out is because Alfred has plenty of money right now from the time he spends taking care of your neighbors' horse.

So he didn't . . . confide in you, she said, regretting the words the moment they had escaped her mouth because she thought they made her sound pathetic: jealous, perhaps, of this woman a mere fourteen or fifteen years older than Alfred.

No, it wasn't like that. It was like, Hey, I'm making a lot of money here, so why would Terry accuse me of taking some? Oops. The minute he said it, he knew he'd made a mistake of monster proportions.

How do you think Terry wants to handle it now?

She raised her eyebrows and offered Laura a small smile. You know, he's your husband. I should ask you that. But here's what does seem pretty clear. He doesn't want to tell you, at least not right now. And, like I said, he didn't call me this morning, so he probably isn't planning on telling me. The fact is, he's never called me, so I tend to doubt I'm tops on his list of people he would even think of talking to.

But he might talk to Alfred some more.

He might. He might also just opt for more discipline. In the meantime, somehow I want to get this out into the open so it doesn't get any worse. But you can't bring it up without getting Alfred in trouble with Terry, and I probably can't—

Why not? she interrupted. Why can't you just tell Terry—maybe Terry and me together—the way you just told me? You said yourself it just slipped out. Alfred hadn't planned to mention it to anybody.

Maybe. But Terry and Alfred don't have, you know, one of those father-son relationships for the ages. Terry might not believe that's exactly the way it happened—

Their relationship isn't that bad!

No, of course not. But it isn't great. That doesn't mean it couldn't become great. It could. But it isn't right now, that's just how it is. And so if I don't do this right, I could really screw things up. I guess that's why I want to have us all together in one room so we can deal with this honestly, clear it up, and then—she tossed her hand over her shoulder, as if she were tossing a ball behind her back—put it behind us.

This, she thought to herself, focusing on a single word in Louise's last sentence, a euphemism for . . . what? For the fact that Terry believed Alfred was stealing from them and planned to run away? Or for the idea that the two of them, her husband and her foster child, didn't get along? Either way, she had a sense that she shouldn't share with Terry that she knew something had occurred that morning in Alfred's room.

He's doing very well here, she said to Louise, hoping her voice didn't sound too defensive. You know that, don't you?

Oh, yeah! My God, the kid's going to school every day and getting B's and C's on his report card. That's huge, Laura, that's huge! And you have to trust me: Your husband isn't the first foster father who thought his foster son was stealing from him. He might be the first who was wrong, but that's another story. No, my hope here is to get through this and, you know, build on it. Make things even better.

So you're not going to take him away? she asked. The question was abrupt and unplanned, another reflex. It, too, was a chain of words she wished instantly she had never spoken, especially when Louise looked back at her—Louise's eyes anxious and worried, just the tiniest bob to her head as if she thought this woman in whose kitchen she was sitting was as unstable as a two-legged chair someone had propped against a wall—and then leaned forward and patted her, an invalid once more, softly on her knee.

There, there, that pat said, you really are fragile. There, there.

AT DINNER THAT night she watched Terry carefully as he ate. He was quiet, and in the past that meant something god-awful had occurred and he needed to be allowed to eat and listen and relax in the normalcy of a dinner with his family. Tonight, however, she was quite sure he'd had a calm day, and his silence had more to do with his fight with Alfred than anything he'd seen on the roads or in some poor battered woman's house. Consequently, she was unwilling to carry the load of their dinner conversation, and so she, too, ate without saying a word. The three of them sat as if they were strangers on stools at a diner, and she allowed the tension in the room to fester. Occasionally he glanced over at her—a further indication in her mind that his day indeed had been fine, and he was surprised that she wasn't babbling on about her morning at the shelter or their afternoon visit from the social worker—his eyes wary, and he would touch his mustache with his fingers with a fastidiousness that annoyed her.

Meanwhile, Alfred ate. He looked at neither of them, and he continued to eat until there was absolutely no trace that the plate before him had once held a large square of spinach lasagna and a piece of garlic bread. She asked the boy if he wanted more and encouraged him to have seconds: She didn't want him to think her silence had anything to do with him or that she thought he had done something wrong. When she brought him his plate, refilled, she kissed him lightly on the top of his head.

And then when dinner was through—when Alfred had finished the brownie she set before him for dessert—she reached for the boy's hand and gave it a gentle squeeze and asked him if he'd like to be excused. He nodded and went upstairs, and she began to clear the dishes from the table. For a moment she was alone with Terry, and she realized she was hoping he would bring up their child. Tell her his version of what had occurred that morning. But he wasn't about to, that was clear after a moment. And so she turned toward him from the spot by the dishwasher where she was standing and said—careful to make sure that although her voice might sound like many things to him, *fragile* would not be among them—You're excused, too, you know.

He wiped his mouth with his napkin and stood. You need any help here? he asked.

She almost answered automatically, *Do I ever?*, but she restrained herself. She looked at the pan and the plates and the pots in which she had boiled the spinach and cooked the sauce, and said instead, Sure. You can have the honors tonight. Then she went upstairs to Alfred's room to see if he wanted to watch television or play a game of Chinese checkers since there was no school the next day.

———

"Both of the Indian girls had been coughing for days, and since Dr. McPherson was not going to visit them and Popping Trees was not about to visit the surgeon, Sergeant Rowe brought the children's plight to my attention; I, in turn, delegated it to my wife, who, like many women, has always been knowledgeable when it comes to certain basic cures."

———

CAPTAIN ANDREW HITCHENS,
TENTH REGIMENT, UNITED STATES CAVALRY,
REPORT TO THE POST ADJUTANT,
JULY 16, 1876

———

Phoebe

I nearly busted open some idiot's head the day after Christmas, he
was saying, that's what I mean. I'm just not . . . focused. The guy was
arrogant, but he didn't deserve what he got.

She rubbed her hand over the fur and muscle on his chest, massaging
the tiny nipple there—the color of coffee, she thought, sweetened with
cream—with the soft skin in her palm, and burrowed her head as deeply as
she could into the small, comfortable valley just below his shoulder.

You stopped him for speeding, she murmured simply. She was happy,
and she wanted him to be happy, too. He overreacted, she continued, and
then you did. It happens, it's not that complicated. You shouldn't be so hard
on yourself.

I shouldn't have been so hard on him.

He hit you.

Still . . . and tonight I get to go home and have dinner with some social
worker with so much silver and steel in her ears that she probably sets off
metal detectors a mile away. What fun.

A part of her didn't want to ask about the boy because she didn't want
their last few moments together to be centered on his family or his life back
in Cornish, but the part of her that would be a mother before another year
passed simply couldn't resist: She wondered—and, yes, worried—about this
faceless child she'd never met. And so she closed her eyes and said, How is
Alfred doing?

Well, let's see. I keep my hunting rifles in a solid-steel Treadlok gun vault
that's bolted to the floor. The key is hollow—nonduplicable. I keep the

ammo locked in a separate sideboard in a separate room. Yet Monday night when I came home from work, I proceeded to remove what had been my father's Savage 99 and my own Browning A-Bolt from the gun case, rounded up my three boxes of shells, and then on Tuesday I took everything with me back to the barracks in Middlebury. The guns, the ammo. The works. I'm storing it all there. Only weapons at home from now on are that Sig Sauer— and he pointed at the handgun in his holster that dangled off the side of the chair beside the motel room desk—and the Remington 870 I keep in the trunk of the cruiser. And I'm pretty sure the lad doesn't even know the Remington exists. So I think that sums it up nicely, thank you very much. That is how little Alfred is doing.

It's that bad?

I caught him planning to run away. The last thing the world needs is a runaway ten-year-old with a bad attitude and his foster father's Browning A-Bolt at his side.

I'm sorry. That's not good, she said, and she watched her fingernails— Casino Red today—carve an invisible line up his chest and his neck. She watched the small goose bumps appear on his skin. Is that why his social worker is coming to your house tonight?

No, I don't think so. She doesn't even know. No one knows but me and the boy. I guess she just wants to see us all together. One big happy family, he said, his voice awash in sarcasm. With his free hand he adjusted the pillow beneath his head.

She saw in the midday light that poured through the drapes the silhouette of one of the motel housekeepers outside their window, pushing her cart with clean sheets and towels and spray bottles of disinfectant. This was a pretty nice motel: It catered mostly to the skiers who were visiting Stowe, and it was likely the young man behind the desk would be more than a little shocked when she checked out barely ninety minutes after checking in. She'd noticed this place—and its vacancy sign—as she drove into Waterbury, but she hadn't anticipated she'd be back here with Terry. They were only supposed to eat lunch. But the last two times they were together, they'd done little more than sit and talk with coffee and tea between them, and the whole idea that they were meeting now for no other reason than the fact that they wanted to see each other was too much. Suddenly it didn't seem so horribly wrong to backtrack up 100 to this motel and shed their clothes and allow themselves a little pleasure. It wasn't as if a person could get *more* pregnant. It wasn't as if anyone, ever, would have to know.

I have some news, she murmured.

Oh?

I'm going to move back here.

To central Vermont?

Yup. Waterbury, maybe. Or Montpelier again. But, you know, this area.

You told your father?

No.

He won't be happy.

I know. But it could have been a lot worse from his standpoint. My family hasn't been hugely supportive of my pregnancy, and I was actually thinking about moving real far away.

How far?

New Mexico.

New Mexico?

Uh-huh. Santa Fe. One year when I was in college in Burlington I lived with a girl who moved out there. And she just loves it. Has a little family, says it's a great place for kids.

You ever been out West?

No, but I think that was a part of the attraction. It would be a complete change of scenery for me.

Still, even Waterbury or Montpelier won't exactly please your father. I think he's going to miss you more than you realize.

But the move will be good for me, and I think he'll understand that, too. Let's face it: When things have gotten to the point in the deep woods that I'm letting Smokey Bear pick me up, it's time to get my fanny back to civilization.

He sighed and his chest rose. We can never make a habit of this, he said. You know that, right?

Of course I do. I know you could get all too used to me.

He squeezed her, pulling her body tightly against his, and he kissed her softly on her forehead. God, Phoebe, what am I doing? What are we doing?

She wrapped her leg over his. We're having lunch, she murmured, happy in the warmth of his arms. That's all. Just having a little lunch.

SHE WOULDN'T BE spending New Year's Eve alone, but she also wouldn't be with Terry Sheldon. A family in her father's church—her church, too, though other than Christmas Eve she hadn't been there since her mother's funeral in August—was having a party, and she knew she would go. She'd play Trivial Pursuit and Boggle and a card game called spoons, and if not for this image in her mind of Terry Sheldon in a nice sports coat or a sweater and khaki pants, she figured she would have a pretty good time. She liked games, and she liked the people who were having the party.

But there was that picture in her head of Terry, and she realized days before New Year's Eve that it was going to cast a shadow upon her evening: She wanted to be spending the evening with him. This was most certainly something she shouldn't be thinking about, she decided, since it was most certainly something she couldn't have. Unfortunately, something was happening to her, that was clear. She was missing him only hours after they'd parted Wednesday afternoon, so much so that she drove on into Newport and went to the bar where they'd had their very first drink. She stood at the bar and chatted with the bartender—a guy who was actually a couple of years younger than she was—and drank a Diet Pepsi, and glanced back every so often at the table where she and Terry had sat drinking their first night together.

It was funny, but she didn't miss beer. She feared that the urge to have one would be overpowering if she stepped inside the bar, but it wasn't. She attributed this to maternal wisdom and protectiveness, and decided that although she was a—and she actually found herself rolling her eyes when the words formed in her mind—home-wrecking slut, she probably wouldn't be a bad mom.

"I don't think [George Rowe] felt guilty. My husband was his enemy. When we got to know each other, he said he'd only brought the Captain's wife to my children because he thought she would be able to make them stop coughing and the fort would be a quieter place. That was a joke, of course. White people didn't think he was very funny because he could be so angry around them, but he really was a very funny man."

VERONICA ROWE (FORMERLY POPPING TREES),

WPA INTERVIEW,

MARCH 1938

Alfred

It was a Wednesday but the school was still closed for Christmas break, and so he called Tim Acker around nine in the morning from the phone in the kitchen to see if he wanted to come over and see the horse. Alfred hadn't introduced Mesa to any of the boys in his class yet, but Paul had said he could, and he'd certainly told a few of them about her. Some, like Schuyler Jackman and Joe Langford, had expressed absolutely no interest, and he presumed at first that this was only because horses were not uncommon in this part of the state—there were two kids in the class whose families he knew owned at least one—but then he began to understand that it was actually because they viewed horses as a hobby for girls. Joe had gone out of his way to inform him that his older sister had taken riding lessons for years at an outdoor stable in Middlebury, and he had dreaded being dragged there by his mother when he was seven and eight years old—too young to stay home alone after school, and so he'd have to accompany his sister to her lessons. The problem—an opinion Joe made clear to Alfred in front of both Schuyler and Tim Acker—was that only girls were interested in horses, and so there was never a boy to be found at the stable. Lots of girls, no boys: a bad combination when you're eight.

Alfred thought he might bring the book about the buffalo soldiers into school someday in January and show Joe the old black-and-white photographs of the black men on their horses. Nothing effeminate about them.

Tim had displayed a little more enthusiasm at the idea of visiting the Morgan—not a lot, but at least he hadn't been negative—which was why he decided to call him first. His mom said he'd spent the night at a friend's

275

house, however (Schuyler's? Alfred wondered. Joe Langford's?), and he probably wouldn't be home much before lunch. Unfortunately, that didn't do him any good because Louise was coming back for another visit in the afternoon, and the last thing he wanted was to have one of the kids in his class meet Louise. The whole idea that there was this person from the state who popped into his life every so often because he didn't have a real mom or dad just helped to set him even further apart.

Briefly he considered calling somebody else, but he decided he didn't want to find out how big the sleepover was, or—worse—inadvertently phone the very house where it was occurring.

He heard Laura coming down the stairs and he realized she'd ask him if he wanted a friend to come over or whether there was someone in town he wanted to see, and he knew he wouldn't be able to bear the look on her face when he said no to both questions. And so he decided it was a nice enough day outside that he might as well lie and ask her to drive him to Schuyler's house. He could probably walk around the village for a while—it wasn't Burlington, but he was an expert at killing time—and then walk back here after lunch. It would take some time, but that was the whole point, wasn't it? He'd tell Laura, of course, that Schuyler's mom had driven him home (he'd even use that word *home* and make everyone happy), and by then it would be early afternoon and he could wander across the street and visit Mesa himself. Get her all ready for when Louise got there, and he could show her just how well he could ride.

———

"Custer may have been a good Indian fighter, but I wasn't vexed by his death. When we were at Fort Sill, our horses were the animals cast off by his illustrious Seventh Cavalry. I've also heard the rumor—as I am sure you have, too—that he was offered a lieutenant colonelcy in the Ninth just after the war, and turned it down because he wanted nothing to do with Negroes on horses."

———

SERGEANT GEORGE ROWE,
TENTH REGIMENT, UNITED STATES CAVALRY,
UNDATED LETTER TO HIS BROTHER
IN PHILADELPHIA

———

The Heberts

A fine blue mist was emerging from the horse's nostrils as he ran his hands down the muscles—as wide as a tire, he thought—that lined Mesa's neck. She turned toward him, her ears pricked, and he slipped her a piece of carrot the size of his thumb. He decided she was happy. She liked him and she liked the boy, and she was warm and well-fed. It wasn't a bad life.

Beside him, Alfred was putting the shovel and the pitchfork back against the near wall in the barn. It was late Wednesday afternoon, and the winter sun had just about set. They would give Mesa her feed—a coarse mix tonight, so she'd eat a little more slowly and give her digestion a bit of a rest—and then they'd be done for the day. That social worker had watched Alfred ride and was now back across the street with Laura. He understood she was staying for dinner.

You know something? Alfred said, and he turned. He noted that sometimes Alfred used the same construction his female students had used when they wanted to tell him something: Begin the statement in the form of a needlessly deferential question. He wondered if it was because the boy was young or because he'd grown up the responsibility of so many adults who frequently didn't care about what he might have to say.

Yes?

In that book you gave me, it said the Indians used to get mad at the buffalo soldiers because they couldn't be scalped.

What?

They didn't have hair an Indian could grab, so they couldn't be scalped.

He tried to read the boy's face, but it was almost expressionless. If an Apache or a Comanche wanted a scalp, he said, I tend to doubt he'd be dissuaded by the difficulty posed by the length of a black soldier's hair.

I'm just telling you what the book said, Alfred went on. I can show you.

Oh, I don't doubt you—or the book.

It was written in a newspaper article.

Ah, I see. No doubt it was a white newspaper, he said, and he explained as best he could his belief that whoever had written the article must have been deeply threatened by the presence of the buffalo soldiers on the Great Plains, and this was a sarcastic dig at their expense.

Still, Alfred insisted, it couldn't have been easy to scalp them.

I don't imagine it was easy to scalp anybody.

Sometimes I wonder . . .

Yes?

Sometimes I wonder why the Indians and the buffalo soldiers didn't band together.

Against the white soldiers?

I guess.

He handed Alfred the two remaining carrots he had left in the pocket of his parka and watched him feed them to the horse. Mesa nuzzled the boy's palm and then chewed with great enthusiasm. Horses didn't really smile, but you could sometimes see how they felt in their eyes, and he thought Mesa's always brightened around the boy.

It's natural to wonder about that now. It really wasn't an issue then.

I just look at a man like Sergeant Rowe—

A buffalo soldier?

Uh-huh. I look at all he put up with, and I just don't get it.

Was he born a slave?

Yes.

He was used to much worse.

That doesn't make it right, the boy said.

No. I suppose it doesn't.

When the horse had finished chewing, she stretched her head out across the stall gate and started nosing against Alfred's stomach and chest in the hope that there might be a pocket there with more carrots.

That's all I have, girl, the boy murmured. Sorry.

He wasn't sure, but he had the sense that Alfred was bringing up the book in part because he didn't want to leave. He'd noticed before that when the child wanted to remain after he was done with his chores—which was usually perfectly fine—he'd bring up a variety of subjects: Why horses didn't eat meat. Why the mane always seemed to fall to the right side of the horse's neck. The regulation that a buffalo soldier couldn't weigh more than 155 pounds. He guessed Alfred was still hanging around because he was apprehensive about the fact that the social worker was at Terry and Laura's house that very moment, and would be staying for dinner. Clearly something was up, and the boy had to know it: It wasn't simply the idea that Louise was back for the second time in three days after having not set foot in Cornish in almost two months. It was the reality that she was back because of whatever had occurred between Terry and the boy early Monday.

He hadn't spoken to Terry since the trooper phoned him the other morning with his odd accusations about the child, and asked him not to allow Alfred to spend any time alone with the horse. He should have called him back, and he wished now that he had. Maybe he could have reassured him that Alfred had no plans to run away, and that the boy certainly wasn't a thief. But he'd been taken aback by the phone call, and he'd decided that Terry needed some distance from his fight with the boy before he could think reasonably.

And now, suddenly, it was late Wednesday afternoon. Early evening, almost.

Louise is a nice young woman, he said, standing beside Alfred and the horse. I like her.

Uh-huh.

You tired?

A little.

You seem a little tired today. You rode fine, I thought, but I could tell you were a bit tuckered. You do anything special this morning?

He shrugged.

Just hung out, huh?

The boy nodded silently, his eyes fixed firmly on the horse before him, and so Paul continued, This dinner tonight. You want me to be there?

How?

He thought for a moment. Getting himself invited would be easy, he could do it with any one of a number of small white lies: He could have

Emily call Laura and say the furnace was on the fritz, and she would most certainly invite them over for dinner. He could ask Alfred for his gloves right that second, bring them by his house early that evening, and then act surprised when he saw the company. Maybe that wouldn't guarantee that he could hang around for supper, but he could certainly get in a few good words for the boy in front of Terry, and make dinner a bit easier on the lad. He and Emily could even, he realized, simply drop in bearing whatever it was that Emily had been baking that afternoon. Pumpkin bread, maybe.

That was an advantage to being old. Older, anyway. You could drop in on people without calling first, on the pretext that you were merely *visiting* and this was how people did it in the past.

He—he and Emily, he corrected himself—should probably just wander by, he finally decided. He didn't want to give Alfred the impression that he approved of lying, even if the lie was small and the cause was just. Still, he wanted Alfred to know that he would see him later on in the evening and so he said, Don't worry about how. You and I are friends and we're neighbors, and this is just what friends and neighbors do.

He could see Alfred was squinting, and he wondered if the boy was merely playing some game with himself—*How tightly can I close my eyes and still see? What does a horse's nostril look like when my eyes are open only a crack?*—or whether the kid was on the verge of tears and trying now to make absolutely certain that not a one ever crept down the side of his face.

———

"The girls got better and I went back to work in the laundry. I didn't go into town, and so the only women I saw were the wives of the white officers, the other laundresses, and the prostitutes. I really didn't have many friends."

———

VERONICA ROWE (FORMERLY POPPING TREES),
WPA INTERVIEW,
MARCH 1938

———

Terry

He could argue that this was either very good luck or very bad, though he had to admit he was more pleased by the news than he thought he should be. He certainly hadn't expected such a small piece of good fortune, but there it was, tangible despite the reality that for the moment it was nothing more than a string of words surfing through space on radio waves. He'd been in his cruiser about thirty seconds—he was barely beyond the parking lot beside the barracks—when the dispatcher radioed him with the news that there had been a B and E at a private residence in Salisbury. He was on his way home, but the night shift was already committed to a car accident on Route 74 and a very messy domestic affair in Starksboro, and since he was on the road and was a shift supervisor, he would need to fill the breach. It didn't sound like a big deal (oh, it would be big to the family who lived there, no doubt about that, but in the greater scheme of things it was hard to get worked up over a stolen CD player and TV set), but it meant that he wouldn't be home for dinner. He'd have to linger over the photographs of the stolen items, do a lot of dusting for prints. He'd need to settle the family down, which would certainly take some time since, after all, a stranger had been in their house and gone through their things, and then there would be plenty of paperwork to fill out.

He probably wouldn't get home much before eight. Make that eight-thirty. Maybe even eight forty-five if the family needed some major hand-holding, and he did the right thing and stayed.

No, not *maybe* eight forty-five. *Definitely* eight forty-five. Who was he kidding? For better or worse, this meant that by the time he walked in his house, the social worker would be gone for the night.

A last-minute stay of execution, he thought to himself, though not without a small pang of self-loathing.

IT WAS ACTUALLY nine o'clock by the time he got home. Laura and the boy were in the den watching a video Laura had rented for them at some point that day, and they were both dressed for bed. Alfred was lying on the floor in his pajamas and a sweatshirt, and Laura was on the couch in her nightgown and a bathrobe. Her hair was damp, she'd already showered.

The cats, he saw, were asleep by the woodstove.

He squatted briefly beside Alfred and patted the boy on his shoulder, and then collapsed on the couch beside Laura. He kissed her on her cheek, but she didn't offer him even a trace of a smile. He realized he was in for a pretty chilly night if only because he was so late, and he knew he deserved it. Still, the idea didn't bother him the way it would have once, and as he sat back against the pillows, he tried to understand why. Was it simply because he'd already had sex that day, so he didn't care whether he got lucky or not? No, of course not, he wasn't that driven by hormones and need. At least he hoped he wasn't. But if that wasn't it, then what was it? Was he really falling so completely out of love with this woman he'd married—this woman beside him right now—that he didn't give a damn that she was pissed at him? In some ways, that would actually be considerably worse.

The truth was, she'd been pretty cold to him for a couple of days now. He didn't believe Alfred had said anything to her about the conversation they had Monday morning—certainly he hadn't as of Monday night when he spent some time with the boy and made sure that every single canned peach and Twinkie was right back where it belonged—but he couldn't be sure.

He turned from the television to look at Laura, aware that he hadn't a clue what they were watching. He saw that Laura was already staring at him, and he tried to read exactly how angry she was by her face. Very, he decided, and he started to speak:

You should have seen the mess this nice family had waiting for them when they walked in their house tonight. Mom and two boys, coming straight home from hockey practice. The place was a disaster, it was like a tornado had gone through the living room, he said, hoping sympathy—for him, for the victims—might defuse the ticking bomb inside Laura. Real nice people, he went on. The Danyows. Got a dog from the shelter a couple years ago. You might even remember them if you saw their faces.

She nodded. Paul and Emily were here for dinner, she said, her voice so calm it was absolutely impenetrable. Louise, too. Of course.

Yeah, I'm real sorry I wasn't here. How come Paul and Emily were? he asked. He wasn't exactly sure why, but the idea that the Heberts had been in this house with Laura disturbed him. He wondered what Paul might have said to her about the run-in he and Alfred had had Monday morning, if anything, and whether the older man might have shared with Laura some inkling of what Terry now knew about the boy.

They just dropped by. So I invited them to stay.

He smiled. Good, good, he murmured, careful to keep his own voice steady. Then: So how was Louise?

She leaned forward on the couch and told Alfred that they didn't want to disturb him so they were going to go in the kitchen to talk—catch up on their days was how she put it—and the boy offered to pause the movie so she wouldn't miss anything.

No, you keep watching, she said to him. You can fill me in on what I miss.

She rose and Terry stood up to follow her, stepping carefully over the child on the floor. Suddenly he was exhausted, and he decided he wanted to be anywhere in the world that moment but where he was.

SHE SAT DOWN at her place at the kitchen table and folded her hands together on the dark wood. He started to sit down beside her, but he realized he would be better off if he remained on his feet—more alert, less vulnerable, in command—and so he opened the refrigerator and got out the container of milk and the makings for a sandwich. He wasn't hungry because he'd grabbed a hamburger and fries at the lone fast-food restaurant in Middlebury after leaving the Danyows, but Laura didn't need to know that. As far as she was concerned, he'd come straight home after leaving the burglary site.

It sounds like you and Alfred had a nice day today.

We had a fine day. Fine enough, anyway.

He stared at the mayonnaise he was spreading on the potato bread, his body facing her as a courtesy though his eyes were focused elsewhere.

Louise get to watch him ride?

Uh-huh.

Paul says he's good. That true?

I think so.

Were you and Paul there when Louise went to see him on the horse?

Paul was. I was here making dinner.

There was a slight edge to her response. It wasn't so much, he thought, that she felt put upon for making dinner, as she was annoyed that he hadn't gotten home on time.

I really am sorry that work intervened, he said as he started to layer the sliced turkey on the bread. What did you all talk about? What did Louise have to say about the lad?

Cut the lad crap. Please.

He looked up. Pardon me? he asked, stalling.

I said to stop calling him *lad*. It sounds condescending.

I don't mean it that way.

Then how do you mean it? You don't say it with even a teeny drop of affection.

He laid the knife down on the counter, careful not to drip mayonnaise on the Formica, and when he looked at her, he saw for just the briefest second the shape of Hillary's eyes—their absolute intensity—when his daughter would be holding a small bat in T-ball. Dribbling the soccer ball down the field. Fighting with Megan over . . . over anything. And while he understood their conversation was about Alfred, he didn't believe that the boy in the next room was in reality the issue. She was angry with him, and he recognized it was because for the last month, ever since Phoebe told him she was pregnant, things had been different between them. Tense. Everything between them had become a small annoyance.

No, that wasn't accurate. With the exception of November—those few weeks when he was trying to make things right after sleeping with Phoebe the first time—everything between them had been a small annoyance for two years. Two years and two months. Either she was a catatonic who couldn't get out of bed—and who could blame her!—or she was angry or . . .

And that was just her. He understood well his own desire to find any excuse imaginable to be anyplace but this house with its ghosts—exuberant banshees one moment, self-contained spirits the next, the shape of the eyes of this woman before him enough to bring them both back—of his dead daughters everywhere. Everywhere! She could take down the fucking photographs, they could box up the toys and books and cart them up to the attic, but you couldn't make them go away so you didn't miss them so much you just grew ornery and short with whoever was present.

Which, often enough, was going to be your wife. Even if some days she was delicate and easily hurt.

I asked you a question, she said. I'm waiting.

He tried to recapture what they were talking about, and he knew it had something to do with Alfred. The way he'd just called the boy *lad.*

He closed his eyes for a brief second because he needed a moment without seeing even a trace of Hillary or Megan before opening his mouth, and then answered softly—the kid was, after all, only two rooms away in the den—Look. I'm sorry. I'm sorry for how I've behaved, I'm sorry for the fact I've been in a foul mood. You know that, right? I'm sorry, really I am. But you know what? It isn't working. I wish to God it was, but it—

It? What do you mean by it?

He held up his hands because he honestly wasn't sure, his palms open and flat. Everything. The boy. Us. This house—

This house? Suddenly you want to move, too?

Too?

Too. You said this house isn't working, either. Like Alfred. And us.

He wondered if he could finish this, and he didn't believe that he could. Not after the deaths of their daughters. But didn't marriages often crumble when a child passed away? Hadn't Laura herself read that in some article she'd come across about grieving, or been told it by some self-proclaimed expert on the subject? What, really, was he protecting her from by not telling her about Alfred and their exchange Monday morning, or about Phoebe and the fact that they were now linked by far more than a drink in a bar? What was he trying to preserve? Their marriage? It was over—or, he told himself, it should be, because he feared he might want another woman more than the woman he'd married, and didn't that say it all? And as for keeping it together for the kids, there were none! Not anymore! If he had a responsibility to any child, it was to the one Phoebe was carrying, not the boy watching TV in the den. That poor, troubled kid was already wrecked anyway, he was already well beyond anything a couple as beaten up as Terry and Laura Sheldon could offer.

She was waiting for him to resume speaking, and spoke herself only when it seemed clear to her that he couldn't decide what he was supposed to say next. You still think I'm a basket case, she said, and you don't want to live with one anymore. Well, I can't blame you. But you know what? I'm not going to lose that boy because of you. I don't know exactly what happened Monday morning, but—

What did Paul tell you?

I talked to Alfred, too, so—

See? That's what I mean. I asked the boy not to—

He told me because I confronted him. And the reason I confronted him was because of what you told Paul.

Well, then, here are the facts from the only grown-up witness who was present. Fact one: He had taken—

Food! He had taken some food! And if he'd been our biologic child or even our adopted child, you wouldn't have considered it stealing! Then you would have just seen it as a kid taking some food upstairs to his room. But because he's Alfred, it's something else! It's theft, it's—

He was planning to run away. Face it.

He was planning to do no such thing. I talked to Louise, and she—

She doesn't live here. How many times has she seen the kid in the last two or three months? Twice? Maybe three times counting tonight? She doesn't—

She does know him. And she knows the behavior. He was only doing what lots of kids in his situation do. He was getting ready in case he got moved again.

Here's the pattern, Laura: You steal something small. Then you steal something a little bigger. It's progressive. You just know he's taken dollar bills out of our wallets, you just know—

He has a job. He doesn't need to do that. If you had any involvement with him at all, you would have figured that out.

And there are—excuse me, were—there were guns in this house. It seems to me, I had—

I think you should leave.

What?

Go. Leave. I think you should leave, and we can talk in the morning.

Tomorrow's New Year's Eve, he said, unsure what he was driving at.

That's fine.

He was aware of a low rumble—a murmur, actually, just loud enough to muffle (though not quiet completely) the sounds all around him. He realized it was the sound of shock. He'd experienced it once before, when he was in the passenger seat of Henry Labarge's cruiser, when the man was driving him home from deer camp after dropping on him the bombshell that his daughters were dead. The engine, the radio, the occasional moments when Henry would open his mouth on the long drive back to Cornish and tell him something were all noises that had sounded to him like they were muted by a thin sheet of water. As if his ears were just below the surface in the bath.

It was like that now. Laura was saying something more to him, something about finding a place to stay for the night, a friend or a motel, it didn't matter to her, but he could only hear select words and syllables through the wet curtain that seemed to surround him.

He nodded that he would leave—yes, yes, for the night, he was saying, and he found that even his own voice was strangely muffled, we'll talk in the morning—and he saw that his sandwich was still incomplete. He'd never finished making it. He didn't need to, because he really wasn't hungry, but he knew he was going to miss it. He didn't know if it would be the very last thing he would do in this house, but it was the very last thing he would do before . . . before this.

This confrontation. This rupture. This . . .

She was still talking to him and he was still nodding, and he realized he should be paying attention. Wasn't this exactly the opening he wanted? Wasn't this what on some level, low and cruel as it was, he'd been hoping would happen? He could never leave her, he'd concluded, but if she initiated it, if she took that crucial first step . . .

But that had all been predicated upon the notion that she took the first step because she found out about Phoebe Danvers. She was kicking him out now, however, and she hadn't said one single thing about that other woman.

Not one word. Still didn't know Phoebe even existed as anything more than a girl he'd once had a drink with in a bar.

And yet she was kicking him out anyway, sending him alone into the night because of . . . the boy. Alfred.

She was actually picking some boy she barely knew over him.

PART THREE

New

Year

"George seemed to be around often that summer. He liked me, I could tell. And I was grateful for what he had done for my children. Then he just disappeared, and he was gone for most of the autumn. His company was on the march. I told myself he was chasing Apaches—maybe the Lipan—because I didn't want to believe he might be fighting my people. But I didn't know for sure, and of course no one would tell me. I missed him."

VERONICA ROWE (FORMERLY POPPING TREES),

WPA INTERVIEW,

MARCH 1938

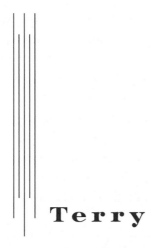

Terry

He drove the cruiser up into Cornish, his first time there in almost a week, and the first time in the new year. He didn't guess anybody would be home: Alfred would be at school, and Laura would be at the shelter. Instead of veering off the main road and returning to the house via the notch, he decided to stay on the River Road. He hadn't planned to visit the river—hell, he hadn't even planned on going to Cornish—but here he was, following the paved road for a change as it curled side by side with the water.

It had been cold and snowy for almost the full week. Winter had finally arrived, and though it had come late, it had come with the storms and icy gales they took for granted. He could only remember two days when he'd seen blue skies and sun in the last seven, and on both occasions it had been so cold that the smoke from the woodstove chimneys he'd glimpse as he drove rose straight into the sky like flagpoles.

When he reached the spot where the girls' bodies had been recovered, he came to a stop and parked the cruiser as close to the drift as he could. He felt particularly alone—more so than usual—because he was in one of those dead spots in the county where the radio wouldn't work. He climbed from his car and guessed the temperature would hit twenty today, perhaps even a few degrees above that. But it was gray and damp and raw, and there was just enough wind to cause him first to blow on his hands, and then reach back into the vehicle for a pair of gloves. Then he started over the snow, telling himself with each step into the knee-deep powder that this was an asinine idea and he should turn around, shake the snow off his pants, and get on with his day.

But he couldn't stop, and he knew that. He'd come this far, he may as well go all the way. So what if his pants got wet? Troopers could always find something to bitch about when it came to their cars, but he had no complaints with the heater. A fucking oven, if he wanted. He'd blast the heater on his legs, and they'd probably be dry by the time he got back to the barracks.

He pushed aside the leafless branches of a pair of sugar maples, stepped over what he guessed was a cluster of raspberry bushes—in the snow he could see only the very tops of the twigs—and stared for a brief moment at the tracks from a snowshoe hare. He wondered if he'd see a river otter or a beaver when he arrived at the water, and guessed there was a chance. At least he'd see signs.

There was a thick wall of ice on the surface of the river, and flat kaleidoscopic filigrees of frost along the smooth surfaces. Frozen white daggers were suspended mid-drip like stalactites from the edges of a great many stones, including parts of the pair of boulders—each nearly half the size of a mobile home—that he knew had caught some of the debris from the village that had been swept downriver in the flood.

He'd been reassured that by the time his daughters had gotten here—this twist in the river with its gloriously big rocks and its nearby pool where his neighbors (though, thank God, not him) had once come to reel in rainbow and brown trout—they'd drowned. Yet what he would never know, and sometimes when he was alone in his cruiser he would see their small bodies pinwheeling through the water, was how much they had felt. How long they had lived. Yes, they had drowned, but there was so much more to it than that. Head traumas. Massive internal hemorrhaging. Broken bones. You don't die instantly when you drown, that's for sure, and that was a part of the problem.

Back at the road he heard a truck rumble by, and he wondered what the trucker thought of the cruiser parked by the drifts here in the middle of nowhere.

He turned around and stomped back through the snow, and through the small tangles of dormant bushes and shrubs. When he was back inside his cruiser, he sat for a moment with the engine idling and felt the warmth from the heater on his ankles—even through his boots and his pants and his socks—and though a part of him still planned to drive by the house (perhaps even wander around a bit inside), already his mind was asking, What for? Really, he thought to himself, what for? The empty house would just depress him, and there wasn't anything there he needed—at least anything tangible he could actually take back with him to Henry Labarge's parents' cabin on Lake Champlain. And so he swung the vehicle around in the thin strip of pavement between the drifts and decided instead he would simply run the roads a bit on his way back to Middlebury.

HE TALKED TO his mother that night on the phone. He spoke with his brother and his sister and, yes, Phoebe as well, but most of the time he had talked to his mother. He actually hadn't planned on speaking to anyone but Phoebe, but first his sister called because she'd heard from their mother that he and Laura were living apart, and she wanted to know what was going on—how serious the rift was. Then, at Leah's urging, he had phoned their mother to reassure her that he was fine and Laura was fine, and she needn't fret: Soon enough, the two of them would solve their problems and reconcile.

Oh, but she would worry, that was clear, and—if anything disconcerted him after his ninety minutes that night on the phone, it was this—now, his mother had said, honestly not trying to make him feel guilty, she was concerned about both her boys. It wasn't only Russell who was going to cost her sleep, it was her older boy, too.

He never liked being paired with Russell. And so he tracked his brother down at his girlfriend's, hoping to regain a measure of separation by calling him up and checking on him. He guessed his brother saw through him, however, because even Russell—Russell with his empty beer cans rolling around underneath the driver's seat in his truck, his weed (and who knew what else) in the glove compartment, Russell with the beaker of anger inside him that seemed always on the verge of boiling over—could see through a need that transparent.

You'll have to forgive me, Russell said, but I really can't chitchat tonight. I haven't been tomcatting around the state of Vermont, and so I actually have a girlfriend I should be paying attention to right now.

When he went to bed that night on an unfamiliar mattress in an unfamiliar house, he told himself things would get better. He knew in reality this wasn't always the case, but he was sufficiently tired when he turned out the light that he was able to believe it and—unlike his mother, apparently—fall asleep.

*"Rule number seven: They are to carry with them
extra horseshoes and nails on the march, even though
it will add extra pounds to their pack. This is just one
more of the ways I encourage them to think ahead at all
times, and this simple precaution has saved the lives of
both horses and men."*

———

SERGEANT GEORGE ROWE,
TENTH REGIMENT, UNITED STATES CAVALRY,
LETTER TO HIS BROTHER IN PHILADELPHIA,
NOVEMBER 18, 1873

———

Alfred

He thought the veins in the horse's forearms stood out like mountains on the topographic map of the United States in his classroom, and gently he stroked Mesa's leg. Then he adjusted the blanket over the horse's withers, careful to make sure it was flat across her back, and fastened the surcingle beneath her. She pounded her hoof on the barn floor.

I know you're bored, he said. I'm bored, too.

Actually, he was more than bored. He was frustrated—exasperated, to use a word Paul seemed to like—because he hadn't been able to ride in days. It was either too cold or too snowy or both. And the lessons that had seemed such a big deal to everyone after he'd fallen seemed to have been completely forgotten. Laura hadn't said a word about them, and he hadn't seen her write any reminders on that Humane Society calendar she kept on the corkboard in the kitchen.

It was so very stupid of him to have allowed his foot to slip from the stirrup after permitting the girl to run a bit, because a second after that he had slid halfway off and it had taken only a small bump to send him flying.

Of course, even if Laura had followed up on the lessons, he wasn't sure he wanted to ride any horse but Mesa. It seemed disloyal. Moreover, every day he had come by the barn this week to do his chores, he had worried that it might be the very last time he would see the animal. Terry had been gone a full week now. The last time he knew for sure that the man had been in the house was New Year's Day, when he'd come back late in the afternoon with some friend of his—a trooper, too—and piled a bunch of clothing into a pair of suitcases and wedged them into the passenger seat of his pickup. Then he'd driven off in the truck, while his buddy had driven away in the cruiser. He and Terry had spoken on the phone twice since then, not about much, and though the man had said he'd be back—and though both he and Laura had seemed as sad as he'd ever seen either one of them—there had been no signs yet that he'd be home anytime soon.

He missed him, but only a little. Still, the fact that he missed Terry at all surprised him. But he did, he missed Terry's stories about work, he missed the times they'd thrown a football in the fall, he missed the way life became a predictable routine when Terry was around.

Moreover, he feared the man's decision to leave put his presence here in jeopardy. Once before he'd been in a house when the man had lit out, and within days he, too, was moved. No reason to believe it wouldn't happen again, and so every day this week he had been careful to eat only the parts of his lunch that were perishable—the yogurt one day, the banana the next— while transferring the small bags of potato chips and snack cakes into his knapsack. (He no longer dared take anything from the kitchen, not after that morning Terry had gone ballistic.) He was usually starving therefore by the time he got home, but Laura hadn't commented on how ravenously he would attack the molasses Anadama bread she had baked one day for an after-school snack, or the fact that he was more likely to eat two apples than one when he'd walk in the door mid-afternoon.

He was careful to keep every penny of the money Paul paid him in his pants pocket whenever he left the house.

And though he tried to pay attention in school, he was finding it more difficult now. Not one kid had called him between Christmas and New Year's—not even Tim, with whose mother he'd left messages twice—and he was finding it hard to view these people as friends during recess and lunch. Besides, Tim and Schuyler were in the math group that was focused on probabilities and beginning geometry, while he was with the kids who were still doing squared numbers and factors. He found this placement galling, because he knew that he could do whatever those two could in math, but his teacher still seemed to doubt him. Most days he didn't even see them a whole lot after lunch.

He was careful not to act up, because he figured if he got in any trouble at all, he'd be out the door in a heartbeat. But he understood that he was angry—he was angry at Terry for leaving, because it meant he, too, might have to go, he was angry at his so-called friends for forgetting that he even existed, and he was angry at the weather because it had kept him off Mesa— and so he resolved to obey Sergeant Rowe's rules and think carefully before he spoke, even if it meant now that he hardly ever said a word.

AND HE WORRIED about Laura. Though he understood Terry was gone because she wanted him gone, that didn't mean she was happy to see him leave. The first few nights she took her cats with her to bed, pulling them out from under the woodstove, where they seemed to sleep in the winter, and carrying them one at a time up the stairs to her room. He didn't hear her crying as she had that night in November when Terry was away at deer camp and she was alone, but he guessed that she was. How could she not? When she told him that she and Terry were going to spend a little time apart, there had been a balneal gauze across her eyes and her voice had been wan.

Most mornings, however, before he would go to school and she would go to the shelter, she was able to rally. She talked freely with him about her children when he was eating his oatmeal and she was packing his lunch. She would chat about the kinds of things nine-year-old girls liked to eat, compared to a boy who was ten (almost eleven, she would add, since his birthday now was only two months away), or how jealous they'd be of the notion that the Heberts had a horse and he was getting to care for the animal and ride her.

He noticed that he and Laura were eating dinner a lot with Paul and Emily—practically every other night, it seemed. Each time Laura would simply join him at the Heberts' house when he was finished with the horse in the afternoon, and the grown-ups would sit in the living room or kitchen talking while he'd watch TV or read or do his homework. He'd listen to the sounds of the voices, sometimes flipping the pages in one illustrated history book or another that Paul would find for him about the Wild West or the cavalry. Occasionally there would be a picture of a buffalo soldier, but most of the time it was as if the black horse soldiers had never existed.

He liked those afternoons more than any other time of the day, though he wasn't exactly sure why. One time he wandered into the room Paul called his library and looked for a long while at the photographs of the Heberts' children and grandchildren, and wondered if the answer might not be as simple as the sensation normal kids had when they saw their grandparents—that Kwanzaa notion of assemblage, of getting all the people together.

He certainly hadn't gotten that feeling the two times Laura's parents had come north from Boston, since that pair clearly viewed him as a stranger. Terry's mother, too. She seemed nice enough—they all seemed nice enough—but none of them knew quite what to make of him. In the eyes of those old people, he was always the foster kid: the kid who wasn't Hillary or Megan, the boy who was only there because their real grandchildren had died.

Not here, though, not in this house. Here was a place where he was accepted and he felt right at home.

THERE WASN'T A lot of sun, but at least there wasn't any wind, and the temperature had climbed above freezing. He was staring longingly at the saddle and the girth, wondering if he should knock on Paul's door and ask if he could go for a ride, when he heard the old man clomp into the barn behind him. The horse was outside in the paddock.

How was school? he asked, offering him a piece of sliced apple from the brown paper bag in his hand.

Okay.

You feel like taking Mesa for a spin this afternoon?

Yeah, I do. A lot.

Thought so. Well, go ahead. You could both use the exercise, I imagine.

Paul handed him the whole bag of apples now—they would feed most of the pieces to the horse—and then grabbed the saddle and a blanket. Alfred reached for the reins and the girth, and then together they started out toward the animal. She was on the far side of the small field, grazing on the hay he had brought her as soon as he arrived here and found her already turned out in the paddock. When Mesa saw them she lifted her long face from the feed, nickered once, and trotted over to the gate.

I made a couple phone calls today, Paul was saying as he started offering the apple slices to the horse. Laura knows. I got our lessons scheduled. Group hour, every Monday afternoon, a place called the Equestrian. We begin next week.

He hadn't expected a group and he grew nervous at the idea. He envisioned a lot of rich white kids who'd know all about horses. How big's this group?

Just two. You and me, we're the group.

Okay, he said, relieved, and he watched Mesa's mouth gnash the apple slices to sauce. She snorted, something she seemed to do when she particularly enjoyed whatever it was she was eating. Another question crossed his mind, and he decided this, too, was a safe one to ask.

Will Mesa smell the other horse on me?

You mean the one at the riding stable?

Uh-huh.

Perhaps if Laura chooses to stop washing your clothes, and you decide to stop bathing. Then, yes, she might. What's your concern?

He shrugged. I don't know. I guess I don't want to hurt her feelings.

The man opened the gate and draped the blanket over the horse. Alfred, my boy, if only grown-ups worried as much as you do about . . .

About what?

About everything. Don't you worry about Mesa's feelings. She won't take offense, I promise.

He followed Paul into the paddock, and suddenly a realization hit him with such force that he stopped for a moment and smiled. If Paul was going ahead and scheduling riding lessons—and Laura knew all about them—that must mean they didn't plan on shipping him out anytime soon.

"I know of three occasions when a white laundress married a colored. And I know of one time when an Indian laundress did."

LIEUTENANT T. R. MCKEEVER,
TENTH REGIMENT, UNITED STATES CAVALRY,
WPA INTERVIEW,
AUGUST 1937

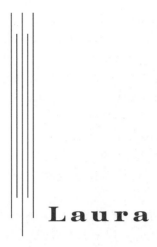

Laura

S he thought the phone was ringing, and she fought through the sheets and the pillows in the dark to reach it, rolling through the wide desert that once had been Terry's half of the bed. When she picked up the receiver she heard only the dial tone, and she realized she'd been dreaming. Something had been ringing in her mind, but not in reality. At least that's what she guessed had just occurred. But maybe somebody was trying to reach her and the phone would ring again in a moment. Maybe it had been ringing for a long while before it pulled her from some preternaturally deep sleep, and the person had hung up only a split second before she finally answered it. Maybe. But not likely, she finally decided.

She fell back into the warmth in the half of the bed in which she'd been sleeping, and wondered at how bright the room was. The moon was not full tonight, but it was large, and a waterfall of light was streaming through the window that faced west. It must be early, perhaps five or five-thirty in the morning. Her alarm would have gone off in another half an hour in any case.

She guessed that if anyone had tried to call her just now, it would have been Terry. Maybe he'd been unable to sleep. Maybe he wanted to talk.

She doubted it was her mother or father, and that something tragic had happened. That was possible, but certainly not probable. If they weren't going to call her at three A.M., she figured, it was doubtful they'd have tried to ring her at five. At that point, they simply would have waited until seven, when they could be sure she was awake.

She remembered vaguely when Terry had phoned her parents with the news that the girls had died. He'd called them the night of the flood, around nine-thirty, from the phone in this bedroom. The phone she'd just touched. She hadn't been in the room with him, she'd been downstairs in the den, surrounded by people. Not a lot of people, but enough. Reverend Cook, though always David or—verbalized in her mind with as much irony as reverence because he was such a down-to-earth man—*Pastor.* His wife, Barbara. The Heberts, Paul and Emily. Her friend Karen, and Karen's husband, Greg. It wasn't exactly a house call, but her doctor, Marion, was there, too— more as a neighbor than as a physician, though she had given her something strong to calm her.

There were a variety of reasons why Terry had phoned her parents instead of her, not the least of which was the simple fact that she had been incapable. She couldn't have made the call. But she had feared also that in some small, unpleasant crevice in her parents' brains—a kind of lobe the two shared after so many years of marriage—they would have been so desperate to find someone to blame that they would have forced her to share with them more details than she could possibly have beared to repeat. Their way through the forest of grief that loomed before them all would be to find culpability—not a reason, because the deaths of nine-year-old girls are always beyond reason—and they would ask and listen and ask and listen until they had a path that would get them through it.

And would they then, in the end, blame her? They'd never say so, even to themselves. Even when the two of them were alone in their house in Dedham, they wouldn't give words to such a thought. She knew that. But she knew also that they would each believe separately that a tragedy such as this would never have befallen their granddaughters had they not lived in Vermont. After all, girls don't get washed over bridges near Boston. Their fathers aren't away at deer camp when it's raining like hell, leaving their poor, fatigued wives alone with the children.

She considered how she should tell her parents that she and Terry had separated for the moment, and whether they would ask her if she wanted to return to Massachusetts to live for a while—come home, they might say, regain your bearings a bit. But then she remembered Alfred and doubted they would suggest that as long as she had the child. And while she did not believe the news of the separation would make them happy, they did not particularly like Terry and they would not be devastated.

She decided she might as well get up a few minutes early, and so she climbed out of bed and went quietly down the stairs. In the kitchen she fed the cats and started to make Alfred's lunch for school, and thought about the coming day at the shelter and the animals there in her care. The Saint Bernard who'd been brought in only yesterday by a loathsome breeder, emaciated and limping because as a puppy something had crushed a front paw and the bones hadn't healed properly. The deaf white cat with a real attitude problem named Josie. The exuberant but wholly undignified stray dog they'd renamed Alexis, in the hope it would give the animal at least the vague aura of a pedigree.

She looked at the line of food she had amassed on the counter—the sandwich she'd made, the bag of potato chips, the pop-top can of fruit cocktail—and started dropping the items into the boy's lunch bag. One of her own cats jumped onto the counter and rubbed up against her arm. She stroked it, and decided she would call her parents before she left for the shelter that morning with the news that she and Terry were spending a little time apart, and Alfred was about to start formal riding lessons. It was an odd commingling, but these were the occurrences that summarized her life at the moment.

The harder call, and one she was less sure how to handle, would be to Louise. At some point she would have to alert Social Services that her—and therefore Alfred's—situation had changed. And though she figured that Louise would be an ally, that call still wouldn't be easy: She felt Terry had let the woman down, and therefore she herself had let the woman down. She reminded herself that her marriage wasn't over, and a little distance now was not an unreasonable need.

Unless it jeopardized the boy.

But even that was a complex issue in her mind. The main reason she was so unhappy with Terry was exactly because he didn't seem to care for the child. Despite his assertions to the contrary—halfhearted, truly, he hadn't even mustered the passion he'd had when she confronted him that night in their bed about what may (May? May? Who was she kidding!) have occurred when he was away at deer camp—more times than not he was either frustrated by the boy or uninterested in him, and so his presence in the house wasn't necessarily the best course for Alfred, either.

And so she grew anxious. She wondered if she had lost her husband and next she would lose the child. Her child. The boy she was beginning to love.

———

"The newspaper reporter wrote that we rode and marched and fought splendidly, in some cases as well as the white regiments he had visited on his tour. He attributed this to his belief that it is easier to recruit the best of our race than his, because we have fewer options. If I see him again, I may offer my opinion that though he is correct we have fewer options, he is wrong in his belief that this company's superiority is the result only of the inferior breed of white man that is enlisting. I am confident we could outride, outmarch, and outfight the very best of his race."

———

SERGEANT GEORGE ROWE,
TENTH REGIMENT, UNITED STATES CAVALRY,
UNDATED LETTER TO HIS BROTHER
IN PHILADELPHIA

———

Phoebe

The camp—it was a term she used only because he did, but in her mind it was much more of a cottage—belonged to another trooper's parents, and it was cozy and comfortable and it had a view of Lake Champlain and the Adirondacks that must have been worth a small fortune. The older couple only lived here through Halloween, however, and then they drove south to a place called New Smyrna, Florida, where they spent the winter and spring in an apartment on a golf course. In her opinion there were a tad too many Hummels on the shelves that lined the living-room walls and in the center of the table on which she and Terry ate breakfast and dinner; moreover, all the furniture seemed a little big for the five small, low-ceilinged rooms that comprised the single-story cottage. But there were big picture windows in both the living room and the bedroom that faced the mountains across the lake, and the few times the sun shone when she was there, she had a glorious view of the winter sunset over Marcy, Haystack, and Whiteface—great snow-covered monoliths now, older and infinitely more primeval than the softer mountains she was accustomed to seeing in northeast Vermont.

She'd been here with Terry since Monday, almost four days now, and she was starting to think about the possibility of getting a job in this corner of the state, instead of one in Waterbury or Montpelier. She figured Middlebury College could always use administrative minions, and there seemed to be a great many small businesses—microbreweries, software entrepreneurs, companies that made awnings or gourmet cheese or wooden toys—that on any given day had a want ad for a bean counter in the local newspaper. In theory she was supposed to be back at work at the general store next Monday, and her father expected her home that weekend . . . but maybe she could give Frank and Jeannine notice (Notice? Notice? she thought. She was leaving the cash register and meat slicer at a general store in the middle of nowhere, for God's sake!) and explain to her father once and for all that it was time she got on with her life.

She discovered that she liked living with Terry—or, to be precise, she liked hanging out with him for a couple of days in what really amounted to an extended vacation. He'd called her the day after New Year's to tell her that Laura had asked him to move out for the time being, and they spoke on the phone a couple of times before agreeing in the second week of January that she should come to the cabin for a visit. She'd have dinner with him on Monday, that was the plan, and though they never verbalized the notion, it was clear she would spend Monday night with him, too. What was she supposed to do, drive all the way home at ten or ten-thirty at night? It was a two-and-a-half-hour drive, and the weather seemed to be in one of those deep winter phases where it was cold and snowy and the roads were often as hard and slick as the skin on a bowling ball. The next day, Tuesday, was one of her days off, but she called Frank anyway to tell him she felt poorly—physically and emotionally—and she was going to take her first vacation since she'd started to work for him and his wife. It wasn't a whole lot of warning, but slicing turkey and ham and selling Slim Jims wasn't rocket science, and he'd be able to find someone to fill in. Then she told her dad essentially what Laura had told Terry when she asked him to leave: They needed a little distance. She phrased it more nicely than that (at least she hoped that she had), but the fact was, her father had treated her like dirt since Christmas Day. She owed him nothing, at least not right now. And if Frank and Jeannine should call for any reason and get her father, well, he might mention her bouts with morning sickness (now, wouldn't *that* get their tongues motoring behind the cash register!), but neither Frank nor Jeannine would be all that upset. They might be surprised and they might worry about her as friends, but they wouldn't give a damn as her bosses. They were shocked and pleased that she'd stayed around as long as she had, and had both said in one way or another that it was time for her to get a real job again, anyway.

———

SHE TOOK THE apple pie out of the oven early Thursday evening while Terry climbed out of his uniform and into a pair of blue jeans and a sweatshirt from the police academy. She'd only made the pie because she had the oven going for a meatloaf and baked potatoes, but she liked the way the apples and the cinnamon made the whole cabin smell. She heard Terry humming to himself, and she was pleased he was happy. Certainly she was. She kept reminding herself that they were really only playing house—this wasn't actually living together, if only because not a soul in this county even knew she was here—but spending time with Terry was proving very easy. During the days she had read and tried out the snowshoes she found in the closet, or driven into Middlebury to go shopping. On Wednesday she'd gone north into Burlington and had lunch with a girl she'd remained friends with since high school, even though they only saw each other once or twice a year.

When Terry emerged from the bedroom, he poured himself a beer and put a mug with water and a tea bag in the microwave oven for her.

So, you really like those snowshoes, don't you? he asked.

I do. They're fun. Up where I live, everyone either rides snowmobiles or goes cross-country skiing.

I was never much for either. Russell has a Polaris; he's probably been living on it the past week. But I never took a liking to the sport. Too loud, maybe.

Oh, I agree. My family are big snowmobilers, all of them, and I just don't get the attraction. I have a niece and nephew in elementary school—and I mean first and third grade—who got their own machines for Christmas. I'll tell you, though, I think they would like snowshoeing, too, if they ever gave it a chance.

Where'd you go today? You get far?

Pretty far. I was able to walk all the way down to the lake, and I couldn't have done that in either boots or skis. Too steep. Too much brush. Then I probably went a mile and a half or two miles south of here. Till I hit that inn.

I hope you didn't overdo it.

It felt good. I'm careful.

See anything interesting?

Some animal tracks. Actually, a lot of animal tracks. And, across the lake, the smokestacks from that big paper mill. I'm sure the people who own that inn—hell, the whole state tourism department—just love the view we have of that baby.

It's a monster, isn't it?

She opened the oven and put a long metal skewer into one of the potatoes to make sure it was done, and then reached for the padded mitt to remove all of them. The bell for the microwave chirped, and Terry handed her the mug with her hot tea.

Cheers, he said, tapping the glass against the porcelain.

Cheers, she said, and then, after she had taken a small sip, he leaned forward and kissed her on her lips. She hadn't planned to, but she opened her mouth and felt his tongue glance off hers: It was cold from the beer, and she liked the taste of the alcohol. They kissed for a long moment, and then she pulled away from him and put the mug down on the counter.

We don't want the meatloaf to get too dry, she said, and she realized she was a tiny bit breathless.

No, of course not, he said, and she heard in his voice a slight tremor. He reached around her and turned off the oven, and she realized he was going to help her get their dinner on the table. They hadn't made love since the night she arrived, as if denying themselves this pleasure once the edge had been taken off their desire allowed them to hate themselves—and what they were doing—a tiny bit less.

SHE TRIED TO convince herself that she really didn't have any serious worries as they went for a short walk later that night after dinner. They bundled up in their parkas and then strolled up the long, thin driveway that led to the road. The driveway was wooded, but the fields around the road were largely cleared and it was like emerging from a forest into the closest thing Vermont had to big sky country. They thought they might see the northern lights, but a thin layer of clouds had moved in and blocked out virtually everything above them but the faint glow of the moon. Still, it was nice to be outside, especially with the knowledge that there was a warm bed and a warm body to come home to. Sometimes he walked with his arm around her shoulder and she wrapped her arm around his waist, and she realized what was gnawing at her was the fact that Terry was going to have lunch tomorrow—Friday—with Laura. She had a sense that Terry was pulling away from his wife of his own volition (she tried hard to believe that she was no more than a catalyst) and she was convinced that she and Terry might even fall in love if they just hung around together long enough. Maybe, in some ways, they already had. Neither of them had said such a thing to each other. But it was clear they liked being together a very great deal, and they were most certainly linked by the little baby inside her.

Nevertheless, there was no way on God's green earth that Terry was going to ask out of the marriage, no matter how much he enjoyed being with her, and there was no way she was going to ask him to even consider such a thing. If his marriage was over, it was going to have to be his wife who said so.

He pulled her close and pressed his nose against hers. We should get you back inside, he murmured. Your nose is as cold as an ice cube.

So's yours. After they had started back she added, It's funny, but I don't think I went for a single nighttime walk this fall or winter when I was home. Not one. I used to walk in the afternoons sometimes, when I was done working at the store for the day. But never at night. I wasn't scared—it's pretty safe. I just never did it.

Pretty safe, maybe. But nothing's completely safe. Fourteen-year-old girls disappear in broad daylight in Brattleboro, female hikers seem to fall off the face of the earth while they're on some major trail up on Mount Carmel. I'm glad you didn't take walks at night alone.

You just worry because you see so much.

I do. Even on a good day, I'm likely to see some real nasty stuff. And I try and help, but a lot of the time—maybe even most of the time—there's very little I can do.

A gust of wind blew across their path as they walked, swirling the snow around their boots and their knees. It sounded to her a bit like an owl.

I imagine you do more than you think.

He started to laugh. My dear, I couldn't even keep my own children safe.

Oh, God, Terry, don't go there. There was no way you could have known your daughters would be in danger that day.

I know. Really, I do. But that's exactly what I mean: Things happen all the time that are completely beyond our control. Even—hard to believe, I know—the control of a sergeant with the Vermont State Police.

But at least you try to make things a little safer, a little better. Look at what you tried to do with Alfred.

I take no pride in anything I did with or for Alfred. We never connected, and that's nobody's fault but my own.

You tried.

Not very hard. Maybe if I'd gotten him a couple years ago—a couple houses sooner—I could have done something for him. Helped turn him around. Hell, maybe Laura still can. Maybe she has a magic silver bullet I don't. That wouldn't surprise me. She was always a great mom.

Well, I'll bet you were an amazing dad with your own girls.

I was okay. Maybe even pretty good. But they were amazing kids, too. Even I couldn't screw them up too badly.

She stopped walking, and he paused with her. I have to say something, she began, and this is important. I have enjoyed these last few days a lot. I've enjoyed all the times I've seen you. But if tomorrow you and Laura figure out that you two should be together, I will be . . . not unhappy. How's that for an honest waffle? I will—

Phoebe—

Look, I'm not being a martyr, she went on, and she took his gloved hands in hers. I believe you'd be as good a father as my baby—our baby—could ever have. And, at least when we're naked, we certainly seem to have a lot in common. But I just found myself actually worrying about your lunch tomorrow, and that's not a good place to be. It's not good for me, it's not good for you.

She felt the wind whipping her bangs into her eyes, and she hoped it was only the cold that was making them start to water. What I'm trying to say, she said, before her voice broke abruptly and she was crying and he was pulling her against his chest.

What I'm trying to say . . .

Shhh, he murmured, shhh, and he pressed one index finger, still sheathed in its leather glove, against her lips.

If she'd finished the sentence, she thought, her mind muddled by tears, she would have said, *What I'm trying to say is I want you to break this thing we have off because I'm selfish and I haven't the strength to do it myself.* But she realized she was too weak to even verbalize the idea, much less push him away and end their affair.

———

"It wasn't until this winter that I even realized I was lonely. It may have been the presence of these tiny Indian girls, but the fact I have nieces and nephews in Philadelphia I've never met has begun to trouble me more than ever."

———

SERGEANT GEORGE ROWE,
TENTH REGIMENT, UNITED STATES CAVALRY,
LETTER TO HIS BROTHER IN PHILADELPHIA,
MARCH 15, 1877

———

Laura

The barracks were within a mile and a half of the county animal shelter on Route 7, but because they were to the south of the building, she never had to pass the site where Terry would usually begin and end his shift. She knew that he, however, had to pass the Humane Society at least twice a day, since he was staying out at the Labarge family's winterized camp on Lake Champlain. The reality, of course, was that he probably drove by the shelter considerably more often than that: Much of his district spread out to the north, and both the courthouse and the state's attorney's office were in that direction. Sometimes, when she was in the room with the cats in the front of the building, or walking one of the dogs and getting some air herself, she would find herself staring at the two-lane state road down the hill from the shelter, half-expecting to see his green cruiser spin by.

She was meeting him for lunch today at a casual restaurant called Rosie's, and it would be the first time she'd seen him since he and Henry came by the house so he could get his pickup and a couple suitcases of clothes. They'd spoken on the phone five or six times since that afternoon, but they hadn't laid eyes on each other. She sat now at a table in the sunniest corner the hostess could find, a woman alone with a sheaf of papers about animal vaccines and contagious diseases, and sipped her tea and waited, wondering what it was she wanted from the lunch—what, if anything, they would resolve.

When he arrived he waved at the waitress behind the counter near the front door, and he had to clap the shoulders of two men who, based on their own uniforms, worked in the service department of one of the nearby auto dealers. Perhaps they serviced the barracks' cruisers. Perhaps they were volunteers with the local fire department or the rescue squad, and their paths crossed with Terry's at small (and, alas, large) fires and accidents.

Even the hostess knew him and they, too, shared a small laugh as she guided him over to her table. Was there anyone in this part of the county Terry didn't know at least slightly? Probably not.

He stood for a brief second before her as the hostess retreated, then awkwardly leaned over and kissed her on the cheek. When he sat down across from her, he was smiling.

It's good to see you, he said. Really good.

She put the papers in the wicker tote she used as a pocketbook and sat back in her seat. It didn't seem fair to her that she'd spent twenty minutes that morning thinking about which blouse and sweater and shade of lipstick she should wear, when he got to slide inside the same clothes every single day. Of course, it was like that to some degree for all men, but it was particularly easy for him.

It's good to see you, too, she said. I didn't notice you pull into the parking lot.

He put his campaign hat on the empty chair beside him. I'm parked around the side. There weren't any spots out front.

She almost commented on how busy the restaurant was, but she didn't: It would sound, in her mind, as if they had just begun dating and needed small talk to get through the awkward moments.

You're looking good, he said when she only nodded. You hanging in there?

I am. It's quiet. Lonely. Must be for you, too.

Can be.

I called the cabin last night. There was no answer.

Yeah, I went for a walk after dinner, he said, and he looked down at the menu. That's where I must have been when you called.

She had a sense that he wasn't telling the whole truth, but she didn't press it because she wasn't here to pick a fight.

You get the chimney cleaned? he went on, his eyes still on the menu. Earl show up on time?

Earl always shows up on time.

He does, doesn't he? And the furnace hasn't been acting up?

You'd know if it was.

I guess. I just feel bad that I'm not there to keep the house pasted together.

The house is fine. I'm a big girl: I can carry in my own wood, I can pick up the phone and call the chimneysweep. I can even read the pressure gauges on the furnace.

You lose power in the windstorm the other night?

We did. I think we've lost power twice in the last week.

Twice?

Neither time for very long. And one time neither of us was even home. You?

Once.

Furnace go out?

It did.

You don't have a woodstove out there. You must have been freezing.

It was a tad nippy for a night, I grant you that. And I had to go get a torch to unfreeze the water pipes the next day. You'd know what to do if our pipes ever froze, right?

She nodded. Of course.

You'd call me.

Actually, I'd call a plumber.

Well, if you can't get a plumber, call me. Please.

He looked briefly back at the menu and then at the specials written in chalk on one of the blackboards in the large room. I always have the turkey here, he went on. Especially this time of the year. I don't know why I bother to look. The open-faced turkey and gravy. He flipped the menu shut and shrugged. So, how's Alfred? he asked.

He's fine.

What does he think about all this?

The fact we're taking some time off?

That's a nice term for it.

He's been through worse, I imagine. He said he lived one place once where the man, his foster dad, just up and left.

And the guy never came back?

Nope.

What a life. He still doing all those chores for Paul?

Tending the horse, you mean? You bet.

He's good about that, isn't he? Most kids, I guess, wouldn't be that responsible. They'd find excuses. They'd go do something else.

What would he do?

I don't know. Most kids would figure it out.

She looked across at him, trying to understand why what he had just said annoyed her so much. He stared back at her and offered a smile that he probably thought was boyish and winning and handsome. Not the knowing look he reserved for people he was about to nail for speeding or because they were driving with more beer in their blood than white corpuscles; it was a smile that once she had found quite attractive.

Alfred isn't most kids, she said simply, but she knew there was a trace of irritation in her voice.

Nope. Has he been paying attention to you—listening to you?

He has.

And he hasn't gotten into any trouble?

When was the last time he got into any trouble, Terry? Seriously?

I'm sorry, really I am. But I know what I saw the Monday morning after Christmas.

You still think he was up to something?

Still do.

The waitress returned to take their order, and she watched the way he teased the young woman good-naturedly about her haircut, and then asked her whether the gravy was thick and fatty enough to come with an angioplasty. Everything he said seemed to make her giggle. After she left, he leaned forward with his elbows on the table and the fingertips on his hands joined in a pyramid, and asked, So, tell me: Where are we? What are you feeling these days?

Well, I would love to see us get back to where we were. It was pretty good once, wasn't it? I don't think I'm making that up.

Nope, not a bit. It was. Remember when we got the girls all the way to the top of Mount Lafayette?

I do.

And the time we left them with Mom and went to Montreal for that long weekend? It doesn't get better than that.

No. That was nice, she said, and though the memories were indeed pleasant—capable, even, of taking the edge off her annoyance—she had the sense that they both were stalling. Certainly she was.

You still have that chemise? The one you slept in?

Somewhere.

You should find it.

There was the small sliver of an ice cube left in her water glass, and she swirled the liquid so that it disappeared. Then: I don't think it'll ever be like that again. I could find it. But we're older now. And very different.

You never know.

Yes, you do. Are you seeing someone, Terry?

Pardon me?

I asked if you were seeing someone.

Don't tell me that you're still obsessed with what my brother said back in November.

Nope. Not at all. But if we're going to talk about me in a chemise, I want to know if you're seeing someone else.

That's why you're asking?

I'm asking because we haven't connected on anything for the last month—

A month is not a very long period of time. People go through phases, you know—

We haven't connected much in two years. You said so yourself. It's the good periods that have been rare.

That's not my fault.

I didn't say it was.

I could ask you if you were seeing somebody. I could—

And you know you'd be acting like a jerk. You know damn well I'm not seeing anybody else. I can say that. I am not seeing anybody. I haven't had a drink with another man in a bar, I haven't kissed one or held one or fucked one. I—

You might want to keep it down if this is going to become an NC-17 brawl.

I was almost whispering.

Words carry in this place. Trust me, I know.

I won't ask why.

Excuse me?

She sat back in her chair, surprised that she hadn't started to cry. She was angry and she was hurt, but she felt strangely composed. She thought she would ask him one more time, though there was no longer much doubt in her mind: So, tell me, she said, it's a simple yes-or-no question. Are you seeing another woman?

Behind him she saw their waitress reaching through the window to the kitchen for the plates with her egg salad sandwich and his open-faced turkey, and she was glad he didn't know their lunch was about to arrive. He might have stalled if he had, knowing the imminent return of the waitress would give him another moment to consider his answer.

He took a deep breath and looked back into her eyes. I am, he said. I'm sorry.

She nodded. It wasn't nearly as painful as she had thought it would be. Perhaps because she had been expecting it for so long, the blow barely nicked her. Is it serious? she asked simply.

It's complicated.

Meaning?

I guess it's serious.

Do I know her?

No. You two have never met.

Can I presume, then, this mystery woman is the person you met in November when you were supposed to be hunting? The woman you *claimed* you only had a beer with in a bar?

Yes. You can.

The waitress arrived, smiling, and placed the egg salad sandwich before her and the hot turkey in front of her husband.

Can I get you anything else? she asked.

Without thinking about what she would do, she reached for her coat and her tote bag and stood, and then—aware that the waitress was gazing at her, confused, and her husband looked vaguely alarmed—she pushed the plate with the hot turkey and the gravy and the creamed squash off the table and into Terry's lap. A napkin for my husband, she said to the young woman. Maybe even a towel: No offense, but that gravy does look pretty greasy. Other than that, I think we're all set. Then she left the restaurant, waiting until she got to the parking lot and was sure that Terry wasn't following her to put on her coat.

It was only when she was in her car and on her way back to the animal shelter that the magnitude of what she had done dawned upon her, and despite what he had told her, she was unable to restrain a small smile: Like all troopers, he had four pairs of all-season uniform pants and an equal number of long-sleeve winter shirts. She was quite sure that half his pants and two of those shirts were in the ironing pile at the house, because she'd seen them there that week. And so although she didn't know exactly how he was spending his evenings at that camp, she realized there was a pretty good chance that he would be shopping for pre-wash stain removers after work, and tonight he would be doing his laundry and ironing.

"I knew he liked me. Maybe if I had been older it would have been harder to like him, given what his uniform meant to my people. But I was a teenager, I was still so young. And he was very handsome."

VERONICA ROWE (FORMERLY POPPING TREES),

WPA INTERVIEW,

MARCH 1938

The Heberts

The riding ring was filled with girls, most of them blond, most of them with long straight hair that (inevitably) they had pulled back into ponytails. For a moment Paul watched a group somewhere in the neighborhood of Alfred's age, five kids nine or ten or eleven (but who could really tell these days, with girls starting to mature so young? For all he knew, they were all third- or fourth-graders) giggling as they fed fast-food French fries to a hitched Appaloosa. They were wearing either leather chaps over their jeans or stretch riding breeches, and they all had boots that laced partway up their shins.

It looks like you and I are the only males here, he said to Alfred.

Maybe some of the horses.

In name only. Count on it: Any male horses here aren't exactly the men they used to be—if you get my drift.

Some of the girls looked up at them, but most paid them little attention.

It's nice in here, Alfred said. Not too hot. I'd thought it might be like a gym.

Nope.

There were two large rings, and a pair of teenagers was jumping over small red-and-white fences in the far one.

A middle-aged woman approached, and one of the girls ran from the hitching post where she, too, had been trying to convince the big Appaloosa to eat French fries, her arms filled with a tangled bridle and a jumbled mass of reins, and intercepted the teacher before she could reach them. The woman, small and athletic with long red hair that fell down her back in a braid, bent over and disentangled the great lump of leather. He was relieved she was an adult—a real adult—not some twenty- or twenty-one-year-old kid. It was bad enough he was taking a lesson, but the notion that he might have been taught by a person barely a third his age had been galling.

When she was done she motioned for the girl to return the tack to a room off to the side, and then ambled over to them.

It looks like you're Paul and Alfred, she said. I'm Heather Barrett. Welcome. She extended her hand first to Paul and then to Alfred, and for a moment the boy looked at the hand, apparently surprised that it had been extended to him so cavalierly.

I understand you've already got a pretty good foundation, she said to him. That true?

I guess.

I taught him, which is probably a mixed blessing, Paul added.

How so?

I'm a good teacher and I ride pretty well for an old man. But I wouldn't even know where to attach a lead line to a bridle.

You ever been on a lead line, Alfred?

The boy looked up at him. Have I?

Nope.

Well, let's get you started and see what you know. She turned to the girls at the hitching post and called out, Are Delta and Thomas ready?

One of the girls stopped laughing long enough to tell her that both horses were saddled, and then ran toward a line of animals at another hitching post at the edge of the ring. They're over here, she called back over her shoulder.

You'll be on Delta, she said to Alfred after they'd started toward the two mounts, and, Paul, you'll be on Thomas. Neither horse is going to set any land speed records these days, and you never know whether Delta will just decide to go to sleep on you. But I think the biggest difficulty you'll have is that they're friends, and sometimes the pony brain gets more interested in his pony pals than the fact there's a human on his back and he has a job to do. Got it?

He watched her turn to get the mounting block, which was about a dozen yards toward the center of the ring, but Alfred hadn't realized he was expected to wait. The girl who'd run ahead had already taken off Delta's halter and tightened her girth, and so Alfred had gone ahead and climbed into the saddle. For a moment Heather paused with the block in her hands when she saw that he had swung himself up onto the animal—she was surprised and she chuckled—but then Paul saw her turn her attention to him.

Think you'll need this? she asked.

I'll never turn down a device that makes my life easier, he said, and she laughed once again in a way that made him happy.

H E   A N D   E M I L Y had dinner that night at Laura's for a change, and he told Laura how well Alfred had done. The boy had spent about a minute and a half on the lead line before Heather had determined he was well beyond needing one, and though she said his form could use work when he posted, he was cantering by the end of the hour. The girls who hung out at the ring after school had watched him with curiosity, and then, Paul decided, grown to respect him if only because he was a boy and he was there. None of the girls, Alfred had told him, went to his school.

In bed that night, Emily's head on his shoulder, they talked about the wounded couple across the street, and they discussed whether the pair would consider counseling. They agreed both that those younger people should and that it was unlikely. Terry was involved with someone else, Laura had told them when Alfred wasn't in the room, and in her opinion he had little affection for the child.

What do you think would happen to Alfred if they got divorced? he asked Emily now, allowing a book he'd been reading to fall closed on the mattress beside him. She was wearing a red nightgown they'd bought at the Corn Palace in South Dakota—emblazoned on the front was a picture of a smiling ear of white and yellow corn with husks for arms and a wild mane of hair made from its tassels—and he noticed that she'd managed to get the smell of bird feed out of the material. The first time she'd tried it on it had looked nice on her, but it had also stunk like the Krazy Korn brand pellets that had been merchandised in great display silos that day beside the official Corn Palace nightshirts and sweatshirts and socks.

You mean logistically?

I guess.

Nothing, I hope.

He wouldn't be taken from Laura?

I doubt it.

But you never know, do you?

No, but I have to believe that people like Louise can see he's better off with Laura than anyplace else he's been lately.

True, true. And Laura wouldn't feel overwhelmed to be raising a young boy alone and decide to give him up, he said. Right?

Good Lord, Paul, of course she wouldn't. She views herself as his mother now. She *is* his mother now!

Oh, I know how much she cares for him. But I worry . . .

She's a little better every day. Why, she's much stronger now than she was three or four months ago.

She is, isn't she?

Certainly. She's had to care for someone again, and I think that's the best thing that could have happened to her.

He thought about that for a moment, recalling Laura and Alfred as they stood in their doorway when he and Emily were saying good night to them after dinner. I would miss him if he left, he said, a remark he made without thinking, and one that surprised him when he heard the words in the air in their bedroom.

Alfred, you mean.

Yes, Alfred. I would—I will—miss Terry, too, if he and Laura don't get through this. But I was speaking of Alfred.

I think Terry needs . . . oh, I don't know what Terry needs. He hasn't been himself this whole winter.

He didn't say good-bye when he left, you know.

You sound hurt.

No, not really. Surprised is all.

Maybe he didn't think he'd be gone all that long.

It just wasn't like him. It seemed so out of control. Here's a man who's seen an awful lot over the years, but he's always been nothing if not in control, he said, and he recalled an August evening some years ago after Terry had spent the day watching the mashed bodies of two mountain bikers pulled from beneath some out-of-state SUV (the driver had died, too, Paul believed, but he wasn't quite sure), and how Terry had come home and mowed the lawn as if it had been just another day on the road, and chatted with Emily and him for ten or fifteen minutes about how much his girls were enjoying some circus day camp in the village.

I wish I knew about this other woman, Emily murmured.

Why?

She sighed and ran her hand over his chest. Because I like Laura. I want to know what he sees in somebody else.

He took her hand and held it: He felt a soreness along his upper thighs and his lower back. Heather had worked him harder this afternoon than he'd worked himself throughout the last month, and he was going to pay the price, he could tell, for at least the next couple of days. He stretched his legs and arched his back ever so slightly, hoping to mitigate the pain; he didn't want to have to get out of bed to get an aspirin, and thereby admit to Emily that an hour on a horse with a real teacher could make him feel so badly beaten up.

―――

". . . and so I may not re-up this fall. I think I need a change."

―――

SERGEANT GEORGE ROWE,
TENTH REGIMENT, UNITED STATES CAVALRY,
LETTER TO HIS BROTHER IN PHILADELPHIA,
MARCH 15, 1877

―――

Terry

Russell took off his boots and his socks—white once, but now the color of a T-shirt that's been left out on the street in the rain—and rested his feet on one of the other wooden chairs that sat around the table near the sliding glass doors.

So this place belongs to Henry's parents? he asked his brother.

Terry counted the beers in the refrigerator, relieved they were down to three, and then pushed the door shut. If he himself drank one more, he decided, then that would limit Russell to another two. Of course, there was also the one that Russell was drinking right now, and the one he'd said he had at a bar in Vergennes on his way here, while waiting for Terry to finish his shift. And so even if his brother had downed two or three cold ones before leaving the tavern, which was altogether possible, he wouldn't have drunk more than a six-pack tonight. He guessed Russell could handle that.

Yup. I called Henry and expected to sleep for a night on some foldout couch in the living room, but he set me up here.

Man, don't leave. Patch things up with Laura, and bring her out here, too.

You really think I should stay? he asked. The moon was completely covered over by clouds tonight, and so the lake and the mountains across the water were invisible. For all Russell could see, outside the glass doors and beyond the wooden deck there might have been nothing more interesting than a parking lot.

I do. Become a squatter. This place is mighty nice, I can tell, and I haven't even gotten to see it in daylight yet.

The views are pretty special, I have to admit.

Laura seen it?

He sat down in the chair opposite his brother's feet, relieved that Phoebe had been gone since Friday morning and wouldn't be back until tomorrow night. Wednesday. He had Thursday and Friday off this week, and their plan was that she would stay here at the camp with him those days.

No, she hasn't been out here yet, he said.

I bet she'd like it.

Probably.

You seen her?

I saw her last Friday. We had lunch. And we spoke on the phone yesterday. I called her.

Russell drained the beer and then rested the bottle on the floor beside him. She's a mighty nice woman, and you two got a lot of years together. A lot of history. I ought to go up to Cornish tomorrow and fix you two back up. Be the peacemaker.

I don't think so.

You don't want your sweet-tempered younger brother to be your marital ambassador?

No. I don't want that.

Well, I presume you know what you're doing.

I'm not doing anything. She kicked me out.

With reason.

Point noted.

Really, this is a woman who takes in all kinds of strays for a living: Dogs. Cats. Now kids. It's just what she does. You must have fucked up in a truly major way for her to kick you out.

When Russell had called from Saint Johnsbury and said he thought he'd use his day off to come see how his older brother was doing, Terry had supposed that he was being sent here by their mother. She remained worried about him—him and Laura, to be precise, given the reality that she'd called Laura at least as many times as she'd called him since New Year's Day—and he guessed that she wanted to get a sense both of where he was living and whether he and Laura might reconcile.

Thank you, Russell, for that analysis.

You want to give me the details?

Not particularly.

Shit, we all know you're seeing someone. I'd bet my truck it's that girl you met up at deer camp.

You'd be risking a lot on a gut feeling.

Laura told Mom you fessed up the other day! And unless you been screwin' around far more than anybody ever realized, it has to be that girl. What's her name? he asked, and he snapped his fingers twice as if that would help him remember.

Phoebe.

Phoebe what?

I really don't want to talk about this, Russell, okay? There's more to it than you know—or anyone knows.

Suit yourself. It seems to me—

It seems to me the last time we talked about this was at Mom's on Thanksgiving, and that conversation did not have a particularly good end.

Hey, I'd had too much to drink that afternoon.

I understand.

I'm sorry.

I know you are.

Want to know what I was going to say—or do you know that, too?

Fine, go ahead.

I think this has something to do with the boy.

Alfred? Why in the name of God would you think this has anything at all to do with Alfred?

He shrugged. You drop a new element into a relationship, and who the hell knows what will happen. Look at me and Nicole, he said, referring to the young nurse he'd been dating for close to half a year.

What about you and Nicole?

She got a puppy, and it's made things a hell of a lot more difficult. Her apartment always smells like puppy shit, and she constantly wants to take the thing outside and walk it. She won't even spend the night at my place these days because of that damn little dog, he went on, before glancing toward the kitchen. You got more of these? he asked, and he motioned down toward the bottle on the floor.

In the refrigerator.

He rose from the chair and said, Incidentally, you'll be happy to know it's a shelter dog. Hound dog and beagle, I believe. Pretty cute, even if he has screwed up my sex life.

A puppy and a little boy are not the same thing.

No, a little boy is a much bigger deal. That's my point. You see the chaos a dog has caused? Well, just imagine what a kid can do. Especially that kid.

He rubbed his eyes for a long moment and pressed his fingertips against the bridge of his nose. His head hurt, at least in part because the clouds hadn't rolled in until mid-afternoon, and so he'd spent the day squinting against the snow and the sun in his cruiser. But Russell, he knew, was making his headache worse. Almost automatically he wanted to defend the boy and defend his wife, but he lacked the energy tonight and so he said simply, Laura's and my problems have nothing to do with Alfred. Okay?

You seen him since you left? Russell asked from the kitchen, after opening the beer and tossing the cap into the metal wastepaper basket.

I'm going to try and see him next week. Go watch a riding lesson or something.

Big of you.

Give me a break, Russell, when would I have seen him lately?

People figure these things out. Divorced dads—

Laura and I are not divorced. And I am not the boy's dad.

You got that right.

Now, what does that mean?

I don't know. Maybe it's just that you treat him like he's Laura's kid. Not yours.

I believe you've seen the two of us together exactly one time.

Russell wandered around the living room, picking up the Hummel figurines and putting them down, and gazing for long moments into the blackness outside the large windows and the sliding glass doors.

And he was too quiet. That wasn't like you, either.

You make it sound like you'll never see him again.

It seems to me if you and Laura split up, the boy goes back to wherever it is he came from. Don't you think so?

I don't know.

Well, I can see you're all broken up by the possibility, Russell said, and he turned toward him with a smirk on his face. Of course, it's probably no big deal to the kid, either. Right? He's probably used to being dumped.

You are one prize asshole when you drink, do you know that? Do us both a favor and don't finish that one, okay?

Russell looked at the beer, saw it was still two-thirds full, and chugged what was left in a couple of seconds. I got some news for you, he said when he was done, wiping his mouth with the sleeve of his flannel shirt.

I can't wait.

Tomorrow's not really my day off.

Don't tell me you were—

Nope. I quit.

Quit.

Well, fired, too, maybe. I guess you could say it was a mutual thing. The dispatcher claimed I had beer on my breath yesterday when I brought in my truck—

You were drinking while you were driving? Are you crazy?

I had one beer when I was done with the route.

Yeah, right.

Truly.

This the first time they ever catch you drinking?

They didn't catch me doing anything.

This the first time they ever accuse you of drinking?

Nah. They've been all over me for a couple months now.

Second time? Third?

He wandered back into the kitchen and left the empty bottle in the sink. I think I will have another one, thank you very much.

This the second time they nail you? he called into the other room, raising his voice a notch to be heard.

Third. But who's counting?

Apparently they are, Terry said when his brother returned to the living room. Mom know?

Nope.

Nicole?

Yup.

What does she think?

Russell took a long swallow and then puffed out his cheeks. Sometimes, Terry thought, his brother looked like the vast majority of people he busted: unkempt, uncivil, and just a little bit dangerous. I don't care what she thinks, he said.

She dump you?

He grinned again. What was it you said to me a couple minutes ago? Let's see: There's more to it than you know. I like that, I like it a lot. So let's try it out: Terry, there's more to it than you know. How's it feel?

I didn't mean to be evasive. I just didn't want to talk about it.

Well, neither do I, Russell said, and he sat down across from him at the table.

You keep this up, and someday you're going to run out of places to work in Saint Johnsbury, he told him. He thought the job with the bottler was his brother's third in five years.

Then maybe I'll move here. Join you in this fine corner of the state. It's warmer. A little less snow. And I'd get to be near you, he said, his voice dripping with feigned sweetness. Maybe I'll even hang around here for a couple of days. Spend some quality time with you.

Terry quickly reminded himself that his brother wasn't a bad sort when he was sober: a little irritating and a tad insecure, but he certainly wasn't malevolent. It was only when he started to drink that he went from slightly annoying to completely detestable. Consequently, he figured the best thing he could do right now would be to get some real food into him and keep him from getting any more drunk than he already was. The last thing he wanted was for his brother to decide to dig in his heels and stay here any longer than necessary—especially with Phoebe arriving tomorrow night.

I have some pork chops and barbecue sauce in the refrigerator, and there's some Minute Rice in the cabinet, he said, consciously ignoring his brother's last remark. Why don't we make ourselves some dinner? You can set the table.

I can, can I?

You can if you want to eat, he said, and he stood. Russell took a long swallow of his beer and then pushed himself to his feet, too. He wondered if he should call Nicole the moment Russell passed out, and insist that she reconcile with his brother: He wouldn't, but that didn't stop him from wishing there was a way he could be sure that Russell would get lost in the morning.

———

IN THE NIGHT he dreamt of Laura, and he was with her in Cornish and they were happy. When he awoke he was briefly disoriented, unsure where he was and unaware that his children—his daughters—were dead. Then he saw the placement of the windows in the room and he remembered, his contentment withered, and he wanted nothing more than to hold Laura and be held by her.

In the living room he heard Russell snoring and he shuddered. He wished he were home; he wished he were better with Alfred; he wished the roots that linked him to Phoebe Danvers were slender, their flowers incapable of efflorescence.

In the morning, he presumed, he would feel better. But he wasn't sure, and he pressed his face into his pillow and tried to find again that dream in his sleep where he was happy and his life wasn't riddled by tragedy and mistake.

"He had a brother in Philadelphia who was a car-penter. We didn't have much money, but we decided someday we would use what we had and go east."

VERONICA ROWE (FORMERLY POPPING TREES),
WPA INTERVIEW,
MARCH 1938

Laura

At breakfast Alfred surprised her. Out of the blue the boy said, I'll probably never know who my dad was, but I think I've found my great-great-great-grandfather.

She lifted her eyes from her tea to try to read the child's face. See if this was a setup for a punch line of some sort. She thought Alfred looked content, but there was nothing in his countenance to suggest that this was a joke.

Go on, she said.

I mean, it's probably not true. But it could be.

And that is?

Sergeant George Rowe. I think we could be related.

She nodded. Is this a hunch or something more? she asked. She understood why he might want to believe he was descended from the cavalry soldiers he'd grown interested in, but she didn't see any link other than the fact that he was black. Moreover, she wondered if this notion might be a harbinger of a more profound wish: the desire to know who his father was, and where his mother was now.

A little of both, he answered. It hit me the other day at the riding ring when Heather said I must have riding in my blood. Well, Sergeant Rowe was a great rider, too, and after he left the Army, he moved to Philadelphia. He had a brother there. He married a Comanche woman, and they settled down in the very same city where my mom was born ninety years later.

I guess it's possible, she said, though she knew the odds were infinitesimal.

I know it sounds crazy when I say it out loud. But when I keep it to myself, it seems like it's true.

The world is filled with crazy things that are true, she said. Trust me, I know. Then she rested her hand on top of his, tenderly rubbing her thumb against the soft spot between his own thumb and forefinger, and looked him squarely in the eyes and asked, Do you want us to try and track down your mother? See how she's doing? Maybe even see if we can discover who your father was? My feelings won't be hurt if you want us to make an effort. It might be fun.

He seemed to mull the idea over for a moment, before shaking his head. Maybe when I'm older, he answered, gazing down at their fingers, but not now. Right now . . .

Go on.

I want to stay here.

Oh, Alfred, of course, she said reflexively, surprised and then moved—she felt a small, rapturous swell building inside her—by the honesty and affection in his short answer. I didn't mean I would *ever* want you to leave.

I like it here, he went on as if she hadn't spoken, and I don't need to know anything else.

She slid her chair beside his and pulled his head to her chest. She squeezed him against her and smiled, and buried her face in the sweet smell of the shampoo that lingered in his hair.

HER MOTHER STILL wrote her letters. They talked on the phone and on rare occasions her mother would send her an e-mail from the computer her father kept in his study, but her mother's favorite way of communicating with her was to write long, handwritten letters every second or third week. Sometimes it was on hotel stationery and sometimes it began on one of the Humane Society note cards she received as thanks for the contributions that she, too, made to the organization, before continuing on white copy paper that she took from her husband's computer printer. The letters were usually long and chatty, and filled with misspellings—an indication of neither her mother's intelligence nor her education, but merely of her entitled disregard for convention. People (especially her daughter) knew what she meant, and she needn't waste time, therefore, looking up words in the dictionary.

Laura had no idea how many correspondents actually wrote back to her mother—or how often—but she didn't believe there were many. She imagined her mother's friends most likely responded by telephone, and in some cases via e-mail, which her father would then print out and deliver like a letter.

In the mail today was one of those notes from her mother, and Laura discovered it in the mailbox when she came home from the animal shelter at almost the same moment that she saw Alfred emerge from the Heberts' paddock on Mesa. She'd had an afternoon meeting today, and so Paul had met the boy at the bus stop. Now as she stood beside her car with her mail in her hands, Alfred rode across the street to her, the horse's hooves rhythmic and loud on the pavement, and she noticed that the animal's eyes were watching the exhaust from her idling car.

Howdy, Alfred said to her, his common greeting this week when he was atop the big animal. His attempt at a cowpoke's accent sounded more Southern than Western, but the very notion that he would offer such a playful acknowledgment thrilled her, and she blew a kiss up to him with her fingers.

How was school? she asked.

Okay.

Only okay?

She could see the shoulders of his parka move ever so slightly. She had scheduled a meeting for the next day with his teacher, hoping that in person she could convince the woman to do what she had failed to make her do over the phone: move Alfred from the math group that was bogged down in squared numbers and factors into the more advanced one that was exploring elementary geometry. She was concerned now that she'd pushed too hard on the phone, however, and so it was possible that the woman had been needlessly defensive around Alfred today—perhaps even hostile.

Maybe better than okay. We had a video about Mount Everest. I liked that.

How was Ms. Logan?

Okay. Her crabby self to some kids, but not to me.

And math?

Boring.

Well, that's what Ms. Logan and I will talk about tomorrow. Have you eaten?

Uh-huh. Paul and me—

Paul and I.

Paul and I had this peanut butter glop Emily made.

I'm sure it wasn't glop.

No, it was glop. That's what it was called. She said it was mostly peanut butter and cream cheese and Cool Whip. They got the recipe from some diner in Oklahoma.

It actually sounds pretty tasty.

It was kind of like pudding, but you knew it was bad for you.

She saw Paul emerging from the barn with a toolbox and a couple of two-by-fours. What's Paul working on?

The outdoor manger. It's a little low.

Mesa's complaining, is she?

She doesn't complain about anything, he said, and he stroked the animal along her shoulder.

You have much homework tonight?

Enough. I'll be in in about an hour, I guess. Paul doesn't think it will take long. That okay?

That's fine. I'll go start dinner, she said, and she watched the boy almost effortlessly back the horse up a couple of feet, and then turn her around and ride across the road to the Heberts'. She climbed back into her car and tossed the pile of mail onto the passenger seat beside her, and noticed for the first time that in addition to catalogs and bills and a letter from her mother, there was a piece of correspondence from the SRS office in Middle-bury. She knew instantly it would be from Louise, and she slit open the envelope with her fingernail to read it that moment.

It was brief and to the point. It was almost time to schedule a case review, and she saw no reason to wait until the end of February—when Alfred would have been with them for a full six months. She wanted to know if there was a day that might work for her in the coming weeks.

Laura told herself there was nothing alarming or threatening about the letter, and she shouldn't read anything into it. She'd known this was coming since Alfred had come into their lives the Sunday of Labor Day weekend.

Quickly she slid the SRS letter into her tote bag and then opened the note from her mother as well. She'd planned on reading it once she was inside and had taken her coat off, but she decided she would get it over with now, too. This way she could put the whole stack of mail in the den and not have to think about it until later, when dinner was made and cleaned up, and Alfred had bathed and gone to bed.

The letter was short and not particularly newsy. Normally her mother would be sure to include her opinions on whatever ballet or show she'd seen most recently in Boston, and a reference to which books she'd just read. She'd have an observation about her father's health (which, in her mother's mind, was always fine, and the aches and pains that came with his age a mere sign of male hypochondria), and she might offer an anecdote she'd heard at a garden club meeting (and why, it seemed to her, Cornish, Vermont, could use such a club). Not this time. She got right to the point: She hadn't stopped thinking about her daughter and son-in-law's separation since Laura had called, and she was very sad for everyone involved—even the boy, who, both she and her father presumed, would now have to be placed in another foster home. Still, she held out hope for a reconciliation. If that wasn't meant to be, however, and her daughter needed to start fresh someplace new, she could always come home. In the meantime, Laura should let them know if she needed money—and, if so, how much. They would, of course, give her whatever she needed to get back on her feet, because they couldn't bear to think of her alone and worried about how she was going to make ends meet.

She thought she should be angry, but she wasn't. This was merely her mother being her mother: as oblivious as ever to what her daughter wanted to do with her life, and why. And so she simply drove the car up to the house, parked it in its usual spot by the small carriage barn, and then went inside to make dinner.

SHE DECIDED SHE had to call Louise. She would imply that the main reason she was phoning was to offer some days and times when she was available for the case review, but then, once they were talking, she would see if there was a way to ask the caseworker what she was thinking—and whether the news that she and Terry were, at least for the moment, separated had had any bearing on the timing of Louise's letter.

She caught the woman when she was just about to leave for the day, and offered to call back in the morning.

No, now's fine, Louise said, and they both looked at their calendars and chose a day in the very first week in February when they would try to get everyone together.

She scribbled a tentative time on a scrap piece of paper and then—hoping the question would sound casual when she actually gave voice to the words in her head—asked, Have you given any more thought to Terry's and my situation?

There was a quiet at the other end of the line, and for a brief moment she wished that she had stalled just a moment longer—found a more innocuous subject to discuss with Louise before getting to the issue that really mattered to her. It might have made her inquiry seem less urgent, and she sound less anguished. But then she stopped herself from thinking like that: This is my child, she thought, my boy, and I will be as urgent and worried as I want.

I guess, Louise said finally. Why?

I was wondering if it had anything to do with your scheduling the case review now.

No. I mean, I wasn't oblivious to it. But what's your concern?

I didn't know if there was a connection—and I wanted to know.

No.

No connection?

That's right. Absolutely none. Even if the two of you wind up divorced, the reality is that single people adopt children all the time. I'm serious: all the time.

Adopt, she said, murmuring the word carefully. Repeating it gave it tangibility.

Yeah, adopt. I presume that hasn't changed. I mean it hasn't changed for me. For us.

No, of course it hasn't changed. I'm just . . . surprised. Pleasantly—no, euphorically—surprised.

What, did you think that because—

It doesn't matter what I thought, she said, her voice almost giddy.

Look, all I want to do at this point is bring in the adoption social worker. That's the main thing I think we'll be discussing at the case review. Okay? I would love for you and Terry to figure out how to solve your problems for a zillion reasons, of which young Alfred is only one. But the bottom line is that the plan hasn't changed. We still want you to adopt Alfred, and I have to assume that's still what you want, too. Right?

More than you know, she said, and she had to swallow hard so she wouldn't cry on the phone. I want that more than you know.

"I can discourage a trooper from marrying, but in the end I cannot prevent it."

CAPTAIN ANDREW HITCHENS,
TENTH REGIMENT, UNITED STATES CAVALRY,
REPORT TO THE POST ADJUTANT,
AUGUST 12, 1877

Alfred

A barn collapsed in Durham and killed thirty-five cows: The rain made the snow on the roof too heavy for the old beams, and the structure bowed and then broke.

In Cornish, the custodian at the elementary school rounded up plastic buckets and left them stacked just outside the kindergarten classroom, the room with the art supplies, and the gym. Apparently at some point the ceilings in these rooms would start to leak because the melting snow on the roof would have to go somewhere, and eventually gravity would lead it inside the school.

And Schuyler Jackman and Joe Langford both wondered at lunch in the multipurpose room how high the river would rise, and it was clear from their tones that this was a subject that disturbed them.

Most of the grown-ups, however, including Alfred's teacher and Paul, tried to talk about the rain and the warm spell as the natural January thaw. It happened every year right about now: There would be two or three days of warm weather and rain at the very end of the month, and most of the snow pack would disappear. This year it just happened to be both a little warmer and a little wetter, and there was a little more snow running off the hills to the east.

Still, Alfred worried. It felt to him as if there had been mountains of snow in the five weeks since Christmas, and now it was pouring and there was still so much rain in the forecast. He wasn't sure what he expected would happen, and when he was falling asleep that night, the rain drumming against the metal porch roof outside his window, he told himself he was only anxious because Laura was. And it was obvious why the rain and the water were so upsetting to her.

WHEN HE CAME downstairs for breakfast the next morning, he heard Laura on the phone. The plastic red bowl in which she cleaned lettuce was on the kitchen counter next to the stove, and every half minute a tiny drop from a leak in the ceiling would fall into it.

No, you don't need to, Russell, really. It's Terry's responsibility. But you're sweet to offer, she was saying, and she smiled at Alfred when she saw him. Look, I'll call the barracks, she continued, and he can come up here when he's done with his shift. That'll be fine.

A moment later she said good-bye and hung up, and after he had sat down at the table and poured milk into his cereal, he asked her what was Terry's responsibility.

She tossed a container of pudding into his lunch bag and a second paper napkin, and folded the top shut. The roof, she answered. Actually, the roofs. She motioned toward the bowl and the leak—he noticed there was a stain on the ceiling the size of a washcloth and the color of rust that hadn't been there the day before—and went on, I don't worry about them collapsing, but we need to get the snow off before the real rains come tonight. Otherwise a lot of that snow is going to wind up here in the kitchen and in my bedroom and in the den. That's where the water trickles in when we have ice jams up there—except it isn't always a trickle. Six or seven years ago it was practically a waterfall. We had to repaint and repaper the den.

That was Russell just now?

Uh-huh. He spent last night at that camp with Terry, she answered, and then her tone lightened slightly. Poor Terry, I actually feel sorry for him. Russell quit his job earlier this month, and it seems at least once a week he's dropped in on his older brother for a night or two. I think he likes that camp. I believe this is the third time he's been out there.

And he's coming here now? he asked, the question a reflex he wished he could have avoided. He was afraid Laura would be able to see how little he wanted Russell up at their house.

Oh, no. God, no. Don't worry about that. The only reason I was even talking to Russell was that I'd missed Terry by a minute or two, he'd just left for work. And so Russell offered to stop by on his way home and shovel off the roofs, since, well, he no longer has a job to get to. It was actually a very sweet offer. But the roofs are Terry's responsibility. And the truth is, I don't want Russell here any more than you do.

He spooned some of the cereal into his mouth and wondered if there was a way he could help. But he wasn't sure he could even lift that metal extension ladder in the carriage barn off the ground, much less carry it through the snow, heavy and thick now with rainwater, to the side of the house. He thought he might ask Paul what he should do if the roof was still leaking when he got home from school, but then he remembered he couldn't do that: The couple was off visiting their daughter in the southern part of the state and wouldn't be back until tomorrow.

WHEN THE BUS passed the Gale River on the way to school, there were massive sheets of broken ice crashing against the banks—some easily the size of the tops of pool tables and the flatbeds of pickup trucks—and the younger children in the bus were shouting, Cool. When the bus arrived at the school building, he saw the custodian was up on the roof over the kindergarten classroom, the ladder flush against the sharply pitched metal, using one hand to bang against ice with a small sledgehammer while gripping the ladder tightly with the other.

In his classroom Ms. Logan was talking to the librarian about the book fair the school would be having in February, and a small cluster of students was already gathered around one of the computers in the corner. What he noticed more than anything, however, was the low rumble that for a moment he presumed was merely the overhead, fluorescent lights, but then realized was the river. Despite the fact that the windows were closed and it was raining outside, despite the fact that the river was across the street from the school, the water was so high he could hear it.

———

"[I was] no admirer of the African, believing he would ultimately destroy the white race . . . [Now I] think the world of the men of my company, and I am proud of what we have done."

———

ANONYMOUS LETTER,
ARMY AND NAVY JOURNAL, FEBRUARY 19, 1887

———

Phoebe

She listened to Keenan Hewitt and Clark Adams talk about the sand truck that had actually wound up off the road, as they poured their coffee into Styrofoam cups and took doughnuts off the wide plate at the far end of the store's front counter. Clark was a warden with Fish and Wildlife, and his uniform looked a bit like Terry's. She knew he was married, and she was pretty sure he had teenage children at home. She guessed he was in his forties. Keenan had run a lathe at the furniture mill until he retired a couple years back at sixty-five, and was a man her father considered a friend. Once when she was in high school she'd gone to a movie with Keenan's son, Tommy, but the boy hadn't been as bright as he was handsome, and she'd been careful to make sure there was no second date. Still, even now—or at least until she'd told him she was pregnant back on Christmas Day—her father would ask her why she never saw that Tommy Keenan.

Likewise, Clark had a nephew just about her age, and every time he was in the store, he would mention how well the boy was doing at the construction company where he was working, and how everyone guessed he'd find a woman soon and settle down.

She wondered now if either of them would try to play matchmaker this morning, or at the very least bring up one of the young men she should consider dating. She hoped not, and when she listened to the wind outside rattle the trees and cause Clark's four-by-four to sway in its spot by the front of the store, she took comfort in the idea that these were the sort of men who found a late January storm—and a sand truck off the road—infinitely more interesting than romance.

———

SHE WATCHED THE sleet outside the store's big glass windows, occasionally glancing at her watch. It was barely ten-thirty. She was working until three today, and so she wouldn't arrive at the camp where Terry was staying much before six even if the roads were any good—which, today, they most certainly were not. She'd be lucky if she got there by seven or seven-thirty. The streets this far north were sheets of black ice and the schools were closed. Only twenty minutes further south it was raining and the schools were open, but other than the interstate (which, alas, she wouldn't be on), even there the roads weren't going to be a whole lot better: In some cases, she knew, there would be small ponds of slush on the pavement, and in other cases the streets would simply be closed and she would have to make short (and, perhaps, long) detours where the culverts were clogged with ice and sludge and the water was streaming over the asphalt.

And, of course, if she was on the road too late into the evening, there was always the chance that all that water on the roads would freeze. Then she'd be in real trouble.

If she hadn't taken that vacation earlier in the month, she probably would have asked Frank and Jeannine if she could leave early, but she didn't want to impose on their good nature again. She'd just have to call Terry so he wouldn't worry, and then take it slow. She'd get there whenever she could, and it was better to get there late but in one piece than to wind up hydroplaning into a ditch or, worse, another car. The last thing she wanted was to get in a car accident with a baby in her tummy, while on her way to—finally—doing the right thing.

Trying to, anyway.

As much as she enjoyed Terry's company—as much as she might even love him—she had vowed that this was the very last time she would see him, at least while he was married. This was it, it had to be. She and her father had fought again last night, this time not because she was pregnant but because, for the third time this month, she was refusing to tell him where she was going. He—her whole family, actually—knew she was going to visit the man who was the father of her baby, and the idea that she still wouldn't tell them who it was was beginning to infuriate them.

As, she realized, it probably should. And while she was able to give lip service to the notion that it was none of their business, the reality was that there couldn't be much future in any activity you couldn't talk about. And so she'd decided, once and for all, there was already too much pain in the world, and she simply would not be responsible for causing this woman who was Terry Sheldon's wife any more hurt than she had already endured.

"Honorable discharge: Rowe, George, Sergeant, B Company, October 13, 1877."

U. S. NATIONAL ARCHIVES AND RECORDS SERVICE, TENTH CAVALRY MUSTER ROLLS, 1877

Terry

He was exhausted by early afternoon, it had just been that kind of day. Still, he hoped he'd be able to get to Laura's—his house, too, he reminded himself, it was still his home, too—before dark. It wasn't merely the ice jams that concerned him, it was the reality that the river was probably roaring by now, and it was only going to get worse, and that would surely make Laura's day particularly difficult. There hadn't been snow the day their daughters died, but it had been exactly this sort of cold, heavy rain.

Today he'd already been on the site of three nasty car accidents, each one triggered by the slippery roads and the bad visibility: There were thick pockets of fog on top of everything else, a result of the warm front hitting all that cold on the ground. There were flood watches across the state, and he just knew there would be whole wading pools of brown water in an awful lot of basements.

He pulled the collar of his jacket up over his neck, radioed in that he was leaving his cruiser, and started toward the old couple by the side of their gray Lincoln. He could see right away they were chilly and wet and annoyed, but otherwise they looked unhurt. The rear of the car looked pretty banged up, and he was almost upon them when he realized that although the front of the vehicle was in the remains of a snowbank, it was the left taillight and that corner of the bumper that were most mangled. He understood then that the couple was not simply frustrated because the man had been driving and lost control of their automobile and they'd had a close call; they were upset because someone else had careened into them, and then driven away and left them by the side of the road.

He shook his head and realized his day was just going to get worse and worse. Phoebe was coming over that night, but even that realization was causing him more stress than pleasure: He really did want to take care of the house first, and he really did want to do a good job. Moreover, how could he possibly go straight from his wife to his . . . lover? Some guys could probably do that, but could he?

He'd have to, he guessed.

Moreover, he'd seen Alfred exactly once in the last month, when he watched the child's riding lesson one afternoon and then gone out for pizza with Paul Hebert and the boy. And though he felt guilty about his almost repellent lack of involvement—especially with the child's case review next week—his life already seemed an unwieldy tangle of relationships (all of which, he had to admit, he was completely mismanaging), and he didn't see how he could find the time to see the boy more. Still, he felt bad. He felt bad about Laura and he felt bad about Alfred, and he couldn't stop thinking about them while he stood in the rain with the older couple as they described the teenagers in their sporty Grand Am who'd been tailgating them for at least two or three miles. When the kids had finally tried passing them, they sent them sliding off the road, banging into the left rear of their car in the process, before speeding away.

According to the woman, they'd never even looked back.

You get a license plate number? he asked, but—as he'd expected—their eyesight wasn't that good. Still they had a description of the car, and they were pretty sure it was from Vermont. That would help. They'd find the kids eventually.

When the wrecker arrived, the fellow from the service station asked them if they'd heard about what was happening over the mountains in Montpelier. Apparently the Winooski was over its banks, and there was a foot of water in the streets within a block of the capitol. Worst flooding since 1991. Then he towed the Lincoln from the ditch, and Terry climbed behind the wheel to make sure it was still working. It was, and so he sent them on their way and continued running the roads himself. He hadn't been driving long when the radio calls started to come in en masse, a deluge from every corner of the county, it seemed, where there were people and there was water. The Otter Creek had taken down a bridge in New Haven, and a part of Route 17 was impassable; the waters were over the top of two stretches of 125, making the strip of highway between East Middlebury and Ripton particularly treacherous; and an ice dam had built up just east of Durham, and the water was pouring into the first floor of a small company that made candles and the Italian restaurant just beside it. There were power lines down and there were phone lines down, and he was one of exactly three troopers in the county on the road at that moment. Three. No one was hurt, at least not yet, and that gave him some small measure of relief. But he also realized the odds that no one would be hurt when he logged off his shift were probably too small to calculate.

———

"I don't have keepsakes or souvenirs, not a single one. I'm bringing with me a family instead."

———

SERGEANT GEORGE ROWE,
TENTH REGIMENT, UNITED STATES CAVALRY,
LETTER TO HIS BROTHER IN PHILADELPHIA,
OCTOBER 14, 1877

———

Laura

The puppy was an Alaskan husky and it sat in her lap in her office at the shelter, attacking the buttons on her heavy cardigan sweater and occasionally looking up at her with its single eye. The woman who brought it in had claimed that the other dogs in her house had attacked the poor thing because it was the runt of the new litter, but Laura hadn't believed that and neither had the veterinarian: The vet had guessed some-one with a boot on had kicked the puppy in the head. Still, aside from the reality that the dog was going to go through life with one eye, it was unhurt and as happy and playful as any of the puppies she saw. She'd named the dog Anya, and she knew both that the animal would find a good home and before it did the photographs of the pup in the Humane Society's newspaper ads would raise the shelter a fair amount of money.

Only one of the three volunteers who were scheduled to walk dogs that day had come in, and Laura was astonished that even one person was willing to walk dogs in the rainstorm, with the roads as bad as they were. The dogs today were being walked on the main street in front of the shelter, rather than the old logging trace behind it: The trail was impassable, a quagmire of melting snow with knee-deep mud underneath.

She tried hard to focus on the animals, which was the reason she was keeping Anya in her office with her, so she wouldn't think about the river and how high the water was, because it was impossible to envision the rapids right now in the Gale without thinking as well of her daughters. She looked at her watch and saw it was almost one-thirty. Normally it was only a half-hour drive back to Cornish, but with the roads as slick as they were, it had taken her forty-five minutes to drive here in the morning. If she wanted to be home when Alfred got off the school bus—and with Paul and Emily gone until tomorrow, she did—she'd have to bring Anya into her assistant's office in another twenty minutes and leave work no later than two.

She shuddered when she thought about the amount of water that was dribbling that moment inside the walls of her house. Terry wouldn't get there until at least four, when he came off his shift, and so he wouldn't have more than an hour to work on the roofs before dark. She certainly didn't want him up there after nightfall. He'd done that once when they were both much younger. The girls had been no more than toddlers, and they were both asleep. For a few minutes she and Terry had watched one of the leaks in the kitchen, and when it became clear that the Sheetrock on the ceiling would have to be retaped in the spring, he had gotten out the ladder and gone to work on the roof with a snow rake and an ax. He'd been standing on the roof over the front porch and slipped, and though he hadn't fallen off the roof—he'd fallen instead into the pile of snow he'd pulled off the higher pitch and was planning next to shovel into the yard—he'd reflexively tossed his ax into the air and it had conked him on the side of his head when it fell to earth. He was lucky it was the blunt edge that hit him, and so he'd wound up neither disfigured nor dead. But he learned from that lump—they both did—that you didn't climb onto a roof in the dark in the rain, no matter how bad the leak was or how competent you believed that you were.

She wondered if Terry would want to stay at the house when he was through, and whether she would let him. She knew that over the last couple of weeks he had had a fair amount of company at the camp where he was staying: His brother had been there a few nights, and though she didn't know it for a fact, she believed that this woman he was seeing had been there, too. It was almost a certainty in her mind.

She was still angry with him, and more hurt than she'd ever been in her life. But she missed him—the Terry, that is, with whom she had fallen in love and who had helped her to raise Hillary and Megan. Even during the past two years she had seen glimpses of that man, though he had all but disappeared in the grief that had enveloped them both. She still liked hearing his voice on the telephone, if only because he always sounded so capable and confident.

Moreover, she believed that he missed her, too—or, again, the woman he'd initially known. Not the woman who, faced with the single worst thing that could happen, she had become.

In the end, she knew that while there may very well have been a part of him that would want to remain in Cornish when the ice and the snow were gone from the roof—and there was clearly a part of her that would like that, too, if only so they could talk in person about Alfred's upcoming case review—it wasn't going to happen. Not yet, anyway, not tonight. Not while he was focused on this person named Phoebe, who, for whatever the reason, had such a hold on his emotions.

SHE HAD JUST ventured into the rain in the shelter parking lot when she heard the siren. She thought it belonged to a state police cruiser, and she turned her head just in time to see one speeding south on Route 7. She wondered if it was Terry, but she didn't consider the idea for long because a moment later, before she had even gotten into her car, she saw a second cruiser, this one without its lights or its siren on, turning onto the access road that led to the Humane Society. Clearly this was her husband.

He coasted to a stop right beside her car, climbed from the cruiser without turning off either the engine or the wipers, and motioned toward her Taurus. Let's get out of the rain, he said, and opened the driver's-side door for her.

He was sopping wet, she realized when they were both settled in the front seat of her car: It was as if he had jumped into a swimming pool in his uniform and his parka.

It's a tad nasty out there, he said, and he gave her a small smile and surprised her by taking her hand.

You're a maniac, she told him.

Nah. It's just water.

Freezing cold water.

I'm okay. More important, how are you?

I want to go home, she said. That's all. I just want to go home.

Well, I'm glad I got here before you left. Be careful.

Are the roads that bad?

They are, and he paused briefly before adding, And while I don't think the town has anything to worry about, I understand the Gale is very high.

The news didn't surprise her, but she still felt a tiny pulse of trepidation when she visualized the roiling brown water, and the foam where it collided with boulders or had to hurtle the massive slabs of ice. She understood he was telling her not simply because he was worried about the condition of the River Road, the road the Gale had torn apart with unfathomable fury just over two years ago now: The reality was she rarely took that way home. He was here because he understood that the very idea that the water might flood would be unnerving, and he wanted to warn her—tell her himself so she wouldn't be cudgeled by the news when she heard it on the radio, or witnessed the high water firsthand because, for example, she simply drove by the general store on her way home to pick up a quart of milk.

Seriously, he went on, his eyes fixed on her, I can't believe it will cause any real trouble again. But, just so you know, the river is—most rivers in the county are—at flood level.

She thought of her girls and she had an image of them on the bridge the day they died, and her anxiety grew more pronounced. And then she thought of Alfred. Anyone hurt? she asked.

No, believe not. She felt him squeeze her hand and then he said, I'm actually going to head up there and check on the roads, so I just might get to swing by the house after all. If you'd asked me an hour ago, I wouldn't have guessed I'd have a prayer in hell. But who knows? There might be a silver lining in all this high water.

I should get going, she said. I want to make sure Alfred's okay.

Don't worry, Paul and Emily will look in on him if the roads slow you down.

They're not home. They're visiting Catherine.

Still, you don't need to fret. He's a big boy, he'll be fine.

I know, that's what I keep telling myself. It's just . . . it's just everything.

He took back his hand and said, Look, I have to go close the road that runs by the quarry in New Haven. That's next. As soon as that's done, I'm going to shoot into Cornish and see about the bridge and the River Road. Then I'll come by the house, I promise.

I hope you're not thinking about the roof. God, at this point don't trouble yourself with that.

No, I wasn't thinking about the roof, he said as he opened the car door and swung his legs back out into the downpour. I was actually thinking about you.

———

"We took a mud wagon for the first part of the trip east. It was supposed to be pulled by six horses, but I remember we had four oxen instead. There was a white officer with us who was going home, too, and a blacksmith. Here's something that made me laugh: Before boarding we were told we could bring all the guns we · *wanted but no alcohol because, of course, we were traveling through Indian Territory."*

———

VERONICA ROWE (FORMERLY POPPING TREES),

WPA INTERVIEW,

MARCH 1938

———

Alfred

It wasn't even two-thirty and he was on the bus home because they were closing the school early. This time the little kids weren't ogling the river in excitement, or shrieking happily when they saw slabs of ice the size of bedsheets and as thick as truck tires careening down the water or wedged upright like firewalls. They were sitting in their seats and facing forward, only glancing at the river with the corners of their eyes. This was frightening to them—to everybody—because even if they hadn't known the Sheldon twins, they'd been told enough by their parents or they'd heard enough from older siblings to know exactly what water could do.

He knew Laura wouldn't be home when the bus arrived at the house, but he wasn't concerned. She would be back from the shelter within half an hour, and it just seemed easier to get on the bus than try to get a message to the shelter—which might have been useless, anyway, because she probably had just left—when he'd only be alone in the house for a couple of minutes. Not a big deal.

When he got off the bus, he thought he recognized the truck instantly. He'd only seen it once before, and that was at Terry's mother's house back on Thanksgiving, but he was fairly confident the dark blue Silverado with the gun and the gun rack and the extra long cab belonged to Russell. It was parked now with its left wheels in a sodden drift along the side of the driveway, causing the truck to tilt ominously.

He paused there in the rain and reflexively felt inside his pants pocket for his house key. Then he started toward the front door, but he hadn't even reached the steps when he heard the sound of metal scraping metal, and he saw Russell emerge from the far side of the house, hefting Terry's massive extension ladder under both of his arms. The ladder was the color of silver, and one long edge of it was caked with wet snow and ice.

Young man, you got yourself a northern exposure with not so much as an ice cube on it, he said, and he dropped the ladder in the snow by the front wall of the house. His eyes were tiny red slits and his hair was a mess: His bangs had been pasted against his forehead by the cold rain, and the strands over his ears were splayed and dangling like frozen bulb roots.

Alfred nodded, unsure what to say. He figured that Laura must have asked him to do this after all, but he couldn't get over his surprise at finding the man here.

No thanks needed, son, Russell said, lowering his voice unnaturally. I am just happy to help your fine family.

Thank you, he said then. He *was* thankful, because if Russell had eliminated the leaks, then Laura would be happy. But he still couldn't get over the fact that Russell was here.

Let's go inside, Russell said. I need me a towel and a beer, but maybe not in that exact order. The man then motioned toward the key in his fingers— until that moment, Alfred had forgotten that he'd actually taken it from his pocket and was holding it in his hands—and continued, I believe that key's my ticket inside. Then he took it from the boy's fingers and marched up the steps and into the house.

RUSSELL BLEW HIS nose into a wadded paper napkin and stood with a towel over his head like a shawl. He took a long swallow of his beer, finishing it, Alfred guessed, and stared at the ceiling above the stove. There was a drop slowly forming where the Sheetrock was taped, but nothing had dripped in the sixty seconds he had stood there and watched the leak.

It may still drip a bit for a while more, he said. Until everything already in the walls has run its course. But I would say you're outta the woods.

Apparently, Russell had been up on the roof with a sledgehammer and a snow rake since well before lunch, banging and scraping away at the ice and the snow that had been melting into the house.

Nasty, nasty stuff, he added, and then he tossed both the towel and the beer can, now empty, into the sink. And on that note, I'm off. The Lone

Ranger is riding off into the . . . well, sure as shit, not the sunset, not today. Into the monsoon, is what it is.

You're not going to wait for Laura?

Russell fell back against the counter in mock astonishment and smacked his hands, open-palmed, against his cheeks. For the love of God, the boy speaks! The boy speaks! It's a miracle, a miracle, I tell you!

I talk, he said.

Hardly. But, no, I am not going to wait for Laura. I kinda like the notion that she'll just get home and then Terry will drive on up, and they'll both see that I took care of the roof. They'll see the slate and the standing seam as clean as the middle of June, and my fine, upstanding older brother and sister-in-law will see that ol' no-account Russell got the job done just fine, thank you very much.

He then walked into the hallway where he had left his boots, sat on the steps to the second floor, and climbed back inside them. A puddle had formed on the wood where he had set them down, and Alfred had a feeling the insides must have felt as squishy as marsh mud. Then Russell was gone, outside the door and the house, and he heard the truck engine start with a growl and the man was driving down the hill toward the village and, Alfred guessed, home.

WHEN LAURA WASN'T back by three-thirty, he called the shelter. He guessed she had probably left by now, but maybe something had come up and she'd called the school and someone had forgotten to give him a message. Or maybe because the school had closed a little early, no one had been able to get the message to him.

Caitlin, the shelter's kennel manager, answered the phone, and he could hear alarm in her voice the moment he asked to speak to Laura. She told him that Laura had left an hour and a half earlier, and as far as she knew had gone straight home. She said that Laura had in fact left when she did precisely because she wanted to be able to meet the school bus when it got to the house.

We got let out early, he told her, not exactly sure why this fact would make the woman feel better, but hoping now, at least, she wouldn't be alarmed by the reality that he had gotten off the bus and no one had been there. Besides, he added, I'm ten. Lots of kids my age get home after school and nobody's there.

Oh, I'm sure, she said. Then: Do me a favor. Would you please have her call me the minute she gets there? I know there's nothing to be worried about—I know some roads are closed, it was on the radio—but I'll still feel better when I know she's back. Okay?

Okay, he said, and after he hung up the phone he decided that he wouldn't wait for the rain to let up to go take care of Mesa. She was used to seeing either Paul or him this time of the day, and he wasn't about to let either the man or the horse down.

Besides, it was one of Sergeant Rowe's rules. You always take care of your horse.

THOUGH HE HAD the hood of his raincoat up and the wind was rumbling like ocean surf, he could hear the sirens in the village in the distance. Not the ambulance from the Durham Rescue Squad, he believed, these were the sirens atop the volunteer firefighters' trucks. He fed the horse and brushed her a bit, and when she was done eating, he decided that he would muck out the stall later. He thought the sirens had gone down the River Road, but he couldn't be sure. They might have been heading south into Ripton. And so even though he still wasn't supposed to ride Mesa when Paul or Laura or some grown-up wasn't around, he carefully unfolded the blanket and placed it atop the horse's back, got the saddle and the bridle off the wall, and decided that he would ride to the center of town. Something was going on, and perhaps if Laura had been home he wouldn't have felt the need to investigate. But she wasn't there and she was supposed to be, and that was exactly the problem.

The horse paused for a moment just inside the wide entrance to the barn, sniffing at the wind and the rain, and he had to squeeze hard with his heels and his legs to prod her outside. There were wide streams of runoff along the sides of the road, and a smooth glaze in the center. Though he knew the road crew would spread sand and salt all night long, if the temperature fell fast enough after dark, the roads would still be impassable in the morning. He wondered if there'd be school the next day.

He saw Laura's car still wasn't back in the driveway, and so he rode across the street to the house, hitched the horse to the front railing, and went inside to write her a note. He couldn't tell her where he was going because he wasn't exactly sure, but he didn't want her to worry and so he scribbled simply that he and Mesa had ridden toward the village and they wouldn't be gone long.

When he emerged back onto the porch and climbed atop Mesa, the wind immediately blew his hood off his helmet. He pulled it back up and over the mound, but it blew off again, and so he listened to the raindrops drum steadily on the plastic shell as he started down the hill at a trot. He was cold and wet and he realized there was something frightening about the sirens and the squalls, but still he pressed on. He pretended he was a buffalo soldier, and sat a little higher in the saddle than Heather would have liked.

HE HEARD THE river before he saw it, and then as he neared the church and the general store, he saw the vehicles parked along the side of the road—there were a half-dozen cars, and perhaps that many pickups—and the people standing near the banks of the water. Then, as he neared the center, he was able to see above the crowd because he was atop the horse, and he saw that the bridge—the bridge made of steel and cement, the bridge that had withstood the wave two years ago that swept away Hillary and Megan Sheldon—was gone. The guardrails and the asphalt and the steel cross beams had vanished. He envisioned the stanchions being pounded throughout the day by those immense chunks of ice, and then one great wave of rainwater and melted snow crashing into the overpass, ripping it vertical—there it was in his mind, standing up on its side for one long, long second, before hurtling back into the Gale—and sending it downriver in pieces. In his mind he saw chunks of asphalt that looked like pieces of meteors, the guardrails twisted like licorice, the cement now rocks in the mud in the channel.

He pulled the horse to a stop when he saw an older woman he recognized whose name, he believed, was Mrs. Wallace. He knew she was friends with the Heberts, because he'd seen her at their house a couple of times that autumn and winter.

When did the bridge go? he asked her, bending down from the horse and raising his voice.

She looked up at him, and he saw that her skin had the gray translucence of block ice.

Alfred, she said, and because she was speaking instead of shouting, he could barely hear her over the torrent. Alfred, she said again, but he only knew she had spoken his name because he could read her lips.

Just now? he asked, yelling.

She shook her head and took a deep breath and sighed.

Is that why I heard the sirens?

A fellow who he knew had children in the first and third grades turned toward him and answered for Mrs. Wallace. The trucks didn't get over the bridge before it went, he said, cupping a hand around his mouth as he shouted. They wanted to get 'em on this side of the river, but they didn't make it.

Where did they go? he asked, and the look of fear on his face must have been obvious: He'd imagined a truck on the bridge at the exact moment the span collapsed.

The road's been chewed up again closer to Durham, the man said calmly, clearly trying to reassure him. They're going the long way around, through Ripton, to see what's happening on the other side of a very big crater. That's what you heard.

The older woman turned toward them. This sort of thing is only supposed to happen every generation or two, she said, speaking loudly enough this time for him to hear her. If that. Now twice in barely two years. It's sad. So terribly, terribly sad.

At least this time no one was on the bridge, the man said. Thank God for that.

Yes. Thank God.

Still. This one's going to be mighty nasty to clean up.

Alfred looked to the west and realized he hadn't seen a single car coming east along the River Road. The road's really gone, isn't it? he asked.

Well, I wouldn't say it's gone, but you can't drive on it. There's a major gorge about half a mile from here, and who knows what's going on beyond that. Probably more damage.

The reins were raw where they weren't wrapped in his hands, and when he stretched his fingers, he discovered just how cold his hands had become. Quickly he curled them back into fists around the leather.

You should get out of the rain, Mrs. Wallace said to him. We all should. There's nothing to be done now.

He turned the horse around, but he couldn't imagine just going home. There was no reason to believe Laura was there yet, not with the roads this bad, and Terry probably wouldn't be coming by now at all. Not with this storm and the damage it was doing: There'd be chaos everywhere he'd have to help clean up. And Paul and Emily weren't at their house, either. And so instead of riding back up the hill, he gave the horse a squeeze and started west toward that immense gash in the road. He'd never seen such a thing, and he might never have the chance again.

Besides, a thought was forming in his mind: Although Laura rarely took the River Road, she had to know that the rains might be washing away whole sections of dirt on the notch way, while turning other long stretches to quicksand. Perhaps today of all days she had chosen to come home via the River Road, and somewhere beyond that great hole in the asphalt she was trapped in the storm in her car.

———

"I had never seen a train. I was unprepared for it to be so uncomfortable and so noisy. I guess because white people rode them, I had expected it would be like a palace. I had been almost as comfortable in the wagon we'd used to reach Dennison."

———

VERONICA ROWE (FORMERLY POPPING TREES),
WPA INTERVIEW,
MARCH 1938

———

Phoebe

She had been driving carefully through country that was almost all snow-covered farmland, and now she was climbing up a series of foothills and at the higher elevation the rain was changing to sleet and—she thought possibly—ice. She was keeping both hands on the wheel at all times, she was pumping her brakes when she needed to slow. She was listening to her music a little softer than usual so she could focus on the conditions of the road and remain alert. Once she looked back to make sure she had remembered to toss her duffel bag into the backseat of her car (she had), but otherwise she stared straight ahead and kept her eyes on the pavement before her.

Generally she had been pleasantly surprised. Once she was beyond Eden Mills there'd been little ice on the roads, and even north of there the pavement had been so thoroughly salted that it hadn't been too bad. And she knew it was warmer still to the south, and soon she'd only have to confront rain. Nevertheless, she realized she still had some dicey conditions before her: She was hearing that some roads had been closed by high water—she guessed her first big test would be the Lamoille near Johnson—and there were power lines down in almost every county. But Route 100 had really been pretty good. The key was simply to be slow and cautious, and leave nothing to chance.

Ahead of her, at the very end of a straightaway on the ridge she had reached, she saw a small SUV with its hazard lights on, but for a moment she couldn't tell through the sleet on her windshield whether it was at a complete stop or simply forging ahead at a creep, and so she leaned closer to the glass to see better between the wipers. It was stopped, and it was only part-way off the road—the drifts to the side had been hammered by rain, but they were still a yard high—and so she started to brake. Abruptly she realized the car was sliding, she'd hit a patch of black ice. She tried to steer into it, aware on some level that this—this patch of slippery glass on the road—was why the SUV had pulled over, but she understood as the rear of her car swung to the side that this knowledge wasn't going to help her. Then she saw she was in the other lane, the wrong lane, and there were headlights coming toward her through the side windows and someone somewhere was pressing a hand down upon a horn. And so she jammed her foot as hard as she could to the floor of the car and rammed the gearshift into park—anything, any-thing at all, to stop—and, much to her surprise, she was airborne. She was actually off the pavement, spinning, and the lights were getting closer and the horn was getting louder—louder even than the wind and the rain and the wipers—and she thought, Shit, I'm going to have an accident and I just can't afford this!

Then, at the moment that she landed back on the ground, her front wheels on the pavement and her rear wheels in the drift to the side, she remembered she was pregnant and she let out a whimper, but she didn't hear the small cry because of the almost deafening crunch of metal upon metal as her car started to collapse all around her.

"And I knew I was pregnant on the train, and that didn't make the ride any easier. I told George, but not the girls. It was going to be complicated enough when we introduced them to George's brother's family. And so mostly on the train I talked about the buildings, and how some would be taller than any trees they had seen. But even that was difficult, because I'd never seen such a building myself, and only knew of them what other people had told me. It was like describing a rattle-snake if you've never seen one—not even a photograph. I think my children expected the walls would be made of animal hides."

VERONICA ROWE (FORMERLY POPPING TREES),
WPA INTERVIEW,
MARCH 1938

Alfred

J ust as there were people at the spot along the river where there had once stood a bridge, a small group had gathered just to the east of the first great fissure in the paved road. Again some had driven and some had walked, and he counted nine grown-ups and five teenage boys. They stood wondering at the sight of the canyon, and he realized as he listened to them talk that their awe wasn't driven simply by the crater's size—easily twenty feet deep and twenty feet wide—or by the high water that even now was carving away the ground in the hollow, but by the reality that nature was pummeling them once again.

There was no one on the other side of the chasm because no one had wanted to risk crossing the water in the bottom or hiking into the slippery woods on the far side of the road. He guessed the teenagers might have tried, but two of them had their parents with them and the grown-ups were not about to permit them to even attempt a crossing.

It was clear from the conversation around him that everyone believed there were other breaks in the road, too: If there weren't, by now cars would have come this far east from Durham, and they would have seen them before the vehicles would have had to turn back. But none had made it this far.

Think people are trapped? one of the teenage boys wondered, and it sounded as if he was reveling in the ghoulish possibilities.

You mean like the Willards two years ago? someone—the boy's mother, Alfred suspected—asked. Even he had heard the tale of how this septuagenarian couple had found themselves on the road between Durham and Cornish when the river had destroyed the pavement before and behind them, and forced them to hike across one of the pits it had hewn from the hillside.

Yeah, the teen said. Like that.

Instantly he thought of Laura, and he wished he knew more about jumping. He wished he knew anything about jumping. Briefly he imagined himself riding the horse into the crevice and then leaping the span where the water was churning up rock and mud. But he could never do that. Not yet, anyway.

He could, however, ride up into the woods. He'd go wide of the gorge, twenty or thirty yards into the melting snow and slick brush if he had to, and then he'd return to the road when he was west of the break. Quickly he sought out with his eyes the widest nearby gap in the maples and pine, and before anyone would be able to grab the reins and stop him, he prodded Mesa into the woods. He heard them calling after him—some calling him by his name and others just shouting Boy! and Son! and You there!—all of them shouting that he should come back. But he was in the woods now, lowering his chin almost to his chest so the thinner branches would glance off the top of his helmet, guiding the horse as best he could between the trees and the brush, aware that the animal was struggling on occasion for purchase beneath the melting snowpack.

And then he was out and back on the road, well beyond the western lip of the crevasse. He could still hear people yelling for him to return, but it was going to be dark soon and so he soldiered on, and it was easier now because he was on pavement. He pushed Mesa harder—despite his sudden misgivings that she might yet slip and be hurt, and he would have injured an animal he guessed he loved more than most humans he had met in his life—and she started to run and the voices behind him faded beneath the sound of the rain and the river and the distance, and after no more than half a mile he saw another crater. This one was smaller than the first, perhaps a dozen feet wide and barely four or five feet deep. In the pocket there were slabs of asphalt, and while it was a barrier no vehicle could cross, the water had receded and so he slowed Mesa to a walk and the horse gingerly stepped down into the rubble and then climbed back up the other side.

He'd ridden more than halfway to Durham, another two or three miles, he guessed, when he saw what looked to him like the searchlights at an airport taking aim at the sky. These weren't as powerful, but he could see them through the fog and the gathering dark. Two of them, he realized as he approached, there were a pair of them. He wondered if he'd reach a chasm and find there a chain of cars on the other side, including one that held Laura.

As he neared the lights, however, he understood by their angle that they couldn't possibly be from a vehicle that was parked on the road. The ground was hilly here, yes, but it wasn't so steep that a car would be able to shine its front headlights almost straight up into the air. Then he saw the break in the pavement and he slowed. The lights were beaming up from inside the rift. He rode to the very edge, and there below him he saw the vehicle that was generating the lights. It was flipped upside down against the side wall of a twenty- or twenty-five-foot-deep hole that less than an hour before had been a hillside with a road, and he could see the wheels and black and brown metal of the undercarriage and the engine. There was water pooling around the automobile and so he rode Mesa to the side of the road where there were trees, got off the horse, and looped the reins around a branch. Then he started down into the hole. He realized no one but him knew this car was here, because otherwise there would have been vehicles on the other side. Clearly there was at least one more break in the road between here and Durham.

HE GROPED HIS way down the sides, careful to make sure the craggy chunks of asphalt were solid before lowering himself upon them, and digging his boots into the muddy ground wherever he could. He'd descended no more than five or six feet when he realized how quickly the water in the chasm was rising: It was now lapping at the rear wheels of the car—the trunk was completely underwater—and he was sure it hadn't been that near them before.

He couldn't make out the color of the vehicle yet, but with relief he decided it was too dark to be Laura's gray Taurus. He wondered if it was possible that whoever was driving had been thrown safely from the vehicle before the water had taken the road out from under it and sent it spinning into this canyon—or, for all he knew, driven the automobile backward into the hole, the water a wave that upended the vehicle like a seashell—but he didn't believe that was likely. He had a sense there would be a person, maybe even people, inside the car. Still, he could hope, and he imagined the driver walking back toward Durham in the rain, cursing his bad luck at having been on this exact patch of the road when the wave had risen up from the river.

When he had climbed down so that he was even with the front grill, he looked beyond the headlights and he could see just enough of a front panel to realize the car was a deep olive green. It was a cruiser; he could see now the inverted lettering on the door and the chipped shards of blue plastic from the roof's strobe lights that had been blown to the sides when the car flipped over. He craned his neck to peer into the driver's-side window—the windshield was buried against the side of the cleft—and though he couldn't see the man's face, he could see someone was still inside. He knew it was Terry, it absolutely had to be, and he was afraid he was going to be sick: For all he had seen in his life, he had never seen a dead body, and he wanted to flee. But the water was continuing to rise and might eventually submerge the vehicle completely, and so he held on to a slab of rock and stepped tentatively onto the vehicle's side-view mirror. He wanted to take a look and be sure that Terry was dead before succumbing to the panic that was swelling inside him, and allowing himself to run away. He bent over and glanced inside the window, recognized Terry's profile instantly, and nearly screamed when the man turned slowly to face him and through the fogged glass mouthed the word *Help*.

"I missed the west, but I was happy. Since I was a teenager I was an outsider, so this was not new."

VERONICA ROWE (FORMERLY POPPING TREES),
WPA INTERVIEW,
MARCH 1938

Laura

She sat in the midst of a line of cars on the notch way into Cornish, watching a backhoe pile earth into a hole that had formed when a mountain stream overran the culvert and carved an impassable trench across the road. She tried to be calm, and reminded herself she couldn't have gone home via the River Road even if she'd wanted to, because that route was gone and everyone was being detoured up here, anyway. She told herself that once enough dirt had been dumped into the crevice before her, she would continue on her way; she'd probably be at the house in another ten or fifteen minutes. Certainly no more than twenty. And though the cell phone didn't work in the hills in this corner of the county, she'd stopped at the bakery in Durham and from there called Mandy Acker, Tim's mother, and asked her to check in on Alfred and make sure he knew she was on her way home. She had convinced herself that he was only feeding Mesa when he didn't pick up the phone at their own house, because even the briefest contemplation of any other possibility would have finished off her already scanty reserves of strength in the face of her memories.

Still, this was just taking forever. There'd been a small fender bender in the corner of the commons in Middlebury, there'd been a power line down just south of New Haven, and she'd been slowed everywhere by the rain that had pooled in the potholes and troughs in the road.

In her head she saw the high water in the Gale River, and she vowed when this was over she would move. With or without Terry, she and Alfred would move. Not to Boston—no, never there. And not to Burlington either, not to that small city where Alfred had almost been lost. But . . . somewhere.

377

With or without Terry, she would leave this hill town with its flash floods and hard winters, the apparitions that could be conjured by wind and rain and the simple sound of the Gale as it lapped at its banks.

But then she decided she was overreacting: She knew in her heart she was incapable of leaving her daughters. This was a storm. Yes, the River Road was apparently a mess, but she rarely took it, anyway. Soon she would be back at the house with Alfred, and the roof might or might not be leaking—Oh, who was she kidding? Of course it would be!—but that wasn't cataclysmic. She was fine and Alfred was fine and Terry . . . Terry was fine, and whether she and Terry were fine together in six months or a year had nothing to do with a January rainstorm.

She flipped on the radio, and whenever a newscaster or disc jockey wanted to report on the flash floods in northern Vermont, she pressed *Scan* and found a station playing music instead.

"It was so humid, sometimes the air was like I imagined a jungle. That's what I remember most about our first summer in the East. Maybe it was just that I was so big with our baby. But the air always seemed sticky. George, I think, would have remembered most how nice it was not to have to ride around all day in the hot sun, chasing my people. Instead he got to chase them at night in our home."

VERONICA ROWE (FORMERLY POPPING TREES),
WPA INTERVIEW,
MARCH 1938

Phoebe

Her skin, she saw in the rearview mirror, had an almost marmoreal whiteness, and the first thing she wondered was why the air bag hadn't inflated. The second, following within seconds, was how in the name of God she could be alive. She glanced again in the mirror and saw that the back of her car was a mass of spiked metal—the gold skin of her own Corolla, the black steel that must have sat beneath the backseats and between her exterior roof and the interior ceiling, and the navy blue shell of the car that had slammed into her vehicle and was pinning it now against a telephone pole.

The wind and the rain had seemed to have gotten louder, more vicious, but then she understood this was only because the back of her car was open and so the sound was no longer buffered by metal and glass. She realized she was cold, and she could see her breath.

She rolled her eyes to her left, and the other driver—a man, a heavyset fellow in a black-and-white woolen jacket with glasses that were askew on his face—was pushing open his own door. He wasn't more than a few yards from her because his car was entangled with hers, and then he was staggering to his feet in the snowbank. She could see his forehead was bleeding, a series of cherry spiderwebs that were pooling together just above those glasses, and for a long moment he stood right beside her, apparently oblivious to her presence. Before them another car was slowing, despite the ice on the road, and she saw its hazard lights starting to blink.

She watched the man press the palm of his hand against the congealing blood in his eyebrows, stare at his fingers for a moment, and then abruptly notice her. Instantly he went to her and pulled open her door—she was surprised at how easily he did it—and she felt the rain stinging her face.

Can you stand? he asked her. From that second car she saw another person approaching, a younger, smaller man with a mustache the color of hay.

She wanted to answer she could, of course, why couldn't she, but she was still so dumbstruck by the fact that she was alive that she was incapable of opening her mouth.

Are you hurt? he asked now, adjusting his glasses, and the other man—a boy, really, he was no more than a teenage boy—was jabbering about whether they should touch her: He was saying he had a cousin on the rescue squad, and he had heard somewhere that you're not supposed to move someone if you think there's a spine or neck injury.

She looked down at her belly and her legs, and then she held her arms before her as if she were sleepwalking. Actually, the only part of her that did hurt was her neck, but it was a soreness only, nothing that unduly concerned or alarmed her.

Maybe you shouldn't move, the man with the cuts on his forehead was saying. I've got a cell phone, I'll call for help.

She turned to talk to him, concluding that she really was uninjured and there was every reason to believe that her baby was, too. She wondered what would have happened if the front grill of her car had been involved and the air bag had exploded after all: She would probably be about the same as she was now, but her child? She couldn't believe the small creature would have survived that impact, and she felt herself shuddering.

You're shivering, the man said. I think there's a blanket in my trunk. Want me to go get it?

No, I think I'm okay, she said. She decided she would have a stiff neck, yes, and though she had perhaps come within inches of being killed—if the car of this man leaning in toward her now had slammed into the front seat of the Corolla instead of the back, if her own car had angled differently into the telephone pole, if the vehicle had flipped onto its side or been toppled over—the truth was that she was okay. She was going to be fine. She dangled her legs out the car and then started to stand, swaying for a brief moment, and allowed the two men to each take an arm and lead her to the teenager's car with its blinking red lights. There she sat in his back-seat, looked out through the window at the spot where she had come so close to dying, and—much to her surprise—realized that her teeth had started to chatter.

"I had my baby, and two years later I had another. They were both boys. I raised our children and George worked with his brother. They built houses. That was our life together, and mostly it was very good."

VERONICA ROWE (FORMERLY POPPING TREES),
WPA INTERVIEW,
MARCH 1938

Alfred

He stood on an upended piece of asphalt the size of the cruiser's long hood, and though he didn't believe he had a chance—he could see the great creases in the metal along the side of the vehicle—he tried to open the door beside the man. Twice Terry shook his head and murmured that it wasn't locked, but Alfred knew he couldn't see where the roof of the car had collapsed onto the top of the door when the cruiser toppled into the ravine. The vehicle was not merely positioned like a rocket before liftoff, as if it were driving up an impossibly steep hill, it was flipped onto its roof. Still he pulled, struggling as much with the looking-glass nature of the angle as he did with the battered door, because already the water was lapping midway up the rear window and it was clear that he couldn't leave the man alone in the car. He could ride fast, but if the water kept rising, Terry would drown before he could return with help—assuming there was even a way for help to navigate the canyons in the road, which he didn't believe there was. How could the rescue vehicles in Cornish or Durham drive over those holes? The fact was they couldn't.

Finally he gave up and crabbed his way back up and over the front grill to the passenger side, and when he saw the way the shell had buckled—the door looked like the metal saucers some of the kids at the school used for sliding on the snow at recess—he tried pulling the handle only because there seemed little else he could do, and so he was surprised when the door gave just a bit. He tried again and this time it opened, and he was able to push it up into the air, the metal groaning above the water—both the water in the river and the water in the hole that was rolling in waves against the vehicle's exposed undercarriage—and there he held it open with his back.

Hello, Alfred, Terry murmured, his voice tired and weak, when he poked his head inside the car. The vehicle smelled of sweat, and it was almost as cold inside the cruiser as it was outside. I'd wave, he went on, but I can't really move my arms. I can move my fingers, but that's about it.

He saw Terry had managed to unclip his seat belt, but he'd been unable to draw the harness up and over his head and his shoulder, and the metal clip still rested in his lap. There was a ruby stain—a damp, viscous jellyfish—clinging to the right cuff of his jacket. He realized if the man's legs or his back were broken, too, there would be no way in the world he could help him.

He crawled inside and allowed the door to fall back against the frame, but he was careful to prevent it from clicking shut. Then he reached across the couch and lifted the belt over Terry's head, and though he tried to be gentle, the man winced. He saw a red mark on the trooper's forehead, just above his left eye. A bad bruise. Perhaps even a concussion.

I think my left shoulder's broken, he said softly, struggling for breath. And this arm—my right. The one that's been bleeding.

Can you walk?

I don't know. You alone?

He nodded.

How the hell did you get here?

I rode.

You rode. How 'bout that.

Terry, the water is—

The radio doesn't work, Terry said, cutting him off as if he hadn't heard him. I don't know if it's because the antenna's crushed or it's just this hollow we're in. Either way, I'm very glad for your company. I don't know how you found me, but it's nice to see—

We've got to move, Alfred told him. You've got to move. The water's getting higher, and I think it's going to come in the car.

Are you serious?

Yes, it's rising fast.

I think—

I know you're hurt, but we have to go now, he said, and he took Terry's right leg and lifted it over the ridge on the floor of the cruiser. When he looked at his hands, he saw there was blood on them, and Terry's green slacks weren't merely wet from the rain in which he'd been working throughout the day.

Don't worry, it's not from my leg, Terry said. It's from my arm. But my guess is the bleeding's stopped. I'd have bled out by now if it hadn't.

Can you slide over? Can you move your hips and slide?

I can, a bit. But feel free to pull, too. I think I'll need any help you can provide.

Okay, he agreed, and he put his arms around the man's waist and yanked him hard across the seat, and though Terry grimaced, he pulled him again, burying himself in the fabric that was wet with sweat and rainwater and blood. He tried not to jostle Terry's arms and shoulders, but he was aware that he was by the horrible way they flopped around his own shoulders like the rag-filled limbs of a Halloween straw man.

Terry groaned from the back of his throat, but Alfred didn't stop until he had pushed the door back open with his foot and was standing in the rain on the stones and the mangled remains of the pavement, with the trooper resting on his back at the very edge of the front couch. The man was shaking his head and shivering, and Alfred told him to crane his neck if he could and look down so he could see the water, within inches now of Alfred's boots, and the way whatever was blocking the current—ice, probably, but maybe there was a whole pile of collapsed asphalt and earth—was causing this hole to fill like a pond.

See it? he yelled over the sound of the storm. See it?

The man gazed at the water for a moment, and then back at Alfred.

Do you see it? he yelled again.

Terry bobbed his head.

I think it's coming in faster now than it was even a minute ago!

Then just go, little man—get out of here, move!

We've got—

Climb, go! I don't want you to drown in this hole!

We'll—

Go! Do as I say!

No!

Alfred, I won't argue with you about this. I—

I'm not leaving! he shouted, and he stared back at the trooper, unwavering. I'm not leaving without you, he said, his voice softer this time.

Terry closed his eyes for a brief second and then asked, Can you help me sit up? Maybe I can walk if you can help me up.

I can sit you up, he agreed, but it'll hurt.

I expect it will. But drowning would be no picnic, either.

And so although the man yelled once more, a short cry but loud, he reached under Terry's back and pulled him upright, and then watched as the trooper swung his legs over the side and out onto the wet ground, gasping with each exhalation. He held the door up and open like the hatchway into an attic so that Terry could duck underneath it and stand, and with the small, careful steps of a very old man start up the side of the ravine.

He let the cruiser's door fall shut and hiked up the slope behind him. He put his hand softly on the small of Terry's back, not so much pushing him as merely steadying him, and he wondered if he'd be able to get the man atop Mesa. He doubted it, but he guessed at this point it didn't really matter. He could find Terry a place in the nearby woods where there was some shelter from the rain, ride back to the village—ride into Durham, in fact, because that town was actually closer now—and let the grown-ups figure out the rest. He'd lead them back here if they wanted, but he was confident they would know what to do.

He imagined Laura was at the house by now since it was clear she hadn't taken this road home from the shelter, and he was glad he had left her a note.

Suddenly he was very, very tired, and the thought of drying off Mesa and bedding her down for the night was almost too much to bear.

"We didn't spend time with white people, and I never saw another Comanche. Once I was introduced to a woman who was a Hopi, but I had never met any of her people before. And a few blocks away there was a family of Arapaho Indians. But mostly we stayed with the Negroes. The white people didn't have any interest in us."

VERONICA ROWE (FORMERLY POPPING TREES),

WPA INTERVIEW,

MARCH 1938

Laura

YOUR LIFE IS *a mess,* she heard herself saying to Terry in her mind, *and you need to make some decisions.*
Your life is a mess, but I still want you if . . .
Your life is a mess . . .

She watched her husband sleep, hours now from surgery and the railed gurney in which he had dozed in post-op, and listened to the wind outside the hospital window. It was no longer raining.

Soon after her daughters had died, someone in the bereavement group she'd gone to that one time told her that a child's death could be a real marriage breaker. The loss of two children, this woman suggested, could be especially destructive, particularly if she and Terry were the sort to grieve differently.

We were, she heard herself whisper now, *we are,* and she turned to see if Alfred had heard her. He hadn't. He, too, was asleep, curled up under a woolen blanket in the larger and more comfortable of the two cushioned chairs in the hospital room.

The hallway outside was quiet and dark. A patient in the next room had been watching TV, but now he'd turned the television set off for the night.

She watched his eyelids flicker and finalized her speech in her head: *It's really rather simple. I am going to adopt this little boy, and you can either be a part of our family or not. The case review is next week, it's up to you.*

That, she decided, once and for all, was how she'd begin tomorrow when Terry was awake.

She stood up, hoping that whatever anesthetic- or analgesic-induced dream he was having was a respite from his pain and his memories and his guilt. She was about to wake Alfred so the two of them could go home when she saw Terry's lashes part and his eyes start to open. He looked up at her— unconsciously he was making a smacking sound with his mouth—and she went to him.

You're awake, she said softly, bending close.

He nodded.

It's very late, she added. Do you need anything?

He looked down at his arms, immobilized now after surgery, and shook his head. His eyes toured the room, landing for a long moment on Alfred, and then he stared up at her.

I'm sorry, he murmured, and when she sighed and said nothing, he repeated himself: I am so sorry. There was a slight shudder in his voice, and she wondered if it was due to exhaustion or the medication or the fact that he was still waking up.

We can talk in the morning, she told him.

I know I screwed up, and I just want you to know how sorry I am, he continued, his voice halting and broken. She placed her hands on either side of his face, and suddenly they were both silently crying.

———

"The men who fought the South—and the Southern-ers, too, of course—were always having reunions. Big parades every Memorial Day, it seemed. But not the Buffalos, I don't recall anyone organizing such a thing for them. Maybe we were too far east. It was only after the Great War ended that someone found him and asked him to ride in a car in a parade. He said sure, and he sat in this elegant open car with four Negroes even older than he was who had fought in Virginia with Ulysses S. Grant. It was cold and rainy and damp, and I teased him that he needed his gum blan-ket. He got sick—everyone was screaming, The flu, the flu!—but it wasn't the flu. It was only pneumonia. He was old, however, and so that's how he died."

———

VERONICA ROWE (FORMERLY POPPING TREES),

WPA INTERVIEW,

MARCH 1938

———

Phoebe

She called up one more time from the phone in the hospital lobby, and when there still wasn't an answer in his room, she decided she had nothing to lose. He might not be there, but apparently neither Laura nor Alfred were, either. Perhaps he'd be back any minute from wherever it was they had taken him.

She wasn't sure exactly what she would say to him, and on the drive into Burlington—in, of all things, her father's truck since her Corolla was about to become scrap metal—she had tried out different formulations in her head. And while they all would end with the news that she was finally going to leave Vermont, she wasn't sure whether she should share with him her belief that she was leaving in part because the two of them had nearly died forty-eight hours earlier, and in her opinion one would have to be pretty damn irreligious not to view that as an omen of some kind of magnitude.

She exited the elevator and followed the blue line that was painted on the tile floor, passing the crowded nurses' station and a small display of paintings that were apparently produced by the children in the pediatric ward on another floor of the hospital, and glanced at the numbers of the rooms until she reached his. Then, almost secretively, she glanced through the doorway in the event that the woman who was his wife and the boy who had rescued him were there after all. They weren't, he was alone in his bed, both his arms incapacitated: His right arm was in a splint from his elbow to his wrist, and his left was in a sling. There was a second bed in the room, but it was empty.

You can come in, he said to her. If you're worried about meeting Laura and Alfred, they're in town getting ice cream.

They don't have ice cream here? she said from the door frame.

Oh, they do. But the flavors are unimpressive and the fat content is low. It's a tad too healthy to be real ice cream.

She wandered slowly into the room and was astonished at how frail and docile he looked in his ivory hospital gown in his bed. His face was swollen and bruised, and she stood for a moment at the foot, afraid suddenly to get too close—as if they barely knew each other and were mere acquaintances.

How did you know I was here? she asked.

The phone rang a couple of times, and by the time I was able to wriggle myself across the bed and reach it, whoever was calling had hung up. You might recall that was your m.o. back in December when you wanted to reach me. And then, of course, you were hovering just now right outside the door.

She smiled. How do you feel?

I have mighty good drugs in me. Very solid painkillers, thank you very much. He wrinkled his nose and then added, I won't be running the roads for a little while. But I'm alive, and that's a good feeling.

You look okay. Better than I would have expected from the news. They said your shoulder was shattered and you'd broken an arm.

This, he said, motioning with his chin toward his left, is a fracture of the proximal humerus. The ball in my shoulder was broken when the door crumpled in. And then over here we have mid-shaft fractures of the radius and the ulna. I probably broke these when my cruiser rolled over and I banged my arm into something.

They showed your car on TV.

Yeah, I was glad to see that even my old Impala got its fifteen seconds of fame. He said nothing for a long moment and she followed his eyes: She looked down at her wrists and saw that she was kneading nervously at the cuffs of her jacket. How long were you at the cottage before you figured out I wasn't going to join you? he asked finally.

I never got there.

He raised his gaze to her eyes and nodded, and she understood instantly that he had read more into her statement than she'd meant. I think you've made a wise decision, he said. Laura and I talked, and I—

No, there's more to it than that. I was in a car accident, too, she explained quickly, straining to keep her voice even as she started to describe for him what had occurred. She knew it wouldn't take long because she'd told the story so many times already, and she hoped his training as a trooper wouldn't lead him to ask more questions than, for example, her father or Wallace had asked. She didn't want to relive the moment with any more specifics than necessary.

When she was through, he asked only one: And the baby?

The baby's fine.

Thank God.

She looked out the window, noticing for the first time his view of the small mountain in the distance called Camel's Hump, and all her imaginings of how she would tell him she was leaving abruptly vanished. I'm going away, she said simply. I have an appointment with a travel agent at four-thirty, and I'm buying a plane ticket to Santa Fe.

One way?

Not yet. Round trip. I want to scout it out first. But yes, my plan is to move there in the spring. I'll stay with my friend from college who lives there. Shauna. I'll stay with her and her family until I find a place. They have an extra room. Then maybe I can get a job with the bean counters who work for the New Mexico government, and make myself some more friends before this baby arrives.

I won't meet this little baby, will I? he said, and she could see a sudden pang of despair flutter across his face like a twitch.

No, she told him, and she was surprised by the composure in her voice.

So, that's it. That's the sentence.

It's not a sentence, it's just—

It's fine, Phoebe. Really. I have a son. I have a family. Still, if you ever need anything, you'll let me know. Right?

Terry—

I mean it.

I'll be fine, she said, and then she repeated the words as much for herself as for him. I will be fine. And you?

Laura and I talked: I know what I want and I know what's right.

I hope they're the same.

They are. I should never have come on to you at the store. I should never have—

You don't have to say it.

I just want you to know I'm sorry. I'm very, very sorry, and I hope someday you'll forgive me. I want to make things right with Laura and Alfred, and—

I don't need to forgive you. I knew what I was doing then, I know what I'm doing now. The thing is . . .

Yes?

The thing is, you really won't ever hear from me again. I'm going to make a nice life for me and my child, and I won't want for anything, she said. Okay?

Oh, Phoebe, if I could—

Don't. I'm serious. I know what I want, too.

Then I'm happy, he said slowly.

And you and Laura? You think you'll be okay?

We'll get through this . . . I hope. I love her. I behaved miserably, but—

Oh, we both did.

She took a deep breath and leaned down on the metal molding along the top of the footboard. She decided her nervousness was shifting, transforming itself now into anticipation, and she allowed the ends of her lips to arc naturally into a smile. She considered blowing him a kiss, but she felt that would be flippant and dismissive, and she didn't want that. And so she pulled herself away from the end of the bedstead, went to his side for the first time since she had arrived in his room, and kissed him lightly. Then she stood back on her heels and left.

PART FOUR

Equitation

———

"When we walked down the street with our children, we might have looked strange to the white people who saw us: an Indian lady and her girls, and a handsome Negro and two boys. That's what we looked like. But we were a family and it worked."

———

VERONICA ROWE (FORMERLY POPPING TREES),
WPA INTERVIEW,
MARCH 1938

———

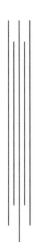

A stiff, cool wind—along with the turning leaves at the very tops of the sugar maples, an early harbinger of fall—was blowing in from the north, and Laura Sheldon stood just outside the ring and watched it blow Alfred's necktie away from his chest. The boy—taller now, only weeks away from seventh grade and the union high school six miles distant in Durham—tucked the necktie back inside his riding coat, checked the front button, and then climbed atop Mesa. The flat class was done and now he would jump, alone for the first time in the ring. Heather Barrett, the woman from the indoor ring who had metamorphosed from teacher to trainer in the year and a half they'd been together, motioned toward the jodhpur strap just below his knee and said something to Alfred that Laura couldn't quite hear, and then left him alone and marched toward the gate nearest her.

Overhead there were immense cotton-ball clouds, and when one would hide the sun, the air would grow chilly. Terry Sheldon stood beside her, and beside him stood the Heberts. Occasionally Emily would curl her cardigan— vertical red, white, and blue stripes, a sweater the woman chose, she said, because it seemed fitting for a horse show, though Laura thought it actually made her look a bit like an image from a World War I recruitment poster— tightly around her shoulders. When Heather joined them, the trainer leaned over the rail beside Laura and blew into her hands.

Cold? Laura asked her, surprised. There was a breeze today, but she wouldn't have thought that a woman as tough as Heather would be uncomfortable.

No, not at all. Just anxious.

You? Terry asked, and he, too, sounded a tad incredulous.

Oh, I get nervous for all my kids. I want them to do well—especially when it's their first show. I think my heart stops completely that moment any one of them approaches their very first jump in a competition.

Alfred admitted he had some butterflies at breakfast this morning, Laura said, and she recalled how he had told them that he was bringing his old buffalo soldier cap with him. Though he could no longer stretch it around his head, he viewed it as a good-luck charm, and right now it was tucked inside a pocket in his blazer.

Aren't you nervous? Heather asked her. You must be.

She smiled. A little.

Only a little?

Actually Terry was the one who didn't sleep a whole lot last night.

It's true, he admitted. Boy's first show, and all. So, yes, I have worried about him. I have worried about Mesa.

You like the braid? she asked Laura.

You mean on her tail?

Yup. One of the girls helped me do that. I thought Alfred was going to die.

It's very elegant.

I think so, too, Heather said, and then her voice grew more serious. Still, looks aren't everything. I really wish we could have had another couple weeks to work with her. I don't know her as well as I do the horses who board at the stable, I don't—

Mesa will comport herself just fine, thank you very much, Paul said, a slight rumble of indignation in his voice, and he pointed the bag of popcorn he was holding in the trainer's direction. None of you has a thing to worry about. That horse will do well, and the young man upon her will do even better.

The announcer called Alfred's number, and Laura watched him swing his horse around to the start of the course. The jumps looked huge to her this morning, though she knew in reality they were a mere eighteen inches high. She counted eight of them, and tried to guess where in the ring he would be expected to change direction.

Are we allowed to stay here, Emily asked, or should we take seats in the grandstand?

Oh, stay, definitely stay, Heather insisted. You might be on your feet, but the best seats are right here at the rail.

Russell's going to be late, Terry murmured, a slight ripple of annoyance in his voice, and Laura was going to tell him it was all right, it didn't matter, when she saw her brother-in-law strutting across the flattened grass in the field just beyond where he'd parked. He was ogling a pair of teenage girls in snug jeans and tight blouses, but he was present and that was what counted today.

She pointed out Russell to Terry, and he shook his head and called out, Mighty nice of you to make it on time!

Russell grinned, satisfied that he managed to keep his brother on edge, and yelled that he had been behind a hay wagon for miles.

She turned back to Alfred and saw him sit up straight in his saddle, his spine a line perfectly perpendicular to the dirt on the ground in the ring, and she saw his fingers open and close around the leather reins. Suddenly, in so many ways, he was a teenager: His chest and his shoulders were filling out, and his new riding boots were a man's size eight and a half. His riding jacket was a man's size thirty-six. And though Laura had not been oblivious to these changes throughout the summer—rather, she had been excruciatingly aware of them—in so many ways she still viewed him as a child who was fragile and small, and she would feel a twinge of unease whenever he was gone from her sight.

Under the small brim of his helmet she saw his eyes, and they were staring straight ahead at the first jump, a pair of horizontal white beams with a pot of gerbera daisies on either side.

Laura took her husband's hand in hers and they watched their son breathe. He squeezed the horse's sides with his legs and then started toward the jump at a canter, the drumbeat from the horse's hooves the only sound she could hear. He moved quickly away from her through the ring, his whole body starting forward with the big animal in two-point and then—the horse's legs extended before and behind her, a carousel pony but real, the immense thrust invisible to anyone but the boy on the creature's back— he was rising, rising, rising . . .

And aloft.

Acknowledgments

I am deeply indebted to Pam LaFave of the Cobble Hill Horse Farm in Middlebury, Vermont; Sergeant Thomas Noble of the Vermont State Police; and William Young, commissioner of Vermont's Department of Social and Rehabilitation Services. Pam taught me to ride a horse (though I still have a great deal to learn), Thomas shared with me the joys, frustrations, and dangers that mark his life daily, and William offered me a small window into the world of foster care in Vermont—a world in which the failures are chronicled often but the successes (of which there are many) are likely to go unnoticed.

Each of them gave me their wisdom and their time, and critiqued this manuscript for me.

In addition, I am indebted to Vaughn Carney, Paul Eschholz, Jay Parini, Sylvie Rabineau, and Judy Simpson for reading early drafts of *The Buffalo Soldier,* and to the following individuals for answering specific questions in the course of my research: Diane Amsden, a family foster care specialist; Dr. Craig S. Bartlett, an orthopedic surgeon; Mark Breen, meteorologist at the Fairbanks Museum in Saint Johnsbury, Vermont; Mary Buffum, a resource coordinator for Vermont's Department of Social and Rehabilitation Services; Susan Eisenstadt, a social worker with Vermont's Department of Social and Rehabilitation Services; Carrie Hathaway, a financial specialist with Vermont's Agency of Human Services; Dr. Paul Morrow, chief medical examiner for the state of Vermont; Towana Spivey, Director of the Fort Sill National Historic Landmark in Oklahoma; and Vaneasa Stearns, the owner of the general store in Lincoln, Vermont.

A variety of books were either inspirational or provided helpful historical information. Four stand out: *Lost in the System,* by Charlotte Lopez with Susan Dworkin; *Loving Across the Color Line: A White Adoptive Mother Learns About Race,* by Sharon E. Rush; *Buffalo Soldiers and Officers of the Ninth Cavalry, 1867–1898: Black & White Together,* by Charles L. Kenner; and *The Buffalo Soldiers: A Narrative of the Negro Cavalry in the West,* by William H. Leckie.

Once again I am grateful to Random House and to my preternaturally gifted and exceedingly wise editor and friend, Shaye Areheart—a reader who never allows her critical eye to blur. I am appreciative as well of all the time and effort that Marty Asher, Chip Gibson, and Anne Messitte put into my work.

Finally, I want to thank my wife, Victoria, for listening to this novel almost a page at a time over the course of a year and a half, reading it chapter by chapter, and maintaining her focus, her patience, and her sense of humor. You are, in all ways, an inspiration.

About the Author

CHRIS BOHJALIAN is the author of eight novels, including *Midwives* (a *Publishers Weekly* Best Book and a New England Booksellers Association Discovery title), *Trans-Sister Radio, The Law of Similars,* and *Water Witches.* He lives in Vermont with his wife and daughter.